"*The Reckoning* is long on miracles, mysteries, secret societies, murderous plots and apparitions."
—San Jose Mercury News

"A highly engrossing, wildly surprising thriller with a stunning premise that thoroughly grabbed me."
—David Morrell on The Blood of the Lamb

"*The Blood of the Lamb* is a really fun read. It has well-drawn characters, depth, and an absolutely marvelous story."
—Whitley Strieber

"Daring . . . the story is irresistible, moving to a mighty climax. Monteleone grabs the reader with his first paragraph and never relaxes the tension. Try not to miss it."
—The New York Times on The Blood of the Lamb

"A vastly entertaining novel of horror and suspense [that poses] difficult questions about the nature of man, God, and the devil."
—Los Angeles Daily News on The Blood of the Lamb

"A terrific book that's as fun to read as it is difficult to put down."
—The Washington Times on The Blood of the Lamb

"Monteleone's prose is a notch or two more sophisticated than that of Tom Clancy."
—The Easton Star-Democrat

"[He has a] knack for the right phrase, dialogue, and imaginative depictions of violence."
—West Coast Review of Books

ALSO BY THOMAS F. MONTELEONE

The Blood of the Lamb
Night of Broken Souls
The Resurrectionist

The
RECKONING

THOMAS F. MONTELEONE

TOR®

A TOM DOHERTY ASSOCIATES BOOK
NEW YORK

This is a work of fiction. All the characters and events portrayed in this book are either products of the author's imagination or are used fictitiously.

THE RECKONING

Copyright © 1999 by Thomas f. Monteleone

A Tor Book
Published by Tom Doherty Associates, LLC
175 Fifth Avenue
New York, NY 10010

www.tor.com

Tor® is a registered trademark of Tom Doherty Associates, LLC.

ISBN 0-812-57524-5
EAN 978-0812-57524-8

First edition: December 1999
First mass market edition: January 2001

Printed in the United States of America

0   9   8   7   6   5   4   3   2

This one is for
Brandon
&
Olivia
and all the baseballs and Barbie dolls,
and dreams forever bright.
Daddy loves you.

Acknowledgments

For a variety of reasons, this book required more than my usual amount of effort to complete. I literally could not have done it without the belief, support, and plain old *work* of the following people: Elizabeth Monteleone for the love and inspiration; Frank Monteleone for those dark days in December; and Melissa Ann Singer for pulling everything together.

Thank you. Thank you. Thank you.

The New York Times (AP) Scientists at the California Institute for Solar Research in Mojave Center have reported observations of unusual and erratic patterns of solar flare activity. "We have never seen anything remotely like this," said Dr. Patrick G. Karger of CISR. "The data indicate our sun is undergoing some very basic changes. All stars evolve through several major identifiable stages, and it is possible that our own star—the sun—is entering a new stage in its life span." When asked what this meant for Earth and its inhabitants, Dr. Karger was initially hesitant to speculate, but eventually admitted that "it is possible the sun could produce a 'flare event' of sufficient size to reduce the earth to a cinder."

PART

1

The mystery of the seven stars which thou sawest in my right hand, and the seven golden candlesticks. The seven stars are the angels of the seven churches: and the seven candlesticks which thou sawest are the seven churches.

–John, *Revelation, 1: 20*

PROLOGUE

Excerpted from the editorial page of *The Catholic Review*, Baltimore, Maryland, May 15, 2000.

In the year since Peter Carenza has taken up Vatican residency as Pope Peter II, it seems the story of his life has been told countless times in every publication and media show on the planet. We have all read, seen, or heard how he was raised in a Church orphanage, became a parish priest in Brooklyn, began performing miracles witnessed by thousands, and escaped assasination at the Los Angeles Palladium Convocation.

But little more has actually been revealed, and there are some of us in the Church who are beginning to wonder exactly *who* our new Pope is.

His unanimous election by the College of Cardinals marked a stunning change in tradition, as Carenza was the first pope to originate from the United States. This fact in itself may not be all that remarkable, but the millennial cult who call themselves "the Nostradamani" believe it to be a signal that the end of the world is imminent (because Nostradamus predicted in one of his quatrains that the "last pope" would come from the New World).

Many, within and without the Church, believe Peter Carenza is the kind of charismatic and revolutionary leader necessary to keep an aging theocratic institution like the Roman Catholic Church vibrant in the twenty-first century. There are, however, hints and rumblings from corners of the Vatican that Peter is constructing an agenda of cataclysmic change—a strategy that might ultimately destroy the Mother Church.

Time will tell.

ONE

Marion Windsor—Vatican City
August 1, 2000

*T*he Pope is getting married."

Peter Carenza's words so stunned Marion Windsor she was not at first certain she'd heard him correctly.

She had been seated by an open window overlooking the Vatican Gardens, a welcome spring breeze weaving through her hair, when he made the announcement. Across the vast drawing room, dwarfed by high rococo ceilings and massive tapestries, sat the Holy Father, Peter Carenza, at a polished marble table. Surrounded by stacks of leather-bound books and piles of paper, he smiled at her like an impish little boy.

It was a smile she had grown to dislike.

"*Married?*" said Marion, getting up from the window seat and approaching him. "Peter—"

"Not just the Pope. Not just me. *Any* clergy. I'm going to make a papal proclamation: Marriage by clerics is now permissible. And of course, the only thing to do is set a good example. I'll do that by marrying *you.*"

A year ago, the idea of marrying Peter Carenza would have rocked her into a passionate fantasy. But Peter had been a different person back then—and so had Marion Windsor. Ever since meeting him, she had essentially sacrificed herself to him and his mission. She had given up her own aspirations, her career, her needs, to follow him, to do whatever he needed.

She'd followed him, all right. All the way to Rome.

And for a while, it had worked—for the first time in her life, Marion had believed she was fulfilled. The miracles by Peter's hand that she'd witnessed had renewed her faith in God, and perhaps more important, in herself. Believing that she and Peter were doing God's work, she felt spiritually recharged. She knew that there was a greater purpose to existence than merely surviving the material world. For the first time in her life, she had been truly content—not merely happy, but actually at peace with herself.

She had more than fallen in love with Peter Carenza; she had been transformed by experiencing the power of his personal aura, basking in his invisible gracelike rays. She'd felt an excitement and a sense of fulfillment her own accomplishments, significant though they were, had never delivered.

Lately, she'd found herself thinking of her Ohio childhood and her past with a wistfulness tinged with wisdom's bitter spice. She'd grown up in a house where her father dominated everyone with the threat of physical punishment and opinions based on prejudice, misinformation, and plain ignorance. Marion and her brothers lived in an atmosphere of constant upheaval, unpredictable as the weather, and far more damaging. She remembered the day that should have been the start of a summer job at a dentist's office. Fifteen years old, wearing a navy blue jumper and a white blouse, she looked like a parochial school girl, but her father thought her hem was far too short. He announced, loudly, that she couldn't go to work "looking like a whore"—and in fact, she couldn't go to work at all. He called the dentist and told him his daughter was turning down the job. Marion never forgot the humiliation of that day, and years later, when she'd been accepted to college, she never told him, never asked him for help with tuition, nothing. "Women don't belong in college getting as smart as men" had been one of Sam Windsor's favorite expressions at the Dayton welding supply factory where he worked.

He had been very surprised to see her walking down the stairs in early September, wearing a navy blue jumper with the hem thigh-high, and carrying a small suitcase. Although the symbolism had been lost on him, he demanded to know where she thought she was going. Marion informed her father that his daughter had been accepted to Syracuse University, that she had a tuition loan from the bank, a job at the college library, and a bus ticket that would take her to the dormitories. She'd shipped most of her belongings ahead. She also told him she wouldn't be coming back to his little bungalow. Ever.

And she never did.

But she did return to her hometown—for his funeral. And she'd done that mostly to appease her brothers and her mother, because Marion had made it quite clear to everyone, especially herself, that she did not need to expiate any guilt over her treatment of her father in life . . . or death. Never again, she'd vowed, would she live under the uncontrolled power of an irrational person.

* * *

So how did she allow herself to become so subjugated to Peter Carenza?

Since coming to Rome with Peter the previous year, she'd been a virtual prisoner of the Palace Vatican.

All right, she thought, maybe not a prisoner, but most certainly not much more than a concubine. She couldn't imagine *why* Peter would feel it necessary actually to marry her.

But then, Peter had become so unpredictable. Marion studied at him for a moment. His dark eyes and chiseled features would always make him physically attractive, but there was an aspect of his demeanor that had caused Marion sometimes to distrust him, fear him, even despise him.

And yet, he exhibited some kind of weirdly seductive power over her and everyone else with whom he interacted. No one could loathe Peter Carenza for very long, it seemed.

"I've done lots of thinking and some research on the issue. And the statistics tell a pretty sorry story," he said, interrupting her thoughts.

"What? What did you say?"

He spoke as he combed through his dark hair with his fingers. "The church is losing its power because young men aren't going into the seminaries."

"I know. You said—"

"And who can blame them?" he said, getting up and walking to one of the high windows, then turning to face her. "Anyone who'd choose to be a Catholic priest these days—he'd have to be crazy, or numb from the waist down."

"You did it yourself, Peter," said Marion with unmasked sarcasm. "Were *you* either of those things?"

He glared at her for an instant. He didn't like being challenged. "It was different with me, and you know it! Francesco had me raised in a Catholic orphanage.

I'd been groomed for the priesthood since I was a little boy! It's not the same when you've been part of some-body's else grandiose scheme."

He was right, but she needed to push him. Part of her had never submitted to him, just as part of her wished he might someday return to being the man she'd fallen in love with.

But that man had been a parish priest. She'd fallen in love with a priest. She'd become so complacent that only rarely did that simple truth shock her. When it did, Marion was forced to ask herself what she was doing and how she'd become the Pope's public rela-tions agent . . . and his mistress.

Peter stared at her with an expression that made no effort to conceal his irritation. Maybe a question would refocus him.

"When do you plan to announce your decision?"

He shrugged, walked toward her. Anyone paying at-tention to his movements would learn much about him. Catlike in his supple, muscular control, Peter walked with a hint of a swagger, barely concealing his arro-gance and his outrageous confidence. He moved as though there should always be a dashing cape swirling in his wake. When he entered a room, even if it was a place in which he'd never been, he imparted the im-pression of having always possessed it. Words like *pres-ence, charisma,* and *power* were used to describe him so often that they made Marion want to vomit.

"Marion, don't humor me, or try to distract me with hollow questions." He grinned darkly. "You don't re-ally care, do you?"

"It concerns me," she said. "Of course I care."

She could see his mood changing as he moved to take her into his arms.

"Well, it's interesting you phrased things that way. I've been concerned with the reality of the act. I think we should make a big deal out of it. Start the publicity machinery this week by leaking to the usual conduits."

Peter teasingly kissed her at the juncture of her neck and shoulder, a move that never failed to send shivers all over her. The bastard.

"Leaking *what?*" said Marion, acquiescing to his embrace.

"That the Pope's going to issue a monumental proclamation! That it will rock the Church to its foundations! I don't know, make it sound good—as ominous and dramatic as possible without giving anything away. Then, sometime next month, we do it."

Releasing her, Peter walked back to his cluttered tabletop. He was dressed in jeans and a T-shirt that said "I Saw the Sistine Chapel." He clearly enjoyed going against the traditions of the Church, even though he dressed so casually only in the privacy of their suites. Peter was far too smart to alienate his colleagues and associates with matters ultimately trivial. He chose his battles carefully and was far more comfortable confronting the College of Cardinals on the weightier issues of Church dogma than arguing the appropriate attire of the pontiff.

"So, what do you think?" He looked at her and grinned, as if to tell her he didn't actually care what she might think of his plans but expected to be amused at her response.

"I think you're asking for trouble," she said, somewhat impulsively.

"From whom?"

"There's a lot of tradition in the Church. You're planning to rip out the heart of what's set it apart from all the other Christian faiths," she said. "The cardinals will have coronaries."

"Then we'll get some new ones," he said.

"Oh, I'm sure you will."

Peter smiled. "I realize the traditionalists will have to put on a public face of disapproval, and it will be the rare member of the old guard who stands up and admits he *likes* it, but secretly, they'll all be dancing the happy dance!"

He chuckled, apparently amused at the image of the old men in their red robes jumping around with rhythmic glee.

"What about the people? The regular Sunday churchgoers?"

Peter smiled dismissively. "You mean the ones who used to sit there and listen to everything in *Latin*? They don't *really* care. They proved time and again they'll ultimately go along with whatever the Church wants to do." Peter chuckled and gestured toward his chest. "Which means they'll do whatever *I* want."

"How magnanimous," she said.

"So where's the 'trouble'?"

Marion looked away for a moment, searching for the courage to say what she was really thinking.

"Well, I didn't just mean any of them—I meant *me*," she said. "Trouble from me."

Peter could not hide the surprise. Quickly, he masked his emotion with another smile, but Marion knew she'd reached him.

"From *you*?" He said it slowly, in a soft, almost playful way, but she knew him well enough to know that he was growing more angry with each passing moment. "Now what, exactly, does that mean, Marion? Just what kind of 'trouble' do you think you're capable of giving me?"

"Well, maybe *trouble* is the wrong word. . . ." Fighting the urge to leave the room, she forced herself to look into his baleful gaze. "But what I mean is—well, what makes you think I want to marry you?"

The words seemed to echo through the capacious room, amplifying themselves.

Peter stood frozen for an instant, just staring at her, absorbing both the venom and the absurdity of what she'd said.

"What you want doesn't really have much to with it—I think you know that." He spoke coolly, in a voice too soft.

"Peter, I don't want to be part of some . . . spectacle." The words burst from her. "You can't do this to me!"

"You know I can. You know I can make you do whatever is necessary. Why are you acting like this?"

Marion backed away from him, across the room, toward the window seat. He slowly advanced toward her, hands in his pockets, trying to look as relaxed and unconcerned as possible.

But she knew him too well. She knew he was beginning to smolder.

"Peter, I've been here since New Year's. I'm tired. I'm going crazy watching you change."

"Change? Into what?"

She shook her head, looked away from him. "I don't know! Into someone I could never love."

"Why does your loving me have anything to do with my plans?" His tone of voice was changing, and she felt herself shudder.

But she stood her ground and spoke from her heart. "Because there was a time when it would have meant *everything*."

That seemed to stop him for a moment, and Marion felt a kind of relief. His outer shell was not yet impenetrable; she could still reach what was left of the original man. She imagined him remembering when they shared the same vision, the same sweet wine of giving, of expecting nothing in return and yet receiving everything.

But Peter Carenza was clearly a different man now—
something dark sought to influence him now, something not Godly but unspeakably opposite. Marion did
not believe he had totally given himself over to the
antipodal powers of the universe, but it was clear that
he swung like a terrible pendulum from one extreme
to the other. She wanted to believe she could still make
the difference in him, to be the unpredicted element in
his life that ultimately swung him back forever to the
side of God and humankind.

And the only way she could make that difference was
to stick it out, stay in the mix for the long haul.

That's why she hadn't escaped from her prison, why
she'd allowed him to control so much of her life, despite her youthful promises. It was why she could not
retreat now.

Peter had been staring at her, as though reading her
thoughts. Maybe he could actually do that—she
wouldn't be surprised. And he seemed to be weighing
his response to her challenge that love could make a
difference in his life mission.

"Well, Peter," she said almost in a whisper. "Am I
right?"

"Sometimes it's not a good thing to be right," he said.
"Sometimes it can . . . really . . . piss people off."

"I just want you to think about your actions, about
who you are, who you used to be, and who you might
become."

He chuckled. "Marion, do you have any idea how
self-righteous you sound?"

"No more than you, I'm sure."

Her last remark seemed to trigger something in him.
His expression flashed from amused tolerance through
annoyance to outright rage.

"You can be so stupid, you know that?"

In a movement so quick she could not even see it,

he'd grabbed her by the throat and was pushing her backward. She had no chance of resisting the power of his hands. She tried to speak, to say something that would stop him, but no sound could escape the closed tube of her throat.

"How could you even *think* of defying me? I'm the fucking pope!" His eyes narrowed as his brow creased into angry folds.

She'd seen him slide toward this kind of rage before, and it terrified her to think where it might lead. Panic surged upward, filling her with a white-hot burst of knowledge that she could die at this exact moment. She stumbled backward against the edge of the window seat, powerless against his fury.

Her vision blurred as the high sculptured ceiling seemed to roll past her.

She was falling backward, slowly, weightlessly, and was only vaguely aware of a cool breeze across her face. There was a smear of lush green across her field of view, and she felt the panic fading as the lack of oxygen began to dampen everything down.

"It's so easy," said Peter.

So easy to kill, she knew. Yet if this was her time to die, it would be all right. Serenity wrapped her in calm comfort.

Then suddenly the pressure was gone from her throat, and air rushed into her like a cold fire. Into her and around her and past her. If she was truly aware that she was falling, actually tumbling through space toward the manicured gardens and stonework below, it was in an abstract sense that required no real concern.

The last thing she remembered was the face of Peter Carenza looking down at her from a tall window.

TWO

Gaetano—London
August 6, 2000

Gaetano sat in the rented flat several blocks from
Victoria Station. From his open windows, the
sounds of endless traffic filled the rooms with an urban
ambiance that over time had become comforting rather
than irritating. He was employed by Lloyd's as an investigator of international claims, but recently he had
become involved in a much more personal project. He
pointed the remote control in his hand at his VCR,
rewinding a tape of events of Christmas Day, 1999.

It was a tape he knew so well, he could replay it in
his memory as efficiently as his video deck, but seeing
its contents somehow made it more real to him.

The machine clicked loudly as it finished the rewind,
and Gaetano pressed the Play button:

A large crowd filtering into a massive bowl, the Los
Angeles Palladium. People stream through every access,
wearing the robes and garments of their various faiths

and occupations. The air crackles with the languages of a hundred different countries.

There are miniprocessionals for each honored guest as he or she enters the vast space and navigates toward a huge central dais, a raised circular platform. The roster ranges from the mayor and his fellow politicos to a seemingly endless list of religious pundits and churchly demagogues.

Gaetano knows that the guests are making their appearances in a gradually ascending order of importance, or more pointedly, of international visibility.

The most exalted guests finally make an en masse appearance. A tsunami of cheers and screams rocks the Palladium, and Gaetano is unable to determine if Father Peter Carenza or the Pope himself is the crowd favorite.

The processional music of the opening ceremonies reaches a majestic crescendo, and the thousand-member choir peaks at just the right moment.

In the gulf of silence that follows the break in the music, the entire arena seems to catch its breath. As all the dignitaries, some sixty strong, take their seats, the huge round platform begins its almost imperceptible rotation—so that everyone in the arena will eventually face the proceedings head-on, even if only momentarily.

The host and leader of the convocation, Freemason Cooper, stands, smoothes his designer apparel, and strides toward the center of the dais.

In studying this tape, Gaetano has always found it fascinating to read the diverse facial expressions of those on the dais. There is the usual mixture of ennui, anticipation, and contentment.

Until he regards the occasional close-ups of the face of the Pope.

The old man's attention seems constantly fixed upon Peter Carenza. The Pope appears puzzled, suspicious, and at times philosophical. Often, the look in the old prelate's eyes is like a rabbit's as it stares into the eyes of a predator. But there is defiance there too, and suppressed rage. There is also understanding—a knife-edge clarity honed by a sudden and single revelation.

Peter Carenza is announced as the next speaker.

This is where it starts to happen, thinks Gaetano. This is where it gets weird.

A man suddenly jumps to his feet and begins waving his arms as he pushes through the assemblage. Everyone is staring at him as he screams, but no one moves to stop him.

"Peter! Stop! Stop! Get away!" His voice sounds oddly dampened and far away, nearly absorbed by the monstrous hush of the crowd.

A security man reacts immediately, moving forward and loosing a dark, ugly handgun from its shoulder holster, trying unsuccessfully to conceal it.

"They're going to kill you!" the agitated man screams as hands reach out for him. "For Christ's sake, Peter! Move!"

Other VIPs are already clearing a path for the sudden madman as they duck for cover. The Pope, however, sits rigidly in his seat, watching events as though he had expected them. Security types of every flavor begin to converge on the dais.

Peter Carenza falls silent at the first sign of the disturbance, though he still stands at the podium.

The yelling man leaps over the railing around the box seats, hurling himself at the stocky man brandishing the gun, who turns, swinging the weapon out like a tank rotating its turret.

18 THOMAS F. MONTELEONE

A brilliant muzzle flash at close range and the shot
sledgehammers the agitator's chest. He is flipped sideways into the air, landing at the base of the dais. Shock
waves ripple outward through the crowd in alternating
rings of recognition and panic. The shooter appears confused for an instant, then leaps off the dais to the edge
of the cinder track.

There is the odd bark of a small explosion off-camera,
somewhere up near the rim of the Palladium.

Peter Carenza cradles the fallen man in his arms.

Gaetano leans closer to the screen, watching more
intently as a new figure appears wearing white maintenance coveralls. Gaetano knows that the man's name
is Targeno, a man of great confidence and swagger. He
moves through the crowd with a single purpose, homing in on the shooter like a cruise missile. Gaetano
smiles, even though he knows what will come soon.

The shooter is now aiming his gun at Father Carenza.

The priest suddenly looks up at him, with a cold
emptiness that locks the assassin in place, keeping him
from squeezing the trigger.

It is the moment needed. A volley of slugs from a
machine pistol rip through the shooter with surgical ef-
ficiency. Bone-shivering impacts dance up the length of
his torso as his entire chest explodes in gouts of blood
and tissue.

Turning, Peter faces the new shooter—Targeno,
dressed in white, weapon still braced for firing, he looks
like an avenging archangel.

The crowd is surging in all directions, seized by terror. Suddenly everyone is pulling out weapons, pointing
them at one another. The man in white, however, low-
ers his gun, and for the first time stares into the eyes of
Father Peter Carenza . . .

... which are endlessly dark, like two black holes drawing in all in their path with a force so powerful that even the light of hope could never escape.

Gaetano always marveled at this point in the video—that even though he was merely watching a media transcript of events, the sensation of time slowing down was inescapable. There was power in merely witnessing the events—a brittle, glass-edged anticipation.

Targeno recognizes something and calmly assumes a classic dueler's pose. He raises his weapon.

Peter lifts one hand, as though in warning or denial, and suddenly the Palladium crowd gasps as one as a tongue of blue-white fire arcs from Peter's palm to touch Targeno.

Gaetano forces himself to watch what he knows is coming. It is a scene he has allowed to be burned into his memory as well as his retinas.

The man known as Targeno erupts into the purest, whitest flame and is suddenly gone. In his place totters an obscene column of charcoal. Greasy smoke wafts upward as the column falls, shattering into shining crystals of anthracite.

All motion stops.

All sound.

Everyone is looking at Peter, and the silence in the Palladium becomes oppressive, choking with foulness. Still no one utters a sound. No one moves.

Until . . .

On the dais, one man stirs to his feet.

Resplendent in his ceremonial robes, sparkling with a kind of pure, brilliant whiteness, the Pope glares at Peter and steps forward.

"Io ti conosco," he says. *I know you.*

Father Peter looks at the old man in the tall miter and Carenza grins a lopsided grin.

The Pope jerks to a halt in midstride like a marionette whose strings are abruptly tangled. He grabs his left arm with his right hand; his jeweled ring sparkles in the midday sunlight. The pontiff presses both liver-spotted hands to his chest as his eyes widen, his round little mouth pops open. He collapses into the arms of his entourage, but he is dead before they can even lower him to stage.

A huge roar rises from the assembly. The great hive thrum of people attuned itself to the overmind of its new ruler.

Gaetano exhaled slowly, drawing strength and inspiration from what he had witnessed. His preparations were complete and he was ready to begin the journey down a tortuous path that led to only one possible destination, at a single moment in time.

Three

Father Giovanni Francesco—Vatican City
August 7, 2000

*F*ather Giovanni Francesco arose from his desk and walked slowly toward his office window. The effort of merely standing and putting himself into motion was a supreme effort, reminding him of how weary and how old he had become. Or rather, how old he *felt*, because he had never before let his advancing age stand in the way of his vital interests. Francesco had always been accustomed to his plans working out precisely as envisioned. A man who expected unquestioned obedience and ultimate success.

He was a member of the Society of Jesus, which de facto branded him as something of a maverick within the infrastructure of the Church, but he had always been known as a radical individualist, regardless of his Jesuit training. Possessing a Ph.D. in political science, Father Francesco proved a formidable opponent in the endless maneuverings and palace intrigues of the Vatican. His official title as Society of Jesus liaison to the papal office was one he'd held for more than a generation, and his peers generally agreed there had never been a more competent, if perhaps ruthless, person in the history of the position.

But regardless of his past performances, Francesco was fast growing weary not only of his work but of his life in general. Ever since the transformation of his protégé from Brooklyn priest to Pope Peter II, Francesco's intricate machinations seemed ineffectual.

Odd, he thought, he'd never imagined feeling so detached from his work, from his mission. . . .

Reaching the high, narrow window, the Jesuit looked out absently, without really seeing anything. His vantage point was the administrative building of the Vatican, the Governorate—a great warren of offices overlooking the Vatican Gardens and a panoramic view of the tiled rooftops of Rome beyond. But Francesco was not regarding the pristine beauty of the gardens or the hazy, terra cotta city in the distance.

Rather, his attention gradually focused upon a building diagonal to his own that contained the papal apartments, to a specific window from which Marion Windsor had . . . fallen.

Fifty feet, landing on her skull and shoulders, she had been killed instantly. However, she remained among the world's deceased for only moments until Pope Peter II raced down to ground level, lifted her into his arms, and performed the miracle of resurrection. The event had happened so quickly that practically no one even learned of it. The Swiss Guards on duty and a few assistants, but that was all.

Indeed, Giovanni himself might have not discovered it but for his long-established network of palace spies and informers. Early on in his assignment at the heart of the Catholic Church, he learned the value of

a flawless system of information conduits. Throughout the political bowels of the Holy See, Francesco
identified *needs* and supplied them in exchange for *favors*. An age-old mechanism that worked well—though
its limits were repeatedly tested by the especially delicate nature of Marion Windsor's relationship to Pope
Peter II.

As a precautionary measure, she had been taken to
the Vatican infirmary for tests and observation, and it
was for word of her condition that Francesco now
waited.

His intercom buzzed politely, followed by the voice
of his secretary: "Excuse me, Father . . ."

For I have sinned, thought Francesco.

". . . Cardinal Lareggia is here."

Returning to his desk, Francesco keyed the device.
"Send him in."

Almost instantly, the double doors to the baronially
ornate office swung open to reveal an obese man in the
traditional cassock of scarlet. Paolo Cardinal Lareggia
was a massive coronary waiting to happen. In his seventies, and perhaps two-hundred pounds overweight,
his face appeared to be pinched into the folds of his
neck and jowls so that he had no real distinguishing
features other than a general doughiness. He did not
so much walk into the room as he tottered back and
forth on thick, trunklike legs, barely executing a forward motion. His gait appeared as painful as it was
slow and ungainly. Lareggia moved to the nearest
chair, lowered his bulk into it like a dockside crane
settling its load.

"Good afternoon, my friend," said the Cardinal.

"Did you see her?"

Lareggia nodded, produced a lace handkerchief to

mop his perspiring forehead. "Yes, I saw her firsthand. She is fine."

"Actually, I expected nothing less," said Francesco bitterly. "It wouldn't make much sense to bring someone back from the dead without conferring good health in the bargain."

"It's so embarrassing!" said the Cardinal. "And we kept it quiet! Can you imagine what it would have been like if the media picked up on this latest mess?"

"He is destroying the sanctity of his office." Francesco moved to his desk, produced a pack of Gauloises cigarettes from one of its drawers. Lighting one, he paused to draw the first puff deeply into his lungs.

"And you are destroying your lungs with that stenchful weed."

Francesco looked at him with contempt. "We all have our weaknesses, don't we?"

"Giovanni, I—"

"You know she didn't 'fall' from that window," said Francesco with a mixture of anger and frustration. "My only question is why he did it in the first place, if he planned to bring her back? What purpose did the entire episode serve?"

"I was thinking it might have been a warning to all of us." Lareggia's tone reflected his respect and his fear of the subject matter. "Or else it was truly an accident."

Francesco gave the barest nod of agreement. "What did we do? What have we loosed upon the world?"

"I know, I know!" Cardinal Lareggia shook his head and smiled desperately. "If this is the Second Coming, then somebody was lying about something."

Francesco began pacing the large office as he continued to smoke the unfiltered French cigarette. His thin frame and jagged movements gave him the aspect of a wary animal measuring the limits of its cage. He'd always acknowledged that his features were foxlike, and therefore shifty, predatory. He'd always used his lean and hungry look to his advantage in dealing with adversaries and allies alike.

"Half a year since he assumed power," said Francesco. "And look what he has done."

"You mean the changes he has wrought?" The Cardinal suppressed an urge to chuckle. "Why should *you* care? Have you not spent your life pointing out how medieval the Church has remained? Have you not campaigned for the kind of sweeping changes Peter has already proclaimed?"

Giovanni held up an index finger to make a point. "Ah, yes, my large crimson friend, but reexamine your words. You said 'the *kind*' of changes! I say: not exactly the ones he has enacted."

"You are dancing on the edge of the monastery wall," said Lareggia.

"No, I don't think so. When one considers the appalling consequences of large families in many South American countries where the economies are erratic or nonexistent, I believe it is possible that birth control—in some church-sanctioned form—*could* be considered helpful, or even humanitarian."

"But?"

"But approving premarital sex is, I feel, going too far—not because of its possible sin quotient as much as the signal that the Church is relinquishing so much *control* over its members." Francesco shook his head to dramatize his displeasure with the idea. "I also think it's a very bad idea to join into global strategies that concern world economies. The wealth of the Church should not be open to public inspection and certainly not invested in risky or politically sensitive areas."

Lareggia nodded gravely. It was obvious he enjoyed

having Francesco in agreement. "And you have no doubt heard rumors Peter has more sweeping changes planned?"

"Of course! And progressive thinker that I am," said Francesco. "I see a case of 'too much too soon.' It will rock the very foundation of the Church. As an organization, the Church has withstood the test of time because of its very nature, its inflexibity, its immutability."

Lareggia grinned. "I never thought I would hear you speak in such tones!"

"I have always lobbied for change in a progressive fashion. Not anarchy couched in the garb of the sensational."

"Well put, Father."

Francesco ignored the compliment, continued. "And frankly, I am surprised he has allowed us to live, since we are part of the few who know his true nature—or at least his origins."

"That's right," agreed Lareggia, still seated, but finally retiring the damp hankie. "His true *nature* is still a matter of speculation."

Francesco stared off, as if remembering a scene from long ago. "Can you imagine the sensation if they knew our secret? "

"No, I cannot. Nor do I wish to."

Considering the sensation the cloning of that silly *sheep* had caused, thought Giovanni, the world media would create a feeding frenzy of speculation and moralizing if they ever discovered that Peter had been cloned from blood off the Shroud of Turin, then brought to term in the teenage womb of a virgin nun.

"How bold we were, eh?" said Giovanni.

"Bold or crazy."

Francesco chuckled softly. "You know, before this saga of Peter Carenza began, I had begun to doubt everything."

Lareggia looked at him, wondering if he understood what he was saying. "You mean a crisis of faith?"

"Precisely. You know the thoughts, the questions, the feelings of abject silliness when you look at the conceptions of some of the Renaissance painters, the simplistic ideologies of sin and punishment . . ."

"Yes, I do." The Cardinal allowed the admission to escape him with obvious embarrassment.

"But along comes our 'godson,' Peter Carenza, performing undeniable miracles, and the work of some greater power, and the proof of its existence, is suddenly right there in our faces."

"Yes," said Lareggia. His voice belied a certain fear beneath the intended joy.

Francesco paused, turned quickly. "Yes, but it is obvious he works with the . . . permission . . . if not the imprimatur, of God himself. *He* has allowed Peter Carenza into the world for a *purpose!* A divine purpose, for certain! But we have not yet discovered what that purpose might be."

"Is it possible we are not worthy of such knowledge?"

"Cardinal, please, we are members of the Church hierarchy. If not men as lofty as ourselves, then who?"

"Giovanni, you are joking, aren't you? Sometimes I cannot tell anymore."

"What does it matter?" Francesco stubbed out the cigarette, immediately fired up another. There was an intensity in his eyes, a light that had remained banked like hot coals. "The thing to seize upon is this: We have been allowed to live for a *reason!*"

"Allowed by whom?"

"God? Or Peter?" Francesco smiled. "It doesn't matter. Don't you see? We have been given a job to do. We are the ones who must discover Peter's purpose here."

Cardinal Lareggia shifted his great weight uncomfortably in the wooden chair. "Why?"

"Because I sense it. I've been thinking about our situation for some time now, and the incident with Marion Windsor has crystallized my thoughts. I see it clearly now."

"You've lost me," said Lareggia.

"Look, will you agree with me that the Holy Mother Church is under siege—by the very presence of Carenza in the Vatican?"

"Of course!"

"What did Peter do today?"

Lareggia was clearly confused, and said nothing.

"He brought Marion back to life!" said Francesco. "If he merely wanted her dead, he wouldn't have done that—which means that something went wrong. Either she jumped, trying to escape from him, or it was an accident."

Lareggia's eyes widened. "Whatever the truth, he was not in control!"

"Exactly. Which means that our Pope is in some kind of metaphysically mutable state. His is a spiritual alloy still being forged, and we are present during the process."

The Cardinal frowned. "Giovanni, please, don't speak in metaphors right now, not when I was just beginning to think I understand what you are talking about."

Francesco shook his head. "All right, let me put this as simply as I can. I think that Peter's soul is still, as the Americans say, 'up for grabs.' That is: Whatever names we wish to ascribe to the pivotal forces in the world—good and evil will suffice—I believe they are still in great conflict over the ultimate control of Peter Carenza."

The Cardinal nodded. "I *hoped* that was a possibility. My prayers have echoed the same desire. Peter is perhaps not yet committed to the wrong side."

Francesco exhaled quickly, held up his index finger. "Precisely, my colleague, but the question we must answer is: *Which* side *is* the wrong one?"

FOUR

Huang Xiao—Beijing
August 30, 2000

*E*arthquake coming.

The thought had always come to Huang Xiao just like that.

Nothing dramatic or somatically painful or traumatizing, just an idea that entered his mind. Naked and alone. Sometimes he would think no more of the quake until it actually happened; other times he received the time and the place as well.

Xiao was a tall, thin boy of eighteen, who spent his days in long, overly disciplined classes on agricultural engineering and his evenings taking care of his grandparents, Li Ping and Dao Tu. Xiao's parents had both been killed almost ten years previously, during a campaign against intellectuals who espoused capitalism as a viable means of economic survival.

Seated at the bench by their dining table, Xiao had been resting before clearing the earthenware from its rough-hewn surface. The house was in a shabby suburb of the city called Kow Pei, a district notorious for its black market activities. So outrageous were the underground dealings in Western commodities that the police and the army had long ago stopped trying to stop them. Many of them were some of the markets' largest traders. Whenever Xiao observed the marketeering, he would think of his parents, who surely would never have been murdered in a climate such as this.

"Mi-mi," he said softly to his grandmother. "I have 'the feeling' again."

His grandmother looked up from her sewing with a grave expression. She had been the first to know of Xiao's uncanny talent, when he innocently discussed an impending quake at the age of five. Since that very first "feeling," he had never been wrong, even though he always wished he might be mistaken.

"There seem to be more happening now, yes?"

Xiao nodded.

"What is happening to the world?"

"I don't know, Mi-mi."

"This latest one . . . do you know *where*?"

He shook his head. "Not yet. Perhaps I will."

"Will you warn them?"

"I must try."

"You must be very careful, my tall boy," said the old woman. "The last time was very bad for you."

She was referring to the stories that the government was looking for him.

"They won't catch me." Xiao stood, stacked the dishes, and took them to the washtub. He tried to occupy himself with a mindless task to keep off the subject of the People's Committee on Natural Disasters, who made it quite clear they would eventually locate the person who had warned the mountain villages near Hsingtai that an earthquake would strike at 3:15 on the morning of April 22.

Being plugged into the university circuit, Xiao knew

there had been much research on animals as tools of earthquake prediction, but very little on the possible abilities of humans.

However, he had recently heard rumors along the corridors of government-sanctioned academia that the military was indeed interested. Among them was a faction that believed the peasant rumors of a willowy, dark-eyed boy who could predict tremors with perfect accuracy. Such knowledge, they argued, could be a most powerful weapon against the enemies of the people.

When Xiao began thinking along such lines, he would become lightheaded and dizzy, feeling as if he might vomit. Just the idea of using his ability to hurt people, to kill people . . .

No!

He would never allow them to use him. He would—

"Xiao!" said the graveled voice of his grandfather. "I will need help with the bags of rice. You will carry them from the granary."

Leaving the plates to soak in the tub, he bowed courteously and moved quickly to obey the frail old man. As he was edging past him toward the open door, his grandmother tugged on his sleeve, pulled him down to kiss him on the cheek. "You are a good boy. All we have in the world—you are the vessel of our dreams and our hopes."

"I know, Mi-mi," he said with respect.

"So you must be very careful. Always careful."

"I am very cautious."

She patted his hand. "Remember, there are those who would capture you like a rat."

"He knows this, old woman!" said his grandfather. "Let him finish his work. Then he can talk to you."

Xiao nodded and moved outside with the old man. As they both grabbed for the bags of rice, Li Ping paused, looked at him. "She does not want you running off to save the world. She is afraid you will never come back."

"I know."

"But you have to run off regardless, yes?"

Xiao half grinned. "I must, yes."

Li Ping nodded. "I understand. I am a man."

"It is the right thing to do. Otherwise, many more people will die."

"You know where it is, do you not?"

Xiao nodded with embarrassment.

"Tell me."

"Kweiyang," he said with obvious sadness. "I did not want her to know it was a place of such distance from here."

His grandfather nodded. "Almost a thousand miles."

"Yes."

"When?"

"Twelve days."

"How will you go such a long way?"

Xiao hefted two bags upward, one for each shoulder, sagging under the burden, but wishing the burden of his strange talent could so easily be borne. "I don't know, but I must."

Li Ping shrugged. "There are trains . . . but . . ."

"I know. Most easy for travel, but also most easy for getting caught."

They brought the bags of rice into the house, placed them in the cupboard. Li Ping signaled that they return to the outside, and Xiao followed him. As they closed the door, an incautious wind swept across the yard, penetrating their jackets. The sun was almost down and the landscape seemed to be closing in on them.

His grandfather led him out behind the granary, hunkered down against the wind, and spoke softly. "Your grandmother knows none of this, but some say the army is looking for someone who fits your description, while others say they already know your identity."

"I have heard these rumors," said Xiao, gesturing them away with a sweep of his hand. "It is the talk of the peasants. What do they know?"

"Tall One, your grandparents are peasants. Are we so stupid?"

Xiao bowed his head. "I meant no disrespect. I am sorry."

Li Ping smiled. "I am not so ancient to forget the impetuous nature of a young man. But we are moving off the main path. Do you know what it means if the peasant rumors are correct?"

"You mean if they are already watching me?"

"Yes."

"It means they wait for me to embark on another journey." Xiao paused to consider what his own admission actually meant. "But, Grandfather, it changes nothing for me. I know why I have this gift—to save lives. I cannot turn my back on that truth."

"There is another truth you do turn your back to. The army will use you for death."

Xiao nodded, whispered as if there might be ears in the wind. "Yes, but every great gift always has the potential for death as well as life. That is no reason never to use it."

Shoulders sagging, his grandfather exhaled in acceptance of Xiao's words. "You are correct, but I wish you were not always so wise."

"Thank you."

His grandfather tapped him lovingly on the arm. "When do you leave for Kweiyang?"

Xiao shrugged. "I have twelve days. I should leave now—to account for any delays."

"Yes, you are wise to do so. Do not tell Mi-mi anything. Leave that to me. It is better if you are simply gone."

"All right. I will prepare my baggage tonight, after she is asleep."

Li Ping nodded. "It is best."

So far, so good.

His freight car rattled over the Taiyuan trestle, spanning a mountain pass on the way to Penyang. Xiao sat by the door, watching a gibbous moon keep pace with the lurching, swaying train. The bleak countryside slipped past him in an unending tableau of villages and rough roads.

Xiao had covered more than two hundred miles in his first full day of travel. He wondered if he had been followed, but had no way of knowing. For all he knew, agents of the government were huddled in the car directly behind him. Of course he had tried to be careful, but he was no expert at the ways of stealth. Shaking his head, he returned to his book, a translation of stories by the American writer E. A. Poe, in an effort to distract his thoughts from possible capture. It was an event out of his control, and therefore he could not allow himself to worry about it.

And he did not, not until very late that night when the freight train slowed to a stop in the stockyards outside the provincial city of Yungchi. Having been lulled to fitful sleep by the gentle rhythms of the rocking cars, Xiao was startled to hear the sounds of the boxcar door sliding open.

He did not move and kept his eyes slitted shut, as if still in a doze. But he could see the moonlight expand to fill the opening of the freight car and the silhouette of a lean young man gingerly climbing aboard. Xiao's body tensed automatically as he prepared for any act of aggression, but the man who entered the car paused as soon as he noticed that he was not alone.

Going by body language alone, Xiao was almost convinced the intruder was genuinely surprised by the presence of another freeloading train rider. The man seemed indecisive as to whether he should retreat from the car and find another.

Xiao watched the man leaning into the open boxcar door, bent at the waist, half in, half out.

The man's head turned as though on a swivel. His eyes caught a dose of moonlight and glowed catlike for an instant as he looked directly at Xiao, assessed the situation, and climbed the rest of the way into the car.

No one stealing a ride on a train would do that, thought Xiao. I am in trouble. They know who I am.

His first thought was to run. But now was not the proper time. If there was one government representative in the train yards, there would surely be more. Better to wait until the odds were more favorable. Xiao had a better chance going one-on-one with the man clambering into the car than with a whole detachment.

The intruder was fully inside now and had turned his back to inch the door shut. As the man was throwing the latch, Xiao stirred and murmured, as though being disturbed in a deep sleep. As he opened his eyes, he saw the man turn slowly to regard him.

"Hey, what's going on?" said Xiao, trying to sound groggy, disoriented.

"Whoa! No cause for alarm, my brother!" The man held up his arms in a nonthreatening fashion, leaned back, farther away from Xiao.

"What are you doing here?"

The man bowed deferentially. "I am no different from you. I am only seeking travel to the south, and this was the only car unlocked."

Xiao looked at him cautiously. "How do you know what I am doing here?"

"Well, I just assumed you were—"

"How do you know I am not working for the People's Railroad?"

"I do not, my brother."

"And don't call me that—we are not related, I can assure you."

Xiao was taking a chance with his aggressive posture, but he needed to see how far they were willing to go in keeping up their ruse.

Suddenly, the train lurched into motion, throwing them both off balance and causing them to roll awkwardly across the dusty floorboards. The freight gradually picked up speed as the two men composed themselves.

"I am sorry," said the intruder. "I can get out if you want. . . ."

Xiao grinned. "Easy to make that offer now that we are moving. Not too practical, I would think."

The freight continued to gain speed as it left the switchyards of the rail hub and headed out into the open countryside south of Yungchi. Xiao peered momentarily through a small slit in the side of the car—the landscape was shadowed by the lowering moon, harsh and foreboding. Still, he had the feeling he was dealing with something far more threatening and unknown inside the train.

"I am sorry I scared you," said the young man, who appeared to be maybe in his midtwenties. He wore loose-fitting athletic warm-ups, which did not wholly conceal his well-muscled frame. "I did not expect this car to be occupied."

"But you entered anyway." Xiao looked at him with total suspicion.

"I had no choice! The signals had turned, and if I

wanted to be aboard this train, I had to jump on!"

"I see . . ."

"I mean you no harm, I swear it!"

Xiao remained noncommittal. The man was very convincing. A good government agent must also be a good actor, he would assume.

"Who said anything about harm?"

Again the man appeared to be deferential. He backed away, bowed, and held up his hands. "You know, it is I who should be wary of you! You have been very guarded and paranoid. What are you hiding, comrade?"

"I am not your 'comrade,' " said Xiao. He could feel the steady rhythm of the wheels against the joints of the rails. They had picked up speed; the locomotive was punching a hole into the darkness ahead.

"No, you are not," said the man, smiling for the first time as he took several steps toward Xiao's corner.

"I know why you are here," Xiao said, slowly standing to face the intruder.

The man nodded. "We did not think you were a dull boy."

"What do you plan to do now."

"We want to know where you are going."

"Sorry," said Xiao. "I cannot tell you that."

The man smiled. "Would you prefer we extract the location from your grandparents?"

"They don't know where I am going."

"Maybe. Maybe not."

Xiao stared at the government representative. It was hard for him to understand how anyone could surrender his basic being so totally to the state. Xiao figured it must be a reflection of how little a person could think of himself.

He shrugged, leaned against the wall, and spoke a painful truth. "My grandparents are old. You cannot scare them. And either would welcome death rather than betray me."

Xiao tensed and was only slightly relieved to see the man produce a cellular phone instead of a weapon.

"Wait!" Xiao said, taking a step closer. He calmed himself, forced himself to become acutely aware of the rocking, swaying motion of the train.

The man, who had begun to key in a number, stopped and smiled knowingly. "I thought perhaps we might be able to talk about things."

"Yes, perhaps we can . . ."

The man nodded, made a big show of folding up the cell phone.

Xiao had an instant to react. He had been watching the government man intensely, waiting for that precise moment when, hearing words of submission from his quarry, he would relax.

Without thinking, Xiao surged forward, grabbing the inner latch on the boxcar door, jerking it downward and pushing forward all in one blur of motion.

The heavy door slid open in a rush, and a blast of cold air hammered both of them. The agent was caught with one arm inside his jacket. He turned to intercede, but Xiao pressed the advantage, kicking him squarely in the testicles.

Everything was happening in a series of rapidly flashing images: the agent's eyes bulging in pain, the search-light glare of the moon through the open door, the howling blast of air, and the blur of the car's interior as Xiao spun around to shove the doubled-over agent into the darkness that rushed past them at death-dealing speed.

Watching him disappear soundlessly masked by the train's clatter, Xiao pulled back from the open door and allowed panic, fear, and tension to rush into him. For an instant, he felt paralyzed by the sudden shock of what he'd done without thinking—probably killed a man.

A man who would have killed his grandparents.

Xiao held the thought—it gave him strength and justification. He closed his eyes for a moment, gathered himself, exhaled slowly into the noisy blast of night air that howled around him.

No matter. He was in control.

As he reached for the heavy sliding door, preparing to close it, he heard the thump of footfalls on the roof of the car.

As Xiao had dreaded, the agent had not been alone. Quickly, he assessed his options—and found them to be few. Straining to see through the darkness outside the thundering freight, he realized he had little time. Whatever terrain blistered past him would have to be sufficient. Better to die in an attempt at freedom than to live under the yoke of his captors.

Above, the footfalls grew louder. Someone was climbing down the handholds on the side of the boxcar. So, using the frame of the open door for leverage, Xiao catapulted himself outward, arcing downward to unseen terrain. . . .

But the expected impact did not happen.

In a flash, a series of impressions registered: He was still falling, accelerating, which meant that the train had been passing over a bridge or next to an embankment; he would either be crushed among trees and rocks or dashed into the icy waters of a rushing river.

As the chilled darkness rushed past, buffeting and tumbling him, he tried to accept the knowledge he was about to die. And that was when he saw the lady, her flowing dress all aglow with an inner light, reaching out to him. . . .

FIVE

Marion Windsor—Vatican City
August 7, 2000

*W*hen she came to consciousness, it was like slowly pulling herself upward through a tunnel so confining that it threatened to crush her at any moment. Her efforts to awaken seemed futile and endless. Darkness held her in its soft glove; the only light appeared as a pinpoint, hopelessly distant and unreachable.

It would be so easy, Marion thought, to surrender to the blackness. But someone was calling her name, extending a tether from reality, a life preserver to a hypothermic castaway. The voice was vaguely familiar, soft, yet insistent. "Marion . . . you will wake up now. . . ."

The voice repeated the phrase until she obeyed, blinking her eyes, clearing them to quickly scan the room that held her. The austere white walls, glucose bag, and monitoring electronic gear shocked her. She'd been hospitalized. For a moment, she felt totally disoriented.

"Marion, you are all right now."

The voice again. Feminine. Slightly accented.

The person at her bedside was a woman. Short. Petite. A nun dressed in the drab habit of the Poor Sisters of Clares bent over Marion, touching her cheek gently, trying to smile and doing a bad job of it. Marion recognized the woman though they had never spoken before. The name came easily to her lips.

"Sister Etienne."

The nun touched a finger to her lips, nodded.

Marion studied her. Although her face was smooth and unlined, the nun appeared to be in her late forties. There is a certain look of maturity, of wisdom that comes with age, and Marion could see it in the angular planes of Etienne's Mediterranean features. This was the first time Marion and Etienne had met, and Marion discovered that an odd sensation filled her—a combination of respect and awe.

Etienne was Peter Carenza's mother.

"Be still, please," said the nun.

"Sister Etienne, why are you here? Did . . . did Peter send you?"

"No, my son does not speak much with me."

"Then why?"

"Do you remember what happened?"

Marion nodded, feeling her face flush. "We were arguing. I fell backward, against the windowsill. Peter—" Her heart pounded as the memory of falling swept through her. Then, she had been calm. Now, she felt panic. Etienne touched her hand gently, soothingly.

"All that matters is that you are all right now." Etienne patted her hand again, smiling. "I am here because I dreamed about this moment, about meeting you here. This has been ordained by God."

Marion listened to her speak—slowly, with the precise pronunciation of someone who had mastered English recently. Marion knew that Etienne's ability to "see" things in dreams and visions had been a subject of discussion and speculation in the Vatican for several years. She had even heard rumors that Etienne had foreseen the previous pope's death, had repeatedly attempted to get an audience with the late pontiff so she could warn him. No one had taken her seriously.

"Do you have these dreams often?" asked Marion.

"No, but when I do, they are significant."

Marion edged herself up higher in the hospital bed. "Did your dream predict future events? Did it involve us?"

Etienne pulled a chair close to the bed, sat down, and looked at her with almond-shaped eyes. "I dreamed I would be sitting here in this room, with you. That we would speak as we are speaking now."

Marion leaned closer, spoke softly, even though they were alone. "No, I mean, were specific events revealed to you?"

"No. That will come later." Marion's frustration must have shown on her face, for Etienne continued, "Please, be patient. I know that you are alarmed, agitated. But we cannot rush the hand of God. He chooses to touch my dreams in his own fashion, and I am familiar with the way he works."

"Okay . . ." Still doubtful.

Etienne smiled. "This dream of meeting *you* is the key, you see. The way God prepares me for what will come next. Since it is happening *exactly* as I dreamed it, I know more revelations will soon be granted us."

Marion said nothing at first, feeling infinitely small and very weak. She sensed the stage being set for a profoundly important series of events and found herself wondering what possible part she could have in the machinations to come. Her old confidence and self-reliance seemed feeble allies now, as she prepared to stand at the very edge of the universe and lean into the wind of destiny itself.

"What will happen to us?" she asked after a while.

"God will protect us. He will show us what he wants of us and the way to make it happen."

Marion nodded as she settled back into the bed. She had never been able to figure out the whole God thing. Throughout the ages, and in just about everybody's sacred texts, some god was always asking some mortals to do something, and Marion had always wondered *why*. If he was really God, then why did he need anybody else's assistance for anything? The oddest thing was that for a little while, when she and Peter had begun their quest to discover his true nature and his mission in the world, Marion had *not* wondered about any divine motives or plans or demands. She had given herself totally to the moment, and for the first time in her life she had been truly at peace.

Perhaps that was the key to finding answers to those sorts of questions. When you became completely immersed in a belief system, it took care of you, comforted you, and removed the need for questions. In her years as a broadcast journalist, she'd covered countless tragedies, interviewed thousands of people whose loved ones had been killed in auto accidents and brutal crimes, by bizarre weather, and in every other kind of lethal encounter. What had always intrigued her was how the people were able simply to go on, to cope with the sudden, irrational death of a child, a husband, or a wife.

When Marion had imagined herself in their situations, she pictured herself as so crushed that there would be little left worth living for. But people had amazed her again and again with their platitudes about God's will and the hereafter and that sort of thing. And thcy had survived. Somehow. Marion saw the power of faith but never understood it.

Then, at Peter's side, she had experienced that power. When it deserted her, it had left a terrible void in her soul. But now, as she looked at this nun, Peter's *mother,* whose faith in God was unshaken despite recent assaults against all that could be divine, Marion realized that there was still hope for her.

She allowed a small grin to brighten her features. "Sister Etienne, I want to ask you a few questions. If you find them offensive or too personal, please tell me and I will respect your feelings. All right?"

"Yes."

"Tell me," Marion began. "Are you afraid of your son?"

"Yes." No hesitation.

"Can you tell me why?"

Sister Etienne stared at the blank white wall of the infirmary room. Marion watched, knowing she was staring into another place and time. Then, abruptly, Etienne refocused on Marion, her ice-blue eyes like bright warning beacons. "It has been many years since I carried him in my womb," she said, "but I remember almost every day of that experience as though it were yesterday. It is a very intimate thing to carry a tiny person within your own body. I grew to know the child very well, and from the very first days I knew Peter was not like other babies."

"How? Was he dangerous? Evil?"

Etienne shook her head. "No. Nothing like that. Just *different.* Not like me. Not like any of us."

An alarming thought occurred to Marion. Sister Etienne had lived most of her life as a cloistered nun, removed from the vast information stream of the modern world. It was possible she did not know *how* her son had been conceived.

There was no way to ask Etienne about this without arousing suspicion or apprehension in the older woman. Marion had to speak to one of the people responsible for Peter's existence—Abbess Victorianna of Poor Clares Cloister or Paolo Cardinal Lareggia of the College of Cardinals. There was another man, a Jesuit named Giovanni Francesco, but Marion so instinctively disliked and distrusted the man that she vowed to have no dealings with him.

As casually as possible, she asked Etienne, "When you say 'different,' how do you mean?"

"I knew from the beginning the child had been, in some way, touched by God. I remember lying in my dark bed, feeling the yet-to-be baby moving inside me and, in his way, speaking to me. He told me he would be special and that he would change the world."

Marion nodded. Mothers often spoke of a special connection, a channel of communication, between themselves and their developing child.

At that moment, Etienne's attention grew sharper still. Her blue eyes stared more intensely, yet she spoke without emotion. "Do you believe me?"

Taken by surprise, Marion hesitated, though her reply was sincere. "Yes, of course—"

"But there is more—you wish to know if I *really* know how my son was conceived."

Marion felt herself blushing with a combination of embarrassment and excitement. "Yes, but how could you—?"

"For the past several years, I have been characterized as 'extrasensitive' by the clergy who have questioned and examined me." Etienne leaned closer to Marion's bed, smiled in a way that was playful but with an edge of steel.

Marion did not reply for a moment, gathering her wits and a newfound respect for the demure-looking nun. "I am so sorry, Sister Etienne. I didn't mean to insult you or give offense."

"None was taken. But please believe me—I know *exactly* what they did to me."

"How? Who told you?"

Etienne spoke softly with a conspiratorial tone. "Last year, when Peter presided over that huge rock music festival . . ."

"MountainRock Ninety-nine," said Marion nodded, remembering it all. She had been there.

"Yes, that is correct." Etienne paused to take a breath. "Just after the accident happened, when Peter raised the river and all those people were drowned—"

Marion interrupted, "They were dying of thirst. He was trying to save them."

"So I understand," Etienne acknowledged. "At that time, I was contacted by Dr. Rudolph Krieger. Having lived in the cloister, I did not recognize his name. I did not know he had won the Nobel Prize for genetics. I did not know why he would want to see me. But he was very kind, very much a gentleman, and I sensed I could trust him.

"He told me that he had been living with a momentous secret for more than thirty years, and the burden had become more than he could bear."

"How did you know he was telling you the truth?" Marion felt that Etienne was confiding things to her that she'd never told anyone else, that the nun was looking for an ally, but perhaps more important, a friend.

"He knew so much about what happened to me, back when I was only sixteen years old."

"You did not recognize him as the doctor who worked on you?"

Etienne shook her head. "Father Francesco had

never allowed me to see the doctor's face."

"I'm sorry I interrupted, please, go on," said Marion.

Etienne nodded. "He told me that I had been selected for the project because I was a virgin . . . because they needed a virgin birth. Abbess Victorianna had told me I had been selected by God to perform a divine duty, but Dr. Krieger made me understand that there was nothing divine about what they had done to me.

"And then, when I finally understood what they'd done, I was rid of the guilt—for sins I did not commit. I should have realized long before then that God was not angry with me. If so, he would not have sent me the gift of visions and prescience."

"Are you certain it's a gift and not a curse?" Marion could not resist the question.

Etienne smiled. "One can receive only *gifts* from the Creator. Problems arise only in the way one chooses to use them."

Marion nodded. She liked Sister Etienne. The nun exhibited a serenity of spirit coupled with great courage and determination. "I don't want to sound presumptuous," said Marion, "but you speak with such confidence, such belief, yet I can't understand why you want to talk to me."

Etienne smiled gently. "You are very perceptive. As I said, we are connected to Peter in very special ways, and I believe God has selected us for a truly divine mission."

Now Marion was certain she knew what Etienne was driving at. It had been at the back of her mind since the nun had begun talking. "Do you really think we can do anything to change him, to stop him?"

Etienne smiled. "I am not certain. God will show me the way when the time is at hand, that I know. Right now, in my heart, I do not wish harm to Peter, only to remove him from the influence of Satan."

"Do you think it is as simple as that?"

Etienne shook her head. "No, nothing is ever simple. Complexity is the greatest beauty of the world."

Marion had never heard it expressed like that, but she liked it. "But what if more is required?"

"What do you mean?"

"Suppose God demands . . . oh, you know what I mean . . . something more drastic? Would you be willing to do whatever would be required?"

"You mean to *kill* my son." It was not a question. "Did he not ask the same of Abraham? Why should my response be any different? What about *you*, Marion?"

"Well . . . I . . ." She was not sure *what* she felt anymore.

"You were in love with Peter Carenza, yes?"

"Sister Etienne, I knew he was a priest. I knew it, but . . . oh, I am so sorry . . ."

Etienne touched her wrist gently, then grasped her hand and squeezed it. "Please, Marion, I do not accuse you. Just because I am a nun, do not assume I do not understand the awesome power of loving someone. I do not blame you for falling in love with Peter."

"I was with him when he discovered what he could do for people, when he discovered who he was . . . or might be, actually." She sighed. "I could use a little more of your wisdom and courage," Marion said. "I have to tell you—I have been close to giving up."

"You are needed. You cannot surrender now. Have you tried prayer? With God's assistance, anything is possible."

"I already believe that," Marion said, "but I feel weak. Are you sure you want my allegiance?"

"Yes. We may be the only ones who really know what he is doing to the church and the world. We may also be the only ones capable of doing something about it."

Marion regarded the nun with growing respect. Her control of the English language was impressive. Her eyes sparked with intelligence and great perceptivity.

"Sister Etienne, I'm not sure what Peter's ultimate plans might be. He might not know himself, not yet anyway, but there's something I should tell you—about one of his most immediate intentions. He's preparing a papal proclamation to announce that clergy will be allowed to get married."

Marion paused, waiting for a reaction from Etienne, but was not surprised when the older woman received this news without expression. All she said was, "I expected this, sooner or later."

Marion chuckled nervously, embarrassed. "Yes, but you must know what that means. He wants to get married—to *me!*"

Etienne nodded. "Yes?"

"What should I *do*, Sister?"

"Marry him, of course."

"What? *Why?*"

"You will be our main conduit of information about him and his activities, his plans. You must become his perceived ally again."

Marion knew the nun spoke sensibly, but it did not make her task any more palatable. Marrying the Pope in an outrageous public ceremony would be the most self-contemptible thing she would ever do. "All right," she said, bowing her head, feeling ashamed of resenting what was demanded of her. "I understand. You are correct."

Etienne patted her hand, then stood up. "You should rest for a while. I have given you so much to think about. I apologize for that, but it was necessary to speak with you."We will do whatever God asks of us—that is our vow to him, and to ourselves. If he requires that we sacrifice Peter to the world, we will know it." Etienne straightened a bit. "And we will do it."

SIX

Father Giovanni Francesco—Vatican City
August 24, 2000

I was sent here to kill you."

The words were spoken by a tall, muscular young man wearing a tailored suit, accessorized by a black alpaca topcoat, a matching fedora, and a chromium-plated 9-mm Glock with silencer.

He stood in the threshold of Giovanni's apartment on the via Cola di Rienzo answering the question that had just been put to him by the old priest: "What the hell do you want at this hour?"

"I am not surprised," said Giovanni with elegant weariness. The man standing before him was obviously an operative of the *Servizio Segreto Vaticano*. "Would you like to come in? Or must you shoot and run?"

The man looked at Giovanni with a puzzled, bemused expression. He hesitated for a moment in the dark corridor, then entered the room. Giovanni backed away from him automatically, noticing that the man moved with stealthy grace of a panther. A sense of control and confidence emanated from him like lethal radiation. With his weapon still leveled at Giovanni, he spoke again: "Most are very surprised. Why not you?"

Giovanni smiled and shook his head. "Listen, son, I've been expecting something like this for quite some time now."

"Interesting." The man looked genuinely impressed with his response. "I must admit I was very shocked to see your name on my 'grocery list.'"

Giovanni continued to back slowly into the room. The assassin mirrored his movements, and slowly they drew deeper into the priest's apartment. Giovanni was not afraid, despite the agent's menacing aspect, perhaps because he believed he deserved whatever punishment the man had come to deliver. "I did not think you were instructed ever to care about such things."

"Normally, I do not, but this . . . *you* . . . are different. Tell me what you know about this. Why did they send me to *you*, of all people?"

Giovanni could not keep from grinning. "You want to know *why*?"

The tall man nodded.

"So, you are not only the executioner but also the magistrate?! *You* will decide whether or not I am deserving of my sentence?"

The two of them had inched into the center of the living room. The man gestured with his glistening gun toward a chair in one corner. "Sit down, Father. I am curious about how a man of your reputation became my target."

"How do you know me?" said Giovanni.

"You worked with Targeno, did you not?"

Giovanni nodded. "Well, technically, he worked for me, but . . ."

"They used to call him 'the surgeon.' He was the best agent we ever had. Maybe the best in the world."

"'A legend in his own time,' as they say?" Giovanni

continued to grin softly as he recalled the verbal spar-
ring in which he and Targeno had often engaged.

"They will be talking about some of his . . . accomplishments for a long time," said the agent, not attempting to mask the respect in his tone.

"And my association with him may save me? Is that
what you are telling me?"

The man shook his head, took a seat on the couch,
then rested the Glock on his knee. It was still pointed
at Giovanni's midsection. "No, not really. But it is a
well-established conviction among us that Targeno was
killed by Peter Carenza. And if it *is* the current excuse
we have for a pope who now wants you dead, then I
must have cause to think."

Giovanni smiled openly. "You know, my son, you
think too much! That's a dangerous attribute in an operative. That was your fallen hero's problem, too."

"Everyone is very much afraid of Peter Carenza,"
said the young man. "This is hardly the proper attitude
toward the Holy Father, don't you agree?"

"Yes, but we live during strange days."

"Father, why does the Pope want you eliminated?"

"What is the usual reason for an assignment like
this?"

The agent shrugged. "You represent some kind of
threat to him."

"Actually, I am flattered he feels that way. It is true
that I believe he should be removed both from his office
and this life, and I *have* plotted and conspired to see
how these ends could be met, but . . ."

"But what?"

Giovanni chuckled. "But I am an old man! My conspirators are a fat cardinal who is older than me and a
nun! What could we possibly do?"

The agent tilted his head in thought. "Men do not

always fear others because of what they can do—but rather what they *know*."

"You are a very shrewd young man."

"Anything you can tell me?"

"I am not certain," said Giovanni as he measured how much he might risk revealing about himself and his past. He did not really trust this dark young man who was doing his best to befriend him. But he was lonely, and he did feel like talking, even if the conversation would eventually be punctuated by a bullet.

He reached for a Gauloise, fired up his Zippo lighter, ignited the cigarette. "You know, I've lately been suffering terrible bouts with an entity I'd believed had deserted me many decades earlier—my conscience."

The agent nodded. "A familiar nemesis."

"Yes, and it is usually late at night, that lonely and brooding time reserved for old bastards like me who can't fall asleep. It's bad when you lie there in the darkness and listen to your parts wearing out. I keep having the feeling that all the unsavory things I've done throughout my life are catching up with me."

The assassin leaned forward to listen more acutely.

"A man's sins are the business of himself and his God," said Giovanni. "But I believe I have been the architect of what could be the greatest sin of pride against God ever conceived."

"That sounds serious enough," said the man with the gun.

"If there is indeed a hell, I surely will be placed at its epicenter."

"I have read Dante, Father. Not for pride, you won't."

Giovanni smiled. "Then let me put it like this: I am responsible for Peter Carenza. Completely. If it were not for me, he would not be our pope; he would not even *exist!*"

The agent regarded him cautiously, probably wondering if he was listening to the rantings of a schizophrenic. After a reflective pause, he said, "You want to bring him down."

"More than anything."

"Are you afraid of him?"

Giovanni puffed on the cigarette aggressively, drew its smoke deep into his lungs and exhaled as he spoke. "More than anything."

The agent suddenly stood up, checked the chamber of his weapon.

"You know, Father, you have presented a very convincing case for sparing your life."

Giovanni shrugged. "I do not think I was actually trying to."

"A man I consider a monster has ordered your death," said the younger man. "I question his motives. Do you know about his mistress? What happened last week?"

Giovanni nodded.

"Stand up, Father."

Giovanni followed the command immediately, rigidly facing the tall, broad-shouldered man. What was going on? Despite the young man's proclaimed convictions, would his orders be carried out?

"Here," said the agent, offering Giovanni his weapon.

"What's this for?"

"Have you ever fired a gun before?"

Giovanni grimaced. "Unfortunately, yes."

"You will need to shoot me—"

"What?"

"Not to kill me," the agent said quickly. "But it has to look good."

"You want me to shoot you with your own weapon?"

The assassin nodded, a smiled hinting at the corners of his mouth. "You have a better idea?"

Giovanni returned the Glock to him. "You expect your superiors to believe that a seventy-year-old priest disarmed you and shot you?"

"I'll tell them you must have been tipped off."

Giovanni chuckled, shook his head. "No. It makes more sense if I shoot you with *my* gun."

"You have one?" The agent could not suppress a smile of mixed admiration and surprise.

In his bedroom, Giovanni retrieved a Smith and Wesson .38 Police Special from his bedstand drawer, then returned to the living room holding it gently like an injured bird. "It hasn't been fired in years, and it sounds like a cannon when it goes off."

"What kind of ammo?"

"Standard load."

"Good. I don't want to get ripped up by a hollow point."

"Where am I to shoot you?"

"In the left arm, through the muscle. It will be clean and will heal quickly."

"Are you certain this is what you want?"

The agent smiled. "In doing what I do, I have learned that sometimes you must work on instinct, which has been telling me I should not kill you, Father. Do you understand what I am saying?"

"Yes."

"Very well. Then the only way I can avoid carrying out my orders is for you to stop me." The agent paused, looked around the room, sizing up the layout, then turned back toward the door. "Is this the only exit?"

"No. There is a back entrance to the alley."

"Good. Let's get on with it."

Giovanni looked down at the gun in his hands. He

fought an involuntary tremble. Could he go through with this? He must. "How do you want to make this play?" he asked tonelessly.

"I'm going to stand outside the front door. You will have been expecting me. You opened the door a crack, fired once, then escaped through the rear. I will fire several shots through this door, obviously missing you."

"All right," said Giovanni, feeling a knot of tension growing in his gut.

Gliding to the door, the agent paused before opening it and looked at Giovanni with an expression of kindness that was neither patronizing nor saccharine. "Ready?"

The priest nodded.

"I will fire the two silenced shots first. Once your thirty-eight goes off with its cannon blast, we will be calling attention to the scene."

"Of course," said Giovanni.

"One more thing," said the agent. "As soon as you fire, you must run for your life. Take with you only what you would be able to grab if you were truly afraid for your life. Do you understand? I will tell them you were tipped off and that you were in the midst of preparing to flee when I interrupted you, so—a small carry-on bag with essentials. That is all."

"I understand."

"Then *presto!* Get a bag—do it now! I will figure out the ballistics of our charade."

Giovanni turned toward his bedroom and regarded the comfortable trappings of the apartment. Having re-sided in the same place for more than forty years, every object and fixture bore his thumbprints both physically and psychologically, representing his likes and dislikes, his fears and his joys. If a stranger had ever entered the apartment, it would be difficult for that person to recognize it as the home of a Jesuit priest. There were no religious icons other than a crucifix, which was almost omnipresent in any Roman domicile. The shades remained drawn most of the time, and the small amount of daylight that leaked into the space did little to enhance the dark oak furniture. The rooms were lean, masculine, unfettered—much like Father Francesco's demeanor and appearance.

It had been his home for a very long time, and now it seemed he might never see it again. Quickly, he pulled down a small piece of airline luggage and began stuffing it with clothes fit for travel, his stash of money, a pocketknife, his notebook/journal, and a Bible. No more than several minutes had passed when he returned to the front room.

"Good. Very good," said the man as he assessed the priest's preparations. "All right, Father, let's get this over with."

Giovanni watched the man position himself beyond the threshold of the front door, then close the door until it was ajar no more than six inches.

"Stand back," said the man, carefully aiming his sleek handgun.

Pffffftttt! Pffffftttt!

Two slugs exited the gun almost silently. One struck the far wall of the room without consequence, the other shattered a framed print of Caravaggio in a glittering blossom of fractured glass.

"*Presto!* Now come to the door, open it wide enough to see me, and aim as I tell you."

Without a word, Giovanni obeyed, allowing the man to position him and his weapon.

"I don't want you shattering my humerus, so we must get this right the first time." The man stepped back, posed himself carefully and with confidence, then, satisfied, held himself stonily like a sculptor's model.

"Now, Father . . . you will pull the trigger please."

Don't think about it.

He squeezed gently, tripping the gun's firing pin. Giovanni staggered backward, recoiling from the shock and the sound of the weapon's report in the close quarters of the room. He caught a quick glimpse of the agent being spun around as the slug ripped through his arm, exploding the rich fabric of his coat into black snowflakes. Giovanni's ears were ringing, his nostrils stinging from the scent of cordite. For an instant, time seemed distended, unreal. He felt disoriented, panicked that he didn't know what to do next.

"Get out of here!" said the agent in a harsh whisper.

Blinking, Giovanni focused on the figure of the agent, slumped across the floor of the apartment building's corridor. With the echo of the gunshot reverberating in his memory, Giovanni heard the first excited cries of alarm and curiosity from neighbors. The agent was right—he had no time to delay.

Turning to flee, Giovanni paused for a second, wanting to check on his felled ally, but the man must have sensed his intent. As he moved slowly to prop himself up against the hallway wall, he flashed him a quick thumbs-up, then slumped down to bleed quietly.

Grabbing his carry-on bag, Giovanni stuffed the still smoking gun into its depths, yanked shut the zipper, and ran for the kitchen egress. As he stepped into the night, an unseasonably cold wind slapped his cheek like an angry woman. It was a pleasurable sensation; it awakened him to the immediacy of the moment, and for the first time in many years, Giovanni Francesco felt undeniably and completely alive.

So strange . . . he wanted to stand defiantly against the night and savor the sensation, but the chase was on. No panic. Just keep moving. Think on your feet. He could not go to the Vatican motor pool or the Swiss

Guard. No way to tell who'd been drawn into Peter's lethal loop.

Steadily, in a half jog, Giovanni moved down the alley connecting with the via Germanico. Any second he expected to hear the sound of pursuit or feel the impact of silenced rounds.

But there was nothing but the ambient whispers of the night and the occasional passing vehicle to punctuate the darkness. For the moment, at least, he had escaped.

Pausing to catch his breath and his thoughts, Giovanni leaned against the wall of a building and realized that he had no place actually to *go*.

He had no friends or relatives to give him refuge. But he *did* have associates and colleagues who would be considered unsavory in many circles of Roman society.

Before he had become a priest, when he was still a young man, he had worked with the OSS in Rome, just after World War II. He had been headstrong, careless, but also fearless, and earned the respect of older operatives because there was no assignment too demanding. His movements brought him into contact with every stratum of Italian culture, and he kept track of favors paid and owed.

Obviously he could not stay in the city. Perhaps not even in the country. There were people who would help him get away.

Checking his watch, Giovanni knew he could not linger in this neighborhood. He worked his way south to the Tiber, knowing he could get lost along the wharves and docks of the lower river. There were men who frequented those places who owed Giovanni favors—and now it was time to collect. He slipped into the backwash of a streetlamp just long enough to cross the street, then blended back into the shadows. The

klaxon bleat of an ambulance grew ever louder as the
vehicle homed in on his apartment. Other sirens com-
peted for his attention: police and other agents.

Giovanni smiled. The Tyrrhenian Sea waited for
him like a dark and familiar mistress. She would welcome him, asking no questions and revealing no secrets.

SEVEN

Peter Carenza—Vatican City
September 2, 2000

I must learn to control myself.

Peter repeated the notion silently to himself as though it were a sacred mantra. Though several weeks had passed, he continued to be haunted by what he had done to Marion. He had only meant to scare her, to send her a message that he was the supreme authority in her life. He hadn't meant to send her tumbling like a rag doll from the apartment window.

What was happening to him?

He'd never been so impulsive, so driven by such base emotions. There were many times now when he felt as if he clung to a tremendous pendulum as it swung from one emotional extreme to the other. In earlier, simpler times, had he heard such a description from one of his Brooklyn parishioners, Peter would have immediately suspected a manic-depressive syndrome. But in his own situation, it was difficult to imagine.

Not only did he have a long history of stability, he

had *powers*. And yet, the notion that he might be vulnerable to something, anything, increasingly plagued him.

That's why he'd decided to act on the impulse to get rid of Francesco.

He paused, drew a breath slowly, then exhaled as he stood by the Leonine walls, the last defense against the Saracens of centuries past. It was very late in the evening, and the droves of tourists had diminished to small pockets of foreigners drifting here and there in the great square of Saint Peter's. They were all dwarfed into insignificance by stone colonnades and fountained water, the obelisk, and the basilica itself. Peter adjusted his baseball cap and pulled the collar of his jacket up close to his jaw. With sunglasses, his disguise was innoucuous enough to draw no attention to himself, and he headed toward his objective with confidence.

Entering the Gate of Saint Anne, he selected the arched road that leads past the *Osservatore Romano* building and walked at a brisk pace. At first he had enjoyed passing incognito among the faithful. There was an impish humor that kept making him do it, just to see if he would ever be discovered.

Tonight, however, was different.

Peter approached the Vatican Library and the Court of the Belvedere, the location of the Secret Archives. As he ascended the ornate staircase to the set of buildings, he noted that the area had been cleared ahead of time by the Swiss Guard, who had been informed of his impending visit. Normally, anyone attempting to enter this area would be checked by several tiers of guards, and finally by the prefect of the archives himself.

But there were no such formalities required of the Holy Father, thought Peter—and that's *me*.

Passing the statue of Hippolytus, the notorious third-century antipope, Peter smiled and nodded in its direction. He felt an odd kinship with the Roman philosopher. Since it was so late in the day, the regular employees had departed, other than a few selected workers who were on call should Peter require assistance of any kind. As he strode down the center of the entrance corridor, he noticed that whoever remained in the building was hidden from his view.

Peter had become aware of the Secret Archives during one of his earliest conversations with Paolo Cardinal Lareggia after his return to Rome and his election to the papacy.

". . . and I thought you might want to discuss your 'mission' at the Vatican," said the Cardinal with obvious anxiety.

"No," Peter had said with a half smile. "I was going to play it by ear for a while."

"Well, I want you to know that I am at your disposal, Holiness, if you have any questions about your office or its protocol. And of course, if the matter is precedental or historical, there is always the Secret Archives."

"The Secret what?"

"L'Archivio Secreto Vaticano," said Lareggia. "It is the repository of all the Vatican's most sacred and important documents. Paul V Borghese established it in the seventeenth century."

"I've never heard of it," Peter said.

"It is listed in the tourist guides. . . . But its materials are not open to the public—only to those high officials within the Church who convince the Pope that their business requires researching the ancient texts."

"How ancient? What kind of material do we have there?"

Lareggia shrugged as he tried to mentally catalog and summarize what lay in the Archives. "The usual papal registers, nuncios, fogli d'avvisi, and miscellaneous fondi. But also many documents and text relating to the earliest days of the

Church. Origins of rites, lists of prophecies, miracles, papal correspondence, discourses of science and medicine . . . there is so much, I cannot mention everything. More than nine miles of bookshelves!"

Peter smiled. "I want to see this place," he had said.

The Cardinal had accompanied him on his first tour of the Archives. It had been a very formal, almost ceremonial adventure, which taught Peter very little, other than the basic layout of the secret repository. It was only during later visits, such as his current one, that Peter was able to explore more fully and discover what lay in its vaults and cases and endless shelves.

Peter's interest in the Archives was not that of an archaeologist or a historian. No. It was something much more primal. He could feel it deep within the core of his being. Like a switch being thrown—*the Secret Archives*. He needed to see them, to explore them, to plumb the depths of their mysteries and forgotten knowledge.

He didn't know why, but Peter couldn't deny the irrepressible hunger he felt burning in him. There was obviously information awaiting him in the Archives, because he'd responded to the Cardinal's revelation of its existence as if he'd been conditioned like one of Pavlov's dogs.

Peter shook his head as he ascended the steep staircase to the oldest section of the Archives—the Tower of Winds, originally built as an observatory. It seemed so long ago since his first trip to this place with Paolo Cardinal Lareggia, but it had actually been less than six months.

Even during those first few visits, Peter had been fascinated by the Archives, and he found himself exploring its niches and rooms with increasing frequency.

His responsibilities as pope included a never-ending series of appointments, audiences, staff meetings, religious services, rituals, and public appearances. The schedule was abusive and unrelenting, but he made it a point to reserve part of each day or evening for the Archives.

He was not sure what he was looking for, only that he would know it when he found it.

And so he combed through the massive indexes of the repository with a careful, expectant patience. A difficult thing to do, considering that the Archives had no cataloging system of card files like its British and American counterparts. Each index was a partial compilation of the materials stored in the Archives, each one a massive tome, and all handwritten by different scribes.

The use of computers was not even a pipe dream.

As he passed the Meridian room, off the Tower, Peter was reminded of something the prefect had shown him there on his initial tour. A single room, adjacent to the Meridian, contained nine thousand packages of documents of unexplored or unindexed documents, each package no larger than a short stack of magazines. Normally, the prefect had said, two of his assistants would need about a week to inventory a single package, and given that as a unit of measure, just the material in that single room would require more than 180 years of bibliographic labor.

Armed with such knowledge before even getting started, Peter had figured that his explorations of the Archives would be quite random and could be expected to produce only equally random results. But Peter also knew he must rely on serendipity and perhaps some sort of supernatural intervention. He had to trust his instincts on this one. He believed he would find something relevant to his "mission on Earth" (as the Cardinal had phrased it, which had always amused him, making it sound as if Peter were an alien . . .).

His seemingly innate interest in the Secret Archives made sense on another level as well. Peter was not blind to the changes wrought upon himself and the world since he had "evolved" into a new person. Just as everyone who knew him shared ambivalent feelings about him and his true identity, Peter himself continued to be wracked by long soul-searching sessions regarding his relationship to his religion, the world, and the mind of God. There were times when he felt totally in control of himself and his place in the world; and other times when he believed he was being completely manipulated, paraded across reality like a marionette.

Perhaps, he'd thought on many occasions, I will find the keys to understanding myself within the dusty corridors of this place.

And he was entertaining the same notion as he entered the room where he'd been most recently at study. The current object of his attention was an *Index of Forbidden Texts* written during the time of Lotario di Segni, better known as Pope Innocent III. The massive volume of calligraphic entries, all in Latin, had been completed in the year 1210 and had been compiled by a cadre of dedicated monks under vows of lifelong servitude to their pope.

Sitting down to a polished mahogany table, Peter focused upon the pages of the *Index*. He was searching for further references to a phrase that had caught his attention during his previous several visits to the Archives: *the Secret of the Seven*. He had found several mentions of this "secret" and their corresponding texts but had yet to locate the actual manuscripts or tomes that might illuminate the meaning of the phrase or, better yet, reveal the secret and the identity of the Seven.

The infuriating incompleteness of the Archives was beyond Peter's power to change. There was so much material sequestered within its miles of shelves and stored inside its vaults, there had never been enough man-hours or manpower to properly codify, classify, and organize all the information. Cross-referencing lay beyond the limited abilities and time of the workers.

The Secret of the Seven.

The first time he read the words, there had been an instant of pure resonance throughout his entire soul, like an electric charge surging and singing across the length of him. He knew the phrase held special meaning, for him and for the world at large.

His search for correlating references proved painfully slow, yet there had been several small discoveries that sparked his imagination and renewed his confidence.

Concomitant references to the book of *Revelation* suggested that the Secret of the Seven might be concerned with the end times as depicted by John. This topic, of course, was of great interest to Peter because he believed he had been selected to be a focal point during the millennium. If, indeed, he symbolized the fate of the world at the time of a great reckoning, then he believed it was his obligation, indeed, his destiny, to discover what his true role was to be.

Some perceived his agenda of foundation-rocking changes in the policies and procedures of the Catholic Church to be insidious, evil, even absurd. Peter had not seen it that way, although at times he felt that his uprooting of so much Church dogma was alternately amusing, experimental, or provocative. He freely admitted, at least to himself, that he'd designed many of the sweeping changes without any objective reasons. He'd simply wanted to observe the world-spanning reactions to his proclamations.

He shrugged as he stopped short of questioning his motives—down that path lay a quirky kind of madness.

Better to wrestle with the heavy, musty *Index* of ancient, cracked leather.

Secret.

The very word tantalized him with its plethora of meanings. Worst of all, it could mean nothing at all. The early disciples of the Church had been steeped in mysticism and superstition. Peter was quite aware of some of the radical interpretations of sects like the Essenes and others. If some of the ancient scrolls and texts had been authored by such theosophical extremists, the "secret" might be nothing more than the distillations of a subtle, religious lunacy.

Granting such a notion, it might be quite possible Peter had launched upon a hideously futile quest. The idea that he could be consumed by a search for something so . . . so silly was repugnant to him. Unacceptable under any circumstance.

No, it couldn't be like that. Besides, there was something significant about the number seven—on that there was little argument. From his days in the seminary and the college courses in comparative religions, he'd always been aware of how prominently the number seven figured in many mythologies and theologies. Checking his notes, as much to sustain his conviction as perhaps to provide a spark of inspiration, he ticked off some of Saint John's references to the number in question: seven churches in Asia, seven spirits, seven golden candlesticks, seven angels, seven stars, seven seals, seven days and nights . . .

Peter shook his head. He'd been over those references many times; and as with much of *Revelation*, there were almost as many ways to explain what John had been writing about as there were people reading his words. After reading, in all or in part, the ancient texts of the Upanishads, the Egyptian and Tibetan Books of the Dead, and even American Indian oral histories as

compiled by Castaneda, Peter had a pretty good idea
of what marked hallucinated writings. He had done a
fair job of convincing himself that Saint John had been
"on" something through most of the creation of his final
book.

But no longer.

He'd been convinced by his powerful, preternatural
attraction to the Archives and its endless shelves of
mysteries and revelations. Specific knowledge lay in
wait for him here, hiding like the slyest of prey, or
maybe a predator. He would find it because he was
supposed to find it. What he would do with the information once obtained was another mystery, but that
didn't matter. Either the events swirling around would
dictate his actions, or he would think of something.

As he sat there, slowly scanning the pages of the
Index, he was suddenly struck by how utterly alone he
was. Not just for the moment, sequestered in a practically unknown building within the Vatican, but personally as well. It seemed like a terribly long time since
he'd had anyone in his immediate circle he could consider a friend.

Leaning back, Peter smiled ironically. Such relationships were now impossible for him. Yes, that was it,
wasn't it? There was no one in the world he could
trust.

The truth of this saddened him more than alarmed
him. Especially since there had been a time when Marion had been the best friend and confidant anyone
could ever hope to have. But he had destroyed whatever bond had existed between them, and he had no
idea why. It happened as if he were following some
precodified program, going through the motions without possibility of contravention. Most of the time, he
didn't pause to inspect his actions or their motivations,
but there was something about the austere trappings of

the Archives that promoted introspection.

And even as he considered his situation with Marion, he could perceive a kind of weird duality in his mind. A part of him missed the unspoken closeness they'd shared, and he would have appreciated her assistance in combing the Archives for additional leads on the Secret of the Seven; yet another part of him felt absolutely nothing for Marion. She was no different from any of the others he must manipulate and use for his own purposes—whatever they might prove to be.

Which reminded him, as he checked his wristwatch—he should have heard from the Vatican Secret Service by now.

EIGhT

Gaetano—Salisbury Plain
September 4, 2000

For more than three weeks, he'd been running.

It had been the first active phase of his physical training, and it was incredibly difficult to establish the routine. He had not played much *futbol* as a boy, in the walled city of Arezzo, and he'd never been a particularly physical person. As an adult he'd avoided the fitness movement as best he could by developing a taste for rich Continental cuisine and sports cars. Working and living in London for so many years had given him a tacit appreciation for the sallow, rickety look of the average Brit. Exercise for its own sake was one of those things, like responding to pollsters, done by other people.

But now Gaetano ran with a purpose, as the beginning of a rigorous conditioning program he'd mapped out for himself. The well-known first step of the thousand-mile journey. As he jogged along the country road, he absently noted that the area was not so much a plain as a series of gently rolling hills. Most of the time he was either dipping down a soft grade or cresting a meadow that concealed a farm or a crossroads. He recalled the first time he'd encountered Stonehenge while driving across the plain, and how he'd been shocked to see the circle of standing stones suddenly appear beyond a gentle grassy knoll. Gaetano had always imagined the great plinths to be standing boldly at the center of a vast, windswept plateau, stark against a wild sky, full of color drama. In reality, Stonehenge lay in a sloping field with all the portent of a roadside barn.

He was approaching the henge now, and as he jogged past the car park area connected to the site by a tunnel, he waved at a passing bus full of tourists. Gaetano smiled as he pushed himself a little harder. His regimen required six miles a day for the next two weeks, then gradually extending it to fifteen over the following six weeks. He could not imagine what kind of endurance machine he would be after that amount of conditioning.

That was if the weather cooperated. England had been hit with some bizarre storms of late, and many rivers had flooded their banks. It had seemed to subside lately, but the fishwives in the villages were still harping on the strange weather all being a sign of the end of world.

He smiled. Silly talk for silly people.

He dismissed the notion and concentrated on his running. He hated the work, but given the task he'd assigned for himself, it was necessary.

At thirty-five years old, it would be hard to abruptly turn himself into a highly efficient, capable physical specimen, but he knew he could accomplish it. Despite his predilection for the finer things of European culture, he had not become an obese pig with an "American belly and butt." Working as a claims investigator for

Lloyd's had given him the chance to travel throughout the Continent and had trained him in the art of intrigue and deception. And having avoided the baggage of a wife or children, he considered himself shrewd, observant, vital, and capable of achieving any goal, meeting any challenge.

In addition to running, Gaetano had begun a carefully researched and mapped-out weight-lifting regimen. As his endurance increased, so would his strength, his power, his confidence. Eventually, he planned to layer in some martial arts training to improve his quickness and coordination.

Reaching his personal six-mile marker, a roundabout spinning off to several small villages, he reversed course and headed back to his auto. Gulping in great breaths, he leaned forward and pushed his pace. The first time he'd run this far, about a week ago, he'd been totally spent by now, but today, he was ready for more, for whatever the road threw at him.

Gaetano grinned as he pounded the asphalt. Yes, he thought, that is exactly the attitude I need. My future is like this road—I must be ready for whatever it lies in wait upon it.

NINE

Charlie Green—Lebanon, New Hampshire
August 25, 2000

Charlie Green rolled his 1966 Corvair convertible down his long driveway to the town-road leading to the Interstate, and although it was technically rush hour, 7:40 in the morning, the highway was not jammed with an endless phalanx of cars—it never was. One of the many reasons Charlie loved living in the region of New Hampshire they called the Upper Valley. As he drove, stress-free, he mused contentedly on how he'd ended up here. About five years ago, Charlie and his wife had fled Long Island's traffic, congestion, high prices, taxes, and crime to this secluded spot near the Connecticut River.

Thinking back, Charlie realized it had been a bold move. After twenty years on the Suffolk County police force, he'd opted for a totally new lifestyle: house in the woods, small town, no job, new friends, everything different.

Well, everything had worked out fine except for the notion that he could actually retire. Charlie had been so active all his life that getting up every day with nothing scheduled had become anathema to him. Reading had always been a passion with him, but he could not read sixteen hours a day. Landscaping, carpentry, auto mechanics, and even his activities within the local Mormon Church—none of it was enough. Charlie discovered he was simply one of those guys who needed a *job* to get up and go to every day.

It wasn't that he needed the money. He, Charlie, needed the structure and the camaraderie of employment. Now he worked for Federal Express. It wasn't that big an adjustment. As a cop, he'd been wearing a uniform ever since graduating from Hofstra, so he didn't mind that; driving was second nature to him, and compared to the department, FedEx paperwork was no big deal. And from jump street, he'd fully expected to have to deal with a whole raft of rules and regs—you don't pick up some guy's box of frozen halibut in Presque Isle, Maine, on Tuesday evening and have it dropped off in Carmel, California, the *next* day unless a lot of people are doing things *right*, which meant by the book.

That was just fine with Charlie. There was a side of him that responded well to order and discipline; just as there was another side attracted to the honest, unsophisticated lifestyle so prevalent in Robert Frost country. He had come to love the small New Hampshire towns with their white church steeples, stone fences, and know-it-all postmasters.

He continued to reflect on these things as he entered the Lebanon station parking lot, slipped the car into a vacant space, and walked into the vehicle barn. Other couriers were already there, some going through their pretrip inspections, others standing in small groups drinking coffee, waiting for the precise moment when they would start unloading the CTV. Charlie went to the tracker room to punch in, got his gear, and headed out to his vehicle, a Grumman step-van that ran like it had a governor set for the old fifty-five speed limits. As he went through the routine truck inspection, he started to feel a little lightheaded, as if he could sense a migraine coming on.

Which he couldn't.

He rarely ever got migraines and wondered why he would even think in those terms. Leaning back in his seat, Charlie took a deep breath, exhaled, and keyed on his radio and onboard computer called a DADS unit—an acronym for a string of techno-words he could never remember. Another weird sensation ghosted through him—like sitting on railroad tracks in total darkness and being suddenly speared by the headlight of a locomotive bearing down on you with unbelievable speed. There was something going on in his head. The feeling of some great event or change impending, looming, ominous and dripping with portent—he actually felt dizzy from it.

What was happening to him?

"Hey, Charlie, you okay?" asked Harold Shaw, the courier in the truck to his right. Shaw had just slapped open his driver's side door, preparing to jump down to the garage floor, when he must have noticed Charlie looking very unstable.

"... I don't know ... I feel funny ..."

He could feel himself losing his balance, and carefully eased himself down to a sitting position on the step-entrance of the van's passenger side. Harold was looking at him with growing concern. When Charlie started speaking again, he heard himself, as if listening to a stranger: *"Ain't no use in yellin'. Cuz there ain't nobody out there to hear you."*

He said the words slowly, heavy with desperation and perhaps something else more like terror. Gone was his distinctive Long Island accent, replaced by a vaguely Western one.

"What'd you say?" said Harold.

"You sure fixed things this time . . . this looks pretty bad . . . oh yeah."

"Charlie, what're you talking about?"

The question acted like a keyword pulling someone out of a trance. Suddenly lucid, but scared, Charlie looked at his friend. "I don't know. I hear myself talking and it's like I'm listening to somebody else!"

"You bump your head or something?" said Harold, smiling in an effort to make light of the situation, but letting it fade when he read the serious expression on Charlie's face.

"Naw, not that I remember . . ."

"Well," said Harold, slapping him on the shoulder, "come on, the freight's coming down the belt, and we're can monkeys today."

"Cans" were the metal freight containers that were configured to fit like giant building blocks into the fuselages of the cargo planes. Every morning, an eighteen-wheeler brought four cans of documents and packages to the station for delivery, and those cans had to be unloaded the old-fashioned way—by hand and by muscle. For the most part, Charlie liked can duty because, at the age of fifty, he wasn't getting much exercise, and he looked on the assignment as having a free membership in a health club.

The rest of the morning unfolded without incident, and so did his round of delivery stops through the towns of Plainfield and Cornish. Charlie loved that route, through the granite-laced mountains and valleys, streams and covered bridges, barns and stone fences everywhere. But while he was on his break, eating a tuna on Jewish rye, the voice started up again.

"*Helloooo!*" he suddenly yelled out, long and plaintive,

tinged with a knowing sadness. "*Anybody out there? Anybody! Goddamn it! Can ya hear me?*"

His voice had acquired that same odd cadence and accent, and it burst from him like epithets from a Tourette's patient, uncontrollable and unexpected.

Is that what was happening to him? Had he contracted some strange malady that was going to creep up him like ivy on a chimney and gradually take him over? Charlie Green shuddered at the very idea. To come to an end so perversely banal seemed like such an unfair way to die. And much too slow for him, but also Joan and his kids, who even though all grown and married, would be required to make occasional pilgrimages back home to see how badly Daddy had deteriorated this particular year.

He'd drive his Grumman off one of the mountain roads first. The thought, though sincere, didn't make him feel any better.

"*There's gotta be somebody out there,*" said the voice. Its tone suggested desperation, smeared with an insufficient lubricant of hope.

Then, just like that, the sensation of hearing another's voice, of being spoken *through*, left him. Not entirely, he felt, but as if whatever force was influencing him had, for the moment at least, turned its back on him.

Feeling totally in control of his thoughts, Charlie made a vow to get to the bottom of this quickly. There was no sense trying to hide it, to make believe it wasn't happening, or worrying about what people would *think* of him. Charlie had always lived with a confidence that his actions were enough to see him through anything.

And it had always been that way. Charlie was one of the good guys. Everybody liked him. He was known to be tough but fair. A guy who would do anything for you, a guy who was thoughtful and helpful without being a martyr.

The first thing to do, he knew, would be to tell Joan what was happening. For almost twenty-eight years, she'd been his wife and his best friend; he wasn't going to start hiding things from her now.

". . . so that's about all of it," he told her that night as he sat on the side of their bed. The room was dark, except for the eerie blue glow of the television set showing the 11:00 newscast.

"Charlie," said Joan, reaching out to take his hand, "you know I believe you."

"I never doubted you would. But we have to do something about it. Can you call Dartmouth-Hitchcock in the morning? See if you can get me an appointment with somebody?"

She nodded.

"I'll call from the road. If not, I'll just roll into the emergency room after work. I'll see somebody sooner or later."

"Charlie, I'm a little scared."

He looked at her and smiled. So different from the freckled redhead he met thirty years ago. More wrinkles and lines, more gray, less color, less sparkle and tone. But it was funny, thought Charlie: She was far prettier now than she'd ever been at twenty.

"Don't be scared. I'm all right. Something's going on, and we're going to find out what it is."

"Okay, Charlie." They kissed. "Good night. I love you."

He remoted off the TV and she moved closer to him, hugging him tightly and not letting go. He couldn't remember the last time they'd slept like this; college, maybe. But he liked it.

". . . *and I'll always love you,*" said Charlie, in that voice that wasn't his voice. He had been dreaming of someplace dark, someplace without air or space. He'd woken himself up with his droning cowboy voice.

"*Margaret, even though I haven't always acted like it, you've always—*"

"Margaret?" said Joan. Her shocked interjection went unnoticed as Charlie continued speaking in a very slow and deliberate manner, as if he were dictating his words to a stenographer.

"*—been first in my book. I'm going to miss you more than you can ever know. It's hard to be thinking like this, but I have to. I'm not sure how the laws go in Arizona, but I know I don't have a will, so . . . when they find this note . . . and I sure hope they find me down here sooner or later . . . I want this to be the proof that everything we've had all these years goes to you.*"

"Charlie!" Joan's voice was high and frantic.

He could feel her fingers digging into his arms, but the pain was not enough to break through the web of whatever held him. He continued speaking in his half-awake state: "*. . . and I'm no lawyer, so I don't know any other way to say this but the way I've already tried. God so help me, in sound mind, Scott Raney.*"

"What're you talking about?" said Joan, her voice penetrating the cocoon that encapsulated him. "Who is Margaret?"

Turning to face her, Charlie noticed that it was almost dawn outside, and the notion danced through him that it would still be dark out . . .

. . . *out where?*

He didn't know.

He had no way to complete the thought. It was as puzzling and incomplete as the fragments of speech that had been escaping from him.

"Charlie!"

"Joan, it's all right. I hear you, sweetheart." He ran

a hand over his head, a habit born of years of pushing his long hair from his eyes, though he was now practically bald.

"Who is Margaret?" Her voice was low, controlled, but he could hear the mixture of distress and hurt beneath the words.

"I don't know . . . somebody that other voice knows, I'd say."

"Other voice?"

Charlie looked at his wife's expression, which told him what she could not articulate—she knew someone else was somehow speaking through her husband, like a voice through a radio, but she wasn't ready to admit it yet, for fear of making it more real.

"You know what I mean, Joan. I can't explain it any more than you can, but there's no sense making believe it's not happening."

"Yes, but . . ."

"But what? Do you think I'm seeing another woman and her name is Margaret?" He sat on the edge of the bed looking at her with an expression that told her he was not trying to cause trouble.

Joan's eye dropped for an instant. "No . . . no, I really don't."

"Now let's try to help ourselves," Charlie said. "We need to keep notes on everything I say and everything I've already said. The more we know about this voice, the easier it should be to figure out what it's all about."

Standing up, he headed for the hallway.

"Where're you going?" asked his wife. "It's the middle of the night."

"I'll be right back," he said, then sped to the desk in the den, grabbed a ballpoint and a spiral notebook from one of the shelves, and rushed back.

"What're you doing? That's for my recipes."

He flipped to the back pages, which were blank.

"Well, it's going to be for something else for the time being," he said, holding up the pen. "Now, I need you to help me out, Joan. Try to remember everything I said. You know, in that other voice."

She looked away from him, wringing her hands together. There were tears in the corners of her eyes. "Charlie, I can't."

He smiled, touched her cheek tenderly. She was scared of what they might find; he was too, but he couldn't let that stop them. "Sure you can—you just don't want to. But you can do it, honey, I know you can."

Joan nodded but said nothing. Charlie tried to kick things off by remembering whatever he could from the incident at the FedEx station, what the guys had told him: that it sounded like the person speaking "through" him had had an accident, that he sounded like he was in trouble or in pain; that he was somewhere where he didn't think anybody could hear him call for help.

Charlie spoke slowly and made a big deal of writing down every item and numbering it in the notebook, then he looked expectantly at Joan. "That's about all I could pull together. Now it's your turn."

Rocking gently back and forth in the bed, his wife closed her eyes and forced herself to remember. "It sounded like you were making out a will; you said you didn't have one and weren't sure about the laws in Arizona, whatever that means, and you were talking about somebody named Margaret getting everything. You said they would probably find you eventually. . . ."

Joan paused, and her expression changed to excitement. "Down here! That's what you said, 'down here.' That might mean something, right?"

Charlie had been writing down everything, nodding at the appropriate moments. "Yes, honey, that definitely means something. Can you remember anything else?"

"You said your name, but I can't remember it exactly. Oh, Charlie, I'm sorry!" Joan looked so sad. "I heard you mention some other woman's name and I guess I kind of pounced on that. I don't know if I was listening to anything else after that."

"You heard it," he said softly. "Witnesses hear more than they realize. Just relax, and we'll see if we can get it to come to you."

Joan sat there, eyes closed, holding back tears, rocking gently, shaking her head. She looked like a little girl struggling to deny the possibility of there being anything evil about something so normal as the dark.

"I'm pretty sure part of it was Scott. Last name or first name, oh God, Charlie, I can't remember. I'm sorry. I'm so sorry!"

Charlie smiled. "Joan, you did great! I have plenty here!"

Even though it was an ungodly hour for most New Englanders, he knew he couldn't sleep anymore. Besides, he had friends he could call back in Suffolk County, guys still working in the department and guys who, even though they'd retired, still knew people in the right places, like the FBI.

Working quickly, relying on his experience and training as a detective, Charlie soon had a hot sheet that would give his law enforcement contacts plenty of leads to follow up. He grabbed the phone and dialed a number he knew by heart at the Smithtown station.

"Suffolk County Police," said a wary voice. Charlie had called in on the "house line," which was used only by officers and staff. "What's up?"

"This is Detective Sergeant Charles Green, retired," said Charlie. "Who's this?"

"Charlie! That really you? It's Moe! Moe Gagne!"

"Yeah, Moe, it's me. How's Rachel? The kids?"

"Can't complain, but, hey! It's four-thirty in the morning. You in trouble or what?"

"No, no, nothing like that," said Charlie. "But I need to get in touch with Emil Pornelos—he's still there, isn't he?"

"Poney? Yeah, sure, he's the big dog around here now."

"Can you hook me into his voice mail? I need to get some poop to him as fast as possible."

"Yeah, sure, Charlie, sure. Now you sure you don't have your ass in a crack, do you?"

"Hey, I told you, man, it's nothin' like that," said Charlie. "Thanks for everything, Moe."

Moe acknowledged with a promise to stay in touch and clicked him through the phone system to Lieutenant Pornelos's voice mail, where Charlie left a brief message, meaty enough to pique the big Hawaiian's curiosity: "Poney, it's Charlie Green! I need you to give me a call ASAP. It might be life or death, buddy."

"So let me give you everything I've got," said Charlie. He held the phone tightly. At 7:30 A.M., Detective Lieutenant Pornelos had called him back. "Someplace in Arizona . . . guy's name is Scott . . . could be first or last . . . wife's name is Margaret . . . and I think he's had a bad accident. He might be lost or stuck or something worse. He said something about nobody ever being able to hear him *'down here,'* which could mean a lot of things."

"And you got this off your shortwave radio?" said the detective.

"Yeah," said Charlie, almost choking on the white lie.

"What frequency?"

"Huh?" The question snagged him like a miscast lure, and he began frantically thinking of an answer that would be correct enough to shut down any further inquiry. "I'm not sure. Why? I'll have to go check my receiver."

"So we can get people to start monitoring it for any more traces of him."

"Oh, yeah, right ... sure," said Charlie, casting about in his memory, back through his hobby days as a ham operator. What the heck would be a band that would make sense? "It was somewhere between ... forty and forty-three meters. I don't remember exactly, and I got so excited I forgot to write it down."

Poney Pornelos seemed to believe him, and the conversation drifted to promises to get right on the police work and then small talk. Charlie was anxious to get off the line because he didn't feel comfortable with his tiny deception. But he knew most cops didn't put much stock in working on "feelings."

Finally, the phone call ended, and he gathered up his notes. Now he just had to convince Joan that everything would be all right.

Poney was chuckling when he called him back. "Don't you folks ever watch the news, Detective Green?"

"Well, we try not to. Why? What'd you find out?"

"A rancher named Scott Raney, married to Margaret Springer Raney, from Randell, Arizona, has been missing for three days. The local sheriff found his horse wandering along their fencing, but no sign of Raney. We put them onto the idea he might be trapped in or under something, and guess what? They found him! Thirty feet down in an abandoned well."

Charlie's cheeks had started to hurt from the ever-widening grin splitting his face. Somehow, he had been selected by God to save a man's life, and he'd done it!

"But you know what?" Lieutenant Pornelos went on.

"What? Is the man okay? Is he still alive?"

"Oh, sure, Charlie, he's fine. But you know what's really funny? Scott Raney didn't have a shortwave radio down there in the well."

Charlie didn't say a word. For an instant he fought the urge to simply hang up the phone, to run away from the whole story.

"Charlie, you there?"

"Yes, I'm here."

"So what do you make of that, huh, pal? Besides that, my technobuddies tell me that a radio might not even be able to transmit that far underground. Pretty weird, huh?"

"Very weird, Poney." Charlie swallowed hard. His lie would now be compounded, and he so hated lying. "I don't know what to tell you—I *heard* that man talking to me. What else can I say?"

"Charlie . . ." he could almost hear Poney grinning slyly. "C'mon, tell me what's going on. How'd you know about this guy?"

"I told you, I heard him talking."

"But not on any shortwave radio . . ."

"I can't explain it, Poney. I swear I can't. What can I tell you?"

"Okay, Charlie, I thought you might have something for me—like how you did it, how you knew. If it wasn't for the stuff you gave us, they probably wouldn't have found Raney before he stiffed on them."

"Thanks, Poney, thanks for everything."

"No problem, Sarge. Stay in touch."

Charlie Green settled back in his reading chair and fell asleep. And had his first dream about the Lady in the Light.

PART

2

And there came unto me one of the seven angels which had seven vials full of the seven last plagues, and talked with me, saying, Come hither, I will shew thee the bride, the Lamb's wife.

—John, *Revelation, 21: 9*

Ten

Peter Carenza—Vatican City
September 14, 2000

$\mathscr{P}$eter watched Marion walk in the door of the papal apartment and close it softly behind her. The detachment of porter, driver, and Swiss Guard had departed, and she looked very vulnerable. She'd been gone for more than a month, having stayed at Etienne's convent for a period of recuperation.

"Welcome home," he said without giving away his current mood. "The doctors say you're fine. In fact, they said that quite a while ago."

"Yes, I suppose I am."

She remained standing by the door with her arms crossed protectively across her breasts. It was a posture he found attractive because she looked so defenseless. Her dark hair and green eyes, accented by the angular planes of her face, had always made her so striking, so distinctive. When she'd been a TV journalist, she'd always looked great on-screen.

"I guess it won't do much good to say I'm sorry." Actually, he wasn't even sure he was capable of being sorry any longer, but he wanted to give it a try. He believed he loved her, yet wondered if any of his emotions were still valid.

"I don't know, Peter. No one can talk to you anymore. You're changing, and if my telling you that makes you mad, well, there's not much I can do about it. Frankly, I can't figure out why you want me around."

"I told you—we're getting married. We have to set an example for the rest of the world."

"Why are you trying to destroy your Church?

"I'm not. I'm dragging it, albeit kicking and screaming, into the new century."

"Is that what you call it?" She started to walk away from him, toward the suite of bedrooms. She had definitely become cooler to him, and he deeply regretted losing control during their last time together. It would be best for everybody of he could bring her back into his circle, and he knew it would take time.

"Well, for exmple, I think it is about time the Church came out for euthanasia. It makes sense—especially if a person wants to go back to God that much faster."

"Peter, do you really believe that is your real reason?"

"It is more important what the world believes, and many of the faithful are in agreement with me—we need change in order to survive."

She said nothing and kept walking. He caught up and touched her shoulder. "You and my mother have become friends, I hear."

"She was so concerned about what happened, she wanted to see me, to console me. I'm glad she did. She is a wonderful person."

He smiled but said nothing.

Marion scowled and pulled away from him. "You would know that, if you spoke to her more often."

"We've never really had the time to get to know each other."

It was her turn to grin sardonically.

"I've been working in the Archives most of the time." He followed her down the hall toward the bedrooms.

"What are you looking for?" she asked, and he noted that she seemed genuinely interested.

This might be the avenue he sought to gain back her support and loyalty. "I'm not sure. But I believe I'll know it when I find it, when I see it."

She regarded him with an expression he could not immediately read; a combination of fear and amusement. He continued, "Marion, I need your help."

"You had it before, willingly, and you screwed it up."

"I know that, but I need you now."

"How do you know you can ever trust me again, after what you did to me?"

"Because you're such a good person, Marion."

"You don't deserve me, Peter. And unless I've been a lot more of a bad girl than I ever realized, I sure as hell don't deserve you." She stalked into the bedroom and shut the door in his face.

ELEVEN

Father Giovanni Francesco—Vatican City
August 24, 2000

*E*very shadow, every sound, practically paralyzed him.

So sharpened were his senses that he felt disoriented, almost confused. Giovanni anticipated trouble everywhere and knew that eventually it would find him. He had to get out of this damnable city! The thought taunted him as he inched his way along a narrow, squalid alley that stank of garbage and gutted fish. Light from an unknown source tried unsuccessfully to sneak around the distant corner. The darkness could be your friend or your enemy, depending on how you looked at it, he thought.

What would it be tonight?

His flight continued to be plagued by a single thought—that Peter Carenza had ordered his death. Hard to believe. However, in one sense, Giovanni felt flattered—Carenza perceived him as a threat. But why? What force could he possibly mount against the young pope, who seemed to be growing ever more powerful?

And what about Lareggia and Sister Victorianna? Had assassins been dispatched to their quarters as well? Were they already dead?

He could not disappear without knowing the answers, without trying to warn them.

At least he had reached the docks of the Tiber without incident. The area was a latticework of warehouses, slips, wharves, and the occasional marina for wealthy Romans. Although he hadn't been here in years, Giovanni knew the riverfront well. Staying to the alleys and causeways, he had worked his way south, toward the dock of a particular fisherman who had performed various services for Francesco and the SSV in years past.

His travel was slow because of his extreme caution. There was no way to know how things had transpired at his apartment, or any way to know if he was being pursued. Better to assume the worst and never be surprised. He would—

Someone lurched out of the shadows, a gaunt human figure who'd been huddled in an unseen doorway. The way he rocked and yawed, the man was obviously impaired—or doing a good job of acting that way. Giovanni melted into the shadows, pressing himself against the dank brick of the alley. The stumbling figure eased past him, continuing his erratic progress toward the opposite end of the passageway.

Giovanni watched him pass as he eased his handgun from inside his jacket and trained it on the figure that continued to move away from him. He was not going to get careless in his old age—if the drunk showed any sign of turning or confronting him, the priest would put a few silenced slugs into him.

But the fellow staggered away, his silhouette dwindling. Negotiating the narrow, damp passageways was like running a labyrinth, but Giovanni moved as if by instinct. The docks had not changed much since the days of his youth, and he remembered by dead reckoning, slipping around corners, avoiding the random pools of light from the occasional warehouse window.

Until, finally, he came to the steps to Enzo's boathouse. The staircase led to a loft and an unlighted door. Giovanni ascended the steps in total silence, turned the knob, opened the door, and slipped inside.

Poorly lit by several oil lamps, the loft reeked of the river and of things better left in the sea. Filled with netting, gaffs, oars, sailcloth, and parts of engines that would never run again, it looked more like a junkyard than living quarters. In fact, it was both. In the far corner, under a single gooseneck lamp, sat a bearded man of indeterminate age, watching a small black-and-white television. If he heard the rear door open, or Giovanni's approach across the cluttered floor, he gave no sign of it.

Then, suddenly, the man wheeled toward him, revealing a speargun that had been stashed alongside his outstretched leg.

"Hold it right there, my friend, before I turn you into fish chum—!" The man's jaw dropped as he recognized his uninvited guest. Slowly, the business end of his weapon dropped.

"Enzo, please, it's your confessor." Giovanni chuckled.

"By the Christ of my Mother! Father Francesco, what're you doing here?" Enzo jumped up, moved close, and welcomed him with open arms.

Taking a seat, Giovanni provided the sailor with a quick summary of the night's events.

"The bastard! I knew something was funny with this one, especially since I heard nothing from you about it. Silence can sometimes speak loudly."

Giovanni looked at Enzo and marveled at his ability

to remain unchanged by time. In the twenty years they'd done business together, he'd always retained the same aspect—roughly trimmed salt-and-pepper mustache, small grapeshot eyes, and the yellowest teeth Giovanni had ever seen. He could be a hard-looking forty or a vital sixty.

"Do you have a phone?"

"Yes, but I'll have to plug it in. I do not use it much. And," he said with a smile, "I expected no calls so late tonight."

Giovanni nodded. "Do you still have the equipment from the SSV?"

"Sure! Why would I get rid of it?"

"Good. It might save your life."

The phone was old, with a slow-moving dial, but connected to it was a small plastic box—a piece of hi-tech that prevented any call placed through this line from being traced.

Giovanni dialed. As he watched the mechanism click and rotate through the numbers, he thought the connection might never be achieved. Finally, familiar ringing sounds buzzed through the line. Giovanni nervously waited, wondering if anyone would answer.

He let it ring for a long time. Not a good sign. He suddenly felt foolish holding the dead receiver to the side of his skull, all the while studied by the flat-eyed, dead fish stare of Enzo.

Then, just as he was moving to hang up, a raspy voice: "Hello?"

"Paolo, are you all right?"

"Huh? Who is this?" The Cardinal sounded thick with sleep. A good sign.

Giovanni identified himself, brought Lareggia up to speed on what happened earlier. His colleague was aghast. "What will you do? What should we do?"

"I must disappear."

"How? Where?" Paolo Lareggia's panic was seizing control of him. His voice had become so high-pitched that Enzo could hear his squeakings through the old phone receiver. The sailor grinned sardonically, shook his head.

"Calm down!" said Giovanni, whispering harshly into the phone. "Listen to me. If they have not come to kill you tonight, then you are probably safe."

"Do you think so?" The Cardinal drew a breath, tried to regain control.

"Yes," said Giovannni, who actually was not certain he believed what he was saying. But at least for tonight, he did not think Paolo Lareggia would be in danger. "But that does not mean you should become lazy or less vigilant. Contact Victorianna. Tell her what has happened."

" 'Vanni, I do not understand these ways . . . you must instruct me."

"Peter has left you alive for a reason, Paolo. He does not perceive you as a problem. I have a feeling he sees Victorianna as even less of a threat."

"So it is you he did not trust."

"That is the heart of it, yes."

"Where will you go?"

Looking at Enzo, Giovanni shook his head slowly. "That I cannot reveal."

"How will we know you are safe?"

"I will have means to get in touch. For now, you must be very watchful, very careful. I may try to contact you. If I do, I will want information. That will be my own armor against Peter and his machinations, whatever they might be."

"I will try," said the Cardinal, "but you know I am not suited for espionage."

"Just do your best."

"What is this all about, 'Vanni? What did we do?

There are rumors that Peter is trying to destroy the Church."

Giovanni chuckled sarcastically. "Oh, it may be far worse, Paolo. He may have the whole world in mind."

"Can he be stopped?"

"I do not know."

There was a pause, and Giovanni could feel the tension and the fear building in his colleague. Then: "I am scared, Father. Very much so."

"So am I."

"No," said the Cardinal. "I do not think you understand—not so much for my life . . ."

"Your soul," said Giovanni. "Yes, I understand. Too well."

"I cannot escape thoughts of it. What we have done, 'Vanni, can God even *begin* to forgive us?"

"If it is absolution you want, I am a priest, remember? *In nomine Patris, et Filius—*"

"Do not be sacrilegious!"

"Then do not talk like a fool. If you believe, then you should know God has already forgiven us. There is no sin so great—"

Paolo chuckled with great frailty. "That was before us . . . and our great idea!"

"Actually, it was *my* idea, if it makes you feel any better. Or should I say less guilty?"

The Cardinal did not respond to this. He cleared his throat, drew a breath. Then: "Is there not anyone here I can trust? Who might help me?"

"I do not know."

"Please, Giovanni. Think!" Paolo's voice was fraught. It was sad to hear a man talk like that.

"Well, actually, there might be," said Giovanni as he nervously stroked his bony chin. "Pay close attention to what you hear in the morning."

"What do you mean?"

"Find out, as surreptitiously as possible, the name of the agent who helped me tonight. He might be able to help you and Victorianna."

"Do you really think so?"

"Paolo, I do not know for certain, but he did take a bullet for me." Giovanni replayed the scene in his mind in that instant. "And I, the perfect ingrate, did not even get his name."

"I will get it," said Paolo.

"Good. Now, remain watchful. You will be hearing from me."

"Thank you, Father," said Paolo. "I did not know you considered me your friend."

Another chuckle, a bit nervously. "I did not know I did, either. Is that why I called you, Paolo?"

"Yes, I think so."

"I never thought I was a man who could have friends, only enemies."

"Wherever you are going, God be with you."

"If he is still with any of us," said Giovanni. "Good night, Cardinal."

Hanging up the receiver, he handed it back to Enzo. "Thank you."

The sailor unplugged the cord, tossed the phone atop a pile of newspapers. He smoothed his mustache, smiled. "Why do I have a feeling that you stopped here for more than a phone call?"

"Because you are a rotten, low-life bastard, and you know the ways of your kind."

Enzo grinned, nodded. "Before our business, some sambucca."

"I would like that, yes."

As the sailor retrieved a bottle and two dusty glasses from a wooden crate under his table, Giovanni leaned back, stretched out the tensely knotted muscles of his neck and shoulders. He considered the irony of his being at this place at this hour. Hardly a place for a high-ranking Jesuit priest to be found. Which was precisely why he felt such a sense of security, in light of the circumstances.

Enzo poured. They touched glasses and sipped the thick liquor that had coffee beans at the bottom. An old custom, Giovanni noted with pleasure. To offer your guest a glass with an odd number of beans meant you were welcome and expected to return.

His glass held three beans.

"So now you will tell me."

"I have nothing to give you in exchange for what I ask."

Enzo shrugged. "Father Francesco, I have never seen you bargain from such strength!"

"Unless it is high drama you desire, because you hold my life in your hands."

"You wish to stay here?"

Giovanni shook his head. "No point in that. No, my friend. I need transport to the sea, to a place where even if they find me, they cannot harm me."

Enzo smiled. "I know of such a place."

"We both do."

The sailor reached for his turn-out coat, shrugged into it. "Then let us be off. We sail tonight."

Twelve

Carlos Accardi—Buenos Aires
September 11, 2000

*H*igh steel.

That is what the Americans called the place where Carlos Accardi worked. It was a general term for any absurdly tall structure—a skyscraper, a bridge, a broadcast tower. This morning, he walked across Tower No. 1 of the city's newest construction—the Río de la Plata Harbor Bridge—the biggest suspension bridge in the Southern Hemisphere. Carlos headed a team of structural engineers who had supervised its design and construction, and now they were out among its girders and cables, giving it a good-bye kiss.

Having lived with the project for several years, Carlos felt a pang of sadness to be finally letting it go. As with any monumental engineering project, you tended to leave a piece of yourself in the work. He had worked all over the world, but nothing had ever given him the satisfaction of completing a job so impressive as this one in his native Argentina.

He looked down from the tower's precipice to the

eight-lane roadway more than three hundred feet below. It had been open to the public for more than a week, but he still felt a great excitement to see tiny, buglike vehicles scurrying across its majestic length. I have made this possible, he thought with a smile. It was not a prideful sentiment, just a reflection of the incredible sense of satisfaction he felt in creating something so beautiful. Carlos did not believe inventive people were capable of pride, only joy in the completion of their unique accomplishments.

A *ping* of workboots on steel sounded behind him, and Carlos turned to see Omar, his foreman, stepping off the access ladder. "How does she look?"

"Better than my drawings could have ever been," said Carlos. Both men knew this last walk-through was more of a custom than a requirement. In the age of CAD and supercomputer modeling, the specifications of this bridge had been so thoroughly tested, over and over, through every stage of design and construction, that an eyeball inspection of the structure was more laughable than serious. "Come, we are done here."

His foreman led the way down the ladder as erratic winds whipped at their clothing and swirled under their hard hats. Carlos followed a safe distance above as they slowly descended to the first landing, where they entered the tower. They passed the electrical bay, which housed all the relays, amplifiers, and power cables necessary to illuminate the bridge at night, and finally emerged at the roadway level.

As they descended, their conversation drifted to the news of the earthquake that had rocked China this morning in a city called Kweiyang. Carlos thought about what such a high-Richter quake would do to his bridge, then tried to bar the twisted image from his mind. The news seemed to be filled with ever more calamities, both natural and man-made, and it made him wonder if God was losing his patience with this small planet.

To the west of the span sprawled the impossibly grand expanse of Buenos Aires. Carlos paused to appreciate the view for a moment, then headed for the single lane closest to the divider, which had been coned off for their company Jeep. Traffic had adjusted, funneling down to three lanes, moving past them in high-speed precision.

As Omar stepped off the curb, striding toward their vehicle, Carlos scanned the roadway beyond their position. It was a vigilance born of long-standing habit; caution on the high steel was always sound policy. He was just about to turn his attention to the Jeep when he noticed an aberrant movement in the distance. A brilliantly red pickup with oversize suspension and tires became visible—not only because of its size and color but also for its erratic motion.

"Watch out," said Carlos, pointing off into the distance where the red truck was weaving in and out of the orderly columns of traffic.

"What a *pendejo!*" said Omar as he reached the driver's side door of the Cherokee.

Carlos moved quickly to the passenger side but paused to keep an eye on the pickup. It was closer to them now, nearing the point where four lanes were merging into three. "He's going too fast!" said Carlos, trying to mask his growing concern.

Indeed, the red truck appeared to be accelerating rather than shifting down. Unable to do anything but stand by, Carlos recorded the events that followed as if they happened in slow motion. He felt a stinging sense of helplessness overwhelm him as the monster truck began to rock from side to side.

The vehicle's wheels locked and it broadsided a small white coupe. Like a cue ball impacting a billiard, the truck ricocheted the diminutive car into several cars ahead. Stunned, Carlos watched the white coupe fly up and over a low-slung sports car. Then, half airborne, it flipped over on its side to slide across the roofs of the vehicles in the outermost lane toward the edge of the bridge itself. He could hear the screams of its occupants as the little white car reached the guardrail and tottered briefly there before pitching forward to tumble end-over-end into the choppy water below.

Transfixed, watching the car fall away from him, Carlos was struck by a sense of unreality, like viewing an ineptly edited video. What he was seeing just did not seem possible.

Time itself seemed distended. The plummeting car seemed to be taking awfully long to hit the water.

Abruptly, everything around him went totally silent. The traffic, the crowd, the vorticing wind. Everything.

Dead silent.

Carlos was leaning against the guardrail, looking down, when he detected light and movement in front him, level with the elevated roadway. Lifting his head to stare into what should be open space, he was stunned by what he saw.

A woman dressed in flowing robes, tan and dark brown, like a nun's, and surrounded by a glowing aura of the most beautiful light he'd ever seen. Floating, wavering, refracting, and reflecting the light, she hung like a Christmas angel before him. She looked like those paintings of biblical figures, of saints, and she was reaching out to him.

Save them.

Only you can do it.

Carlos felt his heart leaping against his rib cage, as if trying to escape. He scanned the faces of the people gathered at the railing.

None of them saw her or heard her.

"I can't do it!" he heard someone yell, then realized it was himself. "I can barely swim."

I need you.

Do this because you are special.

"No!"

Now, Carlos . . .

There was something about the way the glowing woman both asked and commanded him, how she spoke his name, with an intimacy and a caring and a truthfulness he'd never known before.

Only vaguely aware of the crowd all around him, Carlos grabbed one of the thick vertical cables, hoisted himself up to the top of the railing and leaped outward. He did this without thinking, without fear. Instead, he felt a great surge of energy passing through him—the purest, blue-white fire of faith.

The air rushed past his ears as he aimed himself feet first at the olive green surface of the Río de la Plata. His passage downward seemed endless and instantaneous at the same time. Impacting the surface, he felt no shock, no pain.

He did not remember gulping down a final breath, but his lungs were filled to bursting with air, and his vision was remarkably clear as he searched the darkening depths for his target.

I can't swim like this.

But he was. He saw the white trunk of the coupe sinking below him, belching out great misshapen bubbles, lurching deeper with each convulsive release of trapped air. Like a torpedo, Carlos zeroed in on his target. As he drew close he could see the frantic faces of the car's passengers pressed against the windows, screaming soundlessly.

Reaching out, moving too slowly against the heavy drag of his waterlogged clothes, he grabbed the door handle. When he tapped on the glass, the occupants

inside panicked for an instant, then realized someone
was trying to help them. The interior of the car had
almost filled completely with water—which was prefer-
able, because the equalized pressure would allow a door
or window to open more easily. Without forethought
or plan, Carlos motioned them away from the left rear
window, drew his knees into his chest, then uncoiled
them in a burst of strength.

As the glass pane imploded, Carlos arched around,
entering the gaping wound of the window, reaching for
the passengers—three teenage girls. With one hand he
unlatched the opposite door and pushed it open against
the weight of the water; with the other, he guided the
girls out.

One of them was inhaling water. Carlos saw her
body go slack as she began to sink, following the coupe
to an unimagined depth. As the other two girls kicked
and struggled toward the surface, Carlos dove down,
caught the drowning one, and began to yank her upward. Her eyes had rolled back into her head and she
hung limply in his grasp. Looking up, Carlos saw the
surface glittering like an impossible barrier of fractured
glass, and he knew they would never reach it in time.

Too slowly he ascended, feeling the river's grip grow
slightly more tenuous as the last of the air in his lungs
become a bomb primed to explode. He held the girl's
limp body under his arm, her weight like an anchor. It
would be so easy simply to let go—

No!

She was there with him. Smiling and nodding her
head. The lady who glowed like a saint . . .

Not much farther, Carlos.

Just another stroke upward.

And then, suddenly, the sun was burning him and
the canopy of air embraced him, rushed into and over
him, and Carlos could hear the riotous screaming of

the crowds looking down from the roadway high above
and the frantic motorized onrush of the rescue boats.
The air scored his throat like sweet acid as he gulped
it down. His legs felt as if they would fall off from the
supreme effort of fighting the drag of the water. And
then there were hands reaching for him and for the
inanimate body he still fought to keep afloat. Pulled
from the oily surface, he felt himself enveloped in blankets and bobbed across a surface of helping hands.

As they hailed him, he found he had no strength to
share their celebration. The hero in him had run its
course, and the shock of the reality of what he'd actually done was catching up to him. He felt so unbeliev-
ably tired, so completely used up.

Carlos Accardi, who swam with all the style and skill
of an anvil. How had he done it?

But more important: Why?

These were his surprisingly coherent, calm thoughts
as his rescuers and admirers clamored all around him.
The sounds of the boats' engines blended with the hum
and roar of men and women surrounding him.

"Get more blankets!"

"Over here!"

"She's still alive!"

"He did it!"

"Get his name! Somebody get his name!"

The words jumbled together. He heard them but did
not comprehend. All he wanted to do was close his
eyes, and make everything simply go away for a little
while. They were lifting him from the smaller boat to
a larger one. He was vaguely aware of cameras and
microphones, but he had no energy or desire to respond.

If this was how it felt to be a hero, he was thinking

as he gave in to the pull of total exhaustion, then it was terribly overrated.

As the sweet undertow of unconsciousness tugged him down, Carlos hoped he would see her again—the lady in the robes of light.

THIRTEEN

Peter Carenza—Vatican City
September 22, 2000

As he'd been doing for a part of each day for the past three weeks, Peter sat in the wing of the Secret Archives that had once been known as the Borghese Apartments. The interior of the building was appointed in carved mahogany and cherry wainscoting, crown moldings, and threshold trim. The balustrades were polished to a high gloss, and seventeenth-century chandeliers diffused the electric light in every corner of the rooms. As he flipped through the pages of yet another *Index* (this one from the fourth-century *Druidian Chronicles*), he knew he was not giving the task his full attention. Despite being driven to solve the riddle of the Seven, other matters had been distracting him, not the least of which was Marion Windsor.

At this moment she was supposed to be putting together the media release that would alert the world to the impending announcement of a world-shaking event within the Catholic Church: their marriage and a universal removal of the prohibition on marriage for clerics. Ever since her return from the infirmary and convent (no, stop skirting the issue, ever since he threw her out the apartment window), she had been going through the days and nights like an automaton. Sure, she did whatever he asked, but that was part of what bugged him—she did it without emotion, reaction, or involvement.

Peter shook his head slowly. He'd really blown it with her by letting his anger get out of control. No, wait, he thought. Whom did he think he was kidding? He knew he was dealing with a situation far more dangerous than a bad temper. As much as he did not want to think about it, he knew what had happened. Dwelling within him, like some hideous symbiote, coiled a dark force that gained sustenance and power from his outbursts and in some strange way fed the energy back to him and gave him almost unlimited power in the world of men. But to hold onto that power, Peter had to continue to allow whatever twisted in the pit of his soul to break loose and have its way.

Such thoughts so unnerved him, he usually chose to avoid them, to keep them damped down. Better to not go there. As the line from the medieval poems and myths often said: Here there be dragons.

Returning his attention to the prolegomenon of the fourth-century text, he began to scan the paragraphs for any reference that might send him deeper toward the Secret of the Seven. When he was more than halfway through the passage, Father Erasmus, the prefect of the Archives, appeared hesitantly at the threshold of the alcovelike room.

"Excuse me, Your Holiness . . ."

"Yes," Peter said, turning from the heavy vellum pages to look at the middle-aged priest.

"Cardinal Lareggia has requested to see you. He says he knows he has no appointment, but he must see you at once. He says it is of the most urgent nature."

Peter nodded. He could well imagine what the fat man wanted. Better to confront him and get matters done with quickly. "All right. Tell him to meet me presently in the Drawing Room at the Court of the Belvedere. And arrange for us to have lunch there as well."

The prefect nodded and backed out of the room. Closing his notebook, which contained only paltry bibliographic scraps, Peter left the room, passing the Meridian, then through the Tower of Winds itself. Before entering the Archives, he'd been meeting with his newly formed Curial Committee of Geopolitical Affairs, so he was dressed in a white cassock trimmed in the customary gold brocade. He did not wear the "funny hats" of most popes, but he did wear the heavy necklace and gilt cross of Constantine.

Lareggia. There was no doubt why the Cardinal had demanded to see him—Father Giovanni Francesco.

Entering the Drawing Room, a high-ceilinged room of paneled Brazilian rosewood, slatted by thin, tall windows of hand-leaded glass, Peter was not surprised to see the Cardinal waiting for him.

But Lareggia was not alone.

Peter glanced at his additional company. Egon Leutmann, the captain of the Swiss Guard, and Sister Victorianna, abbess of the Poor Clares Convent. Both of them regarded him with expressions that could at best be called dour. "Well, hello, everyone," said Peter. "I didn't know there would be four for lunch."

Paolo Lareggia inclined his round head only slightly. "I thought it best to . . . ah, not tell you."

Peter smiled, looked to the corner of the richly appointed room of dark hand-rubbed paneling where an assistant, a young Christian brother, stood awaiting his pope's wishes. "Tell the cook to make adjustments to the menu."

When the assistant had melted away, closing the double doors behind him, Peter advanced upon the trio marshaled to confront him. He gestured toward a polished wood and marble table. "Please, let's all sit down."

They waited for him to take his chair before seating themselves at the other three sides of the square. Peter smiled again and held his hands open in a classic pontifical pose. "What can I do for all of you?"

"Holiness," said Captain Leutmann, "the Cardinal asked me to accompany him on this audience, and after he apprised me of certain information, I felt compelled to be here."

"Let's not talk in circles," said Peter.

Lareggia had been sitting with his pudgy hands steepled in front of his face. Leaning forward, he dropped his hands flat to the tabletop. "Father Giovanni Francesco called me last night. He was in flight for his life!"

"And he told you why?" said Peter.

"He said you had given the order for his execution. The SSV!"

Peter looked at his three accusers. They all shared a similar expression of temerity, tempered by the resolution of the righteous. That they would dare show up like this and remind him of the fiasco regarding the old Jesuit was enough to get him very upset, but he knew this was not the time to show any loss of control. If there was a lesson learned from his handling of Marion, this was the moment to benefit from it.

There was only one way to handle this meeting: Take them head-on.

"Well, the old man was finally right about something."

"What do you mean?" asked Victorianna.

"Francesco," Peter smiled archly, intending to intimidate. "There was no way for him to be certain that I ordered his termination, but I have no problem admitting the truth of his accusation."

Cardinal Lareggia's features sagged as he looked at him. "Peter, *why?*"

"Because in case you haven't noticed, Father Giovanni Francesco is a very dangerous man. He has killed in the past, with his own hands, and while he lived, I feared not only for my own life but for the very future of the Holy Mother Church."

"You expect us to believe that?" asked Victorianna.

"I expect you to believe in the infallibility of the Pope."

"What?" she said.

Peter continued, "Let me make it more clear: I believed that Father Francsco posed a supreme threat to the future of the Roman Catholic Church. I believed then—as I do now—the most drastic measures were necessary to protect us all."

The captain of the guard had been sitting there, taking it all in. Not even moving other than to smooth down his thinning red hair, which had picked up a static charge and was kind of free-floating all around his head in a wispy nimbus. He had no idea how silly he looked as he regarded Peter with a very serious expression. "Your Holiness," he said softly, "we do not doubt your motives or your beliefs. However, Father Francesco warned the Cardinal and the Abbess they may also be targets."

Peter shrugged. "And . . . ?"

"And I am here to determine if there is any truth to that," said Captain Leutmann.

Peter smiled. "Captain, I think you are here as an insurance policy."

"What do you mean?"

"With you as an impartial witness, and perhaps a concealed wire transmitter, do you not think it would look very bad for me if anything unusual were subsequently to happen to any of your party?"

Paolo Lareggia had tensed for the briefest of moments when Peter had mentioned the wire. That was all he'd needed. They'd thought they were being slick, and that amused him.

"Well, I suppose that is true," said the captain.

"I believe in speaking as frankly as possible," said Peter. "Therefore, I'll tell all three of you the mad Jesuit's fears were unfounded. I haven't put out 'contracts' on any of you. You're all safe from Evil Pope Peter the Second."

He smiled as he paused to gauge their reactions to his words. Their expressions were mostly ones of consternation. Clearly they had expected him to be more recondite, and it perplexed them to be dealing with someone who remained so up-front. "Holiness," said Captain Leutmann, "I am not trying to insinuate that you have done anything wrong or—"

"Oh, yes, you are," said Peter quickly. "But you people are living with your heads in the sand! It's time you woke up to a few things. The Catholic Church is a juggernaut, a sleeping giant, in terms of its geopolitical power. Part of my plan is to completely involve the Church in what goes on in the world politically. The Vatican is a formidable force and I intend to let the rest of the world realize just how powerful we are."

"I am not sure I see the connection," said Cardinal Lareggia.

"Paolo, please. If you choose to play in the political arena, you play by politicians' rules. And one of their prime directives is that you defend yourself from threats—external and internal. And you do this by resolving to eliminate anything or anyone who stands in the way of your survival."

"You're talking about espionage and war," said Captain Leutmann. "That would be the only justification for taking a life."

Peter smiled and nodded. "Consider ourselves at war, then."

"With *whom?*" cried Victorianna.

"With anyone or anything that might threaten the new objectives of the Catholic Church."

Victorianna stared at him for as long as she dared, then said, "I think your 'new objectives' are what concern us."

The Cardinal folded his hands, began wringing them nervously. "Yes, that is correct! Holy Father, please, you are talking about taking stands and making policies that have no precedent, no—"

"That's where you're wrong, Paolo," said Peter, warming to his topic. "Historically, the Church was a true world power for a long time. The Crusades, the Holy Roman Empire! Before that, the Vatican had flexed its muscles for more than a thousand years!"

"Yes," said Victorianna softly. "A time that is now referred to as the Dark Ages."

Peter nodded, grinned. "A mistake that will not be repeated this time around."

Lareggia leaned forward. "What about Giovanni? What will happen to him now?"

Peter shrugged, made a gesture with his hands to indicate his feelings on the subject were *mezzo-mezzo.* "I have not thought about him much. He's probably very far away from Rome now, and is, for the time being, not a direct threat or even an irritating problem."

They were interrupted by the arrival of lunch, served by a small platoon of attendants, who quickly dressed their table with place settings, candles, carafes of wine and other beverages, and baskets of bread, cheese, and fruit, along with the entrees. Everyone waited in silence until the table was complete and Peter had dismissed the staff with a subtle nod.

His three guests waited upon his conferring of the grace and the offering of a toast. "To the future," he said with the hint of a grin at the corner of his mouth.

They all joined him with reluctance, then began to examine their plates with various degrees of interest. Surprisingly, the obese Cardinal was all but ignoring the delicately baked capon. After a few minutes of silent, awkward dining, Lareggia spoke softly.

"So, will you pursue him?"

"I don't know." Peter was being honest. He hadn't made up his mind yet.

"Will you . . . will you tell me when you have reached any new decisions regarding him?"

"So you can warn him?" Peter smiled.

"I don't know . . ." The Cardinal tried to be coy as well. "So I can warn myself might be a better answer."

"Let me put it this way, Paolo. You'll know what's going on—one way or another."

Peter sipped his wine and regarded his guests with an amused gaze. He'd kept them off balance with his candor and his hospitality, and they had no idea what to expect from him. While he didn't actually consider them enemies, he knew they should be kept at arm's length and watched for any signs of treachery or danger. He wondered if this game of palace intrigue really appealed to him. Some people definitely had a mind and a stomach for it, while others proved inept.

History would judge his performance, he thought. No sense worrying about it.

The remainder of the meal became entangled in small talk that served to camouflage everyone's anxieties, and Peter had become bored with them. Having learned all he needed to know about their feelings, motives, and plans, he wanted to dismiss them to their petty fears and get back to his research.

As soon as the attendants finished clearing the table, Peter pushed back his chair as an unspoken signal that their meeting, as well as their meal, had been completed. He stood slowly and made a point of looking at each of his guests.

Adept at such protocols, all three placed their linen napkins on the table and stood up.

"Thank you for staying to dine," he said. "I hope I've been able to clear up any misconceptions and answer all your questions."

They mumbled thank-yous and affirmations. Peter accompanied them to the foyer at the building's grand, stately entrance. As he moved alongside Cardinal Lareggia, he spoke softly: "Tell me, Paolo, have you ever heard of something called the 'Secret of the Seven?' "

Lareggia paused at the threshold as Captain Leutmann guided Victorianna out the double doors and down the small flight of stairs. "In reference to what?" he said.

"I'm not sure. I've been doing some research in the Archives, and I have come across the reference several times. Always enigmatically."

"What kind of 'research?' " Lareggia looked suspicious.

"Apocalyptic is probably the best way to describe it."

"For what reason?"

Peter put a hand on the Cardinal's shoulder, feeling it sink into his soft flesh. "Believe it or not, Paolo, I'm not completely sure what is going on, what this is all about, and I'm trying to find out."

The Cardinal looked at him, shook his head slowly. "I'm sorry, Peter, you will have to forgive me, but, I am afraid I do not believe you."

" 'The Secret of the Seven'—what does it mean to you?"

"Nothing. Absolutely nothing."

"Why don't you ask around? Some of your theologian friends. See if anybody has any ideas."

Lareggia tilted his head. "Do you have anything to . . . ah, trade . . . for this information?"

He looked at the large man for any trace of sarcasm or anxiety. There was none. Lareggia was serious.

"That's fair enough," said Peter. "I'll have to think of a suitable reward."

FOURTEEN

I didn't want to bother you with this, Grace," said
Sheriff DeWayne Davis. "But, God help me, I got
no place else to turn."

Turning from the keyboard of her organ, Grace Allbright regarded the young man who had entered the
First Baptist Church of Hartstown on a Saturday afternoon. Sheriff Davis was medium tall and thin, not frail
looking, but not a hard, hungry lean either. His pale
cheeks were so smooth it didn't appear he even shaved
yet, but Grace knew he was around thirty years old.
His eyes were as dark as ripe blueberries, and they
kinda jumped around in their sockets like he was always on the lookout for something out of whack.

Which was probably a good way for a law enforcement officer to be, she thought with an easy smile.
"What can I do for you, Sheriff Davis?"

"Well, first off, you could put me more at ease by
just calling me DeWayne."

Grace nodded. "All right, DeWayne, I can do that."

She paused for a moment to slip out of her soft, patent-leather flats (the ones she wore only when working the pedals of the old pipe organ) and put on her regular shoes. Then she stood up and gestured toward the door to the church vestibule. "Let's go through there," she said. "We can talk in the garden."

The sheriff nodded and followed her through the little room off to the side and out to a bench set in a manicured space enclosed by a semicircular hedge and accented by late-blooming gardenias and petunias. A soft breeze stirred a variety of pleasant scents. Grace sat on one end of the bench, smoothed out her skirt, and looked expectantly at DeWayne.

"I guess you know why I'm here," he said. His expression added a couple of things to his words—he was feeling kinda scared, frustrated, and silly all at the same time.

"Same reason as last, I'd suppose. You talkin' about the Carstairs thing, right?"

"You been keeping track of the case?"

Grace shook her head. "Not directly, but you can't help but keep hearing about it on the TV and in town, that's what everybody's been jabbering about."

"No doubt. Even though, I'll tell ya," said Davis, "it seems like people are gettin' crazier and crazier everywhere. Seems like there's so many towns all over the country dealin' with killers and crazies."

"Signs of the times," said Grace. "That's what the Bible tells us. You seen any of that business they talkin' about the sun burnin' all funny and not like normal? That's a sign of the times if I ever saw one!"

"Maybe you're right." The sheriff paused. "Now, what do you know about my case right here?"

"Not a lot. I don't have to really pay all that close attention because . . . because, well, you know, if I'm goin' to get a 'shine' on anything, well, I'll just *get* it. And that's that."

DeWayne Davis nodded gravely. He avoided looking directly into her eyes, and she wasn't certain whether it was out of fear or respect. She was at least twice his age, so she hoped he was more respectful than spooked.

"The State police and all my county people are right-well stuck, Grace."

"I know," she said. "I guess I've been wonderin' when you'd be callin' on me."

She smiled gently, touched his hand as if to tell him he needn't be so skittish, and he took it as a sign to go on. His voice took up a hopeful tone. "Does that mean you got something you can tell us?"

"No, not directly. Not yet." Grace paused. She knew what would be coming next. Same thing as always when she was gettin' ready to get a shine . . .

That's what her great-grandmother had called it—The Shine. She could remember being a little girl and sitting on a porch swing with her grandmother and *her* momma, and both old women making such a fuss over her that day she was so upset. Grace's mother was working in a mill outside the Army base in Sumter where they made uniforms for all the soldiers.

All the soldiers off fighting the Germans and the Japanese.

Grace's daddy had been drafted into the war, and her mother said his unit had been one of the first Negro companies to see action in Europe. She had been six years old when he left South Carolina, never to return. Funny thing was, little Grace knew even then that he wasn't coming back.

She never said it to anybody in the family. Not the

day he left, when she got that feeling—that bitter burnt-almond *knowing* that something was true—not until months later. When it happened, she'd been playing in the yard, sitting in a tire swing while one of her brothers pushed her higher and higher into the summer sky. Suddenly she heard bombs going off, the air ripped by thousands of bullets, and lots of men yelling and screaming. And for the briefest instant she was seeing things through the eyes of her daddy: running across an empty street where all the buildings were burned out and half knocked down, him caught flat-footed as a Tiger Tank suddenly crushed into his path, right through the brick wall of a house; a huge, gray machine-monster, wide and flat, it clanked forward an instant, then its long barrel flashed as a shell exploded from it.

That had been it.

The briefest vision and a flash of light. That flash had been the last thing her daddy had ever seen, and it had happened so fast, so clean that he'd never heard the roar of the muzzle blast. Grace knew this because she hadn't heard it either. But she hadn't been thinking of that just then. Like a spell had been broken, she twisted her way out of the tire as the tears escaped her in a hot, stinging burst. She was crying and screaming that her daddy was dead, and her great-grandmother was the first one to reach her and scoop her up into her arms.

Over and over, Grace had sobbed out that her daddy had just died. Everybody tried to calm her down and tell her it wasn't so, that she was just upset, that she was just scared and everything was okay, but she was having none of it. That's when her great-grandmother sat down on the porch swing and lifted Grace to her lap. The old woman's face was weathered mahogany, all full of cracks and fissures, and her eyes were dull blue from cataracts, but she was beautiful to Grace.

"You seen sumpin', ain't you, Dearie?" said Great-Gran. The old woman had been looking at her with an intensity that was almost scary.

Grace had nodded slowly, afraid to say what she'd seen, as if it might make it more real.

"Oh Lawd," said great-Gran. "This little sweet pea, she got *the shine*, she do."

Her grandmother nodded in agreement, and both old women held her close and rocked her and sang songs to her, and it was like that piece of time got frozen and tucked away in her memory where she could go and get it and look at it whenever she wanted and it would always be like it just happened. Just like going to her old cedar chest where she kept a locket with a sepia photo of Great-Gran.

And then about three days later, when her mother got the telegram about her daddy, Grace suddenly understood what her great-grandmother had been talking about. Funniest thing was—they never really *had* to talk about it much. Both of them, the little girl and the wiry, old, half-blind woman, just seemed to know and accept what was going on. (Later, as an adult, Grace imagined that Great-Gran probably had a touch of the *shine* herself, which would have explained a lot. . . .) And as far as the shine, well, it didn't really show up again until Grace was about twelve years old, when she got what Grandma called the "curse of the moon," and even then, it happened only once in a great while. Like when something important or momentous would be about to happen in her life, then Grace might get a feeling that would give her an idea what might be happening.

Or what was goin' to happen.

And it had went on like that—Grace just shining a kind of special "light" on the goings-on of her own life—until about four years back when she was driving her

Ford Escort back to Hartstown and she was only half-listening to the local news broadcast on her radio. Then the announcer was breaking a story that instantly caught her attention—Floyd Wanneker had been shot and killed. He was the manager of the ThriftMart right in the center of town, and Grace had known him most of her life.

Unbelievable. Floyd dead.

Found on the floor behind the cash register counter with a mortal head wound, the announcer said, and—

No, wait . . .

Grace was so struck by the image that rippled through she had had to lean on the brakes and pull the car onto the shoulder of Mulberry Branch Road. She had trouble getting her breath and her hands had started to shake as she suddenly realized what had happened to her.

The announcer hadn't said anything about a head wound or where the victim might be laying or any kind of details at all. But Grace had seen poor Floyd like she'd seen a photograph, and she just *knew* it was true. Leaning back against the seat's headrest, she closed her eyes and let the image flow through her: a skinny kid in blue jeans and a red and white basketball jersey, number 23 on it, and a black baseball cap, big blue-black shiny pistol in both hands as he pointed it at Floyd Wanneker and fired once, then the boy was running around the counter to clean out the register before running out the door to climb into a beat-up old pickup truck with Georgia tags on it.

Grace had opened her eyes and exhaled slowly.

Had she really seen all that? A feeling of dreamlike unreality colored her perceptions. She lost track of time, sitting there like that for a while, before she finally put the little car back into Drive and eased off toward the center of town.

Not sure where she was headed until she found herself pulling into the small parking lot of the county sheriff's office, which was just a small room off the first floor of the Town Office building. An ambulance from Sumter General was parked there, along with two state police cruisers and Sheriff Davis's big white Chevy. Grace turned off the Escort's engine, drew a deep breath, and exhaled slowly. She knew why she was here, and she was going to have to trust in the Lord to give her strength.

She'd figured the easiest way to tell all those men crowded into the sheriff's little office was to just blurt it right out, so she did. She told them things she couldn't possibly know and what kind of vehicle to look for on the state highway.

At first the state troopers were so stunned they didn't believe her, but then they decided only an accomplice could know such details and they wanted to arrest her. It was Sheriff Davis who put a stop to that foolishness and took the time actually to listen to what Grace was saying. He sat down in his office with the door closed and let her explain everything in her own way. He told her he wasn't a closed-minded person and he knew of many cases where psychics helped solve crimes, and if he was looking at one of those situations, well then, he was willing to deal with it.

Grace smiled as she remembered that time. It wasn't like they were looking at anything difficult or complicated. Sheriff Davis put out a BOLO for the blue pickup with Georgia tags, and sure enough, they caught the kid within three hours. He still had the murder weapon under his seat and the money from the cash register in one of Floyd's ThriftMart bags sitting right next to him.

Easy as pie, that's what it had been. Grace had asked the sheriff to keep her part in it quiet, and he promised her he would. In fact he assured he would never ask her about it or for her help unless it was something so terribly awful that she would just know he needed her. She'd really respected him for that and seeing's how he'd kept his word for years now, she understood completely why he'd felt it necessary to see her now . . .

. . . and he was sitting forward on the bench, hands folded as neatly as the ironed and starched creases of his uniform shirt. Grace had the briefest vision of DeWayne's wife spraying and ironing those shirts, and it brought a little smile to her face. Just then he sat up straight, nodded, and gave her that puppy dog look that some men perfect as boys and keep all the way through their man-years. A look that always makes women predisposed to like them and want to do for them.

"Well, then, Grace, I guess I'll be lettin' you get back to your music practicin', and I'll go on back to the office." He stood up, smoothed out his pants, and adjusted the holster that held his big gun. "If there's anything you need on the Carstairs case, you just let me know, okay?"

Grace nodded, stood up with him. "I expect there will be. I'll be giving this whole thing some thought and see what comes of it."

"Don't you think you'll need any of the . . . facts we've been able to come up with so far?"

"I might, but we'll just have to see what comes. This ole shine ain't somethin' I got much control over, DeWayne. It just come over me like, and whoop, there it is."

"Whoop, there it is," he said with a smile. "Wasn't there a song like that?"

Grace nodded. "Yes, but before the song, there was still that ole *whoop*."

The sheriff chuckled, nodded, took her hands in his, and gave her his best puppy dog look. "Thanks, Grace. I mean it, thank you."

"You know you're welcome."

"Whatever comes of this, even if it don't seem like much, it'll be appreciated."

They said their good-byes, and she returned to the pipe organ after she'd watched him drive off. She sat at the bench and started to play "Nearer My God to Thee," concentrating on the sheet music with only a half an eye. Her mind, she discovered, was ticking through the list of things she heard about the Carstairs case and what she knew to be fact and—

—and suddenly she was sitting there, arms hanging by her side, looking straight ahead, and there was stuff running past her like she was sitting at the library turning the crank on one of those old microfilm readers. Everything a blur of high-speed information. Where did it come from and why did it come to her? These questions burned through the flood of images, but they did not actually upset her.

And slowly, like a vessel being filled, Grace accepted the details of Abigail Carstairs's disappearance into her soul. . . .

Two Sundays past, a fourteen-year-old girl named Abby Carstairs had been studying for a big geography test at the home of her best friend, Miranda Jones. At around 4:00 P.M., Abby packed her schoolbooks into a bright yellow L.L.Bean backpack, said good-bye to Miranda, and walked out the front door. Somewhere in the four suburban blocks between the Joneses' house and her own, Abby had vanished. As completely as if she'd fallen into a bottomless pit. The entire city of Sumter had responded to the alarm, but no one had seen a trace of the pretty blonde cheerleader. State, city, county, and even federal agencies had been checking out every possible lead but turned up nothing. Although there was always the possibility that Abby was a runaway, none of the evidence suggested such a thing. The only suspects were a boyfriend and Abby's own parents, but this was based on statistics only, since there was not a single clue linking any of them to the disappearance. The most likely scenario was abduction, rape, murder, or some combination of those elements. So far, there had been no ransom note, no communication or sign of any kind. Abigail Carstairs was simply gone.

But that was not all that filled Grace as she sat motionless, staring at the keys of her pipe organ but not really seeing them. Like the layers of an onion being peeled away, she began to see into the facts of the case more deeply, more clearly. At first, nothing felt *connected* or sensible. Just a continuous flowering of images that gradually took more substance. The yellow backpack, golden hair in a pony tail, black cycle boots with worn-down heels, a weather-gray barn, a billboard for Red Man Chewing Tobacco, a black minivan, strips of wet rawhide, lengths of PVC pipe, a weeping willow tree. Other objects and scenes slipped past her but as though she were seeing through a veil or from a great distance. Not clear or recognizable, but with an underlying belief that all would become clear enough . . . soon enough.

Answers, she thought calmly, usually came to her in dreams.

And they did. Later that night.

After turning off the eleven o'clock news and checking the locks on the doors, Grace entered her bedroom, and dropped down to her knees for her evening prayers. As she began the familiar litany, her eyes touched on the black and white portrait photograph of her husband Herman, who would be dead fifteen years this coming winter. She missed him dearly and lived for the day when the Lord would call her home to be with her husband again. But Grace was patient and totally given over to whatever God had in store for her in the meantime. That's why she could accept her talent for the shine with such an open heart, without fear. And so, after including everyone in her prayers, with special mentions for both Herman and Abby Carstairs, she climbed under her covers waiting for sleep to claim her like a warm tide on a lonely beach.

When it did, Grace dreamed. *An old stone building, looking like a castle or a dungeon, but she knew it was neither of those. Rain pelted the rough stone of the place and a single candle illumined a single open window, and Grace seemed to be hovering above this Gothic place like a circling hawk, but the feeling of flying was neither exhilarating nor fearful. More like just the way things should be. Then she was swooping down and gliding right through the window, past the candle, and down a long stone-walled corridor with an arched ceiling. There was a statue in an alcove at the end of the passageway—dressed in the brown and tan robes of an unfamiliar order of nuns. As Grace drew closer to the statue, it began to glow with a soft inner light, and it was suddenly very obvious that this was not a statue at all but a woman of indeterminate age and a tranquil aspect that made her quite attractive. Grace smiled, and the woman returned the gesture.*

Now what in the world was this? Grace wondered to herself, curiously apart yet totally immersed in the dream.

She'd always had this ability to "step out" of her own dreams and ask such questions, but she'd rarely if ever had the need to do it. But this time, it happened almost automatically—because this dream wasn't like all the rest. She'd never seen that old stone building and certainly never talked to any woman like she was seeing right now. Something looked very Catholic about everything, and that kind of bothered her. The pastor at First

Baptist never had much good to say about them folks. . . .

Clearly somethin' funny goin' on here.

"Here is what happened," said the woman.

"Who are you?" asked Grace, but the Dream Lady didn't seem to hear her. Instead, a new vision began to take shape.

Abby Carstairs left her girlfriend's house just as the sun got tangled in the tops of the trees. Twilight seeped into the streets, turning everything gray just as a black minivan turned the corner and approached Abby from the opposite direction. It drove past her very slowly, and the girl couldn't see who hunched over the steering wheel—the windows were tinted like smoked glass. Abby reached the end of the street, turned right onto the next one, the one that connected to her own. It was a long, wide avenue, covered by a canopy of tall old oaks and poplars and lined by manicured lawns and hedges. A very nice neighborhood, still known as "Pill Hill" by the locals because it had once been where all the town doctors lived. Most of the homes were well off the road, tucked away on sloping swales of lawns and gardens, embraced by boughs and shrubs and not concerned with the traffic. So no one was looking when the minivan stopped at the sidewalk, its side-panel door sliding open like the mouth of a predator, and a gaunt, tall man levered himself out of the vehicle to throw a horse blanket over Abby Carstairs and drag her inside. After he hit her expertly at the base of her skull with a sap, he hog-tied her, gagged her, and drove off on State Road 384 for twenty-nine miles until he reached the intersection of what had once been a town called Conway, now just a four corners with a gas station and phone booth.

Beyond the crossroads, a forgotten Red Man billboard half obscured an overgrown road, but the van did not miss it, turning quickly to rock through the abandoned fields of a farm in foreclosure. The falling-down barn of gray planks accepted the minivan, and again, no one was watching. The tall, gaunt man wore stovepipe jeans, a matching jacket, and cycle boots, and he moved with a stiffness that suggested he was always in pain. He pulled the van next to a large hole he'd already dug into the *floor of the barn. Glowing under the pale light of a Coleman lantern, it looked very much like a grave, and in many ways it was. At the bottom lay an open freezer, unplugged, stained with age and lack of care, and rising up from its open white casket was a wooden painter's ladder. The gaunt man lifted Abby, just starting to stir from her assault, like a fireman rescuing an unconscious victim, and descended the ladder. After placing her in the old freezer, he closed the lid, which had been modified to accept a one-and-a-half-inch-diameter PVC pipe. Quickly, the gaunt man fitted several lengths of the pipe into the lid—high enough to clear ground level—then ascended the ladder, removed it from the hole, and began the slow but inexorable task of refilling the hole with dirt. When he was finished, he unfolded a lawn chair next to the open pipe that extended from the ground to a height of eighteen inches. Sitting in the chair, the man simply stared at the pipe, as if listening for a sound to escape it. . . .*

"What does it mean?" Grace asked the Dream Lady.

"You already know that. And you know what to do about it."

"Yes," said Grace, "I do."

"And when you have finished, I will see you again."

Grace nodded and turned away from the alcove, as though preparing to walk the length of the corridor. But as she took her first few steps, the stone walls began to dissolve and she was drifting through the night sky once again. . . .

She woke up with a start and was surprised to see it was still dark beyond the window. The dream had been so real, so vivid, it was like she now had a memory of being there—actually being with that terrible thin man in the barn. Oddly enough, what she'd watched him do had not upset her as much as outraged her. Grace was not afraid because she believed in the power of God and she knew she had the means to bring the monster to justice. Despite the lack of sleep, her thoughts were clear and sharp, and she moved from the bed, grabbed her robe, and went downstairs to her

writing desk, where she sat each month to pay the bills.
Grabbing a notepad, she began writing.

Grace wanted all the facts right before she called
Sheriff Davis. As she carefully penned the details, she
found herself a bit distracted.

*What's going on here? I'm no Catholic, so who was that nun
who was talking to me?*

She could not get the image of the woman out of her
mind. All the times she'd shined on things, all the
dreams, all the wonderful and terrible stuff she'd seen
. . . she'd never had anything like that vision with the
nun Dream Lady. It was like that woman was right
there, sharin' Grace's dream with her.

And that was impossible, wasn't it?

The question dogged her as she finished making her
list. But she wrote with strength and confidence. She
would prepare everything she could as fast as she
could. The sheriff was going to need to know all the
details if they were gonna save that young girl's life.

And she looked forward to seeing that Dream Lady
again. Had a few questions to be askin' her.

FIFTEEN

Sister Etienne—Vatican City
September 20, 2000

The convent of the Sisters of Poor Clares was un-
usually imposing in its Gothic bulk: large blocks
of stone, tall towers, high windows. Etienne had heard
that it reminded passing tourists of a fortress or a
prison; and she felt that in certain ways it had always
been both of those things. For the women who spent
their lives within its walls, the convent had been a spiritual redoubt against the temptations of the world outside and also a physical jail to keep the members of its
order from ever escaping to a life in mundane society.

To Etienne and the rest of her cloistered soror-
ity, the convent had been a place with precious little
information during what was touted to be the Information Age. A place of minimal technology and less
contact with whatever transpired outside its walls. She
had lived most of her life in that way, right up to the
point when her son had attained the age of thirty.

Ever since then, Etienne had been the receiver of
hallucinated dreams, fugue states, and what some

would term "visions." At times, she had attempted to tell her superiors, Abbess Victorianna or even Paolo Cardinal Lareggia, the content of her visions, but until very recently, no one had been very interested.

Not until their creation, the mysterious Peter Carenza, began to act unaccording to plan, to form, to expectations.

Not until everyone in Peter's orbit had begun to wonder how and why God had allowed such a thing to happen in the first place.

Not until they had nowhere else to look for answers.

Etienne smiled to herself as she entertained these thoughts. She was walking slowly through the twisting stone paths of the convent gardens, awaiting the arrival of Marion Windsor, the single person in the world whom Etienne believed she might be able to truly trust.

Unless her God was cruel, and she could never believe he was, he would not demand or even desire she bear the bulk of her recent experiences in solitude. No, Etienne had decided, she needed to share what she had discovered, what she now knew, or it would consume her.

So lost in thought had she become that she did not notice she was no longer alone.

"Good morning, Etienne," said Marion. She stood by a marble bench, just where the path curved under the bough of a eucalyptus. "I hope I'm not late."

"No, not at all. I am just eager to speak with you."

Marion nodded. She wore a conservative dress, long enough to reach the tops of her fashionable boots. Etienne absently wondered what it might be like to wear clothes other than the habits of her order. "Shall I walk with you? Or sit here?"

"Let us walk a while," said Etienne, reaching to take her hand in greeting. Marion drew near, kissed her cheek. Such a simple gesture, yet it spoke much of the growing closeness between them.

"You sounded very serious on the phone," said Marion as they began to follow the path in a most leisurely way. "Which, by the way, I was surprised to hear you using."

"Our phones are for emergency only, but lately, Victorianna has allowed me to do whatever I believe is warranted." Etienne realized she was speaking very slowly, choosing her words in English with care and some difficulty. She could not control her accent, but she wanted her vocabulary to reflect her thoughts as accurately as possible.

"Really? What's inspired her?"

Etienne shrugged. "I think she is scared."

Marion nodded, chuckled nervously. "I think we all are, don't you?"

"I still believe in whatever God has planned," said Etienne.

"I want to," said Marion, "but it's getting harder and harder."

"Maybe not so much after you hear my story." Etienne paused, cleared her throat. She felt nervous, as though preparing to confess a great sin. Until this moment, she had not realized how difficult it might be to talk about it. But she must. God obviously wanted it.

"You will forgive my English, if I do not have the correct word sometimes?"

Marion smiled. "Your English is fabulous, are you kidding?"

Etienne smiled her gratitude and began. "Marion, you know that in the past I believed I received messages from God."

"Yes, Cardinal Lareggia told me you tried to see the Pope, back when Peter was traveling around the United States. You told him you'd had visions."

"Yes, that is right. They have never really stopped. I feel that God chooses to give me 'signs' or 'messages' because of my role in Peter's creation. I believe Peter was brought into the world for a purpose. God wishes to test humans from time to time, and how the world copes with Pope Peter II will determine how God copes with the world. Now, I know I am going to start sounding crazy—what is the word?—for having delusions, but you should believe me; I have been shown the way . . . by God."

Marion turned to face the older woman and looked deep into her eyes as if searching for something. "Etienne, please, please don't make excuses for what you're telling me. After everything I've seen, everything I already know to be true, there's *nothing* you can tell me that's going to sound too unbelievable."

Etienne nodded. Very well, then, she would just push ahead and stop making prefatory remarks. "I have been having long, complicated dreams," she said. "And sometimes they are more than dreams. It is like I am traveling outside my body. I go to places where I meet with people, special people."

" 'Astral projection,' " said Marion. "That's the term for what you're describing."

"It is very strange, but very real, I can assure you," Etienne said as they began walking again. "The first dream was different. You must know that one to understand the others. I was standing on a vast empty plain, whipped by the wind, and the sky was dark even though the sun was high and full. As I stood watching the sun, it seemed to be pulsating, throbbing like a beating heart. I could stare into its center even though it burned with a white-heat fury. As I watched, fiery arms peeled off, reaching far out into space. I knew I was watching a manifestation of God, that he was showing himself to me in a way I could comprehend.

"And he spoke to me. His voice came out of the wind. He told me of the Seven."

"The Seven *what*?"

"In *Revelation* there are mentions of seven churches. In my vision, He told me there are seven keys to those churches—they are not actually keys but people. They are seven people who are like living saints, in the world today. In the Kabbalah, they were known as the *Zaddikim*, or Righteous Ones. They appear in many religions and beliefs throughout the world, all throughout history. From the *Abbaye* of Babylonia, the *Kanoo-Si* of the Iroquois nation, the *Duc Tran* of Southeastern Asia. Regardless of the culture or the time, there seems to have always been seven people like them. When one dies, he or she is replaced by another. As long as even *one* of the Seven is alive, the world cannot end."

"Seven keys," said Marion. "I'd never heard of anything like that."

"Nor had I," said Etienne. "Although I know of the seven seals. . . ."

"Also *Revelation*."

"Yes, and there is the story of Sodom and Gomorrah, where God asks for one hundred righteous people to save the cities. Which made me wonder—why one hundred for two cities and only seven for the whole world? I studied my Old Testament and discovered that God was probably being sardonic in his request."

"What do you mean?" said Marion.

"He was lamenting that he could not even find one hundred good people, not that he needed that amount."

"Oh, I see," said Marion. "At least I think I do."

"But this reference to seven is more concrete, more real, though I have no idea what it all means yet. I know God will reveal it me at the proper time."

Marion smiled gently at her. "Etienne, I love your

faith! So unshakable. So solid. You're such an inspiration."

"I have seen the power of God," she said simply.

They continued walking slowly along the convent's garden path, neither speaking for a moment. Then Marion urged her to continue. "There is more?"

"Oh, yes. Very much. As I watched the sun in the black sky, I knew I was seeing a possible future, as if this might be the End Times."

Marion looked disturbed by this notion. "Do you believe that it is?"

Etienne considered for a moment. "No, not really. But it *could* be. If we do not please God. My son, Peter, surely plays a large part in what will happen."

"Do you know, or did God tell you how the world must deal with him? Peter, I mean."

"In a sense, yes. I told you I have been appearing before certain people, and—"

"The Seven. You're talking to *them*."

"Yes. Not all of them yet, but I will. On special nights, I encounter them. Each one has been touched in some special way by God, and they are all very righteous."

"What does God want you to do with them?"

Etienne paused on the path, appeared to take great interest in a tall flower, then turned to look at Marion. "There is so much mystery all around us, but I have faith it will be made clear. God wants them for a purpose, and he will tell us that purpose in the fullness of his time."

"Does anyone else know about this?" Marion asked as they began walking again. "Have you told anyone else about your dreams?"

"No, of course not. You are the only person I can trust. Why do you look so worried?"

"Because I think it would be very bad for us if Peter knew what you are experiencing."

"You know, I have been having very like thoughts. It makes me so sad, so terribly sad that I must be afraid of my own son. That I must keep such a wondrous thing from him—because he may be my most feared enemy."

"Peter has plans for all of us," said Marion. "And I don't think he's feeling the kind of compassionate conflict you are."

"No, I fear he is not."

"I am as close to him as anyone can be," said Marion. "He acts careless around me—he doesn't think there's anything I can do to get in his way. But he is involved in some kind of research, and it's got him obsessed. I'm going to pay more attention to whatever he's doing. It might be important to us."

"I am glad you said it that way," said Etienne.

"What way?"

"You said *us*, and that is what it is—both of us, Marion. Even though God is using me directly, he needs us to be allies, to work together."

Marion smiled at her, took both her hands in her own. "Thank you, Etienne. Thank God. You have no idea how helpless I was beginning to feel. But you've given me such strength and something I didn't think I'd ever have again—hope."

"God has a special love for those who never lose hope."

Marion smiled again. "Well, then, I guess I should tell you how much I *hope* you're right."

SIXTEEN

Shanti Popul—Delhi, India
September 14, 2000

The day had begun like any other for Shanti Popul, a young woman of twenty-four. She lived with her husband, Momdar, in a working-class suburb of the sprawling city where he worked as a machinist and she toiled at home as a seamstress. Although their apartment was small and cramped, Shanti had managed to secure enough room for an old treadle-powered sewing machine, where she diligently worked each day to bring extra money to the household.

Though small, their home was warm and filled with paintings, tapestries, family photographs, knickknacks, religious objects, and gifts of sentiment. It reflected both their youth and their dreams, and was a repository of their collective love and dedication to other.

But it was not big enough, and jobs were so scarce in the city, and Momdar so desperate for her to be working, that Shanti felt considerable pressure to do as much as possible. If they could not save some income, they would be trapped forever in such an undesirable part of the city. It was Momdar's dream one day to have a machine shop of his own, but there would be a need for much money to do this. Shanti loved her husband, but she was growing tired of his constant harangues concerning money and working, working and money, money and working. Surely there was more to life than that.

But she did not complain, or challenge his priorities. She served him as a good and dutiful wife, and she spent whatever free time she had as a volunteer for one of the government-established centers for homeless children. Because, like her husband, she too had her own dreams—of having beautiful children and perhaps someday establishing a child-care center. But for now, she would be content with her sewing business, which was growing steadily by word of mouth. Many customers from the surrounding neighborhoods were seeking her services as she became known for her honest work and courteous treatment. Shanti was very proud of this.

Seated at her sewing machine as the noon hour approached, she was interrupted from her work by a knock at the door. This was not unusual, because there were many occasions when a new customer would appear without notice. It was very hot and stuffy in the apartment, despite the windows being open. From the narrow streets, the smells of garbage and human waste were intensified by the heat radiating off the paved stones.

Opening the door, Shanti looked at a man of medium height, apparently in his forties and dressed in the style of a modern businessman. Open-collared shirt, gabardine pants, and fine leather shoes. He carried several garments over his left arm, obviously in need of tailoring, and his soft features gave him a kindly, familiar look.

Too familiar.

The thought struck Shanti instantly, and the truth of it darted deep into the core of her soul. Something odd was happening to her. Just standing there, staring at this man, who was a total stranger to her, was striking some sort of weird, unexplainable resonance in her.

As if someone had thrown a master power switch, or released a main valve, deep in her consciousness, she felt a flood of information rushing into her, a storm-like force. She had no power against it, but the shock of it left her momentarily paralyzed and speechless.

"Are you all right?" ask the man at the threshold. Apparently he could see that she was in distress.

"Oh!" was all she could manage to say. "I know you! I know you!"

"You do?" The man was perplexed.

"How do I know you?" Shanti backed away from the threshold, holding the door for support. She felt weak, disoriented. "Gods protect me!"

"Madam, I have been told you are a very good seamstress, that—"

"Your name is Sevi! You live in Muttra!" She spoke in a loud voice that shocked her.

The man looked stunned. "That's right, but how do you know that? Did someone tell you I was coming?"

"Who? What? No! I have been told nothing. You are the cousin of my husband. My husband's name is Sripak and we have three, no, *four* children."

"I do have a cousin by that name, but how can you know that?" said the man, still standing in the doorway and looking awkward and confused. "And he does have three children."

Shanti felt dizzy, but she was not feeling as scared or confused as before. She still felt a flood of information pouring into her, but it was now more comforting than startling.

And she was beginning to understand what it all meant.

". . . but my cousin's wife's name was Ludgi, and she died a long time ago."

"I know," said Shanti. "I am Ludgi."

It was Sevi's turn to be shocked. Backing away from her, he was now looking at her warily, as one eyes a possible threat. "I am sorry, but what you say makes no sense. It is crazy!"

"I know not what it all means," said Shanti. "Please, come in! Do not be frightened. Let me tell you some things that will help you understand."

Reaching out her hand to the man, Shanti tried to appear as nonthreatening as possible. The man hesitated, clutching his garments as though they could protect him, then exhaled. As his shoulders sagged and he visibly relaxed, he stepped into the room. Shanti gestured him to a seat, which he took quickly.

"When you were much younger we would all meet at your parents' house, remember. I had my babies and your wife, Munga, she had her babies, too. Remember?"

"You know my wife's name!"

"How can I make it more clear? Listen, when I saw you, I recognized you! Seeing you did something to my memories, my memories of the life I lived before. I was Ludgi! I died and I was born again as this new person, the person everybody knows as Shanti Popul."

"Born again? This is unbelievable," said Sevi. "It is not possible."

Shanti smiled. "Yes, of course it is. I am proof of it. Is this not what we mean by reincarnation?"

"How did Ludgi die? Tell me."

"When I was Ludgi, I died giving birth to our fourth child. I can remember the pain and the doctors and the family all standing over me and then . . . nothing more. Did my baby survive?"

Sevi was shaking his head in disbelief, but in a way that made it obvious he understood she was telling the truth. "Yes," he said after a pause. "A boy, who grew up to look like you, like *Ludgi*, I mean. He is studying to someday be a doctor."

"A doctor! That is so wonderful."

"Mrs. Popul, I am so sorry, but I feel so very awkward sitting here with you like this. We are talking of things that cannot be possible, and yet they are making perfect sense to both of us. Perhaps I should just leave and we can pretend this has never happened."

Shanti burst into laughter. "You do not understand! I can never go back to the person I was before I saw you. Seeing you is what did it! Now I have an entirely *new* set of memories, of loved ones, of places and times. I cannot explain to you how strange and wonderful and terrifying it all feels like to me, but you must believe me when I say I cannot just let you leave and forget that anything had ever happened."

Sevi nodded, nervously combed his fingers through his thick, silvering hair. "What you say makes sense, but you have to understand why I am still doubtful, or at least unwilling to accept what you are telling me."

Shanti smiled. "No, sir, I am sorry, but I cannot understand. I am telling you things no one could possibly know unless I was the person called Ludgi."

"It simply cannot be!"

"Why do you not want to believe me?"

"My cousin," said Sevi. "He never married after Ludgi died. He never really got over it—even blamed himself for wanting her to bear more children."

"That is so sad," said Shanti.

"So, let us assume what you tell me is true. It would still be very bad for my cousin. I have no idea how he would react to the idea that his wife was somehow alive and living with another husband. Very odd. Very odd, madam. Do not you see that?"

"Yes, I do," said Shanti. "But I very much want to see my children! They must be all grown up now, and especially the son I never had the pleasure to know!"

Sevi waved his arms at her like a traffic policeman. "No! No! Never, please! I will not tell you anything more about him!"

Shanti smiled gently, reached out to calm him. "You forget, Sevi. I know where the whole family lives in Muttra. I can describe every room in Sripak's house, and your house too! Do you still have the tapestry made by your grandmother, who lived in Calcutta?"

Sevi could not hide the stunned and defeated expression on his face. "It is you, Ludgi. How else could you know such a thing?"

"Yes, as I have been telling you." She stood up, moved close to him, and removed the garments from his grip. "Here, let me take these. Are they marked with the changes?"

"Yes, but how can you speak of this work? After what we have talked of?"

Smiling, Shanti moved back to her sewing machine, draped the new work over an adjacent table. "Because it is the business of life, and we are both living it, Sevi."

"But how can you be so . . . accepting, so comfortable with the knowledge?"

Shanti paused to consider both her feelings and her answer. Sevi had indeed asked an interesting question. And Shanti had no real explanation for the serenity that now suffused her. It was if she'd been living her entire life with a missing piece, somehow incomplete, and never even knowing anything was amiss. And now that piece had been refitted and, in doing so, had imbued her with a sense of *wholeness*, of wellness that could not be articulated, only experienced. There was no disorientation, no confusion, and certainly no fear.

She spoke slowly as she attempted to convey these feelings to Sevi. To his credit, he listened intently and with respect.

"What you say makes sense, and I believe you are comfortable in your knowing. But I am equally certain my cousin would not be so accommodating."

Shanti nodded. "I understand. So what about this?— we will not tell Sripak, my poor husband who grieves still, that his Ludgi lives again."

"Really?" Sevi brightened.

"Yes, but you must allow me to accompany you to Muttra under a pretense—a business associate perhaps— so that I can at least see my children again."

"And you will say nothing?"

"Nothing. I can see that it would only be a disruption in the lives of so many. The past is called the past for a very good reason—it is beyond us, gone, and unchangeable."

"You are very wise for someone so young."

"Sevi, how quickly we forget: I have lived a long time!"

Looking embarrassed, he shook his head, tried to grin. "This is all so odd! So hard for me to keep in mind. I am sorry, Madame Popul."

"Please, call me Shanti, or Ludgi, if you wish."

He paused. "Shanti will be best, I think."

She stood up as he did, extended her hand in a most ladylike manner. "It was so good to meet you *and* to see you again."

He handed her his business card and nodded. "You will call me when the work is completed?"

"Yes, and then we will make arrangements for me to see my other family?"

Sevi shrugged. "Yes, I suppose we can."

She smiled and he muttered a hasty farewell before slipping quickly out the door. Shanti returned to her chair at the sewing machine, literally flooded with emotion. So much to think about. She went about her task automatically as she allowed all the new memories of her prior life to seep into her. At one point she wondered how she would explain what she had learned to Momdar.

The notion truly perplexed her. Remembering how utterly disbelieving, distraught, and helpless Sevi had been, Shanti imagined how much more so her highly pragmatic, all-business husband would be. Shaking her head, she tried to imagine how poorly he might handle this news. Certainly he loved her, but he did so with a high degree of control and a possessiveness that was almost, at times, desperate. No, she thought conclusively, not a good idea.

As she depressed the foot treadle on the old machine, Shanti knew she would avoid sharing her news with Momdar—if at all possible.

But she could not keep her shocking and wondrous enlightenment a secret! What was she going to do? And how would it be possible to live here in Delhi, knowing that her other family (her first family?) was living in nearby Muttra? Such questions she was not yet prepared to answer, and even thinking about them was beginning to make her anxious. And the more she considered hiding her knowledge from Momdar, the more the notion plagued her.

It was not good to keep secrets from your spouse, and in most circumstances, probably one of the more grievous of sins.

You will not sin, said a voice that was not the voice of Shanti's thoughts, but that of someone else.

Someone who had been able to speak to her with

the confines of her own thoughts, but that was impossible. . . .

"What?" she said aloud, turning around in her chair, overwhelmed by the sudden suspicion that she was not alone in the tiny room. As she faced the opposite wall, Shanti was stunned to see a woman standing by the dining table, looking at her calmly.

The woman's features were soft and Mediterranean. Her age lay somewhere between her midthirties and midfifties, and she wore a simple, timeless robe and habit of a religious order, much like the attire of Mother Teresa. Her almond eyes were dark and penetrating but without a hint of malevolence. And a strange, soft, and beautiful light seemed to be emanating either from her or from the thin layer of atmosphere surrounding and somehow containing her.

Please do not be afraid, said the woman.

"I am not," Shanti said as she stood up and stepped away from the sewing machine. "Who are you? How did you get here?"

I am a messenger from God.

"An angel?"

No, just another of his children, like yourself. But God needs you. Now.

"Me?" Shanti smiled involuntarily and with no disrespect. "I am just a young girl! What can I do for him?"

Today you were given the gift of sight into your past. It is a sign of how special you are, special in ways you cannot yet understand. For now you must believe that you are needed by God.

As the woman's words touched her, she felt dizzy, as though they had the power to make her faint. Shanti could sense the aura of great power as if she were standing near a massive, throbbing generator. "I believe you," she said.

Throughout history, there have been times of reckoning. This

*is one of those times, and you have been called to stand against
the corruption in the world.*

"I will not fail you," said Shanti.

*No, not me. I am only an instrument in this. Know this: You
will be called upon and you must do as you are asked.*

"When will this happen? How will I know?"

*As soon as it is known to me, it will be known to you. God
lives in you, Shanti Popul, and you in him.*

And then the Woman of Light was gone.

SEVENTEEN

Gaetano—Scarpino, Corsica
September 18, 2000

Finally, his journey was near its end.

The Tyrrenhian Sea burned in the wake of the setting sun as his boat approached the shoreline. Gaetano leaned against the gunwale and stared at a small harbor dwarfed by a sheer wall of cliffs behind it. His destination was remote, even for a place as out of the way as Corsica.

"You will get your things, *signore*," said the captain of the fishing scow. The short, barrel-chested man spoke as he finessed the helm through the final adjustments to his course. "We will be heaving to in only several minutes."

Nodding, Gaetano turned away from the dramatic coastline, and hustled down to the cabin where his gear awaited him. Two large mountaineer duffels jammed with everything they said he would need. He could feel his pulse begin to jump as he began to dwell on how close he was to his goal. Even though they'd made it very clear to him he was there on the flimsiest of permissions—he would be tested almost immediately, and if he did not measure up, he would not be flunked out of the program.

He would be killed.

It was that simple. And it was a contract to which he'd agreed—without hesitation. For two reasons: He knew he would not fail, and he had accepted the purity of his ultimate mission, convinced that God was on his side.

As he dragged his bags up to the fo'c'sle, he watched the docks grow ever closer. More details resolved, and Gaetano was impressed with the utter anonymity of the fishing village. Ramshackle buildings, a few rotting wharves, and little else. The scow slowed, and its old twin Chryslers belched and farted as their manifolds backed off. Water slapped the prow in short rhythmic chops, accenting the occasional banter from a variety of characters along the docks. And everything smelled like dead fish.

Gaetano smiled. He liked this place. Turning back to the captain, he flipped off a quick salute. "*Ciao, mio amico. Grazie!*"

Just as the starboard hull bumped against the dock, Gaetano heaved his duffels over, then clambered off the gently rocking boat. Before he could lift them and start walking, someone called his name softly, just barely audible but with great timbre and confidence.

"Signore Gaetano, over here. *Avanti!*"

Gaetano saw a muscular man of perhaps forty standing in front of a pile of broken nets. Dark hair, weathered olive complexion, heavy eyebrows, and prominent chin were all his most obvious characteristics, but the battered green baseball cap was all Gaetano needed to see. He walked to him quickly without looking elsewhere.

The man appeared to quickly size him up, allowed

a slight grin of approval to escape his hardened features, then guided him between two narrow warehouses to a waiting Mercedes SUV. After stowing the gear, the man escorted him to the passenger seat and closed the door like a chauffeur. Gaetano glanced around the dim, shabby street; no one took any notice of them. Either the driver and his vehicle were well known, or no one cared.

"I am Verducci," said the driver as they cruised slowly from the harbor. "Welcome to our happy village."

"Thank you, *signore*."

The driver negotiated away from a sickly looking goat crossing the road. Then the Mercedes swung left at a fork in the road and began a steep climb along the cliff side. "I know you must have more questions, since you know none of us. You will get answers—if you survive."

"I'll survive."

Verducci chuckled. "That is what everyone says."

The cliffs above the sea were, Gaetano discovered, honeycombed with caves and passageways. His driver slipped the Mercedes into one of them, an opening in the rock that appeared when a silent mechanism slid an immense boulder out of the way.

After driving perhaps one hundred yards, Verducci killed the engine. "We walk from here."

As he trudged along, following the light from a flashlight, it suddenly occurred to Gaetano that he felt no fear. Even though he had entrusted his life to a total stranger, a stranger who looked as if he could slash his throat without hesitation. Verducci had no interest in killing him; if Gaetano was going to die, it would be by his own failure. He and his guide walked deeper and deeper into the rock, a tortuous path through a labyrinth so complex that he knew he would never leave this place unless someone wanted him to.

After another ten minutes, the endless warren gave way to a small room with three steel doors resembling hatches in a submarine. Verducci keyed an electronic keypad next to the one on the right, and a squeak of air punctuated the silence as the seal of the hatch separated. Slowly, the door swung outward to reveal two figures, one tall, with an unkempt red beard, and a shorter, thick-bodied, bald man. They both wore the robes and hoods of monks, although their hard-edged features did not suggest they were kindly clerics.

"*Benvenuto*, Signor Gaetano," said the bald man. "I am Sforza, the prefect of our order. This is my Second, Domenici."

"It's an honor to be here, sir."

Sforza smiled softly, extended a hand. "You may not believe that to be so twenty-four hours from now."

"I will survive. And I will make you proud to have me in your ranks."

Prefect Sforza nodded. If his gaze were a lance, it would penetrate Gaetano between the eyes. "Pray that you are correct."

"This way," said Domenici, who turned away to lead the group down a wide corridor crowned with Gothic arches, its walls sculpted by endless alcoves embracing statues of the saints. Their path was illuminated by naked electric bulbs hanging from the peak of the ceiling. The general atmosphere was gloomy, dank, and oppressive, but Gaetano had not expected perfumed gardens. It actually looked better than his interviewer had made it sound.

He followed his guides down an intersecting corridor lined with small cell-like rooms, and if they were not for prisoners, they certainly served ascetics of the first

mark. Domenici pushed him into one of the cells, threw
his bags of gear in behind him, then locked the door.
Without looking up, Gaetano listened to the three men
walk away, their passage accompanied by bursts of Si-
cilian dialect and laughter.

Soon, the lights in the outer corridor were extin-
guished, plunging Gaetano into total darkness. He had
nothing to eat or drink, and he soon fell into an exhausted, timeless sleep . . .

. . . from which he was yanked so abruptly and with
such force that his guards almost dislocated his shoulders and snapped his neck. Stunned, he did not resist
as he was dragged to an oubliette for fifty lashes from
a cat-o'-nine-tails.

From there, he was tossed into a well with stone
walls so slick with algae there was no way to climb
out. Grasping at the slimy stone and gaining no purchase would only accelerate his panic, he realized, and
he willed himself to be calm. It was a clearly a test
of resourcefulness, as well as strength or courage.
Therefore Gaetano forced himself beneath the oily surface and blindly felt for an exit. Twenty feet down, he
found a shoulderwide passage parallel with the surface.
But his lungs were swelling with foul air by the time
he found what he was looking for, and he surged to
the surface for a fresh supply of oxygen. Then down
again into the murk, instinctively finding the perpendicular tunnel. He wriggled into the opening and hoped
it was not a dead end. If he wasn't totally disoriented,
the underwater tunnel seemed to slant upward. Then,
barely visible beyond the cloudy water, he saw the ti-
niest spark of light, which grew almost infinitesimally
larger with each surge forward. Was the passage nar-
rowing, like the apex of a cone, or were panic and suffocation overtaking his imagination? He writhed his
body like a fish, rushing forward, and the dim spot of

illumination enlarged until he broke the surface with an expellation of dead air.

Slowly, Gaetano dragged himself from the enclosure, gasping oxygen giddily. Only then, reflecting back on the ordeal, did he feel the total crush of terror—claustrophobia, suffocation, darkness.

Hands upon his arms and shoulders yanked him up like a sawdust doll. No one spoke to him, but he didn't feel like talking anyway. They dragged him up and down staircases, making right turns, and left turns, until he stood facing a doorway cut into the stone that lifted vertically like a portcullis. A single bulb burned in a nearby sconce, casting a pallor over the place. Two men flanked him, holding him under the arms and shoulders. Locking his knees, he forced himself to stand upright, ready to face whatever waited beyond the door. As if on cue, it began to crank upward slowly, revealing . . . *nothing*.

No, wait. As Gaetano's eyes adjusted to the lack of light, he could see a narrow ledge beyond the barrier, maybe eight inches at its widest. Slowly, stars resolved against the black aisle of night. Then they were shoving him forward, slowly so as not to push him past the edge, but inexorably, so he was balanced on the rocky protrusion. Without a word, the two men stepped away from him and the door descended. Quickly he assessed his position. He'd been thrust outside the order's cliffside redoubt, and the ledge ran off in both directions, following the contours of the sheared face. A bracing wind buffeted him. Looking down was a bad idea: five hundred feet to a craggy seawall and an ugly death. Gaetano leaned in, then inched forward to the right. At some points the ledge was barely wide enough for the heel of his boot; at others he could stand naturally. The face of the promontory curved away from him so he never saw what lay ahead. After almost an hour of hideously slow progress, he discovered he'd made the wrong choice—the ledge simply ended. If there was an escape from this predicament, it lay elsewhere. The wind continued to play with him as he sidestepped back the way he had come, more slowly than before, because he knew overconfidence could kill him more easily than anything else. It took ninety minutes to get back to square one at the portcullis door.

He rested, then resumed the awkward side-step maneuver that took him slowly along an equally blind curve of the cliff wall. Twenty minutes to clear the apex of the curve, and he would be able to see more clearly because of the rising half moon somewhere behind him. As he surveyed what lay ahead, it was like getting gut-punched. Twenty yards to his left, the ledge crumbled into broken shards: unpassable. The wall of the cliff sliced deeper into the rock and then back out like a narrow slice from a pie. On the opposite face of the missing slice lay another portcullis door, fronted by a narrow section of ledge—obviously Gaetano's escape route. But how to get from here to there?

Despite the cooling slap of the wind on his face, Gaetano was sweating like a roasting pig. He inched forward, closer to the place where the ledge disappeared, and as he did so, something resolved out of the shadows below. Previously masked in the dark, three fingers of rock rose up from the face of the wall. Like flying buttresses sheered off in midrise, the formations offered a dangerous, almost suicidal route to the door. Gaetano pressed forward, close to the vanishing point of the ledge. From that point, the closest of the three projections of rocks reached out to him like a slightly curled finger. No use thinking about it or mentally measuring it. There was nothing to do but bend down, using the uncoiling power of his legs to propel him as far outward and upward as possible. Flailing through

dark, bottomless space, his forearms slammed against
the half column of rock, and he tried to grab anything
with reach. Scrabbling with his legs, he slowly steadied
himself. Safe—for the moment—and two more to go.

His breathing was ragged and the fire of total fatigue
burned in his arms, yet he held on. Eyeing the next
stalagmitelike section, and then the final one beyond it,
he realized something terrible: There was no way to
leap to the second one and hang on as he'd done with
this first one. It had no flat surfaces, just a clutch of
jagged minipeaks like the circular mouth of a lamprey.
The solution was so absurd he couldn't take the time
to analyze it or plan it. Just do it—and don't look down.
And so he pulled himself atop the projection of rock,
hunkered down on a space no larger than a dinner
plate, like a bird on a tiny perch. From there, he leaped
into emptiness with his right leg extended like a hur-
dler, reaching and pushing off the middle section of
rock, and continuing his leap to the final finger. He
skipped across the open air as a stone off a pond surface, almost flinging himself past his objective. Reaching
out with his left arm, he hugged the stone column close
to his chest. As he hung there, gasping for breath, his
arms aflame with weariness, he knew he had one final
effort to make, and he wasn't sure he had enough
strength left to get it done. Easier just to uncurl his
hands, slide off the rock, and take the high-speed ele-
vator down to the subbasement.

No way. If he died, it would be in the middle of his
best effort. The ledge and the door were only ten feet
distant, but separated by a gulf that might as well have
been a hundred. Weak and trembling, Gaetano feared
he did not have the power to move. But he had to,
because holding up his entire body weight was only
fatiguing his arms and legs more rapidly. He pulled
himself up to the impossibly narrow vertex of the rock,

then leaned out toward the ledge and the door. With the last spring in his legs, he pushed himself into space, arms outstretched as if he were going for a rebound above the rim . . . and reached the ledge with a foot to spare, legs churning, digging, pushing against the face and pulling him to the relative safety of the ledge.

Gaetano screamed in triumph and release of tension. A surge of pure joy at simply being alive at that single moment became the most intense sensation he'd ever known.

He didn't even hear the portcullis cranking upward at a relentless, foreboding pace, and was stunned to feel their hands on him again.

"No! Jesus save me! No more!"

The words escaped him like air from a cheap balloon, embarrassing him with their weakness. But his handlers ignored them, dragging him to what he knew would be his last test, for either he would pass it, or it would kill him.

And oddly enough, it was that very attitude that preserved him. He had no energy left for anxiety or fear, nothing left but the gut instinct to stay alive.

As they carried him along, he allowed himself to lapse into semiconsciousness. He was only vaguely aware of being in motion, losing all sense of time and distance. Not until they tossed him onto the floor of a stone-walled enclosure did he force himself to total wakefulness.

He was in a cell roughly twenty feet square. No windows; opposite the door through which he'd been carried, a second door, painted a dull green and covered with marks that appeared to have been etched by fingernails. Illumination from a single, low-watt bulb hanging from the center of the ceiling. Hard to see anything clearly. No furniture other than a few pegs in the walls where various objects hung—a length of anchor chain, a fishing net, a section of steel tubing, a sledge-hammer. It did not look promising, Gaetano thought, as he willed himself to stand, hoping that would help clear his head. He didn't want to dwell on what awaited him beyond the opposite door, but anxiety began to build in him like air in a stuck pressure valve.

A single, loud metallic *click!* shattered the silence, and the green door swung outward as something cloaked in shadow shambled through.

Gaetano caught the movement in his peripheral vision. His entire body tensed, and for an instant he felt totally helpless. A flash of dark brown or black, moving quickly—and straight at him. An animal of some kind. Wide-eyed, fanged, but moving so fast in the dim light that he couldn't tell what the hell it was. No time to study it anyway. Reacting completely on reflex, he relied on his training and dove at an angle toward his attacker, which usually confused and surprised an opponent who expected a defensive maneuver.

The ploy worked as Gaetano half rolled under the lunging attack of the creature. He smelled its rank fur and heard it growl but still hadn't identified the beast. It slammed headlong into the wall and was scrambling to its feet, shrieking and snarling, as Gaetano too jumped up and into a wary defensive stance. He scanned the objects on the hooks, noting their exact locations, then focused on his adversary.

It stood still for an instant, trying to determine what had happened and why it hadn't landed on its prey. And in that moment, Gaetano realized he was staring at a very angry Kalahari baboon. A big-shouldered male, upward of 120 pounds, equipped with powerful hands and a jawful of teeth that could tear out a man's throat in seconds. The ape glared at him with eyes that bulged from its sloped brow like Ping-Pong balls

It screeched, bansheelike, as it launched itself at him again.

Waiting until the last instant, Gaetano timed its flight and trajectory, then executed a leg kick that caught the beast flat on the jaw. Coupled with its own momentum, the blow was more than enough to slam it hard into the stone wall. It began gasping frantically as it tried to scramble to its powerful hindlegs. Gaetano used the pause to move to the nearest peg and grab the length of chain and the fishnet. The chain was lighter than he expected, the netting heavier. But both were welcome additions to his arsenal because he knew he wouldn't be able to keep the raging beast off balance indefinitely with martial arts stunts.

Holding the chain in his right arm, the spread net in his left, he waited until the big male charged him again. Gaetano whirled the chain above his head, then swung it quickly. The links caught the beast across the left side of its face, shattering a big canine and splitting the flesh covering the lower mandible. An explosion of blood and a furious screeching as the thing flailed at him. One of its paws slashed across Gaetano's chest, opening up three deep gashes and forcing him backward on his heels.

The ape's mouth foamed with blood and gore as it lunged forward again, going for its adversary's throat in a savage burst of animal rage. Still fighting for his balance, Gaetano barely had time to sweep the fishnet up and over its head. They both slammed into the wall, the baboon distracted and irritated by the netting wrapped tightly around its head and wounded muzzle. The creature's momentary hesitation was enough for Gaetano to twist under its bulk and dodge away, retrieving the chain and grabbing the minisledge from its peg. He moved quickly, scrambling sideways like a crab. Though the big male's furious struggles had tangled it even more in the net, the animal could break free at any instant and be on Gaetano.

A surge of confidence jacked through him like good whiskey as he hefted the hammer's lethal weight in his hand. Now it was *his* turn to attack. Gaetano did not hesitate. Realizing he might have only a few seconds before the enraged brute worked free of its restraints, he waded in and swung the hammer in a wide, accelerating arc. The business end impacted a glancing blow across the baboon's forehead—not fatal, but enough to stun the big male into dulled silence.

As Gaetano assessed the damage, he realized something else, something equally important: His strength was leaving him. Total exhaustion lay just ahead, and he understood why he'd had so much trouble swinging the heavy hammer with much power. Arm weary didn't even begin to describe it. His body was trying to tell him it was shutting down.

Beneath him, the baboon stirred, one of its powerful legs twitching.

Do something. Think of something.

Quickly he scanned the pegs on the wall. He grabbed the section of steel tubing, then hustled back to position it over the baboon's chest like a vampire hunter's stake. As the cold metal touched the thing's fur, its eyes abruptly focused and its brow deepened. Its lips curled back obscenely to reveal those curved yellow teeth, and it tensed to rip at him through the netting.

Without thinking about it, Gaetano called on the last of his strength to swing the hammer in an arm extended circle and thunder it down on the top end of the tubing. It slammed with such force that sparks flew and the tube rang like a tuning fork for an instant before puncturing the baboon's chest. Its high-pitched screech was different this time, smeared with shock and pain, rather than rabid anger. Gaetano gave the sledge one last swing, a final, thudding knell of death.

As the tube was hammered into the heart of the baboon, a black-red stream suddenly geysered from its open end. The animal weakly tried to grasp the pipe's smooth surface, but its lifeblood was being siphoned off far too quickly. Its shrieks and struggle became weaker and weaker. Gaetano drew no pleasure from the killing; he felt sick listening to the beast's death agonies. But there had been no room for error—or for mercy. The animal was obviously so maddened, either by hunger or torture, that a fight to the death had been the only option.

Dropping the hammer, Gaetano staggered away from the gore, literally out of gas. As he reached the door, he collapsed, spiraling down into a pit of abject exhaustion . . .

. . . until he was awakened by a pair of rough hands at his shoulders. "Signore Gaetano, you will wake up now."

The voice was familiar but not placeable. As he wiped sleep crust from his eyelashes, he realized his thinking was remarkably clear, his body stable and free of the deadweight of total fatigue. He lay in a simple but clean bed.

Blinking several times, he focused on the prefect of the order, Sforza, the tanned dome of his head reflecting the light of the ever-present naked light bulb. The short, broad-shouldered man was leaning over him, a small grin on his weathered face.

"Congratulations, *signore,* you were correct. You have survived."

Gaetano stretched his arms, legs, flexed his hands and fingers. "Am I okay?"

"More than okay. You performed admirably, with no serious injuries."

"Sorry about your ape. I wouldn't have killed it if—"

"No need to explain. It is regretable, but sometimes necessary, to use such animals in our work."

Gaetano could not hide his relief. "So, now what? Can I join you?"

"Not quite yet, my son. You have earned the *right to apply* for acceptance into our Order. You must now undergo our training, which you may imagine is rigorous, to say the least. After the training, you may join us."

"I knew that. I just meant that—never mind. You know what I meant. You know how important it is that you help me."

Sforza held up his index finger in the universal gesture that said *yes, but wait.* "We are not here to 'help' people, *signore*. We are not a charitable organization. Far better to think that you are helping yourself, and in turn, helping the Order, *capisce*?"

"I understand. But without you, I could not step on the path."

Sforza shrugged. "There are many paths. You just happened to pick ours."

"Okay, so what's next?"

"You will join us for our evening meal, then you will go to the library, where you will begin your training. Mind as well as body."

The meal had been substantial but not exactly elegant. Stone-walled dining hall, long wooden tables, grain worn smooth by many years of simple use. The order conducted its affairs in an environment that lay somewhere between that of a monastery and an army barracks. As he sat at a long table with perhaps forty other men, he surreptitiously surveyed them. Ages between midtwenties and midsixties. All of them wearing loose-fitting, monklike robes, which did little to hide the hard lines of their bodies. Although their faces revealed an array of cultures and bloodlines, they all shared a certain expression that spoke of dedication, strength, and indefatigable toughness. He very much wanted to be part of them.

As he was finishing his food, a man entered the dining hall and walked directly to Prefect Sforza, who was seated at the head of the first table. When Sforza had listened to the message, he directed several of his charges out of the room. The rest of his table buzzed with the news. Gaetano watched it spread to the next table, and then the next—his.

Paying attention, he heard the basic context of the message. Someone had just arrived—Father Giovanni Francesco.

"The Jesuit? From Rome?" He asked the man to his right.

"Of course. Do you know him?"

Gaetano shook his head. "No, but I very much would like to meet him."

The other man nodded perfunctorily. And though Gaetano maintained an outward appearance of calm, he churned inside with anticipation, shock, anger. Francesco! Here? It was incredible. As he sipped his mug of strong Arabica coffee, he forced himself to remain calm, to think clearly.

An hour later, Gaetano had been assigned to the library, a long cavernous room, flanked by countless alcoves of books, manuscripts, illuminations, scrolls, and other incunabula. The first object of his study was a short history, *The Order of the Knights of St. John of Je-*

rusalem. Also known as the Knights of Rhodes or the Knights of Malta or the Hospitalers, they had a long and brilliant record in the service of the Holy Mother Church. Under the aegis of Pope Boniface VIII, they captured the Island of Rhodes from the Muslim infidels and benignly ruled the island for more than two hundred years. After a titanic clash with the Turks in 1522, they moved their operational base to Malta, where they remained until 1798. At that time, during a dispute with Pope Pius VI, the order announced it was disbanding. This, however, was a ruse, which allowed the order to go underground, assuming the profile of a secret society as well as a sophisticated military organization. Throughout the twentieth century, its leaders had made a successful practice of recruiting the best military minds of the age and had used the fires of World War II to forge itself into one of the finest espionage and clandestine ops units in the world. Its ranks supplied leadership and expertise to such organizations as the Mossad, the SSV, and the CIA; it in turn benefited from the shadow technologies developed and deployed by those groups. To call the order an "elite" cadre was very much an understatement, and—

Gaetano was interrupted from his assignment by the opening and closing of a door at the end of a nearby alcove. Footsteps softly padded closer to his place at a long table divided by a row of green-shaded electric lamps. Looking up, he saw a tall man wearing the black habit of a priest. As the man drew near the table, he stopped and said nothing for an instant as he quickly evaluated Gaetano. The man had silver hair in a severe, military brush cut, and the angular face of a fox. His eyes were dark and deep-set, and his mouth the slash of what might be mistaken for a rather nasty-looking knife wound.

"Good evening, Gaetano. I understand you wish

to speak to me." His English, while flawlessly pronounced, retained a Continental flavor, a reluctance to speak without a romantic seasoning.

"You are—" He was stunned, realizing at that instant who it was who stood before him. *The balls!* The bravado of this man was as large as the stories that preceded him. "—Francesco!"

He nodded. "*Father* Francesco to you. What do you want with me?"

"Do you know who *I* am?"

The old priest shrugged. "Not really. They told me you're a new recruit, with good recommendations. Should I?"

"I want to ask you a few things—before I kill you."

Francesco grinned. "You too? You'll have to get into line. What is *your* reason?"

"You knew a man named Targeno."

Francesco nodded.

"I am his brother."

Eighteen

Brother Mauro—Siena, Italy
September 19, 2000

You must not let it upset you," said the Abbot.

Brother Mauro Barzini sat before the austere desk of his superior and nodded his head. He tried to maintain an exterior of serenity and control but felt everything slipping away as his stomach churned and his head throbbed to the rhythm of fear and anxiety. "I am so sorry, Abbot, but I know not what to make of this."

"You must relax now. You have given me every detail, yes?" The Abbot's voice was soft, soothing, like a priest in the confessional.

"Yes, my superior," said Mauro. "Do you think it was the Virgin Mother?"

"No, I do not. She wore the habit of Poor Clares, you said."

"Yes."

"The Blessed Mary would have no need to disguise herself in such a manner."

"But this woman—the Dream Lady—she said God

has plans for me!" Mauro could not quell the anxiety
bubbling within him. "What shall I do?"

The Abbot stroked his beard thoughtfully, adjusted
his glasses. "Mauro, it has always been very clear that
God has special plans for you."

"The stigmata . . ." Brother Mauro sighed. "I have
dedicated my life to the Lord. What more could he
possibly want?"

"You are certain this 'Dream Lady,' as you call her,
you are certain she is real and not a figment of your
own elaborate dreaming?"

"What?"

The Abbot cleared his throat. "Brother Mauro, I
think it is safe to say that we all would like to be contacted directly by God. Perhaps this is—"

"Oh, no," said Mauro forcefully. "I would never
trouble you with something so silly as a wishful dream.
She appears to me when I am sleeping, but she is most
definitely *real*."

"It would be so good to have more tangible proof."

"You do not believe me?" Mauro felt great embar-
assment.

"I believe you. Please, do not feel foolish. But I must
ask questions like this. They will be asked of me if I
take this to my superiors."

Mauro nodded. He understood how difficult it was
to convince anyone of such things. "Yes," he said. "If
you talk to God, they say you are praying; but if God
talks to you, they say you are crazy!"

The Abbot smiled. "I know you are not crazy,
Mauro. Your sincerity and integrity are never in
doubt."

"If I thought this vision could be anything so simple
as a dream, I would never even mention it. No, my
superior, whoever this woman is, she is most definitely
real."

"Yes, yes. I believe you. She said you would be asked to take a stand for God. Certainly you will do it, will you not?"

"Why yes! Anything for my Creator!"

The Abbot smiled, reached out to pat Mauro's bandaged hands. They were always bandaged, sometimes gloved as well, when the flow of blood became heavier than the usual seepage. "There, you see? You are perfectly comfortable doing anything for God."

"I would feel better if I knew her identity—one of the saints, perhaps. And if she would tell me the exact purpose of her request of me."

"In due time, she said." The Abbot tried to sound as reassuring as possible. "And when she reveals it to you, you will share it with me, corrrect?"

"Most certainly." Mauro steepled his hands gingerly in front of his face. "But I am fearful, and I do not know why."

"Trust in God," said the Abbot as he stood up to signal that their meeting had ended. "Come to me when you have new information."

Mauro nodded and stood up to take his leave. The Abbot held him with a gesture.

"I almost forgot! Brother Tomasso is waiting for you in the foyer."

"Why?"

"You have visitors."

Mauro's expression of dismay must have been easily read by the Abbot, who added, "My brother, you must not shirk this obligation. God has given you a special gift, and he intends that you use it to spread proof of his love and his sacrifice."

"Oh, I know, I know!" said Mauro. "But at such a time as this!"

"God asks much only of those who are worthy, Mauro. You are truly holy."

"Thank you, my superior. I am embarrassed by my weakness of spirit. I wish that my faith in myself was as strong as my faith in the Lord!"

The Abbot smiled. "Go. Show your gift to the world. They see in you the signs of Christ's sacrifice, and they return to the Church."

Mauro exited the room, then padded off toward the reception foyer. God forgive such thoughts, but he was so tired of the attention. Every year, as if he were a summer tourist attraction like the horse races in the square, he was sought out by TV and newspaper people. They would park their cars outside the ancient city walls, push their way through the narrow streets, and gather at the steps to the Capuchin monastery, waiting to see Brother Mauro Barzini.

Twenty-two years had passed since he took his vows, and he had never regretted his decision. But sometimes he wondered why God had chosen him for his particular "gift."

Reaching the foyer, he passed a bank of votive candles and opened the heavy bronzed doors to the outer steps. Brother Tomasso, tall and gray and reed thin, stood conversing with three men and a woman. They all turned at Mauro's appearance and regarded him with somber expressions. One held a camcorder, the others small tape recorders. "Good evening, my friends," said Mauro. "You wish to see me?"

"Yes, Brother Mauro," said the tallest of the men, dressed casually, like a tourist to the picturesque Tuscan city. "We are from the television show *Oddities*, and we would like to do a segment of one of our forthcoming shows about you and the stigmata."

"Of course," said Mauro, who had been through this ritual countless times over the years. He nodded to Tomasso, who opened the bronzed door.

"This way, please, we can go to the atrium gardens.

It is a suitable place to speak," said Mauro.

Tomasso escorted the party through the first floor of the old monastery. Mauro's thoughts wandered back to the Dream Lady and what she would ask of him. He did not know why, but he harbored a strong feeling she would be coming to him again very soon.

PART

3

And there appeared to me a great wonder in heaven; a woman clothed with the sun, and the moon under her feet, and upon her head a crown of twelve stars.

–John, *Revelation, 12: 1*

NINETEEN

Peter Carenza—Vatican City
September 22, 2000

"I don't care how many people it requires," said Peter, speaking to Father Erasmus, the prefect of the Secret Archives. "I want a staff working on this research around the clock."

Erasmus sat at his desk in a small office adjacent to the Tower of Winds. He was looking across its surface at Peter with a mixture of equal parts fear and exasperation. "I will have to recruit the seminarians, and—"

"Then do it." Peter rose to end the meeting.

"But, Your Holiness! Those men have other schedules and duties! When will they study? When will they sleep?"

Peter grinned. "After they've found what I'm looking for."

Erasmus looked as if he might ooze down under the desk like a melting candle. "The Archives, they are so vast. This search could take them the rest of their lives."

"Or it could be over tomorrow—if they find the correct reference." Peter held up his index finger as a signal to silence. The matter was at an end. "I'll be expecting a daily report from you, Prefect."

"Very well, my Father."

Peter smiled, turned, and exited the cramped room, which exuded the musty but comforting scent of old parchment and bindery glue. It was a smell that conjured up impressions of past centuries and monolithic knowledge. Although he'd wanted to keep his search for references to the Seven to himself, he had grudgingly acknowledged that a solitary effort could take centuries. The chances of his random discovery of the proper reference were infinitesimal.

And his time was so limited. There were certain things no one could handle but himself. The hunt for Francesco, for one. He had to supervise that personally. Despite the efforts of one of the SSV's best ops, the wily old Jesuit had escaped, and that had very much angered Peter. He'd become determined to find him. Even though his instincts told him he had nothing to fear from Francesco, that the old man would do nothing but cower in some remote and squalid hiding place, Peter still wanted to know where the priest was.

And everything was taking far too long. Marion was supposedly working on her media releases, but she was definitely dragging her feet. He wanted to announce his plans to marry and was getting impatient.

Descending the tower, he exited the Court of the Belvedere and began walking across the lushly landscaped greens of the interior courtyards. He wore a "casual" purple cassock with the usual brocade trim. It was uncomfortably warm, and he would have preferred a T-shirt and gym shorts, but that would upset too many people. Flanked by Vatican buildings as he approached the papal apartments, he could see the cars and media vans already lining up at the West Gate to disgorge journalists for the "history-making" press and TV conference. The day had finally arrived, and it gave a him a feeling of accomplishment—a good balance to the total failure he'd been experiencing in the Archives.

In order to avoid the early arriving interviewers and photographers, Peter continued across the green to a waiting car, staffed by two plainclothes members of the Swiss Guard, which carried him to his building via the private entrance to the underground garage.

As he ascended the green marble steps to his suite, he noticed the high degree of activity throughout the building. The press conference, which would be broadcast worldwide, had generated much speculation, and it amused him to see how much power and influence he'd acquired so quickly. When he entered the drawing room, his private secretary was seated at a large desk checking his speech for grammatical and factual accuracy. The man looked up anxiously as though not expecting Peter but relieved to see him.

"Holiness," he said softly. "I have taken the liberty of preparing copies of your speech for the media, to be given out afterward, and I noticed there are sections missing."

"Yes," said Peter.

"But I do not understand," said the secretary, a sandy-haired priest of Swiss descent.

"The empty spaces are for my most important pronouncements, which will be delivered impromptu." Peter smiled. "They won't need copies of what I'm going to tell them. They'll get it right."

"So I should leave the blank spaces in the handouts?"

"Sure," said Peter. "Why not?"

His secretary's shoulders slumped as he turned away. Peter grinned. He still got a kick out of seeing how his staff reacted to his unorthodox methods.

As he entered the central hall, heading toward his bedroom, he saw Marion crossing from one room to another. She was wearing the semiformal gown he'd selected for the press conference, although she had not yet finished her hair. The new style, a shorter, more fashionable coif, added an element of elegance to her appearance and suggested royalty.

"Looking good, my sweet," he said with a smile. "Ready for the party?"

"Peter, it's hardly going to be a party after they hear your plans," she said in a voice dripping with sadness.

He chuckled at that. What would the world's reaction be? He couldn't wait to find out.

Marion continued looking at him as if waiting for permission to be dismissed, and he held her gaze for an instant, trying to get a read on her thoughts. She'd been acting so differently lately, and he knew he should be paying more attention to such a sea change in a woman. Although he was not exactly expert in the feminine psyche, he knew enough to recognize that something singular was going on with her.

"Whatever the reaction, I'm sure we'll be able to handle it," he said. "How do you feel—nervous?"

She shrugged, held out her arms to showcase the gown. "Not really. This outfit makes me feel a bit silly, actually."

"Don't be ridiculous, you look fantastic."

"Yeah, as the Pope's fiancée. Somehow, I don't think you get the picture."

"It's *them* not getting the picture, Marion. I'm giving them a wake-up call. Welcome to the twenty-first century, folks!"

"Whatever you say, Peter." She half turned away, telegraphing her exit. He touched her shoulder gently, and she wheeled to look at him.

"I feel like I hardly know you anymore."

She looked at him with a flash of anger, tinged with sarcasm. "Well, Peter, I can assure you, I know the feeling."

"No, really. You're so ... so compliant. You never seem to have an opinion, or a feeling, or a preference."

A sardonic grin crossed her features for an instant. "Oh, I have plenty of them," she said. "I just no longer choose to share them with you."

Before she'd died, such a remark would have been delivered with the intent to hurt him, to make him feel guilty or contrite, but something was different now. She'd informed him out of obligation, and her manner had spoken far more than her words: She didn't really give a damn what he thought.

Reaching out, he gently held her shoulders and drew her closer. "Things can change, Marion. They always do. Give me a chance to explore some of what I feel driven to do."

"I'm not standing in your way."

He smiled, kissed her on the neck. "That's the problem, I think."

"Why?" Her green eyes focused on him a little more intently.

"I think I'd feel a little more comfortable if you were."

She looked at her watch. "It's getting late. I'd better get going if you want me to be ready on time."

"You'll be ready."

Taking that as her cue, she casually slipped away from him, gliding down the hall to her dressing room. Peter watched her disappear, feeling a touch of regret, of losing something he knew he would never possess again. Everything had its price; he filed this one under *fragile human relationships.*

*   *   *

Two hours later, he stood at the speaker's podium of
the Press Auditorium in the papal apartments. He was
not dressed in traditional vestments, but rather a business suit—a fashion he'd adopted months earlier as a
visual message that things had changed. Behind him sat
the College of Cardinals and a clutch of other Vatican
officials and dignitaries. Past press conferences like this
one had been the launching point of previous changes
in Church policy—Peter had challenged the world econ-
omy with his creation of the Vatican Stock Exchange,
his announcement of a new currency, and the intention
of becoming a major player in global economics and
politics. Speculation had been flying that this latest
round of pronouncements would have a sexual theme.

A vast sea of faces, hundreds of media representatives all pointing their mikes and lenses at him. Like a
fluid body, the assembled group surged as it reacted to
his new papal decrees: birth control would not only be
sanctioned, but the Vatican would establish a bureau
to assist in the administration and distribution of birth
control devices, especially in third world countries;
abortion would also be henceforth allowed, but not as
a form of birth control; homosexuality would no longer
be considered sinful but an "alternate form of love";
premarital sex was to be encouraged in the hopes that
it would reduce the number of divorces.

With each new decree, a storm of questions swirled
from the audience, but Peter urged them to silence. All
questions were to be held till the end. Behind him, the
red sea of cardinals seethed and roiled in silent outrage. The air in the chamber practically sparked with
emotion and tension, and Peter discovered that he was
feeding off the energy thus created. An unexpected

symbiosis of the spirit and the viscera, pushing him to the summit.

". . . and now," he said, when they were finally quiet. "I have one final decree. The two-thousand-year ban on marriage for clerics within the church is hereby and forever removed."

This one precipitated the most explosive burst of re-action. A cacophony of languages, strobe lights going nova, and the entire assembly of media bodies moved forward like a tidal wave as though they'd been jetti-soned from their seats. Ignoring their questions, Peter held up his hands for order, waiting patiently. Slowly, their clamor receded like a spent wave, and the sound of the crowd reduced itself to a soft buzzing.

Sensing the correct moment, Peter turned from the banks of microphones toward the first row of seats, where Marion sat among the dignitaries. He extended his hand to her, signaling her not only to stand up but to join him at the podium. She did this with grace and style, looking tasteful and elegant, and as she drew ever closer to him, a shock wave of understanding rippled through the assembled masses.

Peter held her hand, raised in his own in symbolic triumph. "I shall show you the way," he said softly, his voice rolling over them with great drama. "May I pres-ent to you Marion Windsor, my future wife!"

He held the pose as a collective gasp escaped the College of Cardinals. It was a sound like stale air leak-ing from a balloon inflated for too long. The media types seemed to be holding their breath, and the mo-ment became distended and awkward, the silence a deafening sound of its own. For that single instant, Pe-ter wondered if he'd committed a terrible faux pas, then decided it didn't matter.

Clearly everyone remained too stunned to react.

And so he would show them. He would *will* them into acceptance of this particular event.

Raising his hands above them, as if bestowing a blessing, he told them what to do. The subtle, unspoken command reached out to them, and a single set of anonymous hands began to clap softly. It signaled others, and geometrically the applause began to build like the approach of a great herd. Peter rewarded them with as bright and broad a papal smile as ever recorded. No spiritual reactionaries here, he thought with satisfying cynicism.

He answered their questions with great verve, surprising them even more with the promise of a pontifical wedding in only six weeks. Actually, he hadn't thought of the date until the journalists pressed him for it, but decided it would be silly to delay the event. And besides, he had a limitless staff at his command to see to every detail. Let them deal with his decisions.

Later that evening, he and Marion dined together. Despite the momentous aspects of the day, their conversation had been almost nonexistent, limited to expressions no more demanding than pass the salt, please. He knew she disapproved of his performance, and he thought he'd prepared himself for that kind of reaction from her, as well as from the cardinals and their staff. But her aloofness was bothering him more than he had anticipated.

"I'm going to the Archives," he said as he finished his meal, immediately wondering why he bothered to share his intentions. But of course he knew why—it was exasperating to have her shutting him out so completely. Face it, he thought sardonically to himself, throwing her out that window had been a bad idea.

"Oh," said Marion, "I thought you'd wanted me to

help you with your project there. Whatever it was."

Her willing response caught him off guard. Better to not show much reaction. Peter shrugged. "Yeah, I did, didn't I. I've decided to get the seminarians involved, speed things up, you know. Make it easier on everybody."

"Make what easier? You never got around to telling me what you were looking for."

Peter took a step away from the table, as if to dismiss her, but on another level he responded to her effort to talk to him.

"Some research, that's all. I think I told you I wasn't even sure myself."

"That's right," she chuckled, possibly in derision. "But you said you'd know it when you saw it, right?"

"Something like that."

"Peter, that doesn't sound like you at all. You're usually so decisive and focused."

"The Secret Archives are so amazing, you know. I was just familiarizing myself with some of the materials there, and I came upon this one phrase that—didn't I tell you this before?"

"What?" she said, without looking up. Obviously trying to feign disinterest, "Oh . . . I don't remember. Maybe you did."

"It was one phrase that just *caught* me," said Peter, deciding he would ignore her little games. "It literally jumped off the page at me."

She looked at him in a way that clearly depicted her doubt. "Peter, really . . ."

"It did," he insisted. "It was a reference to the Secret of the Seven. Have you ever heard of it?"

Marion's gaze centered on him, never wavered. "No, I don't think so. Want me to help you look for it?"

"I told you, I'm putting the seminarians to work on it."

"I'll come with you, if you like."

"Really? Why?"

"I thought you wanted me to. Besides," Marion added, "you've got me curious about it, too."

It was at that point that he realized he did not understand women at all. He'd thought she never wanted to be in the same room with him any longer. Maybe he'd appealed to her professional instincts as an investigative reporter. After all, she been one of the best television journalists in New York when he'd met her.

"All right," he said. "Let's see what they know."

Peter walked around the length of the large table and extended his hand to her, but she ignored it, standing and beginning to walk on her own. A platoon of servants had been waiting at the far end of the room, near the door leading to kitchen, a discreet, respectful distance.

At a single gesture of his right hand, they moved in on the table. Peter followed his wife-to-be, wondering if she would ever feel anything for him again, wondering why she was with him even now.

TWENTY

Pierce Erickson—New York
September 19, 2000

*A*few moments ago, Pierce had been just another
employee in the globe-spanning company of
Providential Casualty Insurance. Now, he was about to
get his fifteen minutes of fame.

He stood outside the Newark Airport entrance to the
under-construction East-Hudson Tunnel, surrounded
by TV reporters, still photographers, and a steadily
growing crowd of passers-by. Beyond his position, a
protective shield of police tape barriers and battalions
of firefighters and EMT personnel. He was still dazed
from the events of the previous ten minutes and was
not thinking clearly. His words and feelings had become so enmeshed that everything just poured out of
him. Everybody was talking and shouting at once and
he struggled to sort out what was going on around him.

"What were you doing down in the tunnel, Mr. Erickson?" a booming male voice asked him.

Pierce looked vainly for the source of the question,
but a sudden silence enveloped him and the crowd as

they all leaned in, awaiting his reply. As though suddenly aware of the attention, he automatically tried to smooth out his longish dark brown hair and adjust his silk tie, which was as waterlogged as the rest of his fashionable ensemble. He cleared his throat.

"I'm an insurance investigator," he said. "I was checking out the details and the evidence for a claim."

"What kind of claim?" asked a woman near the front, holding a portable, voice-activated recorder.

At the same time, the first voice yelled, "How did you know the north tube was going to rupture?"

"Well, I didn't exactly *know* it, I mean, I didn't have any idea until I saw the woman," said Pierce, rubbing the side of head, wishing the throbbing there would subside.

"What woman?" another female voice. A little strident, obviously excited.

"The one who told me the bulkhead was going to collapse," said Pierce, trying to reconnect the sequence of events, to completely recall how he'd gotten from *there* to *here*.

The reporters were working themselves up to a new level of information frenzy, all yelling at him at once. He must have started to reel away from them, because a paramedic stepped into the circle and asked that they give him some room.

But a young, black female journalist had worked her way to Pierce's side, and she looked up at him with an engaging smile. She spoke softly, but her voice had an edge that cut through the general level of noise. "A woman told you about the collapse, you said?"

"Yes, she looked like a nun."

"A nun? Where is she? What happened to her?"

"She's not here," said Pierce. Part of his mind began sending an alarm—*Shut up! Enough already!*—but he continued talking. "She went away after."

"Went away? What do you mean?"

The knot of reporters had begun to lean in again, as they realized that the only way to expand on the scraps of his statements was to maintain a modicum of silence.

"I was standing by the 'lifter,' and that's when I saw her. She just kind of appeared in front of me. She—"

"Where'd she come from?" someone shouted.

"What do you mean, 'appeared?' "

"You mean like a ghost?"

Pierce nodded. "Yes, kind of, but she wasn't a ghost. She was very real."

A few people in the crowd chuckled. Others hushed them. Pierce looked at the crowd with a sudden, new suspicion.

The young reporter at his side touched his elbow, hit him with that big smile again. "It's okay," she said. "Go on, tell me what happened."

"She talked to me. I could hear her," said Pierce. "She was real."

"What did she say?"

"What did she look like?"

"Can you remember her exact words?"

Everybody was talking at once again, and he realized he was getting tired of the whole thing. He wanted to get out of there, get home to his family on Riverside.

"I think I'd better stop now," he said softly, pausing to rub his eyes.

The crowd started making more noise again, and the young woman at his side, the one with the beauty pageant smile, tugged at his sleeve. "Come on, sir, I'll get you out of here."

Nodding, Pierce allowed her to lead him away from the semicircle of reporters, past phalanxes of fire engines, police vehicles, and earthmovers. Lights continued to flash, syncopated to the sounds of helicopter rotors, excavating equipment, sirens, and the blare of horns. With each passing minute, his thinking became less muddled, and he knew he didn't want to be anywhere near the scene of the incident.

"Where's your car?" asked the reporter. "Did you drive here?"

"Company car," said Pierce. "It was right over there, by that access tunnel entrance."

"You mean the one clogged with all that mud?"

Pierce looked at the devastation as if for the first time. It looked as if a giant jar of hot fudge had been tipped on end, its outflow arrested as it tried to surge uphill from the banks of the Hudson. If his vehicle was under there, it would be there for quite a while.

"Yeah," he said shaking his head. "Well, at least it *was* a company car."

"Come on," said the reporter, still holding his arm, walking him toward the parking area outside the chainlink fence of the construction zone. "I'll take you home. Where do you live?"

"Riverside at Eighty-eighth Street."

"That's a good ride from here." She smiled again. "That'll give a us a chance to talk."

He didn't reply as she led him to a car with a Channel 38 decal on the door.

As he was settling into the seat closing the door, she slipped behind the wheel. Wearing a lime green suit that exposed plenty of her long, thin legs, she looked professional but still trendy and hip. Her hair was curled in the latest MTV style, and her glasses reminded him of snowboarder's gear. But she spoke with warmth and respect, and even if she was doing all this just to wheedle a story out of him, that would be okay. He decided he liked her.

Just then, she turned to him. "I'm Shaenara Williamson. Channel 38 News-at-Nite."

He smiled and offered his hand for a professional shake. "Pierce Erickson."

Shaenara keyed the ignition, threw the Intrepid into gear, and started to drive. "What kind of name is Pierce? I'm kind of into names, because everybody's always asking me about mine—how do you spell it, what's it mean, where'd it come from, you know. Well, my mama made it up, that's all I know."

He watched her talk and punctuate everything with a little giggle and that big smile. She was good. A real charmer. Bet she got all the info she wanted.

"Mine's a family name," he said. "My great grandfather was related to the guy who made the Pierce Arrow."

"What's that?"

"It was a car made in the early part of the century. A really nice car, I'm told."

"What happened to it?"

Pierce grinned. "It went the way of the Packard and the Studebaker."

Shaenara looked at him with a mock frown. "More old cars?"

"You know, you really ought to check out the Learning Channel once in a while. A reporter is supposed to know things."

"I thought they were supposed to ask good questions."

"They can't unless they know something about their subject and what came before it."

"Well, I'm trying to find out about you, Mr. Erickson. Because I smell a good story here."

Pierce looked idly out the window as they glided across the lanes of an expressway toward the signs for the New Jersey Turnpike north. Lights from the airport and surrounding industrial complexes imparted an otherworldly vitality to the entire scene.

"Yes, I know you are," he said after a pause. "And I don't mind telling you most of it. It'll keep me from the rest of that mob."

"So I guess you won't mind if I use this," she asked as she reached into her Fendi purse and withdrew a little Sony digital recorder. She pressed Record, then placed it on the console between them.

"Actually, I'd prefer it. Easier to keep the facts straight that way."

Shaenara nodded. "Okay, so you investigate claims for a big insurance company. How long have you been doing it? You want to give me a quick data sheet?"

"I've been with Providential Casualty since college. That was Villanova, fourteen years ago. Married—once and very happily—to a woman named Sydney and we have two daughters, Agnes and Sophia, and a golden lab named Liberty."

"Liberty?" Shaenara grinned.

He shrugged. "It was the girls' idea—I kind of like it, being a Libertarian and all—and they call her Libby. Anyway, we have an old brownstone on Riverside with high ceilings, drafty windows, and lots of crown molding. We collect antiques from New Hampshire and Vermont, we like to ski, hate the beach, and generally like our jobs. Oh yeah, and Sydney's a headhunter for a Canadian company that supplies geologic personnel to the global petroleum industry. Anything else?"

"I'll get to favorite colors and stuff like that later. Okay, now tell me more about this woman you saw, and please, don't make me drag it out of you."

Pierce cleared his throat. "All right, listen: I'm standing there talking to the foreman for Turnbull, the company that owns the machinery we insure, and he's giving me his version of the facts that led to the lifter destroying itself. See, I'm there to see if there was any liability on Turnbull's part, or whether the machine failed on its own, and—"

He stopped as he noticed Shaenara staring his way with a look of definitive disapproval.

"Sorry, let me get a little more focused here. Okay, I'm getting ready to climb into the loader's cab when I see a bright light behind the front end of the machine, like the blue glow of an acetylene torch. I look over there to see what's going on, and I see this woman just . . . *appear!* I mean, one second there's this blue flash and then *poof!*—she is there, standing there and looking at me."

"Were you scared?" Shaenara drifted over the right lane, preparing to take the Lincoln Tunnel exit.

"No, not really. Shocked for a second, then I just knew everything was okay. I knew she wasn't there to hurt me or scare me or anything like that. She was wearing these tan and brown robes like the people in the Bible, and for a second I thought it was the Virgin Mary. . . ."

"Are you Catholic?"

"Yeah, why?"

"Well, I figure most people tend to see hallucinations in terms of what they already believe in."

Pierce chuckled darkly. "So if you've already decided what I'm telling you is a delusion, then, uh, why am I wasting my time?"

Shaenara Williamson looked over at him with that overemphasized expression of disapproval. "Now, come on, Mr. Erickson, it's my job to be skeptical; it's your job to convince me I'm wrong."

"You're wrong. She was real." He noticed that his voice had acquired a harsh tone. Defensive? No, more like assertive. "As real as you are, sitting right there."

"Okay, so you decided she was not Mary . . ."

"Maybe some saint I don't recognize, or maybe she

was just an angel. But listen: She called my name and I was just like, captured, like I couldn't stop listening to her. She told me God had sent her to me for a special reason, and that I would have to want to come to her when the time was right. She also said even though I'd been picked by God to do something special, I could still refuse if I wanted to."

"You know, this all sounds like Crusade fantasies, classical delusions of grandeur, stuff like that."

"And you know you sound like Psych 101," he said quickly.

Shaenara shrugged. "Hey, it's one of the required courses. Sorry. Go on. Did she tell you what you were supposed to do?"

"Yes, but first she gave me proof she was real, that she was sent by God. She told me about the bulkhead, how it was defective and going to give out any minute. I asked her if I had time to warn everybody, and she said yes."

"But nobody listened?"

Pierce had to grin. "Of course they didn't! The guys were looking at me like I was a regular New York nut."

"Did you expect anything else?"

"No, but I was scared—I believed the lady. So I kept yelling and pointing at the weak spot in the wall." He paused. "You ever hear metal start to groan when it gets stressed?"

"No."

"Me neither, but it was a very scary and very loud sound, and when the foremen heard it, they started evacuating the area. Just in time, too. If they'd waited until things started breaking loose, they'd have been buried under miles of mud."

Shaenara slowed down to guide the Intrepid down a long, curving exit ramp that ended with the tollbooth, then opened up onto a straight section connecting to the Lincoln Tunnel at Weehawken. "Yeah, I heard the engineers talking about that. They have no idea how you could have known ahead of time about the structural flaws."

"Well, I'm telling you exactly how I knew ahead of time."

"What happened then, after she warned you to get everybody out?"

"She disappeared. Just like that." He snapped his fingers. "Like turning out a light. And then I started running, and pretty soon everybody was getting into rigs and tractors or just plain running out of there." He paused. "After the sludge finished exploding from the entrance, I saw her again."

"Just like she said you would." Shaenara wasn't grinning now, just listening with quiet respect. It made him feel vindicated.

"I was covered with mud and water, and I'd been helping one of the EMT teams get people onto stretchers. Then, in the corner of my eye I saw that blue flash again, and I knew exactly what it was. I turned around, and she was standing there, smiling very gently. She looked like she might be fifty years old, but when she smiled like that, she looked a lot younger.

"Anyway, she told me she was so happy I'd been able to save all those people, but now it was time to do something very special for her and for God. She told me I had to go to Jerusalem, to the tomb of a prophet named Ahnmet. She would meet me there when I found the tomb and tell me what to do next."

"So, are you going to do it?"

He chuckled. "Wouldn't you?"

"I think I'd try to find out if there is any such place as this Ahnmet's tomb first."

"Ms. Williamson, do you think I'm lying?"

"No, of course not."

"Do you think I just dreamed up this guy's name, the location of his tomb?"

"No, but you might be a biblical scholar, or—"

"Haven't you heard? Catholics never read the Bible. Not until pretty recently, anyway. But believe me, I'm no scholar of anything, especially the Bible."

Shaenara looked at him as they paused at the booth before the tunnel entrance, then paid the toll collector. "You don't have any post-tunnel trauma, do you?" she asked with a small grin. "I mean, the last time you went into a tunnel, it wasn't so hot."

"This one's okay," said Pierce. He liked her sense of humor. "I have a feeling God would tell me if it wasn't."

"Why's that?"

"Haven't you been listening? Because he's got big plans for me."

She aimed the car into the maw of the tunnel, then: "So, you're taking off for Jerusalem. What're you going to tell your wife?"

"The same thing I just told you," he said. "Which reminds me—do you think you could hold off on this story until tomorrow morning? That way she hears it from me first."

"What makes you think I'm going to run with what you told me?"

Pierce shrugged. "Oh, I don't know . . . could it be that you work in television?"

They both laughed, then neither spoke for a minute or two, until the car emerged at Thirty-eighth Street on Manhattan's West Side. Pierce was thinking about what Sydney would say when he told her he had to go look for the tomb of a forgotten prophet. Well, they were only a few minutes from his house. He would know soon.

He drew a deep breath, exhaled. A thought spiked through him: After tonight, he would never see his family again.

Maybe so. But it changed nothing.

TWENTY-ONE

Father Giovanni Francesco—Corsica
September 19, 2000

*H*e never knew Targeno had a brother.

An agent of Targeno's ability and stature was somehow removed from the world of normal people. So much so, thought Giovanni, that you never imagined a man like him as ever having had a mother, or even a childhood. Men like Targeno could not possibly have been googly babies or innocent, smiling, little boys. They had to have been hatched from cold and abandoned eggs like reptiles, only full grown and ready to devour anything stumbling too close to the nest.

Giovanni had spent the last hour listening to the story of the man he knew only as Gaetano. He appeared to be in his late thirties and in excellent physical condition. When he spoke or looked directly at Giovanni, he did it with an intensity and a singular focus the older man had rarely seen. He confessed shock at encountering the infamous Father Francesco at the enclave of the Knights, especially since he'd believed it

would take him a long time to track down the priest
and even more time to maneuver close enough to his
inner circle to effect his assassination.

"So let me see if I have this right," said Giovanni, unable to suppress a wry smile. "You quit your job in
London as a mutual fund manager to train to be a
professional killer?"

"Smile while you can, old man. You heard me correctly the first time," said the dark-eyed man. "But I
didn't quit my job—I own the trading company. My
employees are taking care of things until I return."

Giovanni chuckled. "You mean *if* you return, my
friend. What you have in mind may incur some peril."

"I am already formidable. My brother taught me
many things about survival."

"You looked up to him, eh?"

"He was my brother," said Gaetano. "I loved him
very much."

Giovanni nodded but, did not reply immediately. He
studied the man sitting before him. All his movements
were quick, coiled, wary. He was like a delicate mechanism that had been wound too tightly, ready to fly
apart at any moment. Clearly, Gaetano was a man obsessed, unable to deny or escape the single passion that
fueled his every move and thought.

Revenge.

Giovanni sighed as he considered one of history's
oldest and most provocative motives. The cause of
more conflict and death than any other. Looking at
Gaetano, he imagined how this raw energy, this unfettered power, might be used to a greater purpose.

"All right, young man, I have listened to your story,
but there is one thing I don't understand: Why do you
want to eliminate *me*?"

Gaetano looked at him with no hint of emotion. "It is my understanding that you are the reason my brother was killed."

"Me? I did not kill him. He worked for me. He was the best operative we ever had! I didn't want him to die."

"If he hadn't been assigned to Peter Carenza, he wouldn't have been at the Los Angeles Palladium. Carenza wouldn't have killed him."

Giovanni nodded reluctantly but with his trademark sly grin. "True enough, if you are a fan of crude logic."

"What?"

"You must realize Targeno was *always* in danger of being killed. It was the nature of his job."

"I realize this. That does not change the truth—that you sent him to his death."

Giovanni chuckled, sat back in his chair and lit a French cigarette—no filter, no additives, heavy on the latakia. "I am going to assume that you are intimate with the details of the story."

"I have studied all the video available on the Palladium event."

"Good! Then it must be very obvious to you that your brother was in no danger at all from my assignment, which was to shadow Carenza and *protect* him, if necessary."

"Father Francesco, I—"

"And if you are as intimate with the video as you say you are, then you must have noticed an abrupt *change* in Targeno's manner, in the moments before Carenza torched him."

Giovanni watched the young man pause, his shifting expression revealing his thoughts. It was obvious the young man had indeed noticed the change in his brother.

"I have got you, *Signore*," said Giovanni. "Admit it."

"Well, yes, I noticed what you describe, Father."

"And what did it signify to you?"

Gaetano made the gesture that said *mezzo-mezzo*. "I am not certain. It appears as if he recognized something."

"Do you know what that thing might have been?"

The younger man squirmed.

"I asked you a question, *Signore*." Giovanni pushed his advantage. "What did your brother see to make him pause? Did *you* see it?"

"I . . . I think so."

"Then tell me, *Signore*."

Gaetano spoke slowly, as though remembering an experience. "It happened when the pope was stricken. Just before that, the pope had looked Peter Carenza in the eyes and said, 'I know you.' "

Giovanni nodded.

"Whatever it was the pope saw . . . my brother, he . . . he must have seen it too."

Giovanni clapped his hands softly in mock applause. "*Bravissimo, maestro!* Such skill in perception, in ratiocination."

"Do not try to be humorous, old man."

"Very well." Giovanni assumed an overly dour expression, spoke in low, drawn-out voice. "Then what exactly was it your brother saw?"

Again, the younger man hesitated, as though deciding what he should admit. "You know, it's interesting you have touched directly on this question. I must concede I have spent many hours watching these exact moments over and over on video."

"And your conclusion?"

"My brother saw *evil* in this man Carenza. He *saw* it," said Gaetano, closing his eyes as though reciting a solemn oath, "and realized at that moment he must attempt to destroy it."

Giovanni exhaled a long, thin plume of smoke, then nodded. "Do you believe in the existence of such evil?"

"I do not need to believe in that which I can readily witness."

"Well phrased," said Giovanni. "So then, it must follow that you know in your heart of hearts that I did not send your brother to his death. You do not need me as your scapegoat. You need to focus your rage on the proper target."

Gaetano grinned. "Carenza? Father, what makes you think I have not?"

"Because the only person you seem excited about killing is me!"

"No, you are merely a name on the list. A list always topped by Peter Carenza himself."

Giovanni exhaled and stubbed out the last of the cigarette. He leaned forward into the full glare of the desk lamp, feeling its heat sink into the deep lines of his face. "That name is also at the top of my list," he said.

"Why is that so?" Gaetano looked at him with a trace of new respect.

Giovanni briefly related the account of his attempted termination by the SSV op—under orders of Pope Peter II—embellishing only on the specifics of his courage and resourcefulness.

"Incredible!" said Gaetano. "And we were both driven to this same place."

"It surely means something, *Signore,*" said Giovanni as he extended his hand to the younger brother of Targeno. "We are meant to be allies, not enemies."

"Perhaps."

"I know everything about Carenza and his surroundings. I can get close to him in ways you never could."

Giovanni chucked Gaetano on the arm. "You need me."

"And you need me—to do what the Americans call the 'dirty work,' yes?"

"Very dirty. And yes, I do. We need each other—allies."

The younger man reached out, shook hands. "Strange bedfellows, at least."

Giovanni smiled and lit a celebratory cigarette. "Then it is done. When your training is completed, we will set you off on a course to intercept and eliminate our Holy Father."

"I will dedicate myself to that single task. But what will you be doing in the meantime?"

Giovanni smiled. He liked this younger version of Targeno. He showed the same swaggering confidence, the boldness of spirit. "Good question. It shows you are thinking. The mind as well as the body must be sharpened to its keenest edge."

"I am always thinking, Padre. Now, could you please answer the question?"

Giovanni paused to light another Gauloise, sucked the harsh smoke into his lungs. "I have long-standing contacts within the infrastructure of the Vatican. And along with them, uncollected favors, obligations, and even a few instances of outright fear among the personnel. These are good things, Gaetano, I assure you."

Nodding slowly, Gaetano looked narrowly at him. "Yes, but we need a plan, an objective."

"Of course, but we must first gather as much intelligence as possible. We will want to know Peter's itinerary, schedules, routines, times of solitude, wants and dislikes. . . . In short, everything taking place around him. We will study what we learn, and believe me, a plan will make itself clear to us. When you know that much about your target, you soon realize your plan already exists—sitting there waiting for you to piece it together and merely carry it out."

"I hope you are right, Father."

Giovanni said, "Let us agree to meet here each evening to share what we have learned. Gradually everything will become clear."

"Agreed."

"Very well. Good night, young warrior. You shall soon be a true soldier of Christ."

"Good night, Father."

Giovanni turned away from the table and took several steps toward the door, then paused to looked back at the younger man. "Oh, one more thing, Gaetano. I think it is only fair to tell you—you would have never gotten away with it."

"With what? Killing Carenza?"

Giovanni grinned. "No. Killing me."

"Why?"

"I have been a Knight of Malta since I was eighteen."

Gaetano appeared unfazed by this knowledge. "Which means?"

"Which means the prefect knew all about you before you were admitted to the enclave."

"I did not try to hide anything. My brother had paved the way for me here many years ago. I had a letter from him that detailed exactly what I must do if I ever wanted to follow his path."

Giovanni nodded. "Yes. We know that."

"So it was not by chance that we met here." Gaetano considered for a moment, then stated, "I could still have killed you."

"Perhaps," Giovanni admitted, then smiled sardonically. "But your bones would have never left this place."

"Then it is good we became friends."

Giovanni held up a single index finger in caution. "Allies, my son. The friendship, if it comes, will happen later."

TWENTY-TWO

Marion Windsor—Vatican City
October 29, 2000

The days until the papal wedding had been ripped away from her by the cruelest hands of time. Every minute of preparation, of media hype and pressure, had been an agony. Ever since Peter had made the announcement, Vatican City had been under siege by every communications agency in the world.

They all wanted to record one of the most momentous events in the history of the Western world. There were very few times when you could be certain you would be present for a pivotal instant in History with a capital *H,* and no one wanted to be left·out.

Still a journalist at heart, Marion was in sympathy with what the invading media armies were trying to do. But that did not make it any easier for her to cope with the endless phone calls, E-mail, appointments, interviews, videos, and relentless assaults on her privacy.

And shoehorned into all this tumult were the usual aspects of preparation for a wedding, such as picking out an appropriate dress, completing a personal guest list, deciding on attendants, planning the reception.

She had been determined to keep the wedding from being offensively garish. Everyone in the world would be watching, and she believed it would be best if things were as elegant and tasteful as possible, which might make the entire event more acceptable to Catholics around the globe.

It was too much—especially under the circumstances, which made everything so bittersweet. What a woman was told would be the most important moment of her life had been reduced to self-parody. Every time Marion felt herself getting excited, she would catch herself up short, realizing that the impending ceremony was more of a performance than an event of subtance and meaning.

Peter had encouraged the attention and the endless sorties by the media, his staff made every effort to keep things stirred up. There was no such thing as preferential treatment for any information. No outlet was too small or too sleazy to flay the public's interest. Rumors, innuendo, accusations. No offer refused. Her picture had appeared on covers as diverse as the *New York Times Magazine* and the *Weekly World News*. She had been portrayed as a gold digger, a feminist, a phony, a victim, a harlot, a saint, a social scientist, a martyr.

Throughout the ordeal, she had little contact with Peter. He remained obsessed with his search for references to the mysterious Seven and round-the-clock conferences, appearances, speeches, and conclaves with the cardinals. She couldn't understand why he needed her anymore. There was so little between them but artifice. Still, it seemed certain that Peter had other plans for her in the future.

And she knew they would not be good.

*   *   *

Such were Marion's thoughts as the final day before the papal wedding came to an end. From the west end of her apartment, she could see the courtyard of Saint Peter's, which had been transformed into an outdoor stage capable of hosting almost a million people. Father Cerami, the pastor of the Church of Sant' Anna, would perform the ceremony. His little church was the official, if little-known, parish of the Pope.

When the phone rang, she was surprised. It was the ultraprivate line to which practically no one had access. Peter was at the Archives; she hoped it was not him.

"Hello?"

"You must come to the convent right away," said Etienne. "It is an emergency."

Marion's heart skipped a beat. She could hear the tension in the nun's voice. "Are you okay?"

"I am fine. Please come. Everything will be explained to you."

Before Marion could reply, the line was disconnected.

What was happening? She had to get over to the convent as soon as possible.

She was wearing one of her "media outfits" and suddenly felt foolish in the designer suit. Quickly, she changed into a more utilitarian ensemble of boots, jeans, and a jersey top. She removed her heavy, camera makeup and quickly brushed out her hair, once again reminded of how she had been turned into a modern-day concubine by Peter. The makeup and the artfully constructed hairstyle had been created by a horde of television professionals, who'd unilaterally decided how she would appear to the world.

Outside the apartment, she met a member of the Swiss Guard in plainclothes, and she asked him to please arrange for transport to the Poor Clares Convent.

"A car has already been dispatched, *Madame*," said the tall, thin man. He spoke softly, with much deference.

Her relationship with the Swiss Guard was excellent because of Cardinal Lareggia's close alliance with its captain, Egon Leutmann. The Cardinal had assured her that Leutmann's allegiance was to what many of the Vatican loyalists were beginning to refer to as the "true Church"—the Church before Peter's meddling had so threatened the pillars of its traditions. Marion had grudgingly begun to trust the Swiss Guard even though she knew, ultimately, she should trust no one.

As she entered the subterranean garage, she smiled at the small irony of it. With each passing day, she moved deeper into the political underground, plotting against her ruler. A black Mercedes awaited her near the exit. When the driver opened the rear door to the passenger compartment, she was not all that surprised to see the Cardinal's great bulk occupying almost half of the area's ample space.

Sliding in next to him, she nodded silently.

"Good evening, my dear Marion."

"Your Grace. How are you?"

"Well enough."

"Etienne called you too?"

"She did indeed."

"Do you know what this is all about?"

"I have my suspicions," he said with a sigh. "Marion, it is but a short ride to the convent. Soon we shall know everything she wishes us to know."

"Is Etienne okay?"

He nodded. "As far as I could tell, yes. She told me she has something very important to share with us."

Marion nodded. Recently, Etienne had informed her that she had the Cardinal into their circle of confidence. "What do you think her visions signify?"

Lareggia drew a deep breath, exhaled. "There is evidence that Etienne has been in close contact with God ever since we began to weave this terrible web of deception." The Cardinal rolled his eyes, probably for dramatic emphasis. Unfortunately, the effect was more comical. "It is unfortunate we did not pay more attention to this much earlier than we did. I realize now that God was revealing his message to us through her, and it was through our own sin of pride that we did not listen."

Marion looked at him without expression. "No sense crying about that now. I think we've all made our share of mistakes. I want to know what God wants us to do now."

"We must abide by what Etienne tells us. I believe this is our last chance to heed God's warnings."

"I agree," she said, leaning into the door as the limo turned sharply. Looking out, she caught a glimpse of the lighted portico of the Poor Clares Convent.

"Here we are," said Lareggia, maneuvering himself to depart the vehicle.

As the door on Marion's side was swung open by the driver, it revealed the stately presence of Abbess Victorianna.

"She is expecting both of you," said the elderly nun. "Follow me."

Marion allowed the Cardinal to take the lead as they walked into the foyer of the darkly Gothic structure. Other than the starkest of religious icons, the building's interior reflected a spirit as austere and unforgiving as any dungeon. Despite the pleasant temperatures outside, the convent contained a dank and foreboding atmosphere. Marion shuddered. How could anyone feel comfortable living her entire life in a place like this?

The abbess led them past areas designed for communal dining, prayer, and exercise. At the far end of the corridor, they ascended a circular staircase, and Cardinal Lareggia immediately began to wheeze. As he forced himself upward, his great bulk raging against gravity, his face became blotched with crimson, his breathing increasingly ragged. Marion half-expected him to have a coronary at any moment.

In contrast, Abbess Victorianna, despite her years, appeared almost to glide up the steep, winding stairs without effort.

When they reached the third floor, the nun led the way down to a small room that was usually reserved for private prayer during the canonical and breviary hours. Illuminated by a bank of votive candles, the room was a warm contrast to the rest of the convent. Enhanced by this engaging light, Etienne sat by the room's solitary window. She indicated they should take seats on a bench opposite a kneeling pad in front of the candle stand.

Etienne smiled in greeting, and Marion could not help noticing how serenely beautiful she looked.

"Good evening, Etienne," said Marion. "You look so radiant, so wonderful!"

"Oh, Marion, please! You embarrass me! It is only because I carry the peace of the Lord in my heart."

"We came as soon as possible," said Paolo Cardinal Lareggia, panting.

"Thank you so much," said Etienne. "This is very important. I will need your ears to listen, and then your wisdom."

"Whatever it is," Lareggia's words left him with great effort, "we are here for you, my child." His breathing remained terribly labored, his face covered with a glistening patina of perspiration.

Etienne appeared more relaxed than ever. A small smile hinted at the corners of her mouth. "God has spoken to me again! He has revealed what I must do next. In my dream, I was standing on the barren plain beneath the black sky. I saw a single tree on the horizon, its branches twisting and reaching in every direction, and God's voice passed through me like a warm wind."

"What did he say to you?" asked the Cardinal, whose breathing had gradually calmed.

Marion could detect a trace of impatience in his voice and hoped Etienne did not.

The nun looked off into space as though reliving the event as she related it. "The tree is called Yggradsil, or the Tree Where Man Was Born. It is the tree of life, of form and substance. When I stand in its moonshadow, I will know the location of the Seven Churches. In those places lie the Seven Seals. Only then will I be able to call forth the Seven Keys."

"The seven who are righteous," said Marion.

"Yes," said Etienne. "They will unlock the seals, and each seal will prevent a plague upon the people of the world."

"What then? " asked Lareggia, his tone of voice a mingling of anxiety and dumbfoundment. "What does this have to do with us? With Peter?"

Etienne looked at the large man and smiled enigmatically. "Only *everything*."

"Where is the tree, Etienne?" Marion spoke softly, as if to cue Lareggia to the proper demeanor.

"In East Africa. Kenya."

"Africa!" said the Cardinal. "By the preservation of the saints! You want to go Kenya!"

"Your Grace, please forgive me," said Etienne. "But we are not talking of what I want to do. This is what I have been *commanded* to do—by God himself."

Lareggia produced a handkerchief from his pocket and mopped the sweat from his face. "Yes, of course you are correct. Oh, God, what are we to do?"

"When must you begin the journey?" said Marion.

Lareggia stuffed his hankie into his scarlet cassock, began wringing his hands. "I wish Giovanni Francesco were still here—he would know what to do, how to do it."

"Tonight," said Etienne. "My Cardinal, you must make the arrangements for us."

"Us?" said Marion and Lareggia simultaneously. Then Lareggia leaned forward on the bench. "Sister Etienne, you must realize that travel is very difficult for me. Because of my . . . my size."

Because you're a fat pig, thought Marion. She had been embarrassed by the Cardinal's behavior during the meeting. He confirmed all she'd feared about his weakness of spirit. But she was also thinking of her own situation. Would she be able to safely leave Rome with her face so well known to the world at large? All the pre-wedding publicity had ensured that her image was emblazoned on every periodical and channel throughout the world. And what of the wedding itself? Talk about throwing a wrench into the gears . . . Marion couldn't pass up a chance to sabotage Peter's plans, no matter what risk it involved.

Etienne looked at Lareggia as a mother about to reprove her child. "Forgive me, Cardinal, but you must believe in the power of God. You know that all things are possible in the Lord. You must believe he will provide for your safety as you make this great journey with us."

Lareggia stopped wringing his hands and reached for his handkerchief again. His movements were clumsy and erratic. "You are correct, Sister, I must retemper my faith in the fires of my conviction," he said as he swabbed his brow. "One must not make excuses when God calls him."

"Or *her*," said Marion. "I'll gladly go with you, Etienne."

"I will go also," said Lareggia.

Etienne smiled and looked at the Cardinal. "Can you make it happen? Quickly, before Peter has a chance to find out?"

Lareggia straightened his spine and nodded vigorously. "Yes," he said, as though trying to convince himself. "Of course I can. I will speak to Captain Leutmann as soon as we return."

Marion turned to Etienne. "I will need a disguise. People might recognize me. Do you think the order would like a temporary member?"

Etienne smiled. "I think our abbess would be honored. I will get you everything you will need."

"You know," said Marion, "I don't think it would be wise for me to go back to the Vatican. There's nothing I need from there."

"You are correct," said Lareggia. "Even one step away from there is one step closer to escape."

"Can you imagine the look on Peter's face when I stand him up at the altar?"

"Oh, Marion," said Etienne. "I think he will know your intentions long before the wedding."

"You're right," she said. "If I turn up missing tonight, Peter will send out the Italian Army to find me."

"And this is the first place they will look for you," said Lareggia.

The Cardinal's words struck Marion as if she had been slapped. Paranoia seized her in an instant. Suddenly, she feared that Peter's forces would sweep down on them at any second. She stood up, not knowing what to do next.

"What are we going to do?" Marion realized she sounded helpless and lost. But that's how she felt.

Etienne stood as well and took her hand. "Marion,

come with me. We must see the Abbess. Victorianna will help us gather what we will need for the trip."

Lareggia surged to his feet, trying to conceal the effort this required. "I will call Captain Leutmann," he said.

Less than ninety minutes later, even Marion was impressed with what they'd been able to accomplish.

Captain Leutmann had arranged for the delivery of ample travel clothing and gear to the convent, plus an escort of two loyalist Guards to personally drive them to Ciampino, an airport dedicated to military, charter, and freight service flights. The Vatican Secret Service, while officially under the umbrella of the pope, was more realistically an independent agency. There were plenty of "rogue" agents within its ranks who were willing to do anything necessary to preserve the traditional church. Leutmann had enlisted several of these SSV ops to meet them at the Ciampino airfield and fly them south to Nairobi. From there, they would be met by a Kenyan station op who would get them to their final destination, regardless of where that might be.

"Everything has been arranged," said Lareggia, speaking with ease and confidence, as though he'd been the architect instead of the button man. "No public exposure, no passports, no record of your passage."

Marion looked at him from behind the hooded folds of her nun's habit. The cowl concealed most of her face. "That also means that if anything goes wrong, there won't be any way for anybody to trace us, to find out what happened to us."

Lareggia shrugged. "Welcome to the underground," he said.

Etienne nodded but said nothing, looking out the window as their Mercedes knifed through the darkness beyond the hills of Rome. The twenty-minute ride to the airfield wound through small villages and out-of-the-way train stops. Once they had cleared the Grande Raccordo Anulare, there was little traffic and less interest in their passage along the coast.

Marion spent the time attuning herself to her new clothing and appearance; she knew she would have to be conscious of her demeanor as well. If she wasn't a convincing nun, she would be a red flag to anyone looking for her.

The car left the main coastal road, ascended a single lane winding through the cliffs to a security gate manned by Italian Air Force sentries. They waved through the SSV vehicle without incident. As their limo drew closer to a number of hangars illuminated by banks of auxiliary lighting, Marion could discern the logos of Federal Express, United Parcel, Airborne Express, and other international carriers on the hulls of the jets.

She was surprised at the high level of activity—hundreds of people drove cargo vehicles to and from the planes; conveyors, trucks, lifts, and personnel moved crates and boxes in unrehearsed choreography. Suddenly, their car stopped, and one of their escorts jumped out to open the rear door. He ushered silently them toward the nearest plane, white and green with the logo of International SkyFreight prominent along the fuselage and tail section.

Moving up the steps of the gangway, Marion looked back and down across the tarmac where the ant-colony-like activity continued unabated. No one seemed to be paying them even the slightest attention. She followed Etienne through the cabin door to the flight deck of the jet, then waited while Lareggia struggled up the staircase.

Once all three of them were inside, their escort introduced them to their SSV pilot and his second officer, who guided them through a bulkhead door to a passenger compartment.

"This is not your usual freight plane," said their escort with an ironic smile. "Please strap yourselves in and try to get comfortable. We will be taking off very soon."

Marion took a seat flanking a small coffee table piled with magazines and newspapers from various world capitals. Etienne sat across from her, and the Cardinal eased himself into a wide-body chair that also converted into a bed.

He smiled as he belted himself in. "Now I understand why Father Francesco enjoyed his liaisons with the international community. Very nice indeed."

"Have you heard anything more from Francesco?" asked Marion.

"No," he said, shaking his head. "Not since that single phone call to warn us."

"Do you know where he went?" she asked. Though Marion had never liked Giovanni Francesco, she had learned to respect his courage and his toughness. And she had learned to be rational enough to accept that a person like Francesco was good to have in your corner when things got sticky. "Any idea what happened to him?"

Before Lareggia could answer, the plane began to move, pushed back off its chocks, then towed into position to begin taxiing toward its departure runway.

"Not really," he said, glancing out the window. "There are rumors in the Guard and the Service that he is holed up in different romantic places all over the world—Macao, Patagonia, Corsica, Caledonia, places like that."

"It does not matter where the Jesuit goes," said Etienne, her voice soft and very matter-of-fact. "He will never be free of my son. None of us will be . . . until we stop him."

"I wonder if we will ever see him again," Marion said as the plane began a slow taxi to the end of a dark runway.

"Francesco?" said Lareggia. "If I know Giovanni, and I think I do, that man would spend his dying breath to reach Peter Carenza. Do not be surprised to see him again."

Marion smiled sardonically. "I never thought I'd hear myself wishing that to be true! But you're right—we need him. We need all the help we can get."

No one replied as the plane surged forward, the pitch of its engines rising as its speed increased. Marion leaned back in her seat as the plane climbed off the runway, banked sharply to the left, and glided upward over the Mediterranean.

For some reason, Marion felt vaguely uncomfortable. Something had changed. At first she couldn't put her finger on it, but as the plane achieved cruising altitude and leveled off, she realized what it was. The feeling welled up from deep in her soul. She realized that she had been suddenly unbound. She was free.

At least for now.

Peter would surely be pursuing her, although the odds of him intercepting their journey across East Africa were indeed slim. Marion looked across the cabin at Etienne, who was still staring out the window by her seat. The nun's hands still grasped the armrests tightly despite the smoothness of the flight.

Marion smiled as she realized Etienne had never flown before. She hadn't ever left the comforting embrace of the convent for almost two generations. What a wonder and a terror the takeoff must have been.

She regarded the simple nun with even more respect than before. Etienne possessed the inner strength to escape into a world she knew little about, a world waiting to overwhelm her with its passion and its folly, because she'd been so beautifully touched by God. She never questioned her role in his plan. Maybe that's why it seemed so easy for her.

"Etienne," said Cardinal Lareggia, abruptly breaking the silence.

"Yes?" She turned from the window, looked at him with a lingering awe still shaping her expression.

"When we get to Nairobi, I will have to arrange with our station ops for transport," said Lareggia. "Can you tell us now, exactly where in Kenya we are going?"

Etienne looked at them serenely. "Yes," she said. "It's a place called Olduvai Gorge."

"I've heard of that," said Marion. "Anthropologists call it the 'cradle of man,' I think. I knew a photographer who worked for *National Geographic*—she'd been there a couple of times."

Lareggia leaned forward. "It sounds remote and inhospitable," he said. "Do you have any idea how far from Nairobi it is?"

"Not really," said Marion.

"Me neither," said Etienne.

At that moment the bulkhead door swung outward to reveal the second officer, a ruddy-complexioned man who appeared to be in his midforties. He smiled as he stepped into the cabin. "How is everyone doing back here?"

"Very well," said Etienne.

"Good. We've just logged our flight plan, and we'll be arriving in Nairobi in about six hours."

"Thank you," said Marion.

"Excuse me, *signore*," said the Cardinal. "But do you happen to know how far from Nairobi is the Olduvai Gorge?"

The second oficer tilted his head in thought. "I'm

not certain . . . I've never been there. But I'd guess it's around one hundred fifty miles. Is that where you're going?"

"Ah, yes, it is," said Lareggia. "Will it be a problem?"

The SSV officer allowed himself a brief, smirky grin. "Well, it might. I think we'd better inform the station op ahead of time. They're going to need to secure you a chopper."

"Really?" said Marion.

"Yes, ma'am. You're talking about some very rough terrain. Dangerous, too."

Twenty-Three

Peter Carenza—Vatican City
October 29, 2000

A breakthrough!
Well, sort of . . . Peter mused as he descended
the circular staircase from the Tower of Winds, exiting
the Secret Archives.

The hour was terribly late, but one of the prefect's
seminarians had stumbled upon a reference to a text
titled *The Secret Book of the Seven Abbaye of Babylonia*. This
serendipitous event had set off a flurry of secondary
text searches and, twelve hours later, had already
yielded some promising results.

As was often the case with many of the ancient Middle Eastern cultures—from the Elamites, Sumerians,
Hittites, Assyrians, and Babylonians through the Egyptians and Abyssinians—there existed more than a passing similarity of the various myths. Indeed, much of
the Old Testament could be found in analogous ancient
texts and oral traditions of western Asia and northern
Africa as well as the familiar civilizations of the Middle
Eastern fertile crescent. Using Babylonia as a starting

point, the Archives staff and seminarians began a more focused search among the scrolls and manuscripts for cross references to the seven *abbaye*.

So after endless hours of nothing, they'd finally discovered *something*.

The seven *abbaye* were believed to be the holiest men of the kingdom—those anointed by the gods to represent all that was righteous in man. The Babylonians believed that as long as there were at least seven holy men, the world would not end.

Several of the Archives scholars felt that if there existed an analogue in Christian theology, they would now have a good chance of finding it. Peter instructed everyone to coordinate efforts from this point onward. He didn't want anybody repeating anyone else's work.

As Peter finally left the Court of the Belvedere, the moon was high above the Tiber, casting a gentle light off the basilica's dome and drawing long night shadows across the textured lawns between the buildings. The air was cool but not uncomfortable, as he walked back to the papal suite. Despite the lateness of the hour, he felt very much awake and energized—the small success of his research initiative pleased and excited him.

And the best was yet to come—tomorrow, the Pope was getting married!

Peter was feeling so good about himself he didn't really notice the difference in his living quarters until he was confronted by his personal secretary, Father Strenmann.

"Holiness!" said the young priest, who stood woodenly in the entrance foyer. "We have been waiting for your return!"

"What's wrong?" Peter said. "What's going on?"

"We were reluctant to contact you at the Archives,"

said the secretary hurriedly, anxiety in his voice. "And
we had no idea when you might return. And we
hoped . . ."

"You hoped what?"

"Well, *Signora* Windsor is not here. We assumed she
must be with you, but now that you are returned and
she is not—"

"Marion is not here?"

"No, but she has been out very much over the last
week," said Strenmann. "Everyone has been in and out.
Very busy because of the . . . the wedding."

"But she's never been gone this late."

"Yes, Holiness, we are aware of that."

"So where the hell is she? Did anyone know where
she was going today?"

Strenmann visibly shrank under the shrill blast of
Peter's anger. "I am so sorry, Your Grace, I don't
know! I—"

"Well, tell me what you *do* know, Goddamnit!" Peter
began pacing the foyer like a caged cat, emanating
waves of angry energy like excess heat.

He couldn't believe it!

How could this be happening?

He would never have expected Marion to pull something this crazy. He kept hoping there had been a mistake, a misunderstanding.

But a part of him knew for certain that she'd taken
off. He was gathering more confidence in his sixth
sense, his intuitive abilities, and this was one of those
times when he felt that things had gone terribly awry.

Several other members of the staff had gradually
gathered around him, although he could tell they didn't
want to be anywhere near the angry storm center he
was creating.

"Somebody tell me something! When did she leave?"

"Just after sundown," said one of the kitchen assistants. "I was coming on duty, and I saw her going down the auxiliary stairs to the garage."

Peter looked at his watch. She'd been gone almost nine hours. "Does anybody know anything else?"

"I know she received a telephone call," said Strenmann, "not long before she left."

"Do you know who called her?"

"No, Father."

"Get the switchboard!" he yelled. "Tell them I want a log of every call in and out of here today. Get my guards, and the police . . . and anybody else you can think of!"

People started moving. Peter detained his secretary with a touch on his sleeve. "By the way, I think it's wise if we keep this as quiet as possible. Do everything discreetly, Father, no media yet. None at all, do you understand?"

"Yes, of course, Holiness!" The man moved off quickly down the hall, leaving Peter alone in the foyer like a ship abandoned in the shallows.

He stood there for a moment as a rash of emotions burned through him. Shock at her courage. Outrage at her power to hurt him, to embarrass him so thoroughly in front of the world. Fear that he wouldn't be able to find her. And perhaps most curious of all, a kind of bemusement that something like this could even happen.

Slowly, he began walking toward his study. After all he'd been through, he had become used to the idea he was in some way special, above the range of normal human accomplishment. Even if his true and complete nature had not yet been fully revealed to him, and even though he occasionally allowed himself to ponder his ultimate role and purpose, Peter remained astonished that a screwup like this could still happen to him.

He should have been able to anticipate, and thereby

prevent, this interruption of his agenda. He should know what was going on around him completely and accurately.

That really bugged him.

But he couldn't deny the irony inherent in his plight. So powerful, yet hobbled by the whims of a woman. He would never be so proud as to assume that he understood the human female. Granted, he'd gotten a very late start in even beginning to unravel the feminine mystery, but he had the feeling he'd be just as lost without the intervening years of the seminary.

Entering his study, he knew he needed to clear his thoughts, to attack the situation logically. Who could have phoned Marion? Very few people had access to the numbers, and even those had to be cleared by the switchboard or the secretaries. Soon, he would have a list of all communication, but he began to review a mental roster. There was really only one person Marion had been seeing on any kind of regular basis, and that was his mother.

Marion had escaped with his *mother*?

Peter grinned, shook his head. The idea seemed absurd, yet—picking up the phone, he keyed in the number for the Poor Clares Convent.

"Hello," said an elderly female voice.

"This is the Vatican calling," he said. "Abbess Victorianna, please."

"Oh! Yes, right away!" said the startled woman. "You will please wait one moment . . ."

Peter hadn't spoken to this one of Francesco's conspirators in a while now. It would be interesting to see how she would regard him.

"This is the Abbess." Her voice was well tempered, accented with authority and a certain imperious quality.

"Hello, Victorianna. This is Peter Carenza."

"The Holy Father . . . calling me?" Her tone communicated little respect or much surprise either. "Should I be honored . . . or afraid?"

Peter chuckled just loud enough to be audible. "That is for you to decide. Unless you wish to make a confession, I have no way to know what's in your heart."

A pause, then she said, "What can I do for you, Peter?"

"You sounded like you might have been expecting my call."

"Perhaps," she admitted.

"I'd like to speak to my mother."

Another pause. "Well, this is a cloistered convent."

"And I am the Pope. I think we can stop playing games, Victorianna."

"Very well, then. Your mother is not here."

Peter was not at all surprised to hear this. "I thought she could not leave the cloisters without special permission," he said sarcastically.

"Permission she has received."

"Where is she now, Victorianna?"

"I do not know."

"Don't lie to me!"

A pause, long enough for him to wonder if she had nerve enough to hang up on him. Then, "Holiness, I would never lie to you!"

"You expect me to believe she left the convent without telling you where she was going, and you gave her permission to leave anyway?"

"Yes."

"Why?"

"Well, Father, you told us all in one of your speeches that we live in a time of wonderment and change. You could say I did it in the spirit of that change . . . or you could say I did it because I did not wish to know where she was going."

"You didn't want to have to lie about it later." Peter

spoke evenly, not wanting to give her the satisfaction of knowing she had thoroughly enraged him.

"None of us ever want to lie, Father."

"Have you seen my wife—?" Peter stopped himself, but the last word had already escaped his lips.

He felt immediately foolish. The old Freudian slip? Or was he just pushing the clock? Or worse yet, was this an indication of how much Marion's disappearance had disturbed him?

How stupid he'd been to make himself and his entire agenda dependent on someone else! The clock was ticking down toward the biggest media event of all of human history, and he wasn't going to have a woman to make into a wife . . .

. . . unless he found her, and found her fast.

Victorianna had not been able to repress her laughter. "Your *what*? I didn't know you were already married."

"You know what I mean—have you seen Marion?"

"Tonight?"

"Don't play games, Sister. If I have to, I'll send some SSV people over to talk to you. I understand they have ways of getting answers I've never thought about."

"You can send anybody you wish, Peter. Threats of torture—or torture itself—will change nothing." Victorianna spoke calmly and with a dignity of spirit that irritated him greatly. "I can tell you only what I know, and this is the sum of it: Marion was here to see your mother. They have both left the convent. I do not know where they went."

"I'll find them," he said in a steely voice, as much to himself as to her.

"Perhaps you will," she said. "Your resources are quite impressive."

"You know," he said in a mock-sincere tone, "even

though I believe you, I may send over a few agents to 'interview' you, anyway."

"Peter," said Victorianna, ignoring his attempt to disturb her, "I am truly sorry."

Her remark was so unexpected that he was forced to respond. "What do you mean? Sorry about what?"

The nun exhaled as though with great effort, and in that sound Peter detected weary wisdom and an admission of some sort of defeat. "I am sorry . . . I shared a vision with Lareggia and Francesco. By effecting your birth, so many years ago, we truly believed we were doing something good, something necessary."

"And what was that?" Peter sensed a sudden vulnerability in her, as though she were seizing a chance to reconcile with her Creator, as though she might expiate her guilt by finally articulating her part in what had happened thirty-three years ago.

"Back then, there was so much catastrophe in the world . . . ," she began, her voice acquiring a faraway, wistful quality. "So much disturbance and unrest, so much inequity. There was an evil in the world, Peter, and we believed things could not possibly get much worse.

"But we were too young to understand that that was a fallacy. Because, you see, things can *always* get worse."

"Do you hate me, Victorianna?"

Another pause, then she cleared her throat and spoke serenely. "No, I do not believe I do. Because, you see, Peter, I do not really know who you are. One cannot hate that which she does not truly know. I have never understood what we ultimately wrought in bringing you to the world. And as bad as that may sound, I do not believe you yourself are fully aware of who you are."

"That's very presumptuous of you," he said with obvious sarcasm.

"Well, only you can know how close I am to the truth." Victorianna drew a breath and converted it into another long, labored sigh. "But to me, at least, you are like a prized bone, the object of desire for two alpha dogs. And they have both leaped after you with all their energy. They have both gnawed and tugged at you, and you are beginning to show the stress and wear from that struggle."

"Thank you, Sister. I'd never actually imagined myself as a bone being slavered over."

"A humbling image, no doubt, for most of us. For you, I am not so certain."

"Oh, I wouldn't worry about me," he said. "Goodbye, Victorianna. I'll call if I need anything."

Hanging up before she could reply, he yelled for his secretary, who appeared so quickly that he must have been hiding just outside the room.

"Yes, Excellency?"

"Do you have anything for me?"

"Representatives of the *Guardia*, the *Polizia Romana*, and the *Servizio Segreto* are all waiting to meet with you."

"I don't want meetings; I want information. Do any of them have some of *that*?"

"Holiness, I'm not—"

"All right, where are they?"

"In the receiving hall, downstairs."

"Let's go," said Peter. As he followed the priest, Peter began to realize that he couldn't allow his outrage at being shown up by his mother and Marion to change the way he made decisions. If he did not remain rational, he was going to make a mistake.

No. No way for that. I'm too smart for that. Just stay in control, and the elements will clarify themselves.

What he needed was information, and if he cast his nets with intelligence and patience, he'd catch everything he needed.

Holding that last reassuring thought in mind, he entered the reception hall and approached the three stern-faced men who awaited him. He recognized the short, stocky Molinaro from the SSV, but the other two were unknown to him.

"Your Grace," said Molinaro, "this is Inspector General Olivari from the Central Precinct, and Commandant Dreml from the Guard."

"Where is Captain Leutmann?" said Peter.

Dreml, a tall, muscular man with a great bald head and a handlebar mustache, tensed to attention. "We have not been able to locate him, Holiness."

Peter grunted an acknowledgment, then said, "Let's drop the formalities, gentlemen, I trust you've been briefed . . ."

"Enough to understand the gravity of the situation. We cannot rule out kidnapping or terrorism," said Dreml.

Peter grinned sardonically. "It may be far simpler than that. Have any of your branches come across anything?"

Molinaro shook his head. "Not yet. We are questioning everyone who might have seen anything."

"Someone has to know something," said Peter. He spoke softly, not wanting them to see his high levels of alarm and concern.

He knew there were those within the Swiss Guard—Captain Egon Leutmann chief among them—who were inclined to be loyal to the old ways, to those cardinals and staff who had chosen to quietly oppose him. He could not place much trust or confidence in the SSV. Yet there were those who were weak, who could be controlled, albeit subtly, by Peter's aura of power. By his own will.

If Marion had enlisted the aid of clandestine reactionaries within the Guard or the SSV, they would cover their tracks with proficiency. If that had happened, he would have to hope for someone to make a mistake.

The men before him outlined their hastily assembled plans to locate Marion and Etienne. All of them expressed fear that the trail might already be growing cold because of the women's six-hour head start, and were of course trying to cover their collective asses in the event they turned up nothing.

Peter listened to their presentations with only half an ear. He didn't care *how* they did it, he just wanted it done. He was about to dismiss them when Father Strenmann entered the room, holding a piece of paper and looking very excited.

"Holiness! We have something!"

Peter felt something tighten in his chest. "About Marion?"

The priest's shoulders sagged. "No, the Archives! The prefect wants to see you right away—he says he's found it."

TWENTY-FOUR

Father Giovanni Francesco—Scarpino, Corsica
October 29, 2000

*D*ays and nights at the enclave tended to blend
into one another if you let them, thought Giovanni. It was, after all, not necessary to leave the
confines of the underground installation, unless one
wanted to.

Despite many people thinking he was a rat or some
other kind of slippery subterranean creature, Giovanni
did not particularly enjoy the claustrophobic absence of
sun and sky. And so every few days, he exited the
tunnels through a ventilation shaft maintenance ladder
to recharge his psychic batteries and assure that his san-
ity would not be compromised by living the life of a
mole.

The ladder ended at a hatch that accessed the top of
the promontory. Surrounded by nondescript boulders
and shrubbery, the emergency exit was completely cam-
ouflaged and quite invisible, even to someone standing
only several feet away from it.

Giovanni emerged from the hatch, felt the warm kiss

of the Mediterranean sun on his forehead, and was
instantly renewed. Moving toward the edge of the cliff,
he scanned the horizon, then looked down at the harbor of Scarpino, huddled up against the sheer wall of
rock. It looked as if God had taken a great hatchet and
chopped off the end of the island, then scooped out a
cove at the bottom.

He sat down on an outcropping of granite and let
the sea breeze comb through his crew-cut hair. It was
so peaceful up here, it was easy to forget that not only
might the fate of the world be tilting in the balance, but
that an old wiry Jesuit just might have something to say
about the final outcome.

Giovanni smiled to himself.

He'd been thinking more and more about his role in
the entire drama. For years he'd felt some guilt about
using Etienne, then a young girl just past her convent
vows. Still, he had felt justified in the belief he and his
colleagues had done the right thing. And their plan to
inaugurate the Second Coming had been brilliant. Even
Rudolph Krieger, the Nobel Prize–winning geneticist
they'd selected to do the work, had been impressed
with their vision and boldness.

So what had gone wrong?

None of them had ever dreamed that Peter could
become a tool for Satan. In fact, Giovanni was not sure
this was the case—at least not yet. Peter appeared to be
a theological work in progress. Sooner or later, though,
either ultimate good or ultimate evil would prevail, and
Giovanni was figuring on evil, because Peter had
turned out to be an imperfect creation.

That had been the tragic flaw in their plan: Mankind
was not capable of creating perfection.

Standing up, he walked to the edge of the promontory, looked down again at the harbor filled with its
toylike fishing boats. Despite everything, it felt good to

be alive, and he was reminded of an American blues song that had the line, Everybody wants to go to heaven . . . but nobody wants to die. How utterly true. But Giovanni had good reasons for not wanting to waltz off the stage just yet. He wanted to stop Peter Carenza, and he wanted to make sure he'd receive forgiveness from God for what he'd done.

The idea of forgiveness had gained favor in his mind since he'd received a reprieve from the unnamed SSV operative. Then he'd met Targeno's brother.

Why would these things have happened unless God had further plans for old Father Francesco?

A sound cut through his thoughts like cold blade. The steel hinges of the access hatch screeched loudly behind him. Turning quickly, Giovanni saw Brother Sforza emerge from the camouflage of rocks. He wore classic aviator sunglasses and his standard issue monk's habit. The hood of his robe was pulled back to reveal his totally bald head, which reflected the bright sunlight like a polished dome. The short, barrel-chested man was smiling broadly.

"*Buon giorno,* my good father!"

Giovanni grinned. "Probably wrong on all counts: I'm not yours, I'm certainly not good, and I'm not much of a padre."

Brother Sforza laughed heartily. "You will never change, 'Vanni. Never."

"Too late for that now." He regarded Sforza with some small amount of envy. Although Sforza was more than sixty years old, he hardly looked out of his forties. His lifetime regimen of a healthful diet and outrageous bouts of exercise had obviously been a worthy investment. Francesco had known Brother Sforza for more than thirty years and still remembered when they'd met as if it had occurred earlier that morning.

*   *   *

Giovanni was thirty-six years old, had recently finished his Ph.D. in biochemistry at Ignazio University in Milano, and was planning to teach at a Jesuit high school in Padua. The day he was to leave the dormitory and begin his journey to Padua, he encountered a short, muscular man at the threshold to his quarters.

The man was dressed in civilian clothes but claimed to be a member of the church. He introduced himself as Brother Sforza and informed Giovanni that the younger man had for some time been watched closely by members of his "special order," and that Sforza's superiors had decided that Father Francesco would make a valuable addition to their enclave. Sforza indicated that Giovanni's obvious intelligence, ruthless methods, egomaniacal personality, unique vision, and pugnacious attitude were traits considered necessary to be a member of the order.

Giovanni had scoffed at the invitation, citing his membership in the Society of Jesus—the Jesuits—and expressing haughty doubt there could be a more prestigious or powerful order in the service of God. He told his mysterious visitor to bug off, so that he could finish preparing for his trip to Padua.

Sforza chuckled and said: "So you would rather spend the rest of your life in a small backwater secondary school instead of the Vatican?"

That had gotten Giovanni's attention.

The suggestion that he could build his career within the walls of the holy city-state more than intrigued him, it fired his imagination and his ambition. He did not hesitate in joining the Knights of Malta, whose deep roots reached throughout the most powerful structures of the church. Even more impressively, the Knights had access to the highest levels of governments all over the world.

Knowledge was power. And Henry Kissinger had been so correct: Power was indeed the ultimate aphrodisiac.

Sforza joined Giovanni by the ledge. "I figured you would be here."

"I am no mole. I need the sun, the air."

"There are a few of us here like that. No need to make excuses."

Giovanni nodded. "How is Gaetano making out?"

Sforza chuckled. "He is like a rabid lion. No matter what we throw in his way, he conquers it. He will be completed within the week."

"Impressive." Giovanni reached into his jacket for a cigarette, pulled his old Zippo from his pocket, and fired it up. "What about the rest of your workup on him? Is he clean?"

"Everything he has told us checks out. He is indeed Targeno's brother. That is how he knew so much about the way we operate. That is how he was able to make application to us in the first place. He knew whom to call, what to say. He is very intelligent, very shrewd."

"Can we trust him?"

Sforza shrugged. "As much as one can trust any man so obsessed."

"True. It is a disease with no known cure—but one," said Giovanni, exhaling a thick plume of unfiltered smoke. "So we will use him?"

"Oh yes," said Brother Sforza. "He is perfect for our purposes. He is the x factor, the unplanned element. He is totally unknown in the espionage community. No one has had any contact with him—not even the SSV—

so we can place him close to Peter. He is the perfect assassin."

"How close can we place him?"

"It depends on what kind of conduit I can construct between now and when he is completed."

"That makes sense," said Giovanni.

Sforza paused. "You know, when you asked if we can trust him, I meant to elaborate on my answer, but we went off the track."

"Go on. I am listening."

"Well, as I am sure you agree," said Sforza, "the ultimate test of one's trust is in the action of the subject. In other words, we can discover whether or not Gaetano is trustworthy only by throwing him into the mix, by seeing which way he goes. And that is exactly what we plan to do."

"Isn't that dangerous? Are you not afraid he may give us away?"

Sforza smiled. "One, these are desperate times and we must take risks that might be considered dangerous. Two, he will be watched at all times. If he gives any indication, at any time, that he might compromise us, he will be eliminated. Better we err on the right side of judgment."

"We are going to need somebody on the inside. Somebody they will not suspect. Perhaps Gaetano is not the best choice."

"No one is a good choice at this time."

"I suppose you are right," said Giovanni.

Sforza smiled, tapped him gingerly on the arm. "Oh, yes! I almost forgot—we were able to track down the agent who helped you escape."

Giovanni flipped his spent cigarette past the precipice. "I owe that man my life. What is his name?"

"D'Agostino," said Sforza. "He is held in very high

regard by everyone in the organization. His dossier is exemplary."

"We can use him to place Gaetano?"

"That is the plan, yes. I am working on the details." Sforza leaned forward, rubbed his palms over his knees. "I love this business! Always a challenge."

Giovanni looked at his friend and colleague of thirty years. The bald man appeared so vital, so happy all the time. "Do you ever have any doubts?" he asked him as he returned his gaze to the sea. "About the choices you have made? About our place in God's plan?"

Sforza stood up and began to pace slowly. "When I was younger, when I was full of 'piss and vinegar,' yes, I had plenty of doubts. I would think, I could have been a military leader, a great cockhound of women, an innovative industrialist, even a world-famous *futbol* goalie. It is very natural for a young man to think in such ways. But I can tell you, 'Vanni, as I grew older, I grew wiser, and more comfortable with the choices I made. There is nothing more noble than to be a Soldier of Christ in the oldest, truest sense. Did not the Apostle Peter handle a pretty mean sword?"

"I suppose I already know your answer."

"Spoken like a man who is having a crisis of faith. Do you need to talk about it?"

Giovanni felt himself squirming. "Well, it's not a crisis of faith, actually. I mean, after all the miracles and horrors I have seen since the rise of Peter Carenza, I have no doubts about the deity. Nothing like that."

Sforza chuckled. "Something of a more personal nature, then."

"I want to be more certain of the fate of my soul."

Sforza placed a beefy hand on his bony shoulder. "Giovanni, we all worry about that, because we all fuck up. God loves a sinner, remember?"

"Yes, but I wish I could have a sign that everything

is all right, that I have evened up the accounts, so to speak."

"I saw a sign just recently," said Sforza.

"Really?"

The bald man gestured up toward the bronze-white sun, suspended above them like a Eucharistic host. "Last week, I was up here, communing with God, and suddenly there was a brief glow around everything, as if the sun had for a moment grown brighter. It was an incredible sensation. I was reminded of the Fatima stories."

Giovanni nodded. "Come now, Brother, you know what you are describing, do you not?"

"The solar prominences, yes, I course I do. For more than a year now, they have been subject of great debate."

"I saw several fellows on SNN," said Giovanni. "Scientist types. Some of them think the sun is growing unstable. The others say it is plain silly."

"If we have a G-type star, then it is indeed too young to be so unstable."

Giovanni regarded his friend with mock amazement. "You know astronomy?"

"Enough to be dangerous." Sforza smiled.

Giovanni spoke with intentional sarcasm. "So, do you actually think God had our sun expel billions of tons of its coronosphere just for your benefit and peace of mind—a sign to you that all is well?"

Sforza accepted the friendly jibe as intended. "No, I think it was coincidence. What do you think I am, a medieval pinhead?"

Both men laughed.

"But," Sforza added, "I also think it was God letting us know he is still paying attention."

"I think it is more than that," said Giovanni, articulating thoughts he'd been afraid to speak as though they might be made more real in the process. "I think it is God letting us know that if we screw this latest mess up too badly, He will just wrap things up here and move on to the next world."

TWENTY-FIVE

Marion Windsor—Nairobi
October 30, 2000

"Excuse me, Marion," said a voice that came to her from a great distance and was dampened by a midfrequency hum, "but you should start thinking about waking up now."

Blinking herself awake, Marion was surprised for an instant to see the tiny enclosure of the cabin. So deep had been her slumber that she'd forgotten about their escape, the flight, everything.

"Where are we?" she said, rubbing the sleep from her eyes. "I feel like a little kid on a car ride—are we there yet?"

"About fifteen minutes from Jomo Kenyatta International," said Cardinal Lareggia.

The door to the flight deck opened and the second officer joined them. He put on a respectful little half grin and looked from one to the other as he spoke. "Okay, we've been cleared to land under our Sky-Freight cover, which means a few very important things. One: The authorities here, in Kenya and Tanzania, are notorious for using the law to their own selfish benefit. Given the recent political unrest, it's a delicate situation. I'm talking about local police, the military, even government employees. Have as little contact with them as possible, okay? Good.

"Now, two: Everyone coming into Kenya is supposed to have a passport or a work visa, and you have neither. You are here illegally. The *Servizio Segreto* will protect you and do everything in its power to see that you are not detected, but if you are apprehended, we will be limited in what we can do to help, understand?"

"Yes," said Marion. "But are we going to have SSV personnel with us at all times?"

The man nodded. "It is our intention to have someone with you, yes. I will get to that in a minute. Three: The *Anopheles* mosquito is still prevalent here, which means malaria, which means we must vaccinate all of you. Our field medic is waiting for you at the SkyFreight hangar.

"Now, we have changes of clothes for all three of you. Basic SkyFreight uniforms. You need to change before you leave the plane. That way, no one will question your presence in our facility. You will find everything you need in the next compartment, and I suggest you get started now."

"Thank you," said Marion. "Thank you for everything."

"How are we getting to Olduvai?" asked Lareggia.

"SkyFreight has several helicopters in Kenya, and we are securing a pilot as we speak." He turned toward the flight deck. "You will excuse me for landing duties."

In a moment, Marion heard the pitch of the engines change and the plane tilted slightly to the left as it began its descent. She looked at the rear compartment door and shrugged. "Okay, I'll be first."

*   *   *

Lareggia was the last to squeeze into a SkyFreight jumpsuit. Marion was a bit stunned when the Cardinal
emerged from the cargo compartment and waddled
back to his seat. He looked as though his clothes had
been inflated with compressed air. The jumpsuit ade-
quately encompassed his incredible bulk but empha-
sized just how overweight the man had become.

Etienne, on the other hand, looked petite and cute
in her uniform. She tucked her short hair under a white
baseball cap with the green SkyFreight logo on it and
suddenly looked fifteen years younger.

"Prepare for landing," said the intercom. "Seat belts
fastened."

Looking through the cabin windows, Marion could
see the airstrip swing into view. Beyond it she saw the
downtown sprawl of Nairobi, punctuated by high-rise
office and apartment buildings. The sun had risen less
than an hour earlier, and the city tingled with warm,
dancing light.

Etienne appeared fascinated by the entire landing
process and watched through her own window without
moving or uttering a word until the jet had taxied to a
stop within the protective cover of the SkyFreight hangar.

Things happened quickly then.

A crew of freight handlers swarmed around the jet.
While this activity occupied most of the hangar personnel, Marion and the others accompanied the flight
crew to a second hangar where a small Bell Jet Ranger
helicopter idled in wait. A man with a thick mane of
silver-white hair and a tan flight suit watched them approach.

"*Buon giorno,*" he said with a smile. His tanned face,
with its rugged character lines, radiated confidence.

Marion immediately knew he was someone she could trust. "I am Fabrizzi," he said. "I am told you need to visit the Gorge."

"Yes," said Etienne.

"It is a fairly big place, *Madame*," he said. "Do you have a specific place in mind?"

"I am not sure. I will recognize it when I see it."

"See what?"

"A tree," said Marion. "It is called the Tree Where Was Man Born."

Fabrizzi nodded. "I've heard of it. The Masai have their own name for it, though I can't remember it off-hand . . ."

"Can you find it?" asked Lareggia.

"We will find it," said the pilot. "Come. Let's get your vaccines, then get aboard before any of the local soldier boys get too curious."

Ten minutes later they were tilting into the skies south of Nairobi, zeroing in on the Tanzania, border. Warm, heavy air felt thick and barely breathable, even in the open cabin. The little Bell chopper hugged the terrain as closely as possible, and even Marion clung onto the sides of her jump seat.

The view was spectacular.

"The Serengeti Plain!" cried Fabrizzi as they skimmed across an infinite grassland carved by arroyos, sparkling ribbons of water, and scattered grottoes of trees and watering holes. Gigantic herds of animals surged and flowed across the landscape in amorphous, ever-changing configurations. To the east, Marion could see the peak of Kilimanjaro shining in the sun like a piece of crystal. "A national park and game preserve. And that's Lake Manyara, one of its borders!"

"It is so beautiful," said Etienne full of awe and respect. "And big. I never imagined the world was so big."

Marion smiled, then reached out and squeezed the nun's hand. So pure. So innocent. What a unique person she was.

"See that big circular formation coming up?" said Fabrizzi loudly, over the rhythmic thrum of the rotors. "That's the Ngorongoro Crater. Ancient volcano! Now it's filled with wildlife."

"Is this the area where all that Stanley and Livingstone business took place?" asked Lareggia.

"You got it," said the pilot. "Pretty close to here. More than a hundred years ago! Must have been a hell of a place to go through on foot, yes?"

"Definitely yes," said Marion.

"How much farther?" asked Lareggia, who had been holding on to the base of his seat as though his grip would do a better job than the safety straps.

"Almost there! The Great Rift Valley borders this section down into Tanzania!" yelled Fabrizzi. "Which is about where we are now, and just off to your left is Olduvai . . . there!"

Following his pointing arm, Marion saw the gorge, a gaping wound in Earth's side. Compared to the almost languid beauty of the Serengeti, the Gorge appeared savage. Marion remembered her basic readings in Anthro 101 and the classic citations of Louis Leakey and his australopithecines, and smiled. She had never imagined she would see the place firsthand. She was about to point out an intriguing rock formation to Etienne, when the Bell hit an air pocket and dropped twenty feet.

They all screamed in unison and Fabrizzi chuckled. He adjusted the stick, and the chopper's flight smoothed out. "We can set this thing down anywhere you like, ma'am," he said to Etienne.

"I am still looking. I am sorry, I do not see it yet."

"We have plenty of fuel!" said the pilot. "I can take it down a little lower, a little slower . . ."

"Yes," said Etienne, "that would be good."

Leaning on the stick, the pilot cranked the Bell into a tight swooping curve that dropped the aircraft another five hundred feet, so that they were floating very close to the rugged terrain of Olduvai. Marion didn't imagine it would be too difficult to find a particular tree—there were very few trees in evidence in the harsh environment of the Gorge. She did spot various cordoned-off areas, an access road, and even several parking lots. Pointing them out, she asked their pilot what the installation was.

Fabrizzi smiled. "It's a tourist attraction. Louis Leakey's original archaeological sites. People can come in and look for fossils."

"Is there any chance we will be seen by anyone?" said Lareggia.

"That depends, Cardinal," said Fabrizzi, "on where we put this bird down."

The copter dove into the Gorge itself, and everyone gasped involuntarily at the sudden appearance of the geologically striated walls. Disoriented, Marion closed her eyes and leaned against the outer hull. She'd flown in newscopters when she'd covered Manhattan and the boroughs, but none of her pilots possessed Fabrizzi's skill—or his nerve.

A glance at Lareggia told her he was very close to losing his lunch. His complexion was pale, shading toward a jaundiced green.

Suddenly the chopper lurched to the right and dropped twenty feet or so. Everyone screamed again. Fabrizzi didn't chuckle this time. "Thermal updraft! No need to worry. It's normal, especially when we're this close to the walls!"

Suddenly Etienne cried out, "There! See it?"

As she pressed a petite index finger against the Plexiglas, she again reminded Marion of an excited child getting her first look at Disney World.

Following the direction of pointing finger, Marion spotted an outcropping of rock not far from the rim of the Gorge. Despite the bobbing motion of the copter, she was able to focus on a single object by the edge of the gorge—a large tree with wildly positioned branches and wisps of vegetation that looked like green tongues of flame. Fabrizzi must have seen it as well, because the Bell began to angle toward it.

"Oh my God," said Marion involuntarily as they homed in on it. "It's so beautiful . . ."

"Fever tree!" shouted the pilot. "That's what the Masai call it. Wild, isn't it?"

Marion had never seen anything like it, but the name for the tree seemed so perfectly appropriate. It looked like a bonsai in reverse. Instead of a miniature, organic sculpture, the fever tree was magnificently huge, stark, yet full of grandeur.

"Can you get us down near it?" said Lareggia.

"Close enough!" Fabrizzi yelled above the whining engine. "Just have to be careful with the thermals around the edge!" Then he smiled and worked the stick, playing the helicopter like a skittish colt.

Fabrizzi wrestled the chopper to rest thirty yards from the yawning precipice of the Gorge and the twisted majesty of the giant fever tree. The light of the fiery sun made a coruscating halo around every branch. The thick, sculptured torso of Yggdrasil seemed to pulse with life. When the engine died and the hull stopped vibrating, everyone remained silent, attention focused on the tree with a kind of universal reverence.

Then Etienne broke ranks and slowly climbed from the copter to the dusty terrain. As she began to walk slowly toward the tree, Lareggia spoke softly. "Should we be with her?"

"I think we'll know what to do when the time comes."

"You know," said Fabrizzi, his voice also low. "I've flown the Gorge a hundred times, and I don't ever remember seeing that tree."

"It's so big . . . ," Marion said as she stared at the tree of myth, the tree of life, the tree called Yggdrasil. She could see Etienne, almost directly in front of the thick trunk of the tree. Spreading out in every direction in a tortured asymmetry that was captivatingly beautiful, Yggsdrasil's branches began to move. At first Marion thought it might be due to a strong wind, but the air of the Olduvai was as hot and heavy and still as though it was a solid object.

No.

There was no wind. But the many arms of the tree were definitely beginning to move. A shudder passed through Marion as if someone had passed a cold feather down her back. It was a sensation she hadn't experienced in a long time, not since that night when Peter, in a moment of uncontrolled rage, had killed Daniel Ellington, his best friend. Everyone thought Ellington had died of a heart attack. But Marion had always known what really happened.

The great fever tree undulated, its flamelike leaves fluttering gently, as though moving to a subterranean rhythm, a spiritual score beyond the range of human experience.

Marion watched as Etienne descended to her knees and held her arms out as if to embrace the tree.

The sunlight that had been clinging to all the branches now seemed to be flowing like something alive, as if the tree had suddenly burst into flame.

"Oh, my God! Look out!" Marion shouted as she leaped through the open cabin door into the dirt.

"Wait," cried Lareggia as he began to struggle with his safety harness.

Marion glanced back but kept moving as the giant tree exploded into flame. She feared Etienne was too close and would get caught in the blast. The air had *whoomped!* as all available oxygen had been sucked from the space, and Etienne, who had been on her knees, had been pulled forward onto her face. Marion screamed out the nun's name while rushing forward.

Before she could get to her, Etienne had scrambled to her knees, her attention still intent on the burning tree.

As Marion drew up next to the older woman, she realized that the tree was not actually burning. It gave off no heat, nor was it consumed by the inferno that capered madly through its twisted branches. All fear and dread faded from her mind. Rather, she was filled with a sensation of utter serenity and well-being, and she knew she was in the presence of God. Images resonant of Moses in the Old Testament held her silent and brimming with a fervor she'd never known.

Etienne glanced at her for an instant and smiled. "This is what I came for," she said. "Just like in my dream."

"I know," said Marion.

They were joined by the Cardinal, who staggered forward, threw himself prostrate in the dusty soil, and began reciting prayers in Latin.

Then his litany stopped abruptly.

The great fever tree writhed in ghostly flame, and a sound that was not a sound filled them. It wasn't just in their ears, or even their minds. It was an elemental *awareness* that permeated their collective consciousness.

They all "heard" the voice of God not as individual words but as a more expansive communication that encompassed concept and image as well. Marion gathered the information in an effortless, altogether pleasant manner, as if she were a great sponge simply absorbing it.

The seven righteous ones—keys to the Churches of Revelation—had been contacted by Etienne and awaited only the locations of each of their Churches. One by one, in graphically rich images and sense-laden textures, these destinations were revealed, spread around the globe and across the seven seas. Even the names themselves had the power: Lhasa, Jerusalem, Stonehenge, Delphi, Mecca, Glastonbury, Tiahuanaco. One key to each place, where they must break the seal on each Church, then gather at the ancient focal point.

Time had stretched like taffy, sagging and useless. Staring into the amorphous heart of the flames, Marion saw the fissionable thoughts of God himself, the original high concepts forged in the furnace of creation.

Incredible.

God's plan.

She'd been hanging out at the cosmic water cooler and had overheard the whole deal.

The sardonic notion had popped irreverently into her mind. Suddenly she realized it was something Peter might say.

Had she been under the backwash of his influence too long, or was the thought more sinister? Had Peter somehow discovered them, and tapped in to their celestial connection? Did he *know*? Did he know everything?

Impossible.

Not here. If there was anything such as God's country, then surely the Olduvai was it—a solitary fortress against the time winds, a monumental reminder of the fleeting nature of works of Man and his ego.

Marion swayed to the hypnotic undulations of the flames, sensing that the experience was near an end. She could feel the divine presence withdrawing, like a storm losing its invisible energy. The fever tree began to change, its magical conflagration surrendering to twisted arboreal beauty.

And then . . . the fire was simply *gone*, leaving the three of them alone together in the charged atmosphere of the plateau. Lareggia still lay outstretched on the earth, Etienne knelt, and Marion stood by her side. After a long minute, Marion cleared her throat and spoke.

"What do we do now?"

"God's will," said Etienne. "Did you see the sun, Marion? The black sun! Just like my dream . . ."

Lareggia struggled to all fours, then carefully balanced himself in a squatting position before cautiously standing up. "And the angels! Did you see the angels? The hosts of saints?"

"Yes," said Marion softly. Apparently they'd all seen different things, their own versions of what the Divine should or must be. Better that she not question or challenge the rigorous doctrinal structure of the Cardinal's vision or the intensely personal one of Etienne.

All valid.

All real.

"It was so beautiful," said Marion. "And you've been through this sort of thing before?"

"Never like this," said Etienne.

"Maybe the Masai are correct," said Lareggia. "Maybe this is where he first made us."

"Which explains why I was told to come here—God required a pilgrimage," said Etienne. She reached out to Marion, who extended a hand and helped her up off her knees.

"I still don't know what comes next," said Marion.

"The Seven have been waiting for this day. I must tell them all." Etienne walked to the thick, central bole of the tree, reached out and touched its bark.

"We cannot go back," said Lareggia, staring off toward a distant, hazy horizon. "Do you realize that?"

"I have been thinking the same thing," said Marion. "Peter would stop at nothing to learn what we now know."

Lareggia chuckled softly. "And that is the irony here! What do I know? What could be tortured out of me? I have no idea . . ."

Etienne turned from the tree and walked to the Cardinal, touched his forearm. "Saint John the Apostle told us to await the reckoning with joy as well as fear."

"Tell me more," said Lareggia, "so that I may work on my joy."

"We are gathering together the best of us, Your Grace."

"I know," he said. "It is the worst of us that has me worried."

TWENTY-SIX

Gaetano—Rome
October 30, 2000

*H*e surfaced under a wharf at the Civitavecchia docks. The coastal city lay 120 miles due east of Corsica. Carried there by a stealthy hydrofoil, Gaetano had slipped into the oily water of the Tyrrhenian Sea a half mile from shore, his body in a wet suit, his gear in an unsinkable Waller bag. Moonlight and his wrist transponder guided him to the target. The slap of the low tide against the sea wall sounded like the rhythmic motion of two bodies, in languid coupling.

He smiled at the sexual metaphor. It had been quite a while since he'd been with a woman—since long before his six weeks in a cavern full of militaristic monks! But he had no right to make light of them. They had done their job in spectacular fashion; they had trained him well. He had become a survival machine, a killing machine.

He was one of the few men in the world who could: run a mile in under four minutes; bench-press 350 pounds; remain underwater for more than five minutes; dismantle, reassemble, and operate forty-four different personal weapon systems, and kill a man in more than 130 distinct, highly efficient ways.

The Knights had done that to him.

He'd wanted them to, and now, his life was irrevocably changed. Throughout his training, while he was alone with the Knights, it had briefly occurred to him that he would never be able to return to his brokerage house. He had always dismissed the thought as romantic nonsense. He'd insisted to himself that he would slip back into the mundane world as soon as he avenged his brother's murder.

He'd been full of shit.

Drifting with the ebbing tide under the rancorous docks, Gaetano checked his chronometer. He was three minutes early for the rendezvous.

There was no going back, and he knew it.

Not only did he like his new life, he knew he would never be allowed to go back. He had become one of the men who knew too much. He felt as if a veil had been lifted from his eyes. It was as if he'd been stumbling around his entire life, never really seeing what was taking place right under his nose.

The conspiracy nuts were so close to the truth. Practically nothing was as it seemed. And that revelation in itself was reason enough never to want to return to what was sardonically called the "real world."

The instrument on his wrist beeped once, just at the upper range of his hearing. Time to move. Leaving the cover of the pilings and planks of the wharf, he clambered up to a gangway that led to a cluster of pre–World War II warehouses, most of them still in use despite their utter decay.

Entering the second building was an exercise in total silence, and he relished the opportunity to use his skills. He glided into the industrial space like a ghost. The air was thick and black as hot tar. Exhilarated with his success, he moved toward—

"Stop right there," said a whispered voice. The words were incredibly soft, but they struck his ear as if they were the open palm of a headslap. Gaetano exhaled slowly, feeling no fear or anxiety. This was exactly what he'd been told to expect.

An orange-magenta light lanced into his left eye for an instant, then vanished.

"All right. Take one step forward."

He did.

Suddenly another man materialized from the heavy darkness, so close to Gaetano that he was startled for a moment. To be that close to another person and not give yourself away . . . the operative was very good indeed.

The stranger detected the defensive reaction and chuckled softly. "Relax. Your retinal scan is a match—otherwise you would already be dead, my friend."

"I know that," said Gaetano, getting a clearer fix on the man in front of him. Slightly taller than himself, broad-shouldered and with classic Mediterranean features, the man wore all black clothing and a black watch cap—classic commando ensemble.

"I am D'Agostino."

"I know that, too."

The operative smiled and flicked on a tiny penlight. "Come with me."

Gaetano followed him through a warehouse crowded with shipping crates and interlocking truck containers. They emerged in a deserted alley and climbed into a four-wheel Jeep, also black.

After they had slipped through the narrow streets of the old city, and made the coastal road angling south toward Rome, D'Agostino broke the silence. "About forty miles to the Eternal City," he said. "But the road is not always the best. It may take more than ninety minutes."

"Then I have plenty of time to get out of this wet stuff and dry off." Gaetano climbed into the backseat and pulled some standard-issue commando clothing of his own from his waterproof Waller. He peeled off the thin, highly insulated diving gear and spread it out on the cargo deck to dry.

As he wriggled into dry pants, he saw that the driver was watching him in the rearview mirror. "Francesco told me you took a slug for him."

"That old man is one tough bastard. Yes, I did. It was the only way to avoid killing him."

"Your idea?"

"Yes. My concern was that my story would be dismissed, that no one would believe I could fail to eliminate a man in his seventies."

"And—?"

The agent laughed. "No one said a word! Like I said, that priest carries a lot of baggage, all of it full of dirty laundry. My superiors were not at all surprised that he survived the hit. They were more shocked that he had not managed to get a clean kill on me!"

"The priest said you saved him because he'd worked with my brother."

The driver nodded. "That is the core of it, yes. I knew he'd been Targeno's superior. And they always respected each other. And I knew I could not work for Carenza. If the new pope wanted Francesco dead, then he must be a threat and therefore a possible ally of mine."

"My brother always said there were times when you had to think for yourself."

"I know," said the driver. "He was my mentor, years ago. You look a lot like him."

"So I've been told," Gaetano said as he climbed back into the front seat.

"Your brother was kind of a legend in the Service."

"So I have discovered. He didn't tell me what he did for a living until I was out of university."

"Were you surprised?"

Gaetano grinned. "I thought he sold bathroom fixtures—what do you think!"

"He was the best. If you turn out to be half as productive, you will be an asset to us."

"Thank you. I will not disappoint."

They drove along the coastal road in silence for a minute or two as D'Agostino drew in close behind a dilapidated farm truck, overflowing with produce and creeping along the single lane road as if its operator were pedaling it uphill. As soon as they reached a straight section of asphalt, the agent accelerated past the old truck. Then they entered the outrageously narrow and twisting streets of a small fishing village. As the Cherokee pitched along the main thoroughfare, Gaetano was amazed at how close its fenders were to grazing fences, gates, and even the front door latches of buildings.

When they hit another stretch of open road, D'Agostino said, "You may be aware of the great fracture of allegiance in almost every body of church and government service, but there is more to it than that. No one is completely certain what to make of this new pope. There are arguments for and against him."

Gaetano made a semihumorous snorting noise. "I already know what side I am on!"

"Please, *signore,* I am not asking you to make a choice. I want you to realize the gravity of the situation. Some Vaticanos argue that, given the infallibility of the pope, God would simply not allow Peter Carenza to become pope unless he should actually be there."

"You mean," said Gaetano. "all the changes Peter II is calling for—they are what God wants for His Church?"

D'Agostino nodded. "Following this line of reasoning, yes. And don't forget, if you are a strict dogmatist, then the logic is very powerful. Nobody becomes pope unless God wants it to happen—is that not the ultimate truth?"

"Some would say yes."

"And," said the senior agent, "if this is so, then we should all be following the word of the new pope without question, or even a thought of resistance or disobedience."

"Okay, I follow you."

"There are others who argue that Peter II is a false prophet, as called for in Scripture, and that his presence in the Vatican is an abomination. A way for God to test the faithful and tempt those who may not prove as righteous."

"This seems more sensible to me," said Gaetano. "And to you also."

D'Agostino held up a single index finger. "Yes! But the larger question is: What does one do about it? If you choose to step out against your sworn leader, how do you do it?"

"Carefully."

"The watchword, rookie!" said the driver. "It is times such as these when you never seem to know whom you can trust."

Gaetano had already been considering this problem, but he had no answer. "What is the solution?" he said after a pause.

They were entering another village, not as small or narrow as the first, and D'Agostino negotiated its turns and dips while he spoke. "Treat everyone as the enemy," he said. "Trust no one. Shoot anyone who tries to stop you."

"It may come to that."

"I know, but in the meantime we will take other defensive steps, such as keywords. Any communication you receive from your people will use this . . ." The agent had reached into his pocket and produced an index card on which a single word had been scrawled: PESCO.

He had not spoken the word in the unlikely event their conversation was being intercepted.

"You see it?"

"Yes, of course."

The driver nodded, folded the card in half, and scraped its folded edge on the textured surface of the dashboard. The friction was enough to ignite the paper into a brief ball of blue-white light, and then it was gone. Less than ashes.

"You will use that word for your encrypted E-mail, for your phone scrambler, and even any emergency note you might have to scribble. You must translate into whatever language you are using. If anyone contacts you or tells you anything without using that word in some fashion, you must kill him. If you do not, he will most surely kill you."

Gaetano nodded. "I understand."

"You see, it has come down to what will happen to our immortal souls. Everyone has chosen one side or the other, and they are, quite frankly, betting their eternal fates on their choice."

Gaetano chuckled. "For me, the choice is no choice at all."

"Nor for me," said the driver. "But many people are weak. They prefer that others make decisions in their stead. They wish to stay with the status quo. Rather than follow the warning of their conscience, they fear the price of taking responsibility for one's own actions."

"The story of civilization," said Gaetano. "The doers and the nondoers. Do it, or be done to."

"I like that." D'Agostino chuckled softly. He didn't speak for a moment, then: "Well, now you will get your chance to do some very serious doing."

TWENTY-SEVEN

Peter Carenza—Vatican City
October 29, 2000

T his had better be good," said Peter as he entered the prefect's office. "My secretary tells me you found 'it.' Just what might 'it' be?"

Father Erasmus had been seated at his desk, looking at some notes under a pool of light from a solitary lamp. He was thin, with thin fingers, thin hair, and a reed-thin voice. His complexion was pale and blotchy, and he normally looked unwell. Tonight he looked particularly pallid.

"Holiness, please, have a seat," he said, handing the sheaf of papers across the desk. "Have a look at this."

Peter's heart had started *thruummping* in his chest. Could this be it? Was it excitement that churned in him, or fear? Slowly, carefully, he began to read the prefect's notes—

And the mystery stood revealed.

Seven holy people alive in the world—living saints?

Seven Keys.

Seven Churches.

Containing the Seven Seals.

This was indeed the time of the Reckoning. A time when humankind would tell God if the world should stand for another thousand years, or be tumbled into the eternal abyss. If the Seals were opened by the Seven, the grace and power of God would flood into the world. If the Seals were opened by agents of Darkness, it was a world well lost.

Agents of Darkness.

A world well lost.

The phrases settled upon him like a comfortable old blanket, and that should have bothered him. But it did not.

Interestingly, Peter had stopped wondering about which side he represented in the coming confrontation. What was happening to him bore the fetid stamp of inevitability. He had a feeling of resignation, the way he'd felt as a kid when he'd been picked by what was obviously the losing team.

Even if he wanted to step out of the mold being cast for him, he knew he could not. Something had left him, something elemental.

Peter had lost his cosmic sense of God.

He'd lost his ability to pray.

So where was all this headed? Where was it taking him, and what would ultimately happen to him?

It was a question with no answer. A mystery of anti-faith, to coin a phrase. As he continued to scan the notes, rereading them for anything he may have missed, he felt a terrible friction at the center of his thoughts—a general sense of melancholy grinding against an unformed sense of urgency.

Push on. Go on. There's no place else to go. Nothing else to be doing.

Looking up at the prefect, whose face bore an expression of abject apprehension, bordering on terror,

Peter said, "What are these Churches, and where are they?"

Erasmus tried to smile but failed. "As with much of Saint John's final book, much is metaphor. It is generally agreed the Churches are places, locations rather than actual buildings."

"Yes, I've heard that."

Erasmus proffered a careful suggestion of a grin, a slight curve of the corners of his mouth. He handed Peter a new sheet of paper:

Stonehenge
Lhasa
Jerusalem
Delphi
Tiajuanaco
Glastonbury
Mecca

The names held him with a resonance, as if some other-dimensional tuning fork had been struck. Places of antiquity, of mystical significance, and apparently some power as well. He looked back to Father Erasmus, who appeared ready to wipe a pleased expression off his face at a moment's notice.

"This is a good start, but we will need a lot more," said Peter.

"Of course, Pontiff!" said Erasmus, a little too quickly. "Just tell me what you wish."

Peter leaned forward, gestured toward the list of names. "Come on, Father, use your head. These places—most of them are big places, full of locations where the Seven Seals might be located."

"That is true."

"So where do we go from here? How do we narrow down our search?"

Erasmus scribbled down a few quick notes. "I will get our staff on it as soon as possible! The answers are here, I am sure of it."

"And something else occurs to me," said Peter, speaking out loud but as much to himself as the prefect. "How much time do we have? What kind of deadline are we up against? Do you have any idea?"

"Well, at this point, no, but—"

"Bad answer," said Peter. "You've just scratched the surface. There's a lot more to this, and I'm going to need to know everything."

"Of course," said Erasmus, his voice so low it was barely audible.

"Do you have anything else?"

The prefect's face flashed a *haven't-you-seen-enough?* look for the barest instant, then went blank and weary. "Well, no, not at the moment, but I will have people working around the circuit of the clock."

"Can you bring in more people? Anybody else in the seminary not doing anything?"

"I can ask around. I am sure we can find additional staff."

"Good," said Peter as he stood up and walked to the threshold of the cramped office. "Do it, and call me as soon as you have more."

Several hours later, he found himself awakened by a gentle tapping at his bedroom door. His head was pounding, his mouth dry. Every muscle in his body silently cried out for more sleep.

What time was it?

And who the hell was knocking on the door? He'd cleared out everybody last night when he'd gotten back from the Archives.

As his eyes adjusted to the dimmest of dawn light

through the shutters, he could see the face of his Rolex mocking him. Not enough sleep. Not even close.

Tap-tap . . .

"Yes!" he yelled, with enough edge in his voice to let whoever it was know he was not pleased. "Who's there? What do you want?"

"Excellency," said a muffled voice. Familiar. Deferential. Father Strenmann. Peter didn't like him even a little bit. The man was a little weasel of a priest from Zurich, who'd gotten the papal appointment because of a brother in the Swiss Guard. He was such an uncompromising suck up that it was difficult to tolerate his presence. Peter had been too overwhelmed with other concerns to dismiss him and interview a replacement.

"Yes, Father, come in."

The door opened and the little man entered, carrying some pieces of paper. "I am sorry to awaken you, but this might be important."

"What is it?"

"It is from Erasmus." Peter's attention sharpened as Strenmann handed him a sheaf of laserprint from Internet Web pages, copies of pages from newspapers, and newswire clippings. As he started reading, he noticed Father Strenmann still standing there. "Is there more?"

"There might be. The prefect told me to tell you he has two staffers following up these stories."

"Okay, great. Why don't you let me read this stuff, and you head on back to the Archives and wait."

"Wait?"

"Yes. Wait there, until they have more to show me."

Father Strenmann appeared surprised to be sent away, but he said nothing as he turned and exited the room.

When Peter was again alone, he jumped from the bed and moved to his aircraft-carrier-sized desk, flipping on a banker's lamp. The first newswire piece was immediately arresting. It told of an amazing rescue off a new bridge over the Río de la Plata. A freak accident had sent a car plummeting off the bridge and into the chilly waters, but an engineer named Carlos Accardi, one of the builders of the bridge, had leaped off the bridge into the frigid depths and rescued the people in the submerged and sinking car.

Peter stopped reading the translation from the *Buenos Aires El Clarin*. What could this have to do with what he needed to know?

He was tired and irritated, but he pushed on despite the article's florid style.

> Carlos Accardi, after being examined and released at the Hospital Pirovano, held a press conference where he revealed the complete story behind his daring rescue.
>
> "I had a vision," said the dashing young engineer. "As I watched the little white car splash into the water, I saw a woman appear to me!"
>
> Colleagues working with Accardi on the bridge confirm that he appeared to be shocked and "acting different," said stress analyst Omar Duarte, who was with Accardi when the event transpired.
>
> "She was dressed in long flowing robes," continued Accardi. "And I thought at first it was the Virgin Mary. At first glance she looked like the pictures of people in the Bible."
>
> When asked to clarify what he saw, Señor Accardi explained: "She spoke to me in my mind. She knew my name. She wore brown and tan robes. The more I looked at

her I realized she was dressed like . . . like
a sister in the schools—she was dressed like
a nun."

When asked why a nun would appear to
him, Señor Accardi claimed he had no idea.

Peter put down the laserprint, and massaged his temples. He had no idea how the seminarians or the archivists had found this item, but it had shocked him
even more deeply than the whole mess with Marion
and the wedding.

A churning feeling in his gut was telling him that this
engineer had seen his mother, Etienne.

What kind of forces was he up against?

Again, that sensation of inevitability and lack of
choice passed through him like a chilly messenger of
impending death, and again he did his best to ignore
it. What else could he do?

With much greater interest, he read some of the
other newswire copy.

There were several follow-up articles, some illumi-
nating the details of the lives of the people the engineer
had saved, and including brief additional commentaries
by Carlos Accardi. The most recent, dated yesterday,
from one of the more sensationalistic rags, was head-
lined "Bridge Accident Hero on Mission from God":

Buenos Aires (Knight-Ridder) The odd
and heroic story of Carlos Accardi, the engineer who leaped off a bridge to save three
people, continued today when it was
learned that Accardi has requested a leave
of absence from his prestigious position
with Omar-Chela Steel and Construction.
When questioned about his request, Señor
Accardi announced with obvious religious

fervor that he has been selected by God to embark on a special journey to the ruins of ancient city of Tiajuanaco.

The archaeological site is located in the jungles of Bolivia, and is believed to have been the holy city of a lost culture that later gave birth to the Incas.

"If you must know," said Señor Accardi, who has achieved the status of a great hero in his country, "I had another vision from the nun I call the 'Dream Lady' because when she appears to me I feel like I am dreaming—even though I know I am awake."

Accardi claims to have received a message from the mysterious nun last night and knew that he must take action on her words immediately.

The article went on to corroborate Accardi's character and reputation as a virtuous, respectable, and even, by some friends' accounts, a holy man.

The final adjective struck a jangling chord in Peter, and he knew he'd been handed one of the final players in this weirdly spinning apocalyptic drama.

The Seven.

Clearly, this man was one of them. And even more clearly, he would have to be stopped.

The greater implication being that all of them would have to be stopped, and as soon as possible. Peter would confer with Molinaro of the SSV, who was either a loyalist or simply too terrified to go against Peter's will. Somehow they would have to screen anyone arriving at any of the seven "Churches." Some locations would be much easier to contain than others, but that was Molinaro's problem.

Marion had to be found. She had an appointment at the altar, and she was going to keep it, even if she was late. Every time he thought about the embarrassment and disruption her flight had caused, Peter felt himself losing control. And that couldn't be allowed—he needed complete control over everything. Beginning with the media and the politicos of the Holy See. He would tell them the wedding was being postponed because... Marion Windsor had been kidnapped. Give a few vague details and the press would do the rest.

Peter made some quick notes on a pad, realizing he would need to brief Father Strenmann on all this.

It's too bad there's no one around to help him, he thought. Someone who would always be there, by his side, waiting to carry out a command, to listen to any problems, to offer condolences, or consultation.

For a time, he had had Daniel Ellington, but something had happened to him. Yeah. Peter had happened to him.

And then Marion had filled that role rather well, but something had happened to that relationship too.

Peter leaned back in his chair, realizing he was sinking deeper and deeper into the territory of the maudlin. It bothered him to have such a weakness of spirit. It was a human trait he could do without.

Forget about it. Get back to work.

The second set of papers told a story similar to the first—another seemingly ordinary individual involved in a singular event. Quickly, Peter read the wire accounts of Charlie Green, a retired Long Island cop and part-time Federal Express courier, who'd saved the life of an Arizona rancher who had fallen into an abandoned well. Mr. Green had apparently been psychically connected to the guy and had received telepathic messages from him.

Once again it was a follow-up story that transfixed Peter.

> **Lebanon, N.H.** (from the *Valley News*) Local celebrity and "psychic hero" Charles Green of Canaan, New Hampshire, has attributed the source of his recent newsbreaking experience to a messenger from God—a woman who appeared to him in his dreams wearing the habit of a cloistered nun. The night after he saved the life of Arizona rancher Scott Raney by receiving telepathic messages from Mr. Raney while he lay injured at the bottom of a well, Mr. Green reported to his family and friends seeing a "Lady in the Light, floating in front of me, telling me God had tested me, and now He had an even more important task for me."
>
> Mr. Green, who is a member of the Mormon church, is familiar with that sort of thing. "Everybody in our church has to embark upon a mission, so this will be nothing new for me," said the local hero.
>
> Although Mr. Green did not disclose the details of his spiritual encounter, it was learned from third parties that he has requested a leave of absence from his employers. Other sources indicate that he may be traveling to Glastonbury, England.

Why Glastonbury? Peter asked himself. Why is one of St. John's seven churches located in such an out-of-the-way place?

He thought about the quote from the Charles Green article about God putting the guy to a test.

Something about the God of the Old Testament had always bothered Peter, through his early days of parochial school, the seminary, and beyond—and that was this penchant Yahweh seemed to have for playing games with people. *Job, I'm going to make you the most miserable son of a bitch on earth. I'm going to take away everything that ever meant anything to you and I'm going to give you a world-class case of boils. I'm doing this not because you're a bastard, but because you're actually one of the good guys and I just felt like checking you out to see how much crap you would take before you denounced me. So whaddya think about that?* Or how about Abraham: *Listen, Abe, I have a little job for you, so put down that baby lamb you were getting ready to take up to the top of the hill and decapitate and burn for me. I want you to take your boy, Isaac up there and stick a big knife in his heart. That's right, I want to kill your son, for me, okay? Oh, you will!? Well, hold it! No, don't do it. Just kidding!* And then there's Lot and his wife . . . the list seemed to go on for a while—people, usually good and wholesome folks, getting flimflammed and jerked around by a God who seemed to be either very bored or very mean-spirited or more than a little insecure.

Very weird business, that Old Testament.

Peter smiled as he put the articles on his desk blotter. He had a lot of separate tasks to coordinate today, and an early start was going to help. As he reached for the telephone, he realized something that might help explain The Games Jehovah Played—this God business is a lonely one.

And nobody has to like you.

PART

4

... and they that dwell on the earth shall
wonder, whose names were not written in
the book of life from the foundation of the
world, when they beheld the beast that was,
and is not, and yet is.

–John, *Revelation, 17: 8*

X

TWENTY-EIGHT

Marion Windsor—Nairobi
October 30, 2000

*S*o where do we go now?" asked Cardinal Lareggia, lumbering behind the two women. They were slowly walking back toward the helicopter, dazed by what they'd experienced.

Marion had heard the Cardinal's question, but not only did she have no answer, she was too exhausted even to try to formulate one. She felt psychologically drained, so awed was she by what she'd seen and felt. Thinking seemed like an affront to the power and glory of the presence of God, and she understood how people were forever changed by what the philosopher and psychologist William James had called the "profundity of the religious experience."

When they reached the helicopter, Fabrizzi silently helped them re-enter the cabin, as though he were ushering them into a church pew. Even the cavalier pilot had been affected by what he had seen. Though he had not been directly involved in the event, he realized he'd been a witness to something extraordinary.

Once Lareggia was aboard, Fabrizzi spoke apologetically. "You will excuse me, but we cannot remain here indefinitely. . . ."

"We know that," said Marion. Turning to Etienne, who had leaned back in her seat, looking serenely pensive, she said, "We must leave this place, Etienne. Where are we going?"

The little nun looked surprised by the question. She responded in a tone of voice that suggested the answer was extremely obvious. "We must wait for them now," she said.

"Where do we do our waiting?" said Lareggia.

"In Giza."

"Giza?" said Marion. "Egypt?"

"Yes," said Etienne, closing her eyes and speaking slowly, as if reciting a well-known phrase. "By the Great Pyramid of Cheops they will gather, by the light of the full moon."

No one said anything for a moment, then Fabrizzi grinned. "All right, my friends, at least it's on the way home for me. Why don't we all get comfortable while I get us up in the air and try to log in a flight plan."

The pilot swiveled around to face the controls and kicked the engine into life. Marion strapped herself in as the others did the same. Almost instantly, the chopper lurched upward at an odd angle, heading vaguely north.

No one spoke. Marion reflected on what had happened in the last twenty-four hours and how it had changed her life yet again. Closing her eyes, Marion let the rocking vibration of the aircraft lull her into a hypnagogic sleep. She drifted back to the time when she'd left home. She'd often wondered what her father had thought, seeing her on the evening news and the national satellite feeds. What would he have made of this latest rash of coverage, where she was portrayed as everything from the next saint to the whore of Babylon?

She'd always been able to size up a situation and go after it quickly. That's why she'd been the first reporter to sense that the story of Peter Carenza might be a very big one, a career maker.

The thought shot a sharp pain through her heart. Oh, how she'd loved him. . . .

And his feelings for her had been equally sincere. But so many things had happened since those times of innocence.

Now she was being hunted by various agencies for various reasons—Peter's forces from the Vatican were no doubt searching for her, and she was certain that the rest of the world had been told she was the victim of a kidnapping. At least that was the way she imagined Peter would handle it.

Her imagination raced ahead of the helicopter, trying to figure out what awaited them. Unless Peter was so angry he'd ordered her execution, she was probably safe from anything too severe. Not that she really cared about her own fate any longer. She knew now she had been selected by God—for some inscrutable reason—to be a part of this grand scheme, and that she, like the others, was being tested. It was a test she did not fear because she believed her motives were pure.

Nor did she doubt the others. But she had been wondering what Peter would do if he knew his own mother worked toward his downfall. What a weird situation.

Finally she let the question in her subconscious take full form. Why Giza? And what would be waiting for them there?

And more important: When was the full moon?

TWENTY-NINE

Peter Carenza—Vatican City
October 30, 2000

*G*et yourself more staff," he said quietly into the
phone. "I don't care where you get them—I told
you that before. Just get them. I need answers."

Hanging up the phone, Peter rubbed his eyes. He
needed more sleep, and he wasn't going to get it.
He couldn't sleep, it was that simple. Still no word on
the location of Marion or his mother, and that was
bothering him. The SSV represented one of the best
espionage operations in the world—primarily because it
was comprised of many double operatives who worked
in other nations' intelligence agencies as well. The Vatican operatives were better than good, and yet Molinaro had not been able to come up with the slimmest
scrap of information. Not a single lead.

Peter wasn't buying it.

He'd suspected for a long time that crucial components of the SSV and the Swiss Guard were conspiring
against him. Actually, he had expected it. Loyalists and
reactionaries were not that unusual. Peter would not

waste his time trying to stop any rebellion; no, his greater problem was establishing a strong enough network of counterintrigue that could penetrate the conspirators' inner circle. Getting an organzation together that could be trusted and properly staffed required more time than Peter had to devote. The project had been little more than a mental Post-it Note—yet one more thing he needed to do. At this point, he had little choice but to rely on his sometimes unreliable ability to influence weaker minds.

At the moment, it was obvious that Peter might not be able to do everything alone. Which meant what? he asked himself. What was he really saying here? What kind of help did he mean?

And from whom?

Peter pushed back from the desk and stood. That last thought had pierced the armor of his confidence, and he'd felt suddenly dizzy.

Walking to the window, he looked out over the city of Rome across the river. By now the press releases announcing the postponement of the papal wedding had trickled down to the masses and the commercial interests that were looking to take advantage of the huge crowds, the mass gathering of media, skeptics, and zealots. The news that Marion was mysteriously "missing" would have to be enough for all of them for now. Peter had announced that there would be no papal interviews or audiences until further notice or until Marion's whereabouts became known.

This did not keep the tabloids from hyperventilating, of course. Marion's disappearance had already been atributed to alien abduction, avenging angels, being swallowed into the earth, having been ascended into heaven, spirited off by kidnappers, and even suicide. The mainstream media had handled things with little more decorum. Their ploy was usually to wheel in some sort of "expert" who would then speculate on the reason for Marion to vanish. The more sedate suppositions centered on her unease with the idea of actually becoming the Pope's wife, and how she had felt the weight of the world's attention on her and decided she couldn't take it.

As he concentrated on Marion's fate, Peter's disequilibrium passed, but he knew what had caused it. Just the thought of entertaining help from . . .

No. He couldn't even think it.

Because he'd attended a meeting of such proportion once before—appropriately, in the desert. Arizona. The night Daniel Ellington had died.

A roll of thunder passed over the city, and the building shuddered. Briefly, the sunlight baking the myriad terra-cotta rooftops dimmed, as though a great, ominous cloud had passed overhead.

But there was not a cloud in the sky; the penumbra must have been in his heart.

Or worse . . . his soul.

THIRTY

Gaetano—Vatican City, Rome
October 30, 2000

He looked up at the imposing edifice and nodded. The Seminary of the Society of Jesus of Sant' Ignazio was a magnificent collection of buildings where the church's best and the brightest were armed against the world. And according to the wishes of their founder, Ignatius Loyola, their armament remained a finely honed intellect. Every priest ordained within these walls emerged with a Ph.D as well as a collar. Fields of discipline ranged from Theology and Comparative Religion to include Particle Physics, Anthropology, Biological and Genetic Engineering, Mathematical Theory, History, etc. Gaetano had nothing but respect for the Jesuits and felt honored that they thought him sharp enough to impersonate one of their number.

"Welcome to your new home," said D'Agostino, standing next to him as they faced an ornate set of double doors cast in bronze. Chuckling, he added, "At least for the next few hours."

Gaetano said nothing as the doors slowly began to swing inward, opening wider and wider until he saw a young man wearing a black cassock. "Good morning, my brothers in Christ!" said the seminarian brightly. "Can I help you?"

Obviously, he did not recognize either one of them and had no inkling of the reason for their presence at the gates.

"We are here to see Father Grizaffi," said D'Agostino.

"You are?" said the gatekeeper, surprised that two men dressed like wilderness guides could possibly have an appointment with the rector.

D'Agostino nodded but said nothing, and stepped into the vestibule. Gaetano followed, carrying a large athletic bag filled with various types of gear best suited to one of two endeavors—survival or killing. He wore a backpack filled with the minimum in toiletries and clothes.

"Please wait here," said the priest. "I will be with you as soon as possible."

Gaetano watched the man depart through a second set of double doors, less ornate than the first, then regarded D'Agostino. "You are sure there is no trouble?"

"Trust me," said his senior.

"That is my problem," said Gaetano. "I have no choice. I have to."

They stood silently in the vestibule for not more than sixty seconds before the priest returned. His expression was unreadable, but his body language—something Gaetano had recently been schooled in—revealed a deference and respect not previously exhibited. "The rector will see you immediately," said the priest. "This way . . ."

Gaetano picked up his bag and followed his senior and the priest through a paneled and wainscoted entry hall that ended in a staircase of green marble steps, wide and polished. The place smelled of oiled and hand-rubbed hardwoods, of incense and burning candles. Despite the cavernous quality of the high-ceilinged rooms, the seminary remained warm and inviting. Several connecting corridors on the second level finally led them to an anteroom, a reception area, where another gatekeeper screened visitors to the rector's office.

The receptionist was an older priest with a tonsure of grey hair. He hardly looked at them as Gaetano and the others entered, merely sprang nimbly to his feet and rushed to the door to the inner office. Opening it and entering, he announced them, then ushered them into a large office lined with bookshelves and built-in cabinetry.

Stepping into the room, Gaetano felt his shoes sink into a thick Oriental carpet. Sunlight streamed like rays of God's grace through leaded-glass windows behind the large wooden desk. There was a man seated at the desk but the intense sunlight obscured him in deep shadow. His voice, soft yet limned with a firmness that comes with years of comfort in giving orders, filled the room. "Come in, gentlemen. I've been expecting you."

Gaetano followed D'Agostino to the edge of the desk, as the receptionist faded away, closing the door behind them. The rector stood, and at last Gaetano could see him more clearly. He was a small man with deep lines in his face and a shock of curly hair that was refusing to turn gray. He had large teeth that featured prominently in his smile, thick horn-rimmed glasses that failed to refract the lively spark in his eyes. He was very stocky, and though probably in his late sixties, appeared to be powerfully muscled. He looked more like a leather-tough basketball coach than the rector of a Vatican seminary.

"Hello, Father Grizaffi, I am D'Agostino of the

Knights of Malta." The men shook hands. "And this is your newest seminarian, Gaetano."

The rector chuckled. "Sit down, please, both of you! Good to meet you. Excellent."

Gaetano took a chair, angled it toward the desk, and moved it closer.

"You have been briefed by Sforza," said D'Agostino, not questioningly.

Father Grizaffi nodded. "You have no idea how happy I was to hear from my old friend. I understand that Giovanni has surfaced and is well."

D'Agostino smiled. "He will outlive us all."

Grizaffi swiveled his chair toward Gaetano. "Well, young man, you look like what we need here. How old are you?"

"Thirty-six."

"The best age in the world!" said the rector with an engaging smile. "Now, your primary task is to see that you live to be thirty-seven. I assume you know what your secondary task is."

"Yes, Father. But I must get close to him."

Grizaffi held up his hands like a traffic cop. "And so you will. But have patience with an old bastard like me. I want him dead as much as you do, believe me."

Gaetano smiled. He liked the rector instantly. "Very well, Father. Just tell me what I must do."

Grizaffi sighed, clapped his hands together softly. "You may not know it, but the 'Pope' is at present engaged in some kind of frenetic research at the Secret Archives."

"What kind of research?" said Gaetano.

"I have the details right here," said the rector, indicating a folder on his desk. "You can read it later. What is primary is that he has enlisted an army of assistants to help find what he is looking for. He has raided all the seminaries in Rome."

"And he needs still more?"

"He has the need, yes." Grizaffi smiled. "You will be reporting to the Archives prefect, Father Erasmus, this afternoon."

"Does he know who I am?"

The Rector made a wave-off gesture with his hands. "Gaetano, please, none of them know anything! Beyond this room, no one."

"How close will I get to him?"

D'Agostino touched him on the shoulder. "That is where the training will come into play. You will assess the situation and act accordingly."

"Yes, of course. I know that," said Gaetano. "I am sorry to sound so anxious, but this moment is the culmination of a long journey for me."

Grizaffi nodded. "Understood. But this is not the time to be impulsive or impatient. Trust no one."

"I understand," he said.

The rector stood up, as did the two Knights. "You will be given a room now. Good luck, young man. And please, with God's hand on your shoulder, may you get to crush this scorpion!"

Gaetano smiled. "I will."

Two hours later, after a brief time for solitary introspection, Gaetano prepared to depart for the Vatican. D'Agostino had accompanied him to the small dormitory room, offered him last-minute advice, and assured him he would never be completely alone. Never forget, he'd said before leaving, the Knights had eyes and ears everywhere. Gaetano had studied his maps, blueprints, and other documents, familiarizing himself with every aspect of his environment. Every move he made would require contingency information, if possible. The more he knew about the surroundings, the higher his chances of success.

When it was time to depart, he was led, part of a cadre of fresh-faced young men, through a series of hallways and descending staircases to a courtyard in the rear of the complex of buildings. The fourteen men remained silent until they were ushered into a small, waiting omnibus.

Sitting next to a soft, sandy-haired boy of perhaps twenty-three, Gaetano nudged him in the elbow. "Do you know what this is all about?"

The boy shrugged. "We're going to the Archives. Didn't they tell you?"

"Yes, but not much more than that."

The boy turned and looked at Gaetano, a brief shadow of suspicion scudding across his pinched, doughy features like a storm cloud. "Are you new here?"

Gaetano grinned. "You have never seen me before, correct?"

"No."

"Then you know I am very new." Gaetano continued to grin, but with his jaw set rigidly.

"Where did you come from?"

The bus surged forward as the driver eased out the clutch. It wheeled clumsily and jerkily around in the courtyard, then down a narrow passage, through an arched gate, and into the streets of Rome. Traffic swarmed around them, horns bleated.

"I am Father Gaetano. From our seminary in Arezzo. I am here to finish my doctorate."

That seemed to satisfy the young man, who nodded as though impressed. "I am so tired," said the pale-faced boy. "All we do is study, and now we must do it for someone else."

"Ah," said Gaetano. "But it is for the Holy Father . . ."

The boy made a distasteful expression. "Is that what you call him? I try not to think of what is happening to the Church."

"Then why are you here?" said Gaetano. "Why not challenge the one who dares call himself Peter II?"

"Are you in favor of this Pope? Of what he plans?"

"Did I say that?"

"No, but . . ."

"My friend," said Gaetano, giving him a fraternal tap on the arm. "I am only trying to discover how we have allowed things to get this far out of line."

"Because we are afraid—afraid of what he might do to us if we refuse."

"No," said Gaetano, his voice low, masked by the rumbling engine of the bus. "I think it is worse than that. I think we are afraid, yes, but of what is in our own hearts!"

The young man said nothing for a moment, looked out the window, where the bus was crossing the Ponte Vittorio Emanuele II, then nodded. "If you are correct, Father, then what is to happen to us?"

Gaetano smiled. "Either we must have faith in our God . . . or ourselves."

The truth of what he was saying penetrated the outer shell of the seminarian's faith and slowly sank toward the center of his soul. He said nothing but nodded quickly, as though what Gaetano had said was a truth that had needed to be voiced.

Looking into his dull brown eyes, Gaetano could see the uncertainty, the lack of conviction, and most assuredly the fear.

The bus lurched to a halt. Gaetano saw that they had been stopped at a gatepost, where a Swiss Guard examined the driver's pass, then waved them through.

Moving again, the bus accelerated slowly. The lush greenery of the Vatican Gardens surrounded them as the vehicle turned into a lane flanked by manicured hedgerows. They drove along a row of tall, formidable buildings that comprised the various academy buildings, the Governorate, and the Court of the Belvedere.

As the bus pulled into a reserved space by the set of doors that marked the service entrance to a building housing the Secret Archives, Gaetano wondered why they were called secret when they were clearly not.

"Time to go to the salt mines," said his seatmate.

Gaetano stood and retrieved his athletic bag, which had been stowed under his seat.

"What's that?" said his companion.

"Oh, just a few special tools I thought I might need."

The young man made a humorous snorting sound. "The only tools you're going to need in here are paper and pencil."

Gaetano smiled. "Don't bet on it."

ThiRTY-ONE

Peter Carenza—Vatican City
October 30, 2000

The hours of the morning had run over him like spilled ink on a page, and he felt, with an unarticulated urgency, that something necessary had been overlooked. The feeling nagged him as he pushed on through the unending demands of the morning. The media had been difficult and unreasonable, as expected; his staff appeared to be quietly shaken by the bogus "terrorist abduction." Many seemed unable to perform their duties. Peter felt that if he did not personally carry out every directive, nothing would be completed.

Goddamn Marion! She'd really fucked up everything.

And he was running out of time. Time to stop whatever great wheel his mother had set into motion. That was the most frustrating part in all the machinations clicking into place all around him—time was clearly the missing piece. How much time was required to communicate with the Seven? And how much time were they given to reach their assigned locations? So far, he'd been able to identify only two of them, and nothing had been done to try to stop them.

They could already have reached their Churches. The others might not be far behind them. Peter needed more help. He needed to coordinate a plan, and he needed loyal forces to carry out that plan.

And first he needed a sign, a demonstration of his authority—something to yank everybody into line, lock-stepping to Armageddon.

Peter paused, turning over that last phrase in mind. *Lock-stepping to . . .*

Yes, that's what it really was, wasn't it? All this urgency and upheaval, all this understated terror—it had a purpose, a direction, and a destination. All the old mythologies had something going for them. Somehow, the endless procession of cultures and religions and civilizations all knew what was going on.

Sooner or later it would come down to a confrontation. The unending conflict would be resolved, at least for a while. For a while, because Peter suspected that there was a cyclic nature to the cosmology.

Peter exited the papal apartments and walked across the gardens to the Court of the Belvedere. In the Tower of Winds, Father Erasmus was standing at the top of the circular staircase, waiting for him.

"Good news, Excellency. Fourteen new researchers will be in place this afternoon. They are scheduled to arrive momentarily, and after a brief orientation, I will have them on the job."

"See that you do," said Peter. "What about my private office in the Archives?"

"All has been completed," said the prefect.

"Very good. I will go there now. Do not disturb me unless you have specific information that can be utilized instantly. The only person I want to see is Molinaro,

from the SSV. Call him, tell him I'm here and that he
needs to be here, too. Right now."

"Right away," said Father Erasmus.

Peter nodded, half smiled. "Like I said—anybody
else, he'd better have a pretty good reason if he wants
to see me."

"I understand, Holiness." Father Erasmus backed
away from him, eyes averted.

Turning down the corridor with the gracefully
arched ceiling, Peter walked briskly toward the Archives reading room that had been outfitted for his personal use. He was dressed casually, in jeans and a
sweatshirt, and the several people he passed on the way
had done double takes before acknowledging the presence of God's representative on earth. He always
smiled when that happened. None of these Vatican vet-
erans would ever grow inured to his purposeful avoid-
ance of many of the silly customs that had held the
papacy for hundreds of years.

When he reached his quarters, the heavy wooden
door was closed but not locked, and he entered without
ceremony. The room, although large and high-
ceilinged, was crammed with a research table and
lamps, bookcases, filing cabinets, fax, scanner, photo-
copier, a large computer on a large desk, telephone, and
the rest of the expected executive accoutrements. There
was a second level, accessed by a wrought-iron circular
staircase, that was nothing more than a narrow walkway and bookcases that surrounded the room. A door
at each corner of the walkway connected the library
level to identical spaces in adjoining rooms. The building overflowed with books and documents—no space
had been wasted. Nice. This would do just fine.

Moving to the padded leather chair at the desk, he
sat down and checked the voice-command functions on
the computer to see if it had been successfully net-

worked to the system in his apartment. He'd spent considerable time training the apartment PC so he could now speak to it effortlessly, and he expected the same from this one.

After requesting his notebook files and copies of all wire service clippings regarding anything to do with any of the seven target locations, Peter was satisfied the networking had worked well. He spent the next ten minutes sifting through the hundreds of wire service reports for any possible references to anyone who might be one of the Seven.

He did this until he was interrupted by a knock on the door. Molinaro.

Peter called him in, watched the man in the dark suit enter with great deference. He looked like he'd probably been quite a good scrapper in his prime, which appeared to be about fifteen years past him. His still-dark hair was combed straight back but not slicked down or gelled. His features were softer than classic Mediterranean, but that could be attributable to the little bit of extra weight he was sporting.

"I came as soon as possible, Your Excellency."

"Glad to see you are still on the job, Alfredo," said Peter.

"Why would I not be?"

Peter scowled. "Don't play dumb with me! We both know what's going on in your organization—neither one of us is stupid." Peter spoke firmly. He needed to find out how much crap this guy would take from him. He needed to know if he had a true loyalist here or if he would need more *attention*. Peter had been slowly growing more comfortable with his ability to affect certain individuals' actions, actually to have a form of control over them. "It is obvious we have defectors, reactionaries, or whatever you want to call them."

Molinaro could barely meet Peter's eyes. "It is wise

to look for traitors everywhere, I agree. But I should tell you, they are difficult to catch. My operatives do not make mistakes very often."

Peter chuckled derisively. "Have you caught *any*?"

"Well, no, but there are people we are watching."

Peter nodded absently. "I'm sure there are. Now, to business—you've gone over my memo?"

Molinaro nodded. "I have. Some of the sites will be easier to monitor than others—Stonehenge, Glastonbury, even Lhasa and Tiajuanaco are manageable. In fact, I have people in place at each of them already. It is believed the targets will not have the earmarks of typical tourists, and we will find them."

Peter nodded. "You understand: I don't just want them found, I want them terminated."

Molinaro swallowed hard. "Yes, Excellency, that is most assuredly understood."

Peter studied his minion. Molinaro did not hesitate or flinch—and apparently did not care why Peter had decided the Seven must destroyed. Their death warrants did not bother him. "Now, what can you tell me about the other sites?"

Molinaro drew a breath, let it out slowly, then consulted a small notepad he produced from his breast pocket. "Jerusalem, Delphi, Mecca. All three are larger locations, each containing many possible target sites. I have dispatched as many ops as possible to all three. They will reconnoiter and report on most likely destinations for the targets."

"Can you cover them all?"

"We can do our best."

Peter grinned, shook his head. "Wrong answer. Care to try again?"

Molinaro paused, as if confused, then seemed to catch on. "Yes, Pontiff, we will definitely cover all of them."

"You'd better. I want them caught."

Molinaro ran a nervous finger along the edge of the notebook. "I . . . I, ah . . . should remind you, Holiness, that we do not yet know the identities of five of the individuals you have us looking for. It will be very difficult to locate a person who has no name and no face."

"You are supposed to be working on that too," said Peter.

"Well," Molinaro hesitated and combed his fingers through his hair. "I think we are all supposed to be working on that problem. My men are those of the Guard and the Prefect. We are cross-checking every lead, every possible indicator. We are screening every scrap of info that comes from the target cities. Every lead is being followed up. You are supposed to be getting copies of everything—"

"I am," said Peter.

Molinaro nodded. "Then you can see what we are up against."

Peter smiled. "The only thing I can see is a little man trying to squirm out from under his failures."

"Holy Father," said Molinaro, "I mean no disrespect. I have always faced my responsibilities. I am only trying to show you—"

"No!" yelled Peter, slamming his fist on the desk. "I want results, do you understand?"

Molinaro backed up a step and looked toward the door. "Yes, I do. Forgive me, Your Grace."

Peter stared at him for a long moment. "No can do."

Molinaro looked puzzled.

Peter chuckled. "You don't get it, do you? We're all *way* beyond forgiveness now."

"What do you mean?" said the SVV man.

"I mean there is no one, no being, if you'd still like to believe I am God's representative on Earth, who can forgive us for the path we've taken." Peter glowered at him. "Can I make things any clearer, 'Fredo?'"

The notion seemed to strike Molinaro like an open-palmed slap, and he stepped back another step, obviously eager to leave. "I . . . ah, I understand. Thank you, Holiness."

"Get out," said Peter, "before you start groveling. I hate that. And don't come back until you have something good to tell me. Something *very* good."

Without another word, Molinaro nodded quickly and backed from the room, closing the door behind him.

Returning to his printouts, Peter reflected on what had just happened. He'd been hard on Molinaro because he needed to be sure the man was too scared to do anything but stay in his corner.

That's what it came down to, didn't it? Anybody who'd stuck with him and his "new" Church were the real chickens, weren't they? Too fearful to defy anything, even to doubt, no matter what confronted them.

Which was an interesting contrast to the courage of one's convictions. Of course, it had been like that throughout the centuries, he mused. That's what always separated the leaders from the herd.

And now, for his efforts, Peter had unwittingly surrounded himself with nothing but herd types.

A loud *click* surprised him. It was the latch on the office door opening.

Looking up, he saw a tall man wearing the plain black cassock of a seminarian enter the room.

Unfamiliar.

Uninvited.

THIRTY-TWO

Marion Windsor—Cairo, Egypt
October 30, 2000

Despite the tension that twisted through her like barbed wire, Marion dozed off. The droning lullaby of the SkyFreight jet's engines exerted a strangely calming effect on her. As her eyelids fluttered, she realized she had been dreaming, and that her dream had been a surreal continuation of what had been going on when she fell asleep. Cardinal Lareggia had somehow become tall and thin, and Etienne appeared to be no older than twenty-five, and they had just landed their plane in the desert across a river from the pyramids, which were still being built, to judge by the system of huge ramps and the many slaves dragging stone blocks around. Even as she was dreaming, Marion experienced that over-the-shoulder awareness which told her none of it was real.

She heard a man's voice, sharp and penetrating against the higher-pitched drone of the plane's engines. "...affirmative, Cairo. ETA eighteen minutes. Ten-four."

"Is everything okay?" she asked lazily, pushing herself to full alertness.

Lareggia nodded but said nothing as he found something of interest outside the window.

Etienne looked at her with an openly maternal smile. Marion had become so comfortable in the nun's presence—the woman had become more than a friend, more like a member of her family, someone in whom she could always confide and trust. "You looked so tired. We did not wish to wake you."

"I must have been wiped out," said Marion. "Did Fabrizzi say we're near Cairo?"

"Yes," the pilot confirmed, looking back and flashing her a smile that probably guaranteed him plenty of dates. Fabrizzi added, "We'll be touching down soon enough, but we're going to have to be very careful."

"What do you mean?"

"I've been in touch on a secure channel with our ops station in Alexandria, and it looks like you have created quite a tumult."

"Are we in jeopardy?" asked the Cardinal.

"We must be vigilant," said Fabrizzi.

Marion sat up in her seat, folding her arms against a sudden chill. They were still dressed in tan Sky-Freight coveralls. Both Lareggia and Etienne looked absurd and unlikely to be SkyFreight workers—the Cardinal for his great girth, and Etienne for her lack of size. Marion wondered if she looked equally out of place in her coveralls, then decided that her lean, still-athletic build usually looked appropriate in whatever she chose to wear.

"The 'official' word is a possible kidnapping or terrorist act," said Fabrizzi. "That is how our Holy Father is explaining your disappearance. The wedding will not happen today."

Marion felt a lump form abruptly in her throat and

her breathing tightened. *My God, he's right!* She looked at her watch. *If it hadn't been for that dynamic, little woman over there, I'd be married by now!*

Fabrizzi continued: "They're looking for you everywhere. Official reports mention Sister Etienne as a possible victim in the 'plot' as well."

"What about me?" said Lareggia, like a small schoolboy waiting to be chosen for a team. "What did they say about me?"

"Ah, nothing, actually."

The Cardinal appeared so surprised by this that he had no response. Marion suppressed a grin and looked away for a moment. There were times when she really didn't like Lareggia—for reasons ranging from his obvious gluttony, to his elitist, patronizing attitude, to his outright ignorance of so many things outside the purview of the Vatican—but there were other instances when she felt genuinely sorry for the man. He was truly pathetic.

"What else did they tell you?" asked Marion. "Does Peter know where we are?"

"No," said Fabrizzi. "No one has any idea, although they strongly suspect collusion and cooperation from what they're calling 'renegade elements' of the SSV."

"Well," said Marion, "they're right."

"Who exactly is 'they'?" said Etienne.

Fabrizzi shrugged, hands still on the controls. "Actually, there are several 'theys': the official face of the Vatican Secret Service, under orders of Director Molinaro, who decided to remain allied with the Pope; the College of Cardinals; and the Vatican bureaucracy that interfaces with the world-at-large."

"Why are they so much on Peter's side?" wondered Marion.

Lareggia leaned forward. "I think I can answer that. They are mostly old and fearful of the politics of this world and possibly the next. These are men who have played power-games all their lives. Their natural instincts are to lean to the direction of the power. They are hedging bets, certainly, but the face they show to the world is going to be in total support of the Pope."

"It makes sense in a twisted kind of way," said Marion.

Lareggia held his palms open and upward. "It is the only way they believe they will survive."

Marion returned her attention to Fabrizzi. "So what does this all mean? How safe are we? How easy is it for any of the . . . opposing parties to find us?"

"Good question," said the pilot. "At this point, we are operating within a network based on trust and very little else. We know who we are, and we operate within that limited knowledge."

"Why are you so committed?" said the Cardinal.

Fabrizzi considered the question for a moment, ran a hand through his thick hair. "We who have refused to follow the words of this Pope believe we have no choice. We cannot walk down a path clearly marked to damnation."

Marion grinned. "Well said."

"Besides," continued Fabrizzi, "we could ask you the same question—why do you go against this man? A man who has been so close to you."

Etienne looked at him with a serenity that was frightening. "Precisely because we have been so close to him."

The radio squawked, and Fabrizzi attended to it and did a quick check of his autopilot systems. As he did this, Marion wondered what awaited them in Cairo. What struck her as most interesting was her lack of personal fear. Death held no threat to her—she'd already died once. Embarrassment, humiliation—they were of no consequence. She believed in Etienne, and in what she said God had revealed to her.

Whatever lay ahead, Marion would accept it with the serenity she'd learned from Etienne.

"Okay," said Fabrizzi, speaking to them over his shoulder as he adjusted several banks of controls, then took the stick in both hands. "If you keep watching on the left side of the plane, you will be seeing the pyramids quite soon. We've been cleared to land at Cairo."

The plane's engines had changed to a lower pitch, and the big jetliner angled downward. As Marion shifted in her seat, she looked out the window to see the endless spill of the Sahara tilting up toward them. As the plane continued turning and descending, she caught a brief glimpse of regions to the south, across the Nile, where the pharaohs' monumental tombs pointed toward the stars like a string of celestial markers. Then she spotted the rooftops of the sprawling city in the hazy distance, reaching out toward the sun and wind-scrubbed landing strips of the airport. From their present altitude, everything looked perfectly clean and ordered like a giant game board upon which titans had not yet begun to play.

"When we land," said Marion, "do you have a plan?"

Fabrizzi chuckled. "Me? No, I have no plan. I am a pilot—I can fly anything, but I plan practically nothing. But there *is* someone waiting for you at the SkyFreight hangar, someone I am told who *does* have a plan."

"Who?" said Marion.

"I do not know," said Fabrizzi. "We try to keep radio conversation to a minimum—for obvious reasons."

Marion nodded. "Of course."

As soon as the plane came to rest in a large Sky-Freight hangar, a swarm of handlers wearing familiar coveralls surrounded it like hungry insects.

After the gangway was wheeled up to the door, everyone climbed down from the flight deck hatch to the floor of the hangar. A hideous heat permeated the area, and there was a high level of white noise in the enclosure, a combination of machine sounds and the random shouts of workers. At the bottom of the steps, Marion scanned the hangar and its hivelike activity.

In the distance, she saw two figures—one tall and thin, the other shorter, muscular. Both wore the garb of the bedouin.

They walked with a resolute stride, avoiding the Brownian movement of the freight handlers, and were headed straight for Marion and the others. "Look," she said to Etienne and the Cardinal, gesturing with a slight tilt of her head. "I think they're looking for us."

Marion looked for Fabrizzi, but he was gone.

"I think we should go," said Etienne.

Looking back toward the two men, Marion saw that the shorter one was reaching into his breast pocket.

The Cardinal grabbed her by the arm, screaming, "No!"

THIRTY-THREE

Peter Carenza—Vatican City
October 30, 2000

*P*eter looked angrily at him. "Who the hell are you?"

The man in the doorway did not answer. He stared directly into Peter's eyes while he reached back without looking and shut the door behind him.

It clicked, locked.

"How'd you get in here?"

"Oh, I've always been here," said the man. He chuckled so softly it was almost a whisper. He was not overly tall, but he was thin with narrow shoulders. His hair was cut short, military-style, but thick enough to retain a dark red color that matched his eyebrows. He looked at Peter with a lopsided grin and green eyes so dark they appeared deep and bottomless.

The unknown seminarian radiated an arrogance, a lack of respect that made Peter feel naked and vulnerable. These were sensations he never experienced, but this youngish, puckish character was somehow projecting an aura of such . . .

Menace.

Danger.

Malevolence.

He stood there wrapped in a shroud of silence that roared in Peter's ears. Black smudges began spinning around Peter's head, their frightening high-speed orbits at eye level. Disoriented, he staggered backward, remembering the last time he'd felt like this—when he'd seen the slowly whirling black rose coalesce out of the sunset, when he'd been assaulted by the time-wind that blew over him like the hot, rotten-meat breath of a predator.

No. It was impossible.

Not *here*. Not *now*.

So said his conscious mind as it fought to accept what was taking place in the office. But there was another place, at the core of Peter's being, that was very comfortable with the situation. Way down in that place the neurologists called the R-complex, known more picturesquely as the "reptilian brain." There, this great, shadowy presence would always be welcomed, invited, even needed.

This part of Peter didn't understand the reluctance, the fear, the refusal to accept the way things were. It understood the rules of the game, the necessity of his less-than-holy alliance, and his ultimate destiny.

It saw things so clearly.

Since that evening in the desert, Peter had been like a man who had picked up a piece of radioactive material and then refused to look at the vile, glowing lump that seeped illness and hideous death between his fingers.

"Hello, Peter," said the man. "Long time, no see."

Peter realized he'd been unconsciously backing away, inching toward the corner of the room where the metal stairs double-helixed upward. "I don't get it," he said.

"Get what?" The man's voice was so soft, so controlled. It was if he barely whispered, yet Peter could hear him clearly.

Peter gestured with a single sweep of his hand, up from the man's feet to his head. "This look, this persona . . ."

The man with dark red brush-cut hair shrugged. "Oh, it was the closest thing handy. I'm just borrowing it. Father Gregorio, well, he'll never know what happened."

"He's dead?"

"No, he'll wake up and think he banged his head."

Peter could hear the rushing tempo of his pulse thumping behind his ears, and his hands were beginning to tremble. There was an odd metallic taste in the back of his throat. He didn't want *him* here. Not now. Not ever.

For a time, neither of them spoke. They just stood staring as each other. Finally, Peter cleared his throat.

"All right, what do you want?"

His guest chuckled softly. "You called me."

"I did not." Peter felt surprised.

"You've been feeling very alone lately. You need help. You need me."

"You know, I've tried not to think about you."

The man nodded with great solemnity. "You have tried to forget our last conversation?"

"Yes, I guess I have." Peter put his hand on the back of the executive chair. He stood behind it, as if it were a shield.

The visitor smiled. "But you can't, can you?"

Peter did not answer. He felt a lurching terror building in him, but he didn't really know what scared him more—the entity across the room, or himself.

"That night you killed Daniel," said his visitor with that irritating, uneven, smile. "I still recall it with such pride. One of those crowning moments, really."

"For *you*, you mean," said Peter. "It was *you* that night . . ."

The visitor chuckled again. "Yes, that sounds about right—for you . . . and for this age, in general."

"What do you mean?"

"Ah, Peter, please don't disappoint me. Show me you aren't like all the rest."

"Huh?" said Peter, realizing he sounded dull, yet helpless to do a damned thing about it.

"Why, look around you—victims, everyone! Nobody is ever responsible for *anything* anymore."

The figure took a step closer to him, and the room seemed smaller for it. Peter wanted to back away, but there was no place to go. He was literally backed into a corner.

"Daniel was my best friend. I would have never killed him if . . . if you hadn't . . ." Peter heard his voice trail off, losing steam like a punctured boiler. He sounded incredibly pathetic.

"We both know how it works, Peter. From me, you derive power, power you might otherwise not have, that you might not use in the ways you have."

"Haven't you been paying attention? This power you're talking about—I *haven't* been using it."

"Then you're an idiot. Stumbling around in this dry, dusty cave, looking for little references in the press. What are you working on, Peter, a term paper?" Soft laughter mocked him.

"What do you want? Why are you here?"

"I told you—you need help. You need answers. I have both."

Peter knew he was right, and he knew there was no place else to turn. He exhaled slowly, with resignation.

"That's good, Peter. As the therapists like to say: Give in to your inner child, to the feelings buried the deepest in you."

Peter knew there was no denying it.

"All right! What can you tell me?" he said.

"Well, for starters, I wouldn't worry about getting the rest of the names of the Seven. I can send some of my, ah, colleagues to intercept them."

"*You* can stop them?" Peter couldn't hide the surprise in his voice.

The visitor wagged a finger at him. "Now, now, you know the rules—they have to stop themselves, but my folks might be able to, ah, push them in the right direction, or do something to scare them or trick them. You know, distract them into that fatal mistake."

"You'd do this for me?"

The visitor bowed his head in mock humility, held out his hands like a stage magician accepting his applause. "Well, let's say for *us,* all right?"

"Which means what?"

"Don't you know by now—or are you still in denial?"

Peter frowned, not sure how to respond.

The man held up his index finger, pointing vaguely upward. "You've heard about this business with the sun?"

"The solar prominences? Yes, I've seen some of the stories. Is that you, too?"

"Not exactly. But the scientists are getting pretty smart; a lot smarter than they were a thousand years ago."

"It's all part of a cycle, isn't it?" Peter bit his lower lip, wondering why he was the focus this time.

"You were right when you were thinking that our Adversary is fond of tests. Ever the tinkerer, is my guess."

"So what you're telling me," said Peter, "is that the

sun's going to send out one of those big superflares and—?"

"Well, after Noah, it was promised He wouldn't use water again." The visitor grinned and shrugged. "So, yes, that's our trump card if all goes well, if the world is suddenly rid of its most righteous souls."

"The Seven."

"Ah, good . . . you *have* been paying attention."

"Okay, what else?" Peter stepped out of the corner, the small movement made with great determination.

"You need to be there for the big showdown, Peter. For the shoot out at the O.K. Corral, as it were."

"And where is that?"

Peter stared at him and saw something heave and slouch behind the possessed seminarian's dark green eyes. It chilled him to the core. He might know which side he was on, but the import of that choice . . .

"Well, let's see," his visitor said. "If you had some luck, and maybe another hundred lackeys combing these alcoves, you might find the answer in another week, or in a few minutes, or maybe in fifty years."

"Are you always this irritating?"

"Why, yes, thank you. Giza."

"What's that?"

"Game, set, and match, 'Your Grace.' That's where it all goes down." The green-eyed man smiled with a smugness that made Peter want to smack the expression off his face. "The Great Pyramid. Midnight. In seven days."

"Why are you telling me this?"

The seminarian's body shrugged. "Because I can . . ."

"But it has to be me," said Peter. "I must be the one at Giza."

The visitor nodded. "You *do* know the rules. That's very nice. You understand what must ultimately take place, regardless of your more subtle assaults. You had good ideas, changing things in the Church from the inside out. A good way to subvert the people—the heart spring of that great mechanized juggernaut of faith."

"I was probably working that out subconsciously," said Peter.

"No doubt you were, but that is a long-term investment strategy, and we are short on time."

"So I've got to take the more direct approach," said Peter, who no longer felt so uncomfortable in his visitor's presence. In fact, he suddenly felt better about everything. He didn't think about why. That was probably the source of his recent problems in the first place—he'd clearly been doing way too much thinking.

"Yes," said his visitor. "But before you start packing for Egypt, there is a more pressing issue you're going to have to deal with quite soon—like immediately."

"Really?" said Peter. "What's that?"

The man gestured up over Peter's shoulder, past the circular staircase to the catwalk on the library level. "Well, there's a man in the passage up there, and he's getting ready to kill you."

THIRTY-FOUR

Gaetano—Vatican City
October 30, 2000

*W*hen he heard the guy with syrupy-soft voice give him up like that, Gaetano was momentarily stunned.

All his training, all his controlled rage, all his planning. For that moment, instantly vaporized.

Gone.

And he had no idea what to do next.

After being herded from the bus and into the building that housed the Secret Archives, he and the other seminarians had met with Father Erasmus, who had delivered a short briefing on what the Pope expected of them. It sounded like a good mix between busywork and plain old drudgery, and he was glad he wouldn't be having much to do with it.

Several archivists had then appeared at the door to the cramped room and told everyone to follow them up into the labyrinth of stacks, shelves, alcoves, and repositories. Despite his single-minded urgency, Gaetano could not help but be impressed by the sheer size of the Archives. Endless chambers, all jammed with shelving, snaked in all directions. A man could wander through these spaces for hundreds of years and not come close to plumbing their secrets.

The place stirred his imagination, and he couldn't help wondering what mysteries and revelations lay buried amid those millions of pages. He pushed the thought from his mind as his guide, an archivist named Father Paul, who wore the brown habit of the Franciscans, led him through the Tower of Winds and into what had been the Borghese Apartments.

"The Holy Father has taken a special room here," Father Paul had said with fearful enthusiasm as they passed a carved oaken door. "He is here now, working shoulder to shoulder with the rest of us."

"He's right there?" Gaetano had asked. "Right behind that door?"

"Yes," said the archivist. "Let us be quiet and not disturb his most important work. If you are fortunate, you may see him, or even greet him."

Hey, I'm excited, he'd thought. And, yeah, I have a greeting for him, all right . . .

Gaetano and the other newcomers were given a short tour of their working areas and assigned tables, then shown specific shelves through which to begin combing. His station was a long, gleamingly polished reference room table punctuated by green-glass-shaded banker's lamps. No one had commented on the small athletic bag he was carrying, and that surprised him. He had expected it to be thoroughly searched, but either the Swiss Guards had been tipped by Egon Leutmann to leave him alone, or no one suspected any trouble from a bunch of nebbishy Jesuits.

It didn't really matter, he thought, as he sat down to

his table and slid the nylon bag under his chair. As the remainder of his busmates scattered throughout the wing, he bent down and unzipped the bag. Inside were gray sweatpants and a matching pullover shirt, a white towel, and a pair of heavy-soled, hi-tech basketball shoes.

The bag had no secret compartments, no false bottom, and the contents appeared to be totally innocuous to both the casual observer and someone looking for trouble.

But it contained trouble, nonetheless.

Gaetano picked up the left basketball shoe, held it upside down, and pressed a particular spot on the tread. With downward pressure and a rotation of his wrist, the thick rubber sole axled away to reveal an array of small porcelain and plastic components sunk into cutouts in the bottom of the shoe. He repeated the procedure with the right shoe, then began assembling his Glock 9mm semiautomatic.

No metal parts, no electromagnetic detection.

Nice.

The final piece clicked into place with perfectly fitting precision. He slipped the milky-white weapon inside his loose-fitting cassock and rose to find the lavatory. Once inside the washroom, he locked himself into the stall farthest from the door, then carefully and soundlessly removed the lid from the water tank. Attached by duct tape to the inside of the lid were two thirteen-round clips for the Glock.

D'Agostino was as good as his word.

Gaetano didn't question how the ammo reached its promised location; he simply clicked one clip into the white gun's handle, and remanded the other to his left pocket.

What did they always say in the movies?, he thought to himself with a smile—*lock and load!*

Indeed.

*   *   *

After about an hour of pretend research on an illuminated manuscript from a ninth-century Saxon monastery, Gaetano felt comfortable enough to make his move. The archives were totally silent, save for the occasional whisper of vellum being paged or a volume thumped shut. He could feel the entire building breathing, a subtle susurration that suggested the activity hived within it. Everyone around him seemed consumed by work, and not one person noticed his absence from his table.

Relying on his memorization of digitized schematics of the Archives, he moved smoothly through the corridor to the rooms where Peter Carenza would be found.

The hall remained deserted as he tried the heavy brass knob on the thick oaken door. No one saw him momentarily tense as he realized it was locked. Quickly, he retrieved from one pocket a thin-handled tool that might have been lifted from a dentist's palette. Its business end was covered by a rubber thimble-like sheath, which Gaetano peeled off and held in his left hand. With his right, he inserted the heat-hardened tool into the heavy lock. Feeling the tumblers by extension, he deftly flicked and twisted the point of the tool, then grasped the knob firmly and turned it.

The lock surrendered without a struggle, and he slipped unheard and unseen into the empty room adjacent to the Pope's office. He soundlessly negotiated the furniture in the room and ascended the spiral staircase with total stealth.

When he'd reached the catwalk, he dropped to all fours and began to inch his way along the pass-through, hearing more and more clearly the voices of two men in conversation. It soon became apparent Peter was discussing his intentions with someone of great influence and power.

Gaetano had paused to free his weapon, holding its grip in his hand with of combination of respect and relief.

The man speaking to Peter had a voice so soft it seemed to flow, but with the force of something irresistible, like lava. The man spoke with total control and immense confidence. Gaetano recognized that quality, having heard it in a very few men. It was eerie, and it scared him in a way that few things ever had.

Something weird was going on, but he didn't have time to find out what it was. Gaetano knew he must act without thinking.

The interconnecting hall was less than six feet long and he'd traversed it in complete silence. From the sound of Peter's voice, the Pope had to be standing almost directly below Gaetano, in front of a spiral stairway identical to the one in the adjoining room.

Another few inches and Gaetano would be in position.

Advance and fire, then disappear into the woodwork. Then the man with the voice had betrayed him.

Don't stop!

The thought stung him like acid in his face. No time to hesitate or to consider options.

Springing up, Gaetano surged forward to the railing and the steps of the staircase. He extended his weapon, aiming it over the rail and down. Peter was right below.

Gaetano recorded everything in a blur of motion and color. A man wearing the black robes of a priest was leaping up and over a library table toward Peter.

Just as Gaetano squeezed the trigger and the semiautomatic began stitching the area with HV slugs, the red-haired priest slammed into Peter, chest high like a linebacker meeting a back at the goal line. Carenza impacted with the back wall under the circular stairs, avoiding the cataract of bullets that ripped through the priest's outstretched body.

The volley of shots had attracted a lot of attention, and the door to the chamber burst open to allow an inward flood of black robes and plainclothes guards.

Exhausting the entire clip, Gaetano pulled back from the railing as the plainclothesmen pulled out their Sig-Sauers and aimed at him. Their shots exploded into the thick molding of the threshold as he threw himself down the short passage to the other room. Half sliding on the polished wood floor, he gained his feet like a hockey player sliding across the blue line and vaulted the railing by the stairs in one athletic motion.

The drop to the library table was not as drastic as it appeared, and his legs and knees effortlessly absorbed the impact. Jumping down, he replaced the spent clip with a fresh one as he reached the door—simultaneously with someone on its other side. Pushing it open with his shoulder, Gaetano made a security guard pay for his savvy anticipation by launching him across the corridor and into the opposite wall. Before the man could recover from the collision, Gaetano spun and kicked him under the chin, dislocating his jaw and knocking him cold.

Before the slumping guard even reached the floor, Gaetano was running full speed down the corridor of the east wing. A single window at the end of the hall was his only possibility of escape, even though it was three stories to the gardens below. A solitary square of sunlight, framed by ornate purple and gold draperies, the window grew larger until it was only object in his field of vision.

Escape was his only option now. He knew he would have no more chances to reach Peter.

Behind him, he heard the clatter of boots and hard-soled shoes, and his training kicked in automatically, sending him into a headlong dive. As he slid along the polished tiles on his belly, a volley of shots buzzed over-heard like deadly bees and shattered the glass panes of the window. He rolled to a stop beneath the sill and fired off a quick burst, which scattered his pursuers, giving him just enough time to rise and exit through the window.

A second burst of slugs ripped through the wooden frame just as he cleared it, landing on a decorative ledge only several feet below the window. As his feet touched the solid, flat surface, Gaetano silently thanked the ar-chitect for being so obediently retro in his school of design.

Steadying himself on the narrow ledge, he moved quickly to the left of the fractured window, getting out of the line of fire and also giving him the few seconds needed to discern his best escape venue. Looking down, the height of thirty feet was daunting but not lethal—as long as he found something to slow his de-scent.

Another fusillade of bullets ripped through the rem-nants of glass and frame, inches from his head, but he ignored it. Stay focused, he thought calmly. Scanning the area below he noted no unusual activity. No one had yet noticed him up there, but that wouldn't last long. Directly below him ran a stone-slab walkway, flanked by high, thick, expertly manicured hedges. To the left, the path led to a courtyard, to the right a di-agonal through the bright colors of the Vatican Gar-dens.

The entrance to this section of the gardens was

marked by a large rose trellis in the shape of a classic Roman arch.

A clatter of footsteps and the shouts of angry men just inside the window caused him to turn and fire. The first man who leaned out the window stopped a slug with the side of his head, which erupted like an overripe melon. As he tumbled downward, his colleagues paused in shock, and Gaetano seized the moment to act.

He pushed off the ledge and the outer wall of the building towards the huge trellis below. There had been no time to worry about the consequences. He tucked himself into a cannonball position and hoped he'd calculated enough arc into his plunge. The red and white splash of the rose trellis expanded until it filled his vision, then he bull's-eyed into its verdant center.

The latticework of wood splintered with a loud crackling explosion, and a thousand thorns slashed into him like scalpels, shredding his black cassock and ribboning his flesh. The middle of the wood and vine arch collapsed, sagging inward so that the entire trellis cupped him like a pair of hands and placed him on the earth with an unexpectedly gentle touch.

Gaetano only needed to thrash his way free of the razorlike thorns and splintered wood. No easy task, that, but it beat hell out of the alternatives.

As he worked his way free, the air began to fill with sounds of panic, outrage, shock, and retribution. Sirens, gunshots, screeching tires, people screaming—all good sounds to him.

It meant a lack of a plan to handle a loose cannon like himself.

By twisting and rolling, tucking and turning, he extricated himself from the thorny prison in fewer than ten seconds, just about the time it took for the gunmen at the third floor window to reorient themselves and resume firing. Ducking through the nearest hedgerow, he escaped the latest volley and emerged on the other side, engulfed by an ocean of hydrangeas. He rolled through the pungently sweet blossoms and came up running.

As his legs pistoned furiously through the gardens, he realized that his cassock had literally been shredded into long, black tatters and strips. His legs and arms poked through, streaked with crimson. What a fucking mess!

Where the hell was he going to go, looking like he'd narrowly escaped a close encounter with a wood chipper?

He ran parallel to the hedgerow, staying with the cover of the flower and shrubbery bed whenever possible. Incredibly, no one had yet spotted him, but that would change in a hurry. As soon as he reached the access road and the parking lots, they'd have to be blind to not spot him.

But he didn't have much choice.

Crouching low, he moved quickly through the greenery, gasping for breath, fighting a cramp in his side. A couple of substantial cuts across his forehead kept streaming blood into his eyes, and it was an effort to see clearly. Sirens and klaxons filled the air.

Goddamn, he'd made a complete botch of things!

But it wasn't his fault. Somehow, the other guy in the room had *known* he was there!

And that couldn't be possible—unless somebody gave him up, unless he'd been some kind of pawn all along. But *why?*

None of it made any sense.

Gaetano scanned the terrain ahead; he was fast running out of landscaping to use as cover. His best chance would be to find a car on the access road, yank the driver, and hijack the vehicle. He hated the idea, but it might be the only way to survive this mess.

He cleared the hedges and scanned the roadway.

The scream of tires on asphalt made him jerk his head in the opposite direction. A black Mercedes SUV, windows opaqued, was power sliding around the far corner. Gaetano watched all four tires churning as it leaped forward like a sleek jungle cat.

Straight at him.

Veering off at the last instant and hitting the brakes, the four-wheeler lurched to a halt in front of him. The smoked glass window powered down to reveal D'Agostino behind the wheel.

"Get in! Hurry!"

Gaetano exhaled in relief, grabbed the handle, and ripped open the passenger-side door.

He was smiling as he vaulted into the cab and pulled the door shut behind him. But then he noticed the Colt semiautomatic in D'Agostino's right hand.

It was pointed at the small region between Gaetano's eyes.

ThirTy-Five

Peter Carenza—Vatican City
October 30, 2000

Chaos churned all around him, but he seemed oddly insulated from the screaming and all the running around.

Peter knelt over the body of the priest with the odd smile and the dark red hair, a body so brimming with malevolence that he could almost feel its radiation upon his flesh. Dark green eyes bored into him. The body was alive, but only barely, and Peter could sense an urgency in the presence that inhabited it.

"Why did you do that?" Peter asked, cradling the man's head.

The barest suggestion of a shrug. The man spoke with immense effort. "The rules. No direct intervention. All choices . . . all actions . . . must be . . . through human . . . form."

"Who was that?"

"Gotta go . . . now."

"Wait!"

"Can't. Can't . . . be trapped in here . . ."

"No, wait! What about Giza?" Even as he spoke, Peter could see the light behind the green eyes suddenly blink out. A chill passed through him as the entity departed, and the priest's body sagged.

Without thinking about it, Peter placed his hands over the yawning chest wounds. Warmth built beneath his palms. Ozone tinctured the air with its distinctive scent, and a faint blue aura surrounded his hands. As though a disconnected third party, Peter watched the azure light begin to flow out of his palms and into the chest wounds, crackling with vital energy.

For an instant Peter was engulfed by vertigo. The sensation of being sucked into a terrible vortex of infinite darkness was overwhelming. He resisted the urge to pull away, to protect himself.

He was touching the stuff of death itself—the ultimate entropy of all things. The absence of existence yawned before him, and he imagined it beckoning to him like a seductive woman. He nodded, mostly to himself, in recognition of the innate appeal of the consummate void.

How effortless it would be to become part of it.

Peter opened his eyes, not realizing he'd closed them. When he looked down at the priest's lethal wounds, he was surprised to see they hadn't begun to disappear, to heal. The savaged flesh had not smoothed out, and the cyanotic color in the man's face had begun to darken.

He removed his hands. The aura faded, and Peter watched the priest's eyelids flicker and then close.

They would never open again.

A chill raced through Peter as he realized what had happened . . . or rather, what had not.

His gift of life and healing had been far too . . . Godly . . . to withstand his latest round of self-revelations. This idea struck him amidships like a torpedo up the gut.

Peter looked down at the dead man; earlier in his life he might have wept at his failure to save the priest. Now, at this moment in the spinning universe, he regarded the man with a coldness that scared him.

The moment passed, and suddenly there were people filing into the room, everyone talking at once, crowding around. The Swiss Guard pushed through the throng, trying to get to him. They formed a protective ring, and Peter had to tell them over and over that he was unharmed.

He asked some of the onlookers to do something about the dead man beside him, hoping that no one would wonder why he had not helped the man in the most miraculous of fashions.

Plainclothesmen and uniformed officers arrived, attended to the body, and helped Peter out of the room. Only then did he truly realize that someone had tried to kill him. Amazingly, the notion held no terror for him.

Indeed, there was a certain appeal he could not yet articulate. With a small, wry grin, he looked at the senior agent. "Did you get him?"

"He was like the wind," said the man.

Peter frowned. "I'll take that as a no."

THIRTY-SIX

Marion Windsor—Cairo
October 30, 2000

*A*ll around them, the SkyFreight handlers heaved packages on and off the conveyors like worker ants. No one seemed to notice the three people trying to get away from the two men in the bedouin garb. Or if they did, they obviously didn't care.

"Stop!" said a familiar voice.

Marion looked more closely at the taller man as he walked directly toward her. It was Father Francesco, and the object he'd produced from his long linen duster was not a gun but a manila envelope.

Before she could say anything, Cardinal Lareggia had begun lumbering toward him with his arms extended. "Giovanni! It *is* you! I thought I recognized you, even from way back there."

Francesco smiled his vulpine smile and hugged the large Cardinal briefly and perfunctorily.

"So, you made it! You are safe," said Lareggia.

"Yes, with a little help from some friends," said Francesco, looking at his colleague's coveralls with obvious mirth. "This is quite a change from your usual ensemble."

The Cardinal flushed with equal parts anger and embarrassment as Francesco gestured toward his partner. "Etienne, Ms. Windsor, this is Brother Sforza. He is with the Order of the Knights of Malta." The shorter man stood by with a stolid expression. He looked like a marine drill instructor with a lantern jaw and birdshot eyes. His frame was muscularly compact and he looked like he was in great shape for someone no longer in his forties.

Greetings were exchanged as the activity of the freight hangar buzzed all around them. Despite their ages, the two men had presented a dashing, adventurous image, and their confidence was infectious.

"How did you catch up with us?" asked Lareggia.

"We tracked you through the SSV. Our facilities are top-notch," said Francesco. "What's this been all about?"

"It is part of God's plan," said Etienne.

"But it will take some explaining," added Marion, looking around the busy hangar. "This is probably not the best place."

"Of course not," said Brother Sforza. His voice contained the inflection of one accustomed to giving orders. "We have made arrangements for you to be sequestered in Cairo. Not against your will, of course, but you must realize that Peter Carenza's people are looking for you."

"Oh, yes," said Marion.

"We also want you to know about this man," said Francesco, handing Marion the manila envelope. "His name is Gaetano. He is working with us—to assassinate Peter."

Marion was opening the envelope when he said those last two words, and despite how she felt about

Peter and what he'd become, she still felt her entire body seize up for an instant. The idea that someone would want to kill Peter was shocking, but to think of him as *dead* was hard to imagine.

"Assassinate him? " said Lareggia, his voice colored by shock.

Marion pulled a black-and-white photo from the envelope. It depicted a man in his thirties with dark hair and deep-set, intensely dark eyes. He had a strong jawline and nose—handsome in a rugged, unassuming kind of way. He looked oddly familiar; she had the eerie feeling she'd seen him before.

"He is Targeno's brother," said Francisco.

So much for familiarity, thought Marion. She looked at Etienne, who had said nothing. If the idea of someone killing her son disturbed her in the least, she revealed it not at all. In that respect she was no less resolute in her faith than the biblical Abraham, who'd been ready to sacrifice his son at God's command. But, she thought wryly, that's probably the way you were supposed to act when you got a direct line from God.

"I hope he serves the Church as well as his brother did," said Lareggia.

"Are we meeting up with this man?" said Marion.

Sforza shook his head. "It is not part of the current scenario, but one never knows in this business. I just wanted you to be aware of his presence in the equation. Should you encounter him, you will know he is on our side."

"You are certain of this?" said Lareggia.

"We feel confident, Paolo," said Francesco. "But he is being watched by other operatives."

"His most attractive feature is that he is totally unknown in the spook business," said Sforza.

"Completely invisible," said Francesco.

"Where is he now?" asked Marion.

Sforza said, "He is inside the Secret Archives as we speak. We should know more very soon. But for now, we would like to get you to a safe house and some more suitable clothing."

The Cardinal stretched his arms in the tight coveralls. "That sounds like a splendid idea. I can't wait to get out of this thing!"

Everyone chuckled as they followed Brother Sforza to a side door in the hangar, which opened onto a narrow alley between the buildings. A Mercedes sat silently in wait, and everyone climbed inside. After Sforza guided the vehicle free of the hangar area, he began to operate various unrecognizable pieces of electronics that had been wired into the dashboard and center console. Marion assumed the gear was some sort of antisurveillance package but did not ask.

Apparently satisfied with the data on the instruments, Sforza pressed the accelerator, and everyone sank a little deeper into the leather seats. When the sleek sedan had slipped onto the airport road, heading toward the center of Cairo, Sforza looked back at his passengers. "Where will you be going from here?"

"Giza," said Etienne. "The Great Pyramid."

The Maltese Knight grinned. "Impressive. When?"

"When the Seven Keys are here."

Before Marion could begin the tale, she was interrupted by the electronic chirp of a sat-phone. Sforza pulled it from his breast pocket and flipped it open. The conversation was brief. When finished, Sforza said, to no one in particular, "We have trouble."

THIRTY-SEVEN

The Seven

CHARLES GREEN

The drive from Gatwick Airport was not as bad as he'd expected, since he'd rented a Taurus with an automatic transmission—and so what if the steering wheel was on the wrong side of the car! Charlie smiled to himself as he drove down a two-lane road toward the town of Glastonbury on the "wrong" side of the highway.

Actually, he wasn't having a tough time driving, and he wondered if his dyslexia had anything to do with it.

He'd always seen the world differently and had to adjust to what other people called the real world. Still, he knew that just about everybody else was wrong and he was right.

Other than Joan, nobody thought it was a good idea for him to go on his mission to England. The guys at work, his friends in town, the reporters, the whole bunch of them. Nobody except the general authorities of the Church of Latter-day Saints. When Charlie had told his story to them at his temple, and they found out he might have had contact with a spirit or a holy apparition, they had encouraged him to investigate it as thoroughly as possible. Charlie's reputation as a devout and righteous man instilled confidence in his Mormon elders—so much so that they had funded his journey.

A road sign flashed by telling him he'd closed the distance to Glastonbury to only three more kilometers. Good thing, too. The jet lag from the overnight flight had finally caught him by the short hairs. He was exhausted and hungry and despite what he'd always heard about British food, he planned to consume mass quantities of it, no matter where or what it was.

He probably should have gotten some sleep after the flight, but the thought of putting off the greatest day of his life was unthinkable—even though he kept denying a really annoying feeling that he wasn't going to make it back from this adventure.

The notion simply would not leave him, regardless of whatever prayer he whispered. It upset him to think that God's price for his service and devotion might be that he would never see his wife again.

Not that that would change his decision or his devotion to his God. No sir, Charlie Green wasn't that kind of guy. No, the lady in his dreams had told him he was a key to unlock one of the Seven Churches, and Charlie knew his Bible well enough to know what *that* reference was all about. And frankly, the idea of maybe being alive for the Rapture excited him.

The town of Glastonbury came into view. First several scattered houses, a bed-and-breakfast or two, and some red phone boxes, then, abruptly, the main intersection, an off-center plot of grass held together by a traffic curb, with a small concrete obelisk in its center.

Glastonbury was clearly not the urban presence Charlie had imagined from the travel guide descriptions he'd read on the plane.

Charlie motored slowly past the tiny roundabout and looked for a place to leave the car. There were spaces all over the street, and the pedestrians paid him not the slightest attention. After parking, he stood outside the vehicle and noticed a newspaper rack for the *Globe*. The headline was about the sun becoming unstable. Well, if it is, he thought, maybe that has something to do with this job God picked out for him.

The end of the world as we know it . . .

Wouldn't that be something? he mused as he stretched his back. Well, that was okay with Charlie. He'd been living all his life for that moment when he would meet God.

But right now, his back was killing him. Even though he drove for a living, he'd never gotten used to sitting in one position for extended periods of time. Best thing to do would be to start walking, get all the kinks out. He caught a glimpse of himself in the window of a roadside shop and decided he could pass for a Brit just as well as a Yank. Dressed in khakis, turtleneck, and a poplin jacket, he looked like any other fifty-year-old guy out for a walk on a balmy day.

With a vague map in his head from the travel books, he oriented himself toward the Glastonbury Abbey and had no trouble locating its imposing bulk, the thick walls standing defiantly, although the roof was gone and the floor was overgrown with grass. Charlie could see three distinct layers of stone in the walls, each one more sophisticated in its masonry, each like a geologic layer of time.

For an instant, Charlie felt dizzy. The absolute oldness of the place embraced him like a long-lost relative. Something began to pulse in the center of his soul, like a metal detector or a Geiger counter. He was both repelled and attracted by the sensation.

Psychically sensitive people, he thought, had been right about Glastonbury. It was a special place, a holy place. You could just feel it. As he continued to walk through the ruins of the abbey, he remembered seeing in one of the books that some New Testament scholars believed that Joseph of Arimathea had crossed the Channel in a Roman galley with Jesus when he was just a boy. Now Charlie knew it had happened. Perhaps along this very path the young Christ had walked.

The Dream Lady had told him he would know the Church when he came upon it, and the Church would likewise know him. And Charlie was not so naive to think he needed to find an *actual* church—especially since *Revelation* was known to be heavily tilted toward excessive metaphor. He paused to read a plaque at his feet, which suggested that he stood over the graves of Arthur and Guinevere, and told a brief tale of bones discovered by monks and later scattered by a vengeful Henry.

Continuing to walk, he eventually found himself in a garden on the opposite end of the abbey grounds. Although the abbey held him with its special, ancient grace, he knew this was not the place that sought him.

As he returned to his car, he thought about Arthur's grave and the legends of that great king. It was believed that Glastonbury itself marked the original location of Annwn, which was the entrance to the Underworld. Could that be the church he sought?

Charlie grinned to himself as he keyed the engine to the sturdy Taurus. If Annwn was his destination, he was in trouble—it wasn't marked on any tour guide maps.

But another place was, a place called Avalon.

As he sat there on the side of the road, he picked up

one of the guidebooks from his L.L.Bean carry-all and thumbed to the page with the proper roadmap. Working on a feeling, not unlike those first tentative impressions he'd had of poor Scott Raney lying all busted up in that well, Charlie selected the route to his next stop. He maneuvered the sedan down a narrow side street out of town to a section of rolling meadows partitioned by hedgerows, and parked on the verge.

A short walk through the hedges opened up on a pristine valley, goldened by the sun, with a mound in its center that looked like a volcanic peak in miniature, no more than several hundred feet high. Sheep grazed on its steep slopes, and a path spiraled around it, all the way to a small tower at the top.

Some historians speculated that this place might have been the Avalon of legend, with the little tower at the top of the hill being the Tor of Merlin. The closer Charlie ambled toward the conelike mound, the more certain he became that the historians had been correct. He had the feeling of walking ever closer to an immense electric generator. His skin seemed to be tingling. One of the books he'd found on Glastonbury had mentioned what the mystics called "sacred geometry." A visionary, Alfred Watkins, had theorized that all the holy places on earth were connected by invisible lines of forces beneath the earth. He called them "ley lines"; the Chinese had called them the "path of the dragon," and other cultures had bestowed equally dramatic and mysterious names.

But Charlie knew it all meant the same thing, led to the same conclusions. Geomancy. There was power in the earth.

And it was there because God put it there.

As he ascended the spiral path, the details of the Tor became more distinct. The galvanic, skin-tingling sensation increased so much that he could almost hear a humming sound in the air. Sunlight cast everything in warm tones. Charlie felt totally at peace.

The grazing sheep had also been working their way up the hill, and their shepherd, a young man wearing a white cable sweater and a matching tam-o'-shanter, half jogged up the slope toward them, calling them downslope and waving his staff. The animals largely ignored him as they continued to nibble the grass.

Charlie reached the base of the Tor. It was open on all four sides and looked very much like a two-story giant chess piece. Suddenly he *knew* he must stand in the exact center of the Tor.

Just like a key in a lock . . .

The notion seemed so right that he found himself smiling as he took the final steps to the top of the mound. Below, the countryside surrounded this place in a great circle. That might have been the bed of a long evaporated lake.

"That's going to do it, mate," said a voice from behind him.

"What?"

Turning slowly, just several feet from the Tor, Charlie saw the white-sweatered shepherd. Large yellow teeth were the most prominent feature of his thin, raw-boned face. The man was pointing a pistol at Charlie. It had a silencer screwed into its barrel.

So this is what God had writ for him? thought Charlie the instant he saw the gun. The moment everyone wonders about, the moment of exactly *how* he would die, was suddenly and harshly revealed to him. For some reason God had wanted it this way. Charlie smiled and nodded. That was fine with him. He would have to wait only a little while to see Joan again.

Charlie looked benignly at his assailant. He felt a hideous burning in his stomach and realized that the silent weapon had spat a big slug into his midsection.

Like napalm, the pain enveloped him. His knees disappeared and as he began to collapse, he felt the man place the warm snout of the weapon against his forehead—

Huang Xiao

It seemed as if he'd been falling through the darkness of the night for most of his life. When the Lady in the glowing light spoke to him, all time and motion just went away, and Xiao stopped thinking while he listened.

God had selected him to go to the Holy City of Lhasa!

After an unknown time, the Lady had faded into the night, and suddenly Xiao was aware of his stomach-ripping fall into blackness. Terror rushed in to fill him like an empty pot, but he hardly had time to think of how scared he should be—he'd just landed in something thick but yielding.

Like taffy, the substance surrounded him, cushioning his weight, absorbing his gathered velocity. Xiao could feel the cool surge of thick mud trying to swallow him whole. He began thrashing and kicking, hoping to touch something solid as the rank putrescence of the bog fell over him like a heavy tarp. Panic sparked erratically through him as he arched his neck back to keep his nose and mouth from sinking into the foulness of the swamp. How ironic that the very thing that had saved him could now destroy him.

Just as the ooze lapped at the corners of his mouth, his foot thumped on something solid, deep in the thick mire. A buried stump, a rock, it didn't matter—it gave him a respite, a place to pause and collect himself. Far away, he could hear the faint rattle of the departing

freight train. Ambient starlight provided him his only
illumination, but it was enough to see that he foundered
at the edge of a quagmire. A little more vigorous kicking and struggling should quickly get him to firmer
ground.

Soon he lay on harder earth gulping grateful breaths
and trying to collect himself.

Incredible had been his first thought, until he realized
he'd been brushed by the hand of God. Then he remembered his original reason for flight, but he knew
in his heart that warning a single city district of an
earthquake was far less important than his responsibility to the entire planet. Without the Lady in the Light
ever really saying anything specific, Xiao knew that this
all had something to do with the superflares on the sun.
His talent for sensing oncoming danger in the earth had
a corollary in space as well.

Something was coming for the world.

He was not yet certain whether it might be good or
bad, but he knew he was inextricably connected to it.

But Lhasa! How would he ever get to such a place?
And what to do when he arrived? And what about the
people's agents of justice? Their efforts to find him
would surely be redoubled when they learned of his
escape from the train.

This last thought made Xiao smile as he imagined
how angry the district bosses would be. It was not a
good thing to lose face to a peasant boy. Orienting himself against the stars, he began walking toward Yungchi.

The trek lasted three days, and he found it strange that
he encountered no resistance, that no one appeared to
be looking for him. Regardless, he kept to the sides of
the roads, leaping into undergrowth and ditches to
avoid being seen by anyone passing by. He traveled by

cover of night and rested during the day, stealing food and clean clothes from cooperatives, distribution centers, and the occasional semifree enterprise market.

In Yungchi, he spent several days hanging around the warehouses and truck depots, listening and saying nothing, waiting to hear of a shipment to Kangting or beyond, into the Thanglha Mountain district. Not many trucks went there, so he had to be patient as well as invisible. He slipped in and out of shadows, fed himself by stealth, and was ever watchful. Xiao carefully studied the day-to-day routines of the shippers, drivers, expediters. Even from his clandestine locations, he was able to deduce much of how procedures were carried out, schedules adhered to, people supervised.

Maybe because of such patience and cunning, Xiao was rewarded so well. Or perhaps it was the face of God smiling in his direction? He wished to believe it to be a serendipitous combination. The truck in which he had sequestered himself during the midday meal break now rattled and bumped along poorly maintained roads. It was filled with crates of replacement parts for small gasoline engines and bound for a string of border towns in the foothills of the Himalayas, adjacent to Nepal. The trip lasted for two days of long, arduous travel, sunk in the darkness of the cargo cabin with nothing but a stolen blanket to insulate him during the cold nights. By the time the truck reached a warehouse in Tsangpo, Xiao felt as though he'd been held at a government information facility for interrogation. He had bounced around so much that his rear end and knees had become one large bruise.

But that evening, after the driver quit his rig for a few drinks at the local entertainment center, Xiao forced himself to move with speed and silence. He slipped into the back streets and crosscutting alleys, always moving south, closer to the border.

He glided through shadows and pools of light like a thief, and no one paid him a second glance, or often even a first one. But he had to be careful to not be overconfident; the sin of pride brings down the best. Better to treat every moment as if he were being pursued. Vigilance would keep him free.

In recent years, he knew, the patrols along the Nepalese border had become less frequent and less fanatical, and he found it almost ridiculously easy to creep through a starlit meadow into the land of the Dalai Lama. He walked through the remainder of the night, without food, without rest, always ascending. Close to his target, he'd become fueled by the power of his faith, his belief in the righteousness of his mission.

Although he was technically safe beyond his homeland's borders, he knew his government would ignore international protocol with impunity to get what they wanted. He planned to walk until dawn, then rest during daylight, but now realized how close he'd come to his quarry.

The Lhasa gates soared up from beyond a distant rise on the road, twin towers where sentries have stood for centuries. Even in the pale light of the firmament, they gleamed like bleaching bones. When he crossed beneath the pillars, he could feel the oldness of the place, the timeless presence of thousands of lives trafficked through narrow alleys and wide boulevards.

In the predawn, the streets lay practically empty, other than robed and coveralled workers who cleaned the gutters and sidewalks, and the earliest of the merchants who opened the outdoor markets and street-corner vendors' stalls. Xiao's heart had begun to pound as he neared his goal. He felt himself smiling, not in any kind of smug victory, but with the simple joy of accomplishment.

The temples and monasteries of Lhasa occupied the

high ground in its geometric center, reached by a series of staircases cut into the stone. As the sun fired the tips of their tallest spires, Xiao began his ascent, knowing that the final stop of his journey lay close at hand. Somewhere up there, within the maze of ancient buildings, a sacred place awaited his presence. He knew that was all that was required—to place the key within the chamber.

The steps passed many terraces, gardens, and doors into lower buildings, and as he passed a door painted bright red, a monk in orange robes emerged.

"You are from our neighbor's house," said the monk. "We have been expecting you."

Bowing, Xiao averted his eyes from the holy man. "I mean you no harm."

"This we know," said the monk. "You have a holiness about you. No one will stop you."

"Do you know about my . . . mission?"

"Every one has a mission. The tragedy is that some never discover what it is."

Xiao nodded and looked upward.

The monk touched his shoulder, saying, "I will accompany you."

Together they climbed the final distance, walking silently, as if following a secret homing beacon, to a small garden enclosed by a circle of ornate columns. The sun seemed to collect here like molten gold, pooling and flowing over the stones, warming them with a special magic.

Xiao looked from the columns to the monk, who nodded with great deference and smiled. "Yes," he said, "it is so."

Xiao moved slowly, but with confidence. His limbs felt feathery and light, as though supported by the hands of angels. Each step was so effortless he believed he could be floating. Never had he experienced such a feeling of surrender, of total serenity. If this is what it was like to be eternally within the presence of the Creator, then he would welcome his death, whenever it might come.

As he passed within the circle of columns, he felt the hands of God upon him. Entering the Church of Saint John's *Revelation,* the seal was opened.

So clean.

Simple.

And for an instant, as in a glimpse through a briefly open door, he saw the future of the world unrolling like an endless carpet. And it was a good thing; he sensed no terrible outcomes, no damnation. Was it his imagination, or did the sun seem to be burning a little more steadily? Xiao smiled as he gazed at the sky. His task had been to help initiate a new beginning, not an end.

When he stepped from the columns, he knew that the Lady in the Light still needed him. His journey was not at an end. He must go to her, because she needed his strength and because he now bore the mark of God's hand upon his spirit, like a beacon of light cutting an unstoppable swath through the darkness. He saw a long pathway twisting away from the place where he now stood, and he saw where he must now go. All of these things he knew as if they'd always been a part of him.

Bowing to the monk who had been watching him on bended knee, Xiao walked slowly toward the stairs, already beginning to calculate how far and how long it might take him reach the banks of the Nile.

CARLOS ACCARDI

Why had all this happened to him?

Carlos had asked himself this question over and over

since the day he'd leaped off his bridge, and he'd received no answer until last night. The Lady in the Light had appeared to him again and told him he must enter Akapana, the Fortress Tomb of the Gods.

He'd never even *heard* of Akapana, but somehow he knew immediately where it was. Bolivia. The mountain jungles of the Andes, the oldest city in the world . . .

Tiajuanaco.

He sat in the jumpseat of the chartered Sikorsky as it twin-rotored northwest from Buenos Aires at three-hundred miles per hour. When he informed his bosses that he would need a short leave of absence, they not only complied but obtained a pilot and chopper and arranged for visas and clearances, to make his trip as easy as possible.

This was the way a grateful people treated its heroes. And there was no way Carlos could turn away from such kindness, even if he so desired.

The flight lasted almost five hours, and as they homed in on the coordinates of the ruins, Carlos felt the bottom falling out of his stomach. He knew he stood at the edge of something vast and incomprehensible. Something of frightening power, able to produce either unexpected ecstasy or extraordinary confusion.

Whatever it was, Carlos would rely on his faith as his compass. With God at his shoulder, he believed all things were possible, and he would fear nothing.

"I'm going to drop her down to thirteen thousand feet," said his pilot, a short stocky man named Coco Barboza, who'd been flying with the company for the twenty years.

"How much farther?" said Carlos.

"Any time now. The coordinates are just about on the money. Now we have to make a visual."

Carlos nodded. Tiajuanaco lay buried in the thick vegetation that had been slowly reclaiming its grandeur for more than fifteen thousand years, if you believed the archaeologist H. S. Bellamy, whom Carlos had discovered to be the undisputed authority on the ruins. No one claimed to know the exact date of the city's birth, or the name of the people who built it, but everyone seemed to agree with Bellamy that the technology needed to construct Akapana had become lost to the world for another ten thousand years.

Even though Coco had slowed the chopper's speed to one hundred miles per hour, spotting the ruins would not be easy. The jungle devoured the city stone by massive stone, and Carlos alternated between using Zeiss fieldglasses and the naked eye to scan the scrolling terrain. Without any beacons or landmarks to signal their approach to the target area, Carlos knew there would be as much luck as skill in finding it.

"We should be right over it!" yelled Barboza.

Carlos scanned the dense green barrier below them, punctuated by the occasional outcropping or volcanic mesa. Suddenly black spots danced and whirled before his eyes and he felt feverish. His hands began to tremble, and he felt as if he might pass out. The site was close at hand. He could feel it reaching out to him. Perhaps there was a beacon, after all.

"It's down there," he said, nudging his pilot. "Close. I can feel it!"

Barboza looked at him with surprise. "*Señor*, are you all right? You look terrible!"

Carlos nodded, then slid back the Plexiglas side panel. As the slipstream screamed into the can, he leaned out, as far as the seat belt would allow, and puked. As the long, bilious stream trailed downward, he began to feel better.

His eyes were watering, and as he blinked to clear

them, he saw the blazing white stones of the city, poking free of the greenery like the ribs of a carcass drying in the sun.

Pointing and shouting, Carlos trained his binoculars on the location and felt a spike of adrenaline notch up all his senses. As the Sikorksy angled down, Carlos registered more and more detail of the ruins. Wide boulevards, multitiered levels of roofless structures that could have been shops or stables or apartmentlike housing.

"Can you believe it?" said Carlos loudly. His nausea had passed, absorbed by the sheer joy of discovery.

"I have never seen anything like it, *Señor*. It is beautiful!"

"Look! Look how big it is!" Where did they come from? The people who conceived of such a place hidden in the middle of the densest of jungles. Where did they get all those fantastic white blocks of stone? And how did they transport them here?

"Do you know where you want to set this thing down?" Barboza yelled over the *whumping* of the blades.

"Not really. I am looking for Akapana—it is called the Tomb of the Gods."

"What does it look like?"

"I don't know, but I have a feeling I will know it when I see it."

Barboza nodded, tilted the stick expertly, and dropped closer to the canopy of trees and vines that had crept into and over the stones of Tiajuanaco. Almost as soon as he did this, something bright and brilliantly white caught the full glare of the sun and momentarily flashed, as though signaling them. Carlos felt that same feverish rush pass through him for an instant and pointed at the exact spot.

As the pilot angled in, Carlos could see the facing of what was obviously the apex of a pyramidal structure.

Great slabs of polished granite formed the outer shell, but many had been weathered and dislodged, breaking loose to reveal a deeper level of huge, solid blocks. As the Sikorsky hovered almost directly above the peak, Carlos could see from the angle of declination that the structure was extremely large, as well as higher than the tallest trees.

And when they passed over the exact center of the pyramid, he felt as though a hot blade had sliced him in half. What a sensation!

Akapana.

There below him.

"Down!" he cried. "Right here! This is the place!"

"I cannot get in between the trees, Señor!"

"As close as possible, then!"

The pilot nodded and began scanning the canopy for the nearest opening, a place where the rotors could turn without fear of fouling. Carlos literally tingled with excitement and a hideous anxiety. All the weirdness and mystery and the thrill of being touched by a messenger of God . . . for this moment.

"This looks good," said Barboza. He pointed to a break in the foliage where the stone slabs of what must once have been a grand boulevard struck boldly through the jungle toward the mighty bulk of Akapana.

Carlos closed his eyes as the chopper cleared the tops of the trees and was immediately enclosed by deep green shadows. As soon as the Sikorksy touched down, Carlos ripped off the seat belt and climbed down. To his right, he could see the path of stones, wide and flat like the deck of a carrier, leading to a staircase and platform that at one time must have supported a grandly official entrance to the great pyramid.

As he and the pilot advanced on Akapana, he saw evidence everywhere of the inexorable creep of the jungle. Vines and roots had spent millennia working between the seams of the stones and slabs, slowly lifting and pushing, eventually wedging every block apart. And what blocks they were! Based on his knowledge of structural materials, Carlos estimated that each had to weigh at least 150 tons.

Regardless, given enough millennia, the jungle would take this place apart, stone by stone, grind it up and drive it all back into the loam and soil.

But not yet.

As they to climbed up, they recognized what had once been a colonnaded and cantilevered platform with a double staircase at either side—a place where priests might have performed rituals before the assembled masses.

"In there," said Carlos, pointing to the entrance. He adjusted the small utility belt he wore, automatically checking to see that a variety of tools remained available.

The dark, half-collapsed aperture in the side of the pyramid awaited them like the open mouth of a great beast. Barboza hesitated, then said, in a voice that revealed his embarrassment: "Maybe I should wait for you out here, *Señor.*"

"You are frightened," said Carlos. "Do not be ashamed of that."

"But you have been such a great hero, a good person. My fear makes me feel worthless in your presence."

"Coco, my fear is equal to yours, but I do not allow myself to think about it. In that lies the only difference between us." Carlos chucked him on the shoulder in a gesture of macho appreciation. "Besides, it is smarter for you to remain here, to keep the chopper ready to lift off at a moment's notice."

Coco grinned. "You think so, *Señor?* I will be ready!"

Carlos moved on, picking his way through the rubble. Each step filled him more with a combination of excitement and dread. As he neared the entrance, he noticed an odd sound, a whispery droning that seemed to come from everywhere and nowhere simultaneously. It made him think of insect wings beating furiously, but in slow motion. He'd never heard this sound before; there was something innately frightening about it. Looking back at Barboza, he could see that the pilot too heard the odd noise and was scanning the jungle and sky for its source.

The susurrations grew steadily louder and more eerie. Ducking into the cool darkness of the passageway into the pyramid, Carlos listened keenly for any sounds emanating from its interior. He noticed that the seams of the blocks were perfect, the edges where they joined so snug they could have been cut with a laser. He did not move, made no sound. The ancient structure was equally silent.

As he unhooked a flashlight from his belt, ready to go deeper into the passageway, he turned for a final look outside, and source of the soft droning was suddenly revealed. Descending through the canopy into the open space where Barboza stood transfixed, it looked like a giant dragonfly.

Carlos realized he was looking at an object of modern mythology made suddenly real. Long a favorite of conspiracy proponents, the sleek, black helicopter hung motionless for a moment above the Sikorsky, its engines barely a whisper, then settled to the stone boulevard without a sound. When a half dozen armed men were disgorged from its belly to surround Barboza, Carlos moved without thinking, turning to run as fast as he could into the bowels of the pyramid called Akapana.

The floors were covered with dust that had accrued for more than ten thousand years. The path sloped downward at a slight but steady angle. The beam from his flashlight was strong and penetrated far into the corridor. The feverish sensation had returned, and Carlos knew he was approaching the target of his mission, the heart spring of the ancient edifice. Its builders had called it the Tomb of the Gods, but it was one of St. John's mysterious, apocalyptic Churches.

Carlos broke into a light jog, his boots slapping the stone floor. The sound of his passage seemed to boom through the corridor like thunder. The men in the black copter were looking for him, he knew, but he didn't care what happened to him as long as he did not fail the behest of his God.

Time lost all sense of proportion as he plunged ever deeper into the giant structure. Several times, the passage forked and twisted, like a maze, and each time Carlos continued unerringly, not even thinking of what path must be the correct one but simply choosing and moving.

Behind him, the sound of pursuit. Growing louder, closer.

His fever increased, and he felt as though his blood neared the boiling point. He wanted to stop, to collect himself, but he knew he could not. He felt all his senses becoming more acute, like a radio receiver getting louder and stronger as it neared a transmitter.

The farthest reach of his flashlight beam abruptly touched something very bright, and he knew he was close to the end. Picking up the pace, he raced down the stone passage toward the unresolved brightness.

And then he could see it. Carved from a solid piece of white quartz, like a giant ice sculpture, an exact miniature of Akapana rested in a central pyramid-shaped chamber. A pencil-thin beam of light touched the apex of the miniature at the perfect angle to fill it with prismatic light. Carlos flicked off his torch and stood in the eerie illumination, then moved close enough to see the shaft that lanced straight up through the heart of the pyramid to the point that still poked through the canopy of the forest. It collected the sun's light and heat and focused it here, on the model.

"Stop, *Señor* Accardi!" a voice cried out, but Carlos had already leaped forward like a man diving into a lagoon.

He landed with his arms outstretched to embrace the miniature pyramid, and for an instant the feverish heat that pulsed with him and the focused prism light of the quartz structure became one. The instant of fusion filled him with the white-heat fire of pure joy, and he knew he had opened the Seal.

Spectral light filled the chamber as he rolled off the quartz replica and blinked his eyes to see the armed men from the black helicopter surrounding him. He smiled at them, not caring what might come next, safe in the knowledge he'd done what was asked of him.

"Get up, Accardi," said one of them.

"You are too late. The Seal is open," said Carlos, slowly rising up from his knees.

"As long as we have you, we are not too late," said the group's leader, a muscular man in his late twenties.

"Who are you?" said Carlos.

"The Pope sent us."

Carlos was truly stunned. "The Pope! He wants you to take me to him!'"

The man in the black and green fatigues chuckled. "No, *Señor*. He wants us to *kill* you."

ThiRTY-Eight

Gaetano—Rome
October 30, 2000

"$\mathcal{B}$efore you do it," said Gaetano, "will you first let me tell you what happened?"

D'Agostino remained rigid and silent. He wore a pair of dark sunglasses with round lenses, which gave his long, angular face a distinctly skull-like aspect. He kept his weapon pointed directly at Gaetano's face. "Why should I?"

"Why are you going to shoot me?"

The man with the gun chuckled. "Because you really fucked this one up."

"It wasn't my fault!"

"Our Order cannot be compromised." D'Agostino shrugged.

"Just hear what I have to tell you, then decide," said Gaetano.

"This is not the place to have an extended discussion," said D'Agostino. "We have to leave this area."

Putting his hands behind his head, Gaetano sat up

in the seat, stretched out his legs. "You have my word as a Knight . . . no tricks."

"They told me not to trust you."

"And I am telling you, you can." Gaetano's gaze remained steady. No subterfuge intended or implied.

D'Agostino said nothing, but he lowered the weapon. A police klaxon sounded somewhere.

"We must get moving. No tricks." The agent punched the accelerator and expertly guided the car down the narrow street.

Gaetano exhaled and inhaled as naturally as possible, even though the sudden break of tension left him wanting to gulp in great chunks of breath. He kept his hands clearly visible above his head, confident he was safe as long as he gave the agent no reason to shoot him.

When D'Agostino slipped into traffic on the via Crescenzio, he began weaving in and out of the lanes at high speed, changing positions like a piece on a checkerboard until he almost sideswiped a bus, taking a right at the Piazza Adriana practically on two wheels.

"We need to get across the river!"

"Where are you going?"

"South!" was all he said as he yanked the car into a powerslide right-left, and another right onto the Ponte Umberto.

Across the bridge, D'Agostino slipped from one side street to another, working steadily east and south toward the via delle Terme, which would eventually deposit them on one of the main arteries out of the city. The street names flipped by with speed and confusion: del Corso, dell'Umiltà, Plebiscito . . . Gaetano had lost all bearings.

At an intersection at Teodoro, a small delivery van was in the wrong place at the wrong time.

"Hang on," said D'Agostino, burying the pedal.

Tires screeched and the big Mercedes leaped forward like a Harrier jet, expertly clipping the front fender of the van at just the correct angle. The mass and velocity of the big sedan slammed the other vehicle into the side of a parked car.

Hardly slowing, the big Mercedes continued south, dodging pedestrians and traffic like a single-minded *futboler* on a mission to the goal. They careened past Monte Celio, and the traffic began to thin out.

"Well, if they weren't looking for this car," said Gaetano, "they will be now."

D'Agostino depressed the accelerator and they were quickly doing ninety miles an hour. "See anyone interested in us?"

"If they are, they are in the wind."

"Good. Keep your hands where I can see them."

"Where are we going?" Gaetano rested his hands on the dashboard, palms down.

"Eventually? I am going to Anzio. You—I am not so sure."

Another sharp turn, past an outdoor market. As the car slid into the curve, vendors and shoppers alike ran terrified from the stalls. But there was no one in pursuit, and that didn't seem right.

"Nobody behind us. What do you make of it?" Gaetano said.

"I don't like it. Too easy."

The road ahead straightened out and patches of open lawns, gardens and fields began to appear. Rome's environs were spreading thinner. They reached the intersection with Route 7, and the Mercedes hugged the soft right onto the highway. The asphalt snaked lazily through a series of rolling hills.

Neither man spoke for several minutes, and Gaetano continued to scan their position in all directions. He was about to comment again on the lack of pursuit when he noticed the shadow.

Cast off to their left side by a westering sun, it appeared whenever they passed a large enough object like a house or barn or copse of trees. But such things had become less frequent in the open countryside, and both men had missed it until now.

Although its shape was indistinct, there was no question what it could be. The chopper hung directly over them, keeping pace.

"Trouble," said Gaetano, pointing at the menacing shadow.

"Goddamn! One of the black dragons."

Gaetano knew of the black helicopters with the whisperjet rotors, but had never seen one. They were so deadly silent it was hard to believe. "They have not hit us for a reason," he said.

D'Agostino nodded. "They want to see where we might lead them. Big mistake. For them!"

The agent continued to drive as if they had noticed nothing amiss. He pointed to the console between the two front seats. "Open it," he said.

Unlatching the lid, Gaetano looked down to see ammo clips for a variety of weapons. "Which one do you want?" he said, inwardly steeling himself for the trouble about to begin.

"Uzi. The piece is under your seat."

"So now you trust me?" He picked out three clips he would need.

D'Agostino smiled. "Better the devil you know . . . than the one you're about to meet."

"Funny you should mention him . . ."

"Who, the devil?" D'Agostino chuckled. "Why?"

"I'll tell you later," said Gaetano as he leaned down and felt the familiar configuration of the venerable Israeli weapon. Pulling it out, he popped a clip into the breach. He had become very familiar with this incredibly light yet highly lethal little automatic. Although it was not one of those guns that settled into your grip like an old friend, it quickly won you over as soon as you squeezed the trigger. Even though you could release a stream of bullets so quickly and with such force that you could literally cut down a palm tree—or cut a man in half—the recoil on the weapon was practically nonexistent.

"Ready?" said D'Agostino, as he gradually increased the sedan's speed. He pushed a button on the steering wheel and glanced upward for an instant at the sunroof as a smoke-tinted glass inner window slid silently into its roof recess. Beyond was an outer panel flush with the roof, still closed.

Gaetano nodded.

"When I open the outer door, you're going to have only a few seconds before they realize what's happening."

Gaetano unstrapped his seat belt, got up on his knees, and braced the Uzi on the leading edge of the sunroof. "Hit it," he said.

Instantly the seal around the outer roof panel was broken and air rushed in. Before it had slid an inch, Gaetano was spraying slugs up into the belly of the black chopper. So rapidly did the gun fire that the bullets looked, for an instant, like a thin black line drawn from the roof of the car to the aircraft. The closeness of the "black dragon" surprised Gaetano—it had been pacing them, hanging so close he could count the rivets on its metallic seams and read the little warning decals about refueling.

When the first clip of slugs reached the undercarriage, they sparked like a magnesium flare, and Gaetano knew the ship carried light armor. But something must have been vulnerable, because the chopper immediately yanked up and right. Dropping down, Gaetano powered down the passenger door window, resting the Uzi's stubby barrel on the sill, fighting the slipstream to keep it pointed in the general direction of the chopper. The black dragon was hanging about twenty feet off the ground, drifting first ahead, then in back of their speeding sedan. It had developed a distinct wobble, like a gyroscope getting ready to tip over. Some of the slugs must have ripped into the twin rotors, which were not armored.

Onboard the aircraft, he could see several things taking place—the pilot wrestling with the stick and the controls just to keep airborne, and some goons in the midsection sliding back a small hatch, which meant that some kind of weapon would soon be poking its way out of the opening.

"I'm going to give them another blast, then you hit the brakes!" he shouted to D'Agostino.

Without waiting for a reply, he squeezed off another superclip, and the bullets ripped out of the little gun, swarming all over the side of the chopper, pinging and sparking.

Simultaneously, from the dark interior of the hatch, he saw some sort of muzzle flash, and then he was being thrown violently from his seat, as D'Agostino hammered the brakes. Grabbing the seat belt with his left hand, Gaetano pulled against his sudden momentum to soften his impact with the thickly padded leather of the dashboard. Tires wailed in protest and something exploded in the road surface ahead of them, sending up a billowing cloud of liquid fire. The chopper had fired a heavy round at the spot where they *should* have been.

Stunned, Gaetano forced himself to get up and get focused. D'Agostino yanked the wheel hard left to avoid the explosion, and the sedan slammed into and across a shallow ditch on the opposite side of the road. The open countryside was hilly and the road full of swerving contours. Several miles ahead, Gaetano saw the spires and rooftops of a hill town. If they could make the relative cover of the buildings, the chopper could not hang so close.

But it was very doubtful they would get that far without some luck and a lot of skillful dodging.

D'Agostino struggled to get the car back on the highway, the Mercedes's stout suspension system admirably absorbing the punishment. To their right, the black helicopter had recovered enough to edge back alongside. Gaetano clanked the seat belt buckle into place, slammed another clip into the Uzi, and stitched up the area around the chopper's open hatch.

The chopper's wobbling flight was more pronounced, but it still managed to hang close to them. Another flash from the belly of the black ship, and a missile floated by the onrushing hood of the Mercedes like a torpedo missing the prow of a ship. Gaetano watched the object impact on the hillside to the left of the road. The debris and the shock wave moved the sedan sideways for several feet, but the car clung stubbornly to the road. Gaetano scrambled to fire a fourth clip, snapped it into the Uzi, and emptied it in the general direction of the black ship's twin rotors. Sparks flew, and a thin plume of ink-black smoke began to stream from the turbojet engines. Now the craft was no longer "whispering"—rasping or grinding was more like it.

Stealing a glance ahead, Gaetano was surprised to see how close they were to entering the hill town, less than half a mile. They might make it.

"Hang on!" D'Agostino yelled as he whammed the brakes, and the chopper surged ahead of them again. Before the pilot could recover, Gaetano emptied yet another clip into the tail section, and the aircraft started to pitch wildly to the right.

"Nice shooting!" said D'Agostino, as he began to accelerate again.

The black helicopter's flight was getting more erratic with each second. Like a broken kite, it dipped suddenly, the angle severe and unforgiving. The whispery hush of its rotors had been replaced by a grotesque ratcheting sound that intensified when the wildly turning blades sliced into the soft earth to the right of the highway.

Just as the Mercedes shot past the point of impact, the chopper crashed into the ground and blew up. The roll of fiery heat lapped at Gaetano's face as he swiftly turned away from the blast. Thousands of chunks of twisted metal razored into and shredded the side of sedan. Gaetano ducked down behind the passenger door, avoiding the deadly wave of debris, but D'Agostino had no chance.

The shrapnel sliced through his right arm just above the elbow, almost severing it, and sending artery-driven blood everywhere, as if from a sheared-off hydrant. Then it continued on through his chest and out the other window. The agent was so stunned by the violent impact that he simply collapsed in shock. The Mercedes left the road at high speed but sank its left-side tires into a drainage ditch full of mud, which quickly brought it to a stop.

Scrambling as quickly as he could, Gaetano popped both seat belts, jumped from the car, ran around to the driver's side, and eased D'Agostino out onto the verge grass. The gush of blood had slowed somewhat, but the worst damage was to the man's upper torso, where too much of his rib cage was exposed. He was also hemorrhaging through the nose and mouth, and Gaetano figured he didn't have more than a few minutes left.

"Can you hear me? Squeeze my hand if you can," he said softly. Beyond them the air crackled with the burning wreckage of the chopper, and farther away came the first sounds of alarm and interest from the village in the nearby hills.

Squeeze.

Then, ". . . Good . . . job."

"Do not try to talk," said Gaetano. He looked desperately around for something to stem the terrible bleeding, even though he knew it was futile.

"If . . . not now . . . then . . . never . . ." The words half whistled from D'Agostino's throat and bubbled from his savaged chest.

Gaetano nodded.

"I . . . was not . . . going . . . kill you . . ." D'Agostino's eyes were losing focus, his grip getting very weak.

"That's good to know. I didn't want to have to kill you, either."

Squeeze. "You . . . leave . . . now . . ."

"I can wait. Help is coming."

Squeeze . . . Stronger this time. "No!"

Gaetano cradled the man's head a little closer, gentler. He bent down to whisper into his ear, to ensure that D'Agostino heard him. "No man should be like this . . . alone."

For a moment, D'Agostino's face filled with color, and his eyes brightened. "My . . . savior . . . waits for me. I am . . . not alone. I never . . . will be."

"I cannot leave you here," said Gaetano.

"You must . . . Peter knows . . . you stop . . . him.

"I can stop him," said Gaetano. "I will."

D'Agostino performed the ghost of a nod. "Go . . . Anzio . . . shoemaker . . . Solotano . . ."

The agent gasped for air. The color in his face was draining quickly. The temporary flush of energy had burned as brightly as it ever would, and now it retreated.

"What about him?" said Gaetano quickly. "Solotano—what for? What do I do? Do I say something to him?"

"Tell . . . him . . ." He stopped.

"Tell him what?" Gaetano whispered urgently, trying not too sound too harsh. But inwardly thinking; You simply cannot leave me twisting in the wind like this.

". . . Sonny-boy . . . is . . . home."

"Sonny-boy is home."

The man's eyes blinked, rolled upward. "Good . . . good-bye . . ."

D'Agostino expelled a weak breath—his last. Gaetano laid him gently on the verge grass.

Time to get out of there. He did not want to explain anything to anybody—even small-town mayors or constables. As much as he disliked the idea, he quickly searched D'Agostino's body for weapons, money, or anything else that might prove useful. Then, getting up, he ran to the Mercedes and gathered up more ammo clips, identifying papers, and the Uzi, before running dead left away from the roadside through the high grass. He crouched as low as he could without sacrificing speed. Loping along like a drunken orang, he picked out an immediate target—a small hillside with a large clutch of trees spilling over its ridge.

He was sorry to abandon the Mercedes, but there was no time to work it free of the ditch. The local authorities would sound an alarm that would not be overlooked by whoever it was that owned stealthy helicopters. It would not be long before the place was overrun with bad guys.

Which meant he had a choice to make—either get as far away from the area as possible, or get lost in the village for the night and make an exit when the situation dictated the highest chance of success. If they were looking for him very seriously, they would be using heat-mapping scanners from aircraft and possibly satellites, which would pinpoint his body-temp signature no matter where he was hiding in the surrounding area.

But if he went right into the village, his body-heat image would be lost among those of the townspeople. He would be hiding right under their snouts.

Better. Much better.

He waited until several cars had arrived at the crash scene before working his way down the back side of the hill, staying just within the running edge of the trees, angling south toward the village, which he would enter from the opposite, or south, end. Soon the sun would be down, and the cleanup and investigative activities would be hampered till morning.

Which was just fine with him. Plenty of cover for him to skulk around, or to find a source of more appropriate clothing and perhaps a means of escape. Being attired in a torn and bloody Jesuit cassock branded him with a unique appearance, and he needed to get rid of it as soon as possible, but a B-and-E at an apparel shop *plus* an auto theft in the village would be like leaving a personal calling card for Peter's people.

None of it would matter as long as his crimes were not discovered till morning. With Anzio only an hour away, he would have vanished into the underground network with many hours to spare. His trail would be very, very cold.

Gaetano followed the line of the trees for as long as they led him closer to the outskirts of the village. He went to ground in a mulberry copse, full of succulent berries and a thick green dome of cover. Loamy scents of the earth and the leaves surrounded him in a comfortable embrace. From there, on the downward slope of a hill leading down to the highway, he enjoyed a full view of the crash scene and the village.

At nightfall he would make his move.

In the meantime, his thoughts returned to the immensely psychotic events of the day.

Honey, I'm home! How was my day? Well, let's see: I impersonated a Jesuit priest, tried to assassinate the Pope, interrupted a conversation with Lucifer, and shot down a helicopter with a small gun. How about you?

Gaetano chuckled wryly.

All true.

He had been trying to avoid thinking about D'Agostino. For all his training, he had never watched a man die like that. To hold him in his arms and *feel* his life force, his soul, escaping like steam from a broken valve. All the memories and impressions, the ideas and hopes and terrors—everything that makes a man what he is, what he was . . .

To feel it all evaporate into some cosmic ether was something he would not soon forget.

Funny how a single moment could mark you, he thought as he watched the sun descending toward distant hills like a glowing host of benediction. He hadn't known D'Agostino very well, but the intimacy of sharing his death had touched him deeply, and in one sense, he now knew the man better than any other in his life.

Looking at the wreck of the Mercedes, where a handful of vehicles had gathered, Gaetano saw some people struggling with the mangled body of a Knight of Malta.

Good-bye, my friend, thought Gaetano. I never got to tell you about that devil you *didn't* know. . . .

THIRTY-NINE

The Seven

GRACE ALLBRIGHT

*T*he soldiers led her to the center of the square, where a large crowd had gathered to watch the fate of an infidel. A tall, shirtless man in billowy pantaloons stood waiting, his hands resting on the hilt of scimitar whose tip was driven into the sandy earth in front of him. Next to him a small fountain, decorated with exquisite carvings and mosaic inlay, pulsed with a weak plume of water.

As Grace walked to the designated location, she was thinking of Herman and her lord, and how she would soon be with them. Recent events played through her mind, and she clung to the memories because they would be her last in this earthly life.

It seemed like it had been only days earlier that Grace had climbed from her bed with her head just *filled* with stuff—some of it from the shine, and some of it from that Catholic Lady in her dream. In fact, she had had so much important stuff in her mind that she hadn't known what to commence thinking about first.

Actually, that wasn't wholetogether the truth, she remembered thinking as she drove her little Escort over to Sheriff DeWayne Davis's office. It was right after she'd had a quick breakfast of fresh-baked cornbread and black-as-the-devil coffee. The last such breakfast she was likely to ever have, as it turned out. Sheriff DeWayne was so glad to see her walking in with her little notepad that she thought he might jump up and hug her. But he didn't, and he waited for her to tell her story—which she knew so well she hardly had to look at her scribblings from the night before.

But she did check to make sure she had the number of the State Road right before describing the long ride to the broken-down barn past the old Conway Crossroads. Sheriff Davis had been so excited by the time she finished telling him what the lady in the dream had given her that he could hardly dial the State Police boys and tell them to go on down to the old crossroad and sneak up on that skinny man in the stovepipe dungarees. Yessirree, she remembered, she could still see that place with sun-faded sign for Red Man Chewing Tobacco as if she'd been traipsing around in it herself.

Those young boys, in their pressed and starched trooper uniforms, drove down Route 384 to that falling-down barn where Abby Carstairs was breathing through a piece of bathroom plumbing pipe ... and they had dodged some bullets and shot some of their own.

The newspapers told the rest of the story of how the crazy man had fired his shotgun and been killed in self-defense by the State Police. The newspapers had called them heroes and credited the raid and rescue of Miss

Carstairs on a reliable tip from an anonymous "eye-witness."

Grace didn't really care how her help was described to people. She had always been happy knowing she used her gift to do God's work, and it hadn't ever been important that the police didn't want anybody to know they were getting their leads from a little old black lady who taught choir.

She had driven straight from the sheriff's office back to the house to begin making preparations. It took a few weeks to get the trip—from Florence City County Airport to, eventually, Gatwick in London, then to Jidda, and finally a bus to Mecca—booked at a price she could afford, plus she had to get inoculated for some awful ailments and get people to fill in at the choir. She'd put it all on her Discover Card because she knew the Lord would provide for the cost. It was his will she followed, and her faith had always provided.

She'd always hated flying and made sure she slept most of the way. It was some kind of hot in the Middle East, and she would have never elected to go to a place like this unless God had asked her to do it—which he had. The temperature flirted with one hundred degrees, but Grace felt surprisingly comfortable in her long, loose-fitting robes of cream and baby blue. Her head was covered by a matching burnoose in the style of the Afghani tribesmen—it was traditional clothing she'd bought in an airport shop at the suggestion of the travel agent.

She had studied her guidebooks enough to speak the standard tourist phrases, and had trusted the Lord would see to a way for her to get into the holy city of Mecca, even though she was an infidel. Having checked other Westerners' accounts of their visits to this sacred site of Islam, she decided the best course was to seek safety in numbers. She would join one of the almost continuously organized pilgrimages.

She boarded the old Grumman bus that would take and her "fellow Afghanis" away from the Red Sea port through fifty miles of desert. The almost three-hour ride would end in a valley surrounded by low hills at the fabled city of Makkah or, as it was known in the West, Mecca.

When the school bus, its paint buffeted by a generation of wind-swept sandstorms until burnished a dull beige, pulled to a stop, the driver announced their destination. Grace had stood and shuffled out with all the Afghani faithful. Many of them were chanting prefatory prayers and walking with a slow, deferential gait that communicated their devotion. Grace looked at the long lines of people that snaked toward the narrow gates that filtered the pilgrims into the inner circles of the city, and eventually to the inspiring open spaces of al-Haram, the great mosque.

She'd looked at them with the same lack of understanding she usually saved for the poor people of Hartstown, whom she would see on a Sunday, streaming down the steps of churches that were not Baptist churches. She wondered how they could possibly not see the error of their choice of religions—especially when she would be driving past that big, stone, castle-looking Saint Charles Catholic Church.

Now, here she was going to unlock one of the Seven Seals at the request of a *Catholic* nun, surrounded by a million people who not only weren't Baptist, weren't even Christian. . . .

And suddenly Grace realized that it just plain didn't matter.

After all, had she ever checked on the religion of any of the people she'd helped with her shine?

Of course not.

"Excuse me, ma'am . . ."

She stopped and turned, looking for whoever it was who was talking to her—in English!

"Yes?"

And realized instantly that she'd made a mistake.

Large, rough hands grabbed her by the shoulders and yanked her so hard that her neck snapped to one side, stunning her for a couple of seconds. Totally without strength, Grace had been dragged from the line by men dressed in soldiers' fatigues. They threw her into the backseat of a humvee and drove through narrow back streets until they reached the electrified link fence and sentry gate of a small Saudi military compound.

Grace was half carried and half dragged from the vehicle into a spare, dim barrack building, where two men in dark suits were waiting for her. They were swarthy but did not look like Arabs. The younger of the two sported a goatee. The older man was balding.

"You are an American," said the older man, directing her to a cheap folding chair.

Grace said nothing, trying to act as if she did not understand.

The goateed man chuckled. "Please, no dramatics, *Signora!* We know you are Grace Allbright from South Carolina, America."

Defeated, Grace shook her head. "Who are you?"

"We are soldiers of Christ," said the balding man. But he spoke without reverence. "We have been scrutinizing the customs papers of everyone coming to this city from any foreign venues. We have been looking for someone very carefully, and I believe we have found her."

"The Lord's gonna protect me," Grace said, lifting her head and speaking in a regal tone. She was proud to be on the side of the redeemer.

The man with the goatee smiled. "And he will need to do just that."

The bald one added, "You are on a mission against the Pope."

Grace had almost laughed out loud. *The Pope!* "I'm on a pilgrimage. I haven't done anything wrong."

Just as she said that, three Saudis in traditional Bedouin garb entered the room and sat at a fold-up table, facing her. They'd sat stiff and formal, as though presiding over a tribunal.

The goateed man smiled. "We are part of the international law enforcement community. We share information with agencies all over the world, and the name Grace Allbright appears in both the FBI computers and the ones of the State Police of South Carolina, USA."

"What?" Grace was truly surprised.

"You solve cases by extrasensory means," Goatee announced. "And you purchased a trip to Mecca on short notice."

"I don't know what you're talkin' about." Grace did not like lying, but these men had begun to scare her very much. "What do you want with me?"

The bald one began ominously, "We need—"

"I am afraid there is a problem," interrupted the Saudi minister seated in the middle of the trio.

"What is that?" said Goatee, who looked at the Arabs sharply, obviously irritated by the intrusion.

"This woman has violated both civic and religious proscriptions. She is an infidel, and she attempted to enter the holiest of the holy places in all of Islam. What she did is forbidden and must be punished."

"What is the punishment?" said Goatee.

The Saudi minister held out his hands, palms up, and shrugged, as if the answer were obvious. "It is death."

When she heard those words, Grace felt like she

might faint and just slip out of her chair, like molasses spilling off a table.

But at the same time, she'd felt an immense relief settling over her, filling her with warmth like the whiskey and honey that her mother used to give her when she was laid up in bed with the grippe. Grace thought of all those nights she'd had to go to sleep without her Herman—fifteen years' worth, and her always wondering when she'd finally join him again. Well, it looked like the wondering was over.

"We have seen enough. The law is very clear," said another of the Saudis.

"So it is written," said the trio.

The three men stood and indicated that Grace should stand as well.

When she did this, the one in the middle said, "In the square of al-Haram, in the morning, as the sun touches the highest minaret, you will die. May Allah be your final judge."

"You will allow us to be present?" asked the bald one.

"It is allowed," said the minister on the left.

Then the soldiers took her to a bare room with a cot and a galvanized bucket in the corner. Nothing else. No food. No water.

Now of the soldiers led her to the fountain. "You may wash away your sins," he said.

The water sparkled in the early dawn light. It seemed like the most beautiful sight Grace had ever seen. She stepped forward to dip her hands into the flow, and suddenly she knew—

This was it!

A wave of heat passed through her like a fever. Then the touch of the water cooled her, suffusing her with the most complete peace she had ever known. Her fear evaporated in a burst of white light that radiated from the center of her soul.

Along with that serenity came knowledge. Thousands of years before, this spring had been used by Moses and the Israelites during their forty years of wandering through the desert. Here, Miriam had summoned water from the sands to save her people. It was a sacred place, a place of life.

In the sky, there was the briefest change in the light of the sun, as though a cloud or a great hand had passed over it. Everyone looked up, wondering what had happened. Only Grace received the gift of understanding.

The Churches of *Revelation.*

The Seal.

She had done the work of the Lord!

As she patted some of the water to her face, Grace began to smile, then turned to face her executioners. The soldier helped her kneel and gently positioned her head.

Thank you, Lord.

Grace was thinking those words as she heard a collective gasp from the crowd, everyone holding their breath as the sword was raised. It was the last sound she ever heard.

SHANTI POPUL

"Out of the question!" Momdar was pacing back and forth in the small apartment, his face flushed several shades darker by his rising anger.

Shanti wanted to go to him, to touch his cheek and try to calm him. But she had never seen her husband in such a state. "But you have seen the truth of what I say. God is telling us something, my husband!"

Momdar, ran fingers through his black hair in absent frustration. "God? There are many gods and there are none! These are modern times, Shanti!"

"Did I not show the proof with those dear people in Muttra? They were my family when I was Ludgi."

"You were never Ludgi!" Momdar screamed at her, more furious than before. "You have been hypnotized! Tricked!"

"Tricked?" Shanti wanted to laugh, for what he said was so silly, but she knew he would become even more enraged if he thought she was laughing at him. "By whom?"

Momdar paused, caught by his own words for an instant, then, "By that man who came here!"

"Sevi?" Shanti moved the opposite end of the small room, keeping a couch between herself and her husband. "But, Momdar, for what reason? Why would a man want to do something like that to me?"

He began pacing again, holding the sides of his head with both hands, as if in great pain. "I don't know!" he screamed. "But I know it must be a trick, because what you say is not possible."

Shanti looked at him with no expression, although inside, she boiled with emotion. Her memories of her other family, her babies of so long ago and the sight of them now, and how seeing them had filled her with such joyous pain . . .

Finally she spoke, as softly as possible. "Momdar, you were with me. You drove me to Muttra, to the house of Sripak! How could I know where everything was located? How could I know so much about them?"

Glaring at her, he turned away, looking out the window above her sewing machine, as if there was something of great interest to see. He spoke without looking at her. "I do not know how or why, but for some reason, my wife has decided to deceive me."

"Momdar, you hurt me when you say such a thing. I wish you no harm. I love you as I always have."

"Yet you say you loved this . . . Sripak?"

Is that it? she thought quickly. My husband is jealous? "That was another life! Another me. I cannot explain it. I only know it happened. Just having the vision and the knowledge of it . . . is a gift from God."

He turned, regarded her with an expression no less agitated. "And this . . . trip you want us to make. What is that?"

"God gave me the memories to show me that I am special," said Shanti, lowering her eyes as she realized how prideful she sounded. And so she added, "Special for His purposes."

Momdar's expression softened for an instant. "Shanti, do you have any idea how many items you must sew to pay for plane tickets to England? To Stonehenge of all places!"

"I have been taking extra work for six weeks! I have saved every rupee. But I did not think it proper to put a price on the wishes of God."

Looking up at the ceiling, Momdar held his hands in tight fists of frustration. "A price? Did you put a price on our future, Shanti? What about our dreams? My machine shop? Your sewing store?"

"I believe we will be provided for. . . ."

"You know," he said, as though the words he spoke had a bad taste, "I always thought your morals were of such good quality, but now, I am . . . ashamed."

"Oh, Momdar, how can you say that?"

"Because you are going to ruin us!" The words issued from him like a lava flow. He screamed at her. "England! Stonehenge!"

Shanti knew she could not stay in the little apartment much longer. Her husband danced upon the edge of violence, and she could not bear to see it. The rooms were like a tiny cage into which two shrews had been thrust, with space for only one. Shanti, backed toward the front door, fearing what might come next.

"Where are you going?" Momdar shouted.

"I cannot stay, my husband." Shanti began to cry. She hated for him to see this—he would interpret it as weakness. Really it was the expression of her infinite sadness, at losing him.

"He was right!" shouted Momdar, his expression strangely bright, almost triumphant.

"Who, Momdar? What are you talking about?"

His gaze locked into hers as if looking through a gunsight. She had never seen him look so . . . so dangerous. "A beggar . . . I almost walked right over him in the street. I looked up and he was suddenly right there in front of me. I ignored him, tried to step over him," said Momdar, his voice suddenly calmer. "And he reached out with a skinny hand, like a bony claw, and he grabbed my leg! He forced me to look at him. I was ready to kick him in the face, but his gaze was so clear. . . ."

"What happened?" Shanti edged closer to the door, hoping he would not notice. He seemed to be in a trance and spoke as though recalling a nightmare.

"He said something that made my bones go cold. He said, 'Your wife will try to leave you today. And you must stop her . . . any way you can.'"

The way he recounted the words told Shanti that the man had been no beggar—and probably not even a man.

As Shanti put her hand on the door, Momdar pulled a knife from the wood block in the kitchen. Its serrations sparkled with cruelty, like the teeth of a smiling predator. She was transfixed by its unworldly brightness.

"Do not move!" said Momdar, each word higher and

more shrill. His jaw muscles throbbed as he extended his lower teeth in a bizarre parody of a smile.

Shanti had seen more than enough, and she pulled open the door.

A great mass slammed into her, shoulder high, and she was jammed roughly against the threshold of the open door. Something struck into her back, below her left shoulder, something that burned with a cold fire. Momdar screamed unintelligibly as he jerked the serrated knife down savagely. When it jammed between her ribs, the pain became a black shroud enclosing her. She tried to cry out but he reached around, placing his hand over her mouth and yanking her head back.

And suddenly there was a great rush of cold down her throat, filling her chest, and then an explosion of heat, wet and slippery.

Momdar released her and she felt herself collapsing, felt her life spilling down her chest and pooling on the floor at her feet. She felt so sleepy, so lazy and weak; everything seemed to be rushing away from her as though she were in a long tunnel. The only thing that remained constant was the piercing ache of her husband's scream.

But then, even that went away.

BROTHER MAURO

It had been so long since he had been on a train that he was newly fascinated by the endless passage of Italy beyond the window of his private compartment. The towns rolled past, their names like poetry—Arezzo, Cortona, Ascoli Piceno, Ortona a Mare, Lanciano . . . As Mauro sat with his face close to the glass, like a small boy, he experienced a sudden epiphany, and realized why he was enjoying the train ride so much.

It was his earliest memory. He was sitting on his mother's lap, riding on a train, probably between Catania and Messina, where his grandparents lived. The memory was not much, just flashes of color and the muffled rattle and thunder. He was warm and safe, sitting on the lap of his mother.

Outside, the sun was flirting with peaks of the Apennines, and soon his train would be rocketing down the endless blue aisle of the night, and would not stop until Termini Otranto. From there, in the morning, Mauro would catch the ferry across the Adriatic, to Levkas. Then, another glorious train ride to the mythic city of Delphi.

Mauro took a pillow from the overhead rack and stretched out on two of the padded seats, dozing until the train's next stop at San Severo. The lurching halt almost tipped him off the edge of the chairs, and he awoke with a startled cry. Embarrassed, he was glad he was alone in the compartment.

And then, there was a gentle tapping on the etched glass, so light that he was not certain that he'd heard it.

Tap tap.

Yes, he did hear something. "Enter," he said.

The door slid back to reveal a woman with thick dark hair and hazel eyes that were almost golden. Her face was classically angular, and she had a long, slender neck. She wore a black, loose-fitting dress of several gauzy layers that still managed to reveal her slender frame as she stepped into the train carrying a small piece of exquisitely tooled leather luggage. She looked like an aristocratic artist or gypsy, and she was smiling at him.

It was the most intriguing, friendly smile he had ever seen.

"Oh, excuse me, Father," she said, averting her eyes

for an instant. "The conductor said this compartment was empty."

"No, please! Come in, *Signora*!" he said as he pushed the pillow into the corner behind him and struggled to stand up. As he did so, the train surged forward, and he almost fell over.

She giggled daintily and stepped forward, closing the door behind her. Mauro was transported by her scent, her perfume, her sheer impact. She sat down, crossing her legs, which extended provocatively from beneath her long skirt. Her shoes were all thin straps and high heels. "Thank you, Father," she said, after she had settled comfortably into the seats opposite him.

"I am not a priest," he said. "I am a brother. Brother Mauro Barzini. It is very good to meet you."

She nodded. "Gabriella di Pietro. I am an actress."

"I am not surprised. You look . . . very dramatic."

"Oh, thank you! But there is not very much drama in Bolognese television. I am a 'balloon girl' on *Take It Off!*"

She laughed lightly, almost musically, and flashed her golden eyes at him. The effect was radiantly powerful, and Mauro wanted to look away, but he could not. He had never been seated this close to a woman like this before.

"I am afraid I do not see very much television."

"Is it allowed in your . . . home?"

"I live in the Franciscan abbey in Siena."

"I love that town!" she said, clapping her hands together. "I once saw an incredible horse race there, in the square, drinking wine, eating mozzarella and bread. I was a young girl and it was very exciting."

Mauro could think of nothing to say, and he found he was kind of gaping at Gabriella.

"Are you cloistered?"

"Ah, no, we can come and go as we please."

Gabriella smiled and tilted her head, then reached into her handbag and produced a bottle of red wine and two glasses. "I am always prepared," she said. "Would you join me in a glass of Bardolino?"

Mauro was so shocked by her invitation that he felt his heart begin to thump in his chest. He was certain she could hear it too. His hands, wrapped in gauze and covered by white cotton gloves, had begun to tremble.

"Well, I don't know . . ."

Gabriella smiled and placed the two glasses on the ledge under the window, then uncorked the bottle and poured each glass half full. She picked up a glass, then looked at him.

"Very well," he said, managing a pathetic imitation of a smile. He lifted the glass.

"*Salute!*" she said, and quaffed the entire glass in one swallow.

Mauro sipped politely as she poured and drank another glassful of the wine. Despite his frequent contact with the media, Mauro was not worldly-wise. He was, by turns, awkward, embarrassed, and excited.

This woman seated across from him was like no other woman he had ever encountered. Keeping his vows had always been easy, and he often wondered why God had made it so. He sometimes saw his colleagues struggling with desires and temptations, but he often could not grasp their predicaments. When he'd first received the gift of the stigmata, he'd often asked God the reason, wondering if it was a reward for his success with the stringent vows of his order.

But now . . .

Gabriella had uncrossed her legs and stretched them out across the space between the facing seats. Her dark hair spilled across her shoulders in a fashionable way. Her every move, her whole attitude, was casual and relaxed, never wanton or cheap. She poured yet another glass of wine for herself, and her smile became wider, her teeth whiter, her lips more full.

"You don't like your wine, Brother Mauro?"

"Oh no, it is very good. That is why I prefer to sip it."

She laughed. "Life is short. Take big bites. Wash it down with lots of wine!"

Gabriella leaned forward, and despite the loose layers of her blouse Mauro could see the swell and swing of her breasts beneath the cloth. He imagined their fullness in his hands.

Shocked at his own thought, he sat bolt upright in his seat.

"What is the matter, Mauro?" she said. "You look suddenly upset."

He decided he should be honest with her. Deception might lead him farther astray. "Miss di Pietro, you are a beautiful woman. I confess to having an impure thought regarding your person."

She laughed that musical laugh again, then looked at him with a curious tilt of her head, a slant of her eyes. "Tell me, are you one of those people who believe the thought is the same as the deed?"

"Why yes, that is the teaching of the Church."

"Well," she said with mock frown, "if that were really true, then the Church, when the collection basket was passed down the pews every Sunday, would be satisfied with people merely thinking about giving their money to the priests, instead of actually doing it!"

Mauro could think of nothing to say. He had never heard that argument before, and wished he'd paid more attention to his classes of logic and philosophy. Finally, he said, "I have a feeling there is a fault in your reasoning, a flaw in comparing one set of variables to another. 'Specious' is the term, I believe . . ."

"So you still believe the thought equal to the deed?"

"Yes, I do."

"Interesting," said Gabriella. "Do you have any idea what I do on television?"

"You said you are an actress."

She batted her eyes in self-parody. "Mauro, I was being kind—to myself."

"I don't understand."

"I appear on the set wearing a costume made entirely of balloons. It is a game show, and the contestants compete for either money or the chance to pop my balloons with pins."

As she described the activity, his mind created lewd images worthy of the *Decameron*. He could not believe this was happening to him! Without thinking, he gulped the rest of his wine, relishing the tangy rush down his throat. "What happens," he heard himself asking, "if they break all your balloons?"

Gabriella looked at him with the slyest of grins. "Well, what else could happen? I am naked, of course!"

Mauro said nothing—he could not speak, in fact. His mind was filled with feverish imaginings of what this fantasy woman must look like unclothed. He felt a stirring in his penis, a feeling he had successfully ignored since he'd been a young adolescent. The sensation was at once repugnant and wildly exhilarating.

Gabriella refilled his glass. He did not object. Then she sat next to him, and he could feel the animal heat of her thigh where it touched his. He had no idea anything could feel like that. Her perfume was the merest suggestion of sweetness mixed with something deeper, darker.

He felt an electrical current race up his arm, and looking down, he was surprised to see that she was touching his gloved hand. "Did you hurt yourself?" she said.

"No," he said, knowing he should withdraw his

hand. He could not. He simply could not do it. "It does not hurt. Ever. It only bleeds. My hands, in the palms."

"You have the marks of Christ," she said.

"They call it the stigmata," he said with as much dignity as he could muster.

"And you wear the gloves always?"

"Yes. Almost all the time."

Gabriella looked into his eyes, and he could not look away from those dark pools of gold.

"So you touch nothing?"

"After a fashion, no . . . I suppose I don't."

Leaning closer to him, she placed her glass on the shelf beneath the window. She did not move away. Her lips lingered near his ear and she spoke in a husky whisper. "But you would very much like to touch *me*, wouldn't you?"

"Yes!"

The word exploded from him without design or intent. It was the most natural, most human response he could have ever uttered, but in that instant he knew he would never reach Delphi. In a flash of bitter prescience, he *knew*.

Outside their compartment, the night rattled past, but he felt so isolated that he and this siren woman could have been adrift at sea or sealed in a derelict satellite. Gabriella was looking at him, her golden almond eyes grown so large that he could see her lust writhing behind them. She unbuttoned her dress, and it fell to the floor in a whisper of soft fabric as her magnificent breasts rose up toward him.

"Say it again."

"Yes!"

Mauro had never felt such stirrings in his life. As if overcome by a hideous fever, he had no control over his actions. He felt totally consumed by an atavistic response. Reaching out, he put his arms around the nude Gabriella, instantly absorbed into her aura of sweet musky scent, her body heat. Never had he imagined anything like this. His hands glided over the length of her and he was utterly transfixed by her skin, impossibly soft yet defined by toned muscle.

In a fog of desire, he stripped off the gauze and the thin cotton gloves, feeling for the first time the unspeakable smoothness of a woman's flesh.

He became aware again of the trundling rhythm of the railroad car, and he realized he had come full circle—the rocking comfort of the train, the pliant security of a woman's body. His mother, holding him as the smallest boy on a train such as this, had launched him on a voyage to this moment. All his life, he had been seeking this kind of well-being and never finding it, always burying the undying need.

Until this moment.

Until this abdication of all that ever had meaning to him.

Gabriella sighed under his touch, then took his hands and raised them to her parted lips. She kissed them gently, then with greater fervor. Abruptly she stopped, then lowered their linked hands slowly, like a curtain on a closing act.

"Mauro, my sweet Mauro," she whispered. "Look! It is a miracle!"

He had been lost in the maelstrom of her gaze, beyond the capacity to think with clarity or wisdom. With incredible difficulty, he focused and saw . . .

. . . hands, white and smooth, unviolated.

His hands.

It was the most horrible sight of his life. Something shifted in the deep vault of his soul, forcing its way up through a throat much too small. When it broke free, it was the most terrible sound he'd ever heard—not really a scream as much as a cry of abject loss, of recognized damnation.

Tears burst into his eyes like acid, and he reeled back, stumbling away from Gabriella, holding up his unwounded palms in stunned disbelief. Mauro reached for the latch, sprung it frantically, and slid back the frosted glass panel. As he stumbled into the narrow passage, the mocking laughter of the slut reached out for him like a serpent from a tree.

In a flash of utterly coherent perception, he knew that laughter had not come from the throat of a woman, but from something usually unknown to humans. . . .

His vision blurred by the glaze of his tears, he pushed through the door that connected his car with the next and found himself whipped and battered by the roar of steel against steel and the ragged wind of the train's passage. Below, between the cars, beyond the huge couplers holding each other like clenched, black fists, the smear of the roadbed and railroad ties awaited him.

Mauro sealed off the unending scream that still leaked from him and stepped forward to be ripped beneath the wheels.

PIERCE ERICKSON

Blinking his eyes, he looked up to see the machines flanking him like robots in a cheesy sci-fi flick. They were all beeping and monitoring and adjusting, and he knew he was in a hospital.

What?

The last thing he remembered was getting out of that reporter's car, going up the steps to his house, and . . .

. . . and what?

Pierce couldn't think straight—every notion, every

memory a supreme effort to form and consider with acuity. What the hell was wrong with him? Drugged? Possibly, but why? There was more to remember, he was certain, but it would be so hard to bring it back, to pull it up from the deeps. He began moving his fingers, clenching and unclenching his fists, then testing his legs. Everything felt rubbery, unresponsive. Definitely drugged, maybe wearing off, but were those machines going to notice his coming to consciousness and send him another dose of lotus blossoms?

I don't think so, he thought forcibly, and it was the first truly clear thought he'd enjoyed since awakening.

He moved his arm, hoping it was really moving and not just some drugged memory of what it felt like to move an arm, and reached for the IV tubing that snaked down to a taped needle tapping a prominent vein on the back of his left hand. One yank and it was out. Now, even if the machines didn't like what they were seeing, they couldn't do anything about it.

Slowly, with no sense of time, he waited until images and impressions and finally snatches of entire events bubbled up to the surface of his mind.

He had to be patient and hope no one came to check on him. When it occurred to him to look out the window, he saw darkness through the thin slats of the blinds. Which meant that the hospital, or whatever it was, was most likely running on a skeleton crew; therefore he had less chance of being discovered off his pharmaceutical tether.

Gradually the past clarified itself.

The vision, the tunnel, and the cave-in, the escape ride with the TV reporter, entering his home . . .

That's when things got hazy, more weird, as though his subconscious was trying to skirt what followed. No way, he thought, I have to push through this mess.

. . . he was standing in his living room, Sydney hold-

ing him close as he told her everything, and she was
reacting with the expected incredulity and shock. But
she'd hung in there, not flinching—he remembered that
in a sudden burst of memory. His wife had been where
she'd always been: right by his side. No ridicule, no
chastisement or accusations. That was Sydney.

They'd begun to discuss the details of how he would
get to Jerusalem as quickly as possible. Right there in
the living room, she'd started making plans with him.
She not only believed him, but she believed in him,
which made *everything* in his life easy.

Until the banging on the front door . . .

Somehow, they'd found out where he lived. From
the wreckage of his car and its registration papers, or
maybe even from the reporter—what was her name?—
who'd sworn to say nothing. They laid siege to his
house on Riverside: newspapers, television and radio,
the rescue teams, the paramedics, even army engineers.
Everybody determined to get a piece of him for his or
her own purposes. No sooner had Sydney slipped the
latch than they literally stormed his home like pillaging
barbarians. The clamor of the invasion had awakened
his little girls, who stared down from the second floor
in terrified confusion. Pierce remembered screaming at
them all to get out and leave them alone, but nobody
was listening. A huge crowd of people, all jacked up
from the tension of the tunnel accident, all locked onto
the scent of a great story or the promise of more information.

This man, Pierce Erickson, who had saved so many
lives, belonged to them now.

They swarmed around him in overwhelming numbers, and he became enraged. Shouting and pushing
made no difference. Microphones and cameras bobbed
across the sea of bodies like buoys in a storm. Someone
shoved someone, arms and hands were flying in all

directions. Pierce saw a hand grab Sydney and spin her around to face the obscenely prying eye of a camcorder. He lunged for the offender, his fist landing squarely in the man's face, and the melee had escalated quickly out of control.

He remembered being thrown to the carpet and people falling all over him. He'd been pummeling them, struggling to get up, to help Sydney, to find his daughters! They pushed him back down, and someone jammed a needle in his arm, right through his white shirt, and the whole scene went spiraling downward into darkness . . .

. . . and now he lay there seething all over again. The bastards! Who did they think they were? And as soon as they found out he was conscious they'd be all over him again. Nothing but a bunch of leeches lining up to suck him dry.

No way.

Sitting up, Pierce fought a moment of disequilibrium, then methodically disengaged himself from the rest of the monitoring devices. If he was setting off alarms in the nurses' station, he would deal with it later. First things first. And first was out of this rear-ventilated hospital gown. Dim ambient light leaked in through the blinds from sodium-vapor parking lots. He used it to find the closet at the end of the bed, which held his suit, shirt, and shoes. His wallet and his house keys were gone, but they'd left his reading glasses in their case in his breast pocket. Good, very good. Quickly, he fumbled his way into the clothes. As he was tying his wingtips, the door to his room opened, partially obscuring Pierce behind it.

A small-framed man in surgical greens paused in the doorway, trying to assess what was happening. "What the fu—?"

Pierce put his shoulder into the door and slammed

its edge up against the guy's temple. It was like hitting him with a hammer; he collapsed and didn't move as Pierce stepped over him and out into the corridor.

It was empty, but might not be for much longer, and he leaned forward to run on his toes to the closest exit sign. The stairwell was illuminated with hard, cold fluorescent light, and he had to be careful as he tried to run down the steps. Still fighting the residual effects of the drugs, he was feeling dizzy. But he kept going, three flights to the bottom, which opened into a deserted hallway that ended in double doors under another exit sign.

He hit the doors running and found himself in an alley that led to the hospital's loading dock. He ran to the nearest street and quickly assayed his position. They'd taken him to Columbia Medical, which meant he was not too far from his house, but there might still be lots of confusion and crowds there.

He needed to get away from everyone, contact Sydney to assure her he was all right, and somehow get to Jerusalem as quickly as possible. He would never forget the image of the woman who'd appeared to him; her words of warning and her message that God needed him.

Pierce knew he had to act fast. No telling how much time before the nurse woke up. Taking out his glasses, he reached into a side pocket and pulled out two things he would need—two spare car keys and a debit card. He smiled, thinking of Sydney who'd always made fun of his obsessive need to have those emergency items on his person. And he'd always explained to her that the two things he most worried about were losing his wallet and getting his keys locked in his car. Hence the survival kit in the little leather case he'd ordered from Levenger's catalog years ago.

And so, after hitting the ATM for the cash limit, he

hailed a cab to JFK's international terminal. By the time he got there, the sun was almost up and the terminal was coming to life. Going to the nearest phone, he dialed an 888 number that keyed him into his company's computers. Providential Casualty Insurance had been a pioneer in same-day claims investigation and settlement for its largest corporate customers, and the state-of-the-art cybernetics were a big part of making it happen. Pierce was about to use it to his advantage as well.

When the digital system greeted him and asked for his password, he keyed it in and entered the flight reservation submenu, which afforded claims investigators next-flight access on a company LearJet to any part of the world at a moment's notice. Punching keys quickly, he received passage clearance out of JFK to Tel Aviv. Departure in less than ninety minutes—that's why his company was the best. He could call Sydney from the plane.

He took a shuttle bus to the private hangar of Providential Casualty and signed in with Dan McClory, Director of Flight Operations for the company.

"Good morning, Mr. Erickson," said Dan. "Last-minute plans as usual, eh?"

"You betcha." Pierce smiled as he passed through the security scanner. "That's why they pay me the big bucks!"

McClory chuckled and waved him into the executive lounge to wait for boarding. "They're getting your plane ready for you now, sir. It will be only a few more minutes."

He used the time to wash up and shave in the men's room and decided he didn't look too beat up, considering what he'd been through in the last twenty-four hours. After he finished fresh coffee and pastry, he felt renewed. When the call came to board, he was feeling extremely good about everything.

Climbing into the passenger section, he was welcomed by his pilot and second officer. The compartment resembled a studio apartment. Outside the craft, the ground crew scurried about, attaching the tractor for push back to the runway. Absently, Pierce watched the activity out the window. He was already planning his moves after arriving in Israel, when he thought he saw something that clearly *shouldn't* be.

As the Lear began backing up, one of the ground crew on the fuel truck, a young black woman, turned to look at the plane, then directly into the cabin windows, at Pierce. It was not a passing glance, but a purposeful stare, and she continued to track the plane's movement with her gaze until she was certain Pierce had not only seen her but also recognized her.

It was impossible! She could not conceivably be here . . .

Raising her right hand, the woman who'd called herself Shaenara Williamson smiled her perfect television camera smile and waved *bye-bye*.

FORTY

Giza
October 31, 2000

MARION WINDSOR

She was awakened by a plaintive wailing sound.

It wasn't quite a scream, somehow softer and filled with an infinite sadness. Marion realized the sound was coming from Etienne who lay beside her in a trancelike state.

Should I touch her, wake her?

The thought filled Marion with alarm. Etienne might be traveling out of her body, performing one of her "visits," as she had once phrased it.

There was a tapping at the door to the room, and Marion slipped from the straw pallet to hold it open several inches. Francesco and Sforza stood poised for trouble.

"What is the matter?" asked the Jesuit, looking more gaunt than usual.

"She's sleeping, but she's having some sort of dream

or vision or something." Marion looked past them. "Where's the Cardinal?"

"He sleeps like a dead man," said Francesco.

And the sound stopped. Just like that. The two men eased into the room without a sound. Marion turned around and saw Etienne, propped up on one elbow, looking at the three of them.

"Things are going badly," she said, as if she were in the middle of a conversation.

"What do you mean?" said Francesco, walking over and hunkering down beside her.

"The Seven Keys . . . Peter must know about them."

"Why? What's happened, Etienne?" said Marion. "Tell us."

"Some of the Seals remain unopened."

"Is that bad?" said Sforza.

"I don't know. But only *one* of the righteous still lives!" She recounted her latest vision in which she witnessed the fates of those she'd summoned. Everyone listened without interruption.

"What does this mean?" Francesco said softly. "Is that bastard winning?"

"Not yet, but he can," said Etienne.

"Are we clear on what the Seals represent?" said Sforza.

Francesco looked at him. "How clear have we ever been on what *Revelation* is all about?"

"That is true," said Sforza. He swiped a hand over his bald head reflexively, a mannerism he performed with enough frequency to be noticeable.

"Father, I feel so responsible," said Etienne. "I summoned those people to their deaths."

"No," said Francesco. "God did that. You were only his instrument."

"In my heart I know that, but I watched them die.

All of them so brave, so trusting." Etienne shook her head, then stood up. "We must go. Now. This is the beginning of the next full moon."

"Interesting," said Francesco. "Tomorrow is All Souls' Day."

"So this is All Hallows' Eve." Lareggia spoke with a great solemnity. "The time in antiquity when Evil was given its freedom."

"It is a time for caution," said Etienne. "We must move quickly."

"What?" said Marion. "Where?"

"To Giza. To the Great Pyramid. We must be there before Peter."

"He is coming to Giza?" said Francesco.

"Oh, yes. He knows what is at stake, and he has no options. He is in the hands of the Adversary. He is committed now to seeing this through."

"Somebody must wake up the fat man," said Francesco. "I am certain he will not want to miss the show."

Sforza chuckled. "Come, we will all prepare."

Marion watched the two men exit the room, then turned back to Etienne. She felt a growing, undefined terror. "Something bad is going to happen, isn't it? What does it all mean, Etienne?"

"The Seals are gateways to each new era. In themselves they are not important, other than as symbols. By opening them, we are showing God that we want the world to continue."

"Why does Peter want it to end?" Marion kept thinking of how much he had changed, how twisted he had become. How could he have chosen to be such a monster?

Etienne smiled wanly. "In his heart, he may not; but he now serves one who wants this world removed, so that another—more pleasing to him—might take its place."

"It's the sun, isn't it?" said Marion.

"You remember my dream about the black sun?"

"Yes," said Marion. "And I've seen pieces in the news. The scientists have been recording strange activity."

"It may all be connected, yes."

Marion could not speak for a moment. To think the world could actually end . . . how could it . . . ? Oh, God, *how* . . . ?

Etienne looked at her with an expression of complete serenity, and Marion wished she could be like this woman. "Marion, have faith . . ."

"But you said things are not going well. What happened to the Seven? How did Peter stop them?"

"He hasn't yet," said Etienne. "As long as there is one to affirm God's supreme glory, the world cannot end."

"But there's only one left!"

"We need only one, and that's why we must be at Giza to meet him. We can protect him from Peter's wrath. We can end it there."

"Why Giza?"

Etienne shrugged. "It is one of the most sacred places in the world. Probably the oldest location on earth, and therefore the most important. There are geomantic lines in the earth, like transmission cables. They connect the holy places. Giza is a focal point. All lines pass through there. The pyramids are like prisms of spiritual energy."

Marion grinned ironically. "So there really is such a thing as 'pyramid power.' "

"Yes. Nothing to joke about."

"The Egyptians knew this?"

"If they are the ones who built the pyramids, yes."

Etienne turned and went into the washroom of the falling-down hovel where Sforza's people had hidden them. Built late in the last century by enterprising British hoteliers, the building had since become a tenement in the Algerian neighborhood. The stucco walls were filthy, the plumbing barely worked, and the electricity was erratic and minimal. When they'd told Marion she would be taken to a safe house, this was not what she had imagined. But it had indeed been safe—no one paid them any attention.

After taking her chances with the unpredictable plumbing, she joined the others. They were all dressing like amateur archaeologists, in a style that reminded her of the apparel catalogs offered to people who wanted to pretend they were dashing and adventurous.

Marion climbed into the backseat of a vintage Land Rover obtained by Sforza. The stocky, muscular man drove through the back streets of Cairo with the elan of someone who knows it intimately, and she imagined that his familiarity with hundreds of cities had become one of his primary survival traits. Marion closed her eyes against the rising sun above the low rooftops. She had not been prepared for how densely crowded were the streets of this city—not just with people, but with *everything*. Trash, vehicles of every year and sort, cats and dogs, all competing for precious space.

The Rover hugged a tight corner, and they were suddenly near the waterfront, where their pointed quarry loomed in the hazy distance.

GIOVANNI FRANCESCO

His life was winding down.

He could feel it. Not because of the creaking effort required each morning as he struggled up from fitful sleep that never left him feeling rested. No, it was more of a spiritual creaking—a fatigue that could no longer be replaced by the driving energy of curiosity or tasks undone. He believed he had seen and done enough to comprise one lifetime, and he wondered what came next.

As the Rover headed for the gangway to the al-Tariq Ferry that would get them across the Nile, Giovanni considered the justifications and excuses he'd been feeding himself and his God all his life to excuse his renegade behavior. He had not been a very good priest, except for keeping celibate. While so many of his colleagues had either forced their natural urges down avenues of the perverse, or simply surrendered to an occasional prostitute, Giovanni had been oddly untroubled by that kind of desire. His lust was of a different sort. With each tempting dram of power, he found himself drawn to ever more of it.

It was always for power. To keep a pope or world leader in power, to acquire more for himself, to see that others did not obtain it. He'd found global intrigue and espionage to be his fatal aphrodisiac, which explained his part as the impetus for the birth of the monster who now called himself Pope Peter II.

How stupid he'd been to believe he could control or even manipulate such a creation! Little Mary Shelley had known the folly of that thinking, the utter madness that cultivated such pride. But Francesco's creation would be better than all who had come before him. God wouldn't dare swat him down.

No, God would not. Giovanni would do a far better job himself.

And now, as in the poem, the hour was coming round at last . . . but it all might very well end in fire instead of ice. All the poets, after all, could not be correct, he thought with a smile colored by his erudition. What he needed now was a means to rectify everything he'd done wrong for so many years.

He felt like one of those sheriffs in the American Western movies he so much loved when he was young—the man who walked into the center of town, knowing he faced certain death at the hands of the outlaws, but doing it not so much because it was the right thing to do, but because it was the *only thing left* to do.

Etienne said that Peter was on his way to this spot. Good, he thought. I have been running from one thing or another all my life, including the truth of my most terrible creation. It stops now.

PETER CARENZA

No turning back now.

The thought kept replaying in his mind like a warped sector on a music CD, nudging itself between other notions at random moments. Irritating but tolerable. And in one sense he actually liked the intrusion, because it underscored what was happening and the path onto which he'd finally, completely stepped.

Peter did not like to think of anything so Calvinistic as having everything totally worked out ahead of time. It simply did not make sense. No, God obviously liked giving people tests, although Peter could not remember getting any specific test himself. It was as if God had decided early on he was . . . tainted goods and therefore not worth saving.

That was okay with Peter. He was finally comfortable with the role of Necessary Evil.

He smiled as his private helicopter angled down low over the Mediterranean, passing just west of Alexandria's harbor and continuing south, following the compass of the Nile. The brass barge of the sun had just begun its voyage across the ancient land below.

Necessary Evil. He repeated the concept to himself.

How perfectly Zen. The need for an endless cosmic symmetry was an issue many Western, Christian philosophers had ignored, gingerly skirted, or missed altogether.

One of the most important aspects of this symmetry was that the concepts of good and evil lost their meaning. The balance in the universe is no more or less than the basic antipodal nature of protons and electrons. Neither can be pronounced any more "good" than the other—only different.

As *I* am different, thought Peter.

Is the antelope any more "good" than the lion that slays and eats it? And wouldn't the antelope eat the lion, if it could? What about the microbes that burrow and multiply throughout the fabric and tissue of everything on the planet? Does painting them with a moral brush make even the slightest bit of sense?

Peter at last understood his place in reality, and had grown comfortable with it. He had communed with the one he'd been taught all his life to shun and revile, and honestly, it had not been "bad" at all.

"Touchdown in twenty minutes," said his pilot.

"Do the Egyptian authorities know who we are?" Peter looked down, studying the jeweled meanderings of time's most storied waterway. A ferry eased across the slick surface like a wounded waterbug.

His pilot grinned, shook his head. "They don't know the Pope is here, if that's what you mean. They think we are from the NATO Security Agency, looking for one of our agents."

"Which means?"

"Which means their own ops will watch us, but they will leave us alone. Unless we do something out of line."

Peter smiled. "You know, I was thinking, maybe

they *should* know the Pope is here. It might make our job easier."

ETIENNE

The Rover had completed its river crossing, and Sforza headed through Giza, following the signs to the Pyramids area. As they drew closer to the world-famous tourist mecca, Etienne noticed how quickly everything changed from severe poverty to outlandish commercialism. On the Alexandria Desert Road they passed many posh hotel complexes that would not be out of place on the Vegas strip. She said, "Take the Western Desert Road, down to the Dashur pyramid."

"But that's south of where you want to be," said Sforza. "Are you sure?"

"Yes," said Etienne. "There is another way to the Great Pyramid, a way untraveled in many thousands of years."

"Something tells me that is all about to change," said Paolo Lareggia, who looked vastly more comfortable in his loose-fitting white cotton blouse and voluminous safari shorts, though they were already stained with large patches of perspiration.

"Don't be afraid," said Marion, with a brave smile. "This lady usually gets it right."

Etienne looked at Marion and smiled. She liked the young woman, especially because she had never allowed herself to become closed-minded or cynical. Marion could easily have surrendered to the forces that consumed Peter, but Etienne believed she possessed an inner strength that was only now beginning to be tapped.

They drove past the familiar collection of four-sided peaks, continuing to the outskirts of an archaeological site that received little or no tourist attention. Etienne saw an odd shape in the distance. The Dashur pyramid lay just beyond the partially excavated series of ancient gardens, boulevards, and temples. "There it is," she said.

"It looks different from the other ones," said Francesco.

"It's called the 'bent' pyramid," said Etienne. "No one knows why its lines bend out like that."

"Strange," said Francesco. "I've never heard of it."

"This is far enough," said Etienne to Sforza. "Pull off the road. We must walk to the base. Make sure we have flashlights—we will be needing them."

There was little activity in the area, and if anyone saw the small group homing in on Dashur, they paid them no attention. Etienne led them to an area several yards south of the pyramid's base, to a series of stone slabs that appeared to be part of the floor of a wide boulevard or promenade. Some of the slabs had been removed to reveal a sloping entrance into a subterranean passage.

"We go in here," said Etienne.

"Where is this going to take us?" asked Francesco, flicking on a large flashlight and falling into line behind Etienne.

"Inside the Great Pyramid," said Etienne. "To a location called the Queen's Chamber."

The Cardinal, with Marion following, walked single file behind Francesco, leaving Brother Sforza to establish a rear-guard position. The passage was approximately seven feet high and wide, and paved on all four sides by polished limestone. The joints of the stone were close to seamless, and the floor was extremely level. They walked in silence for a while, although Etienne could feel questions, as well as tension, building in all of them. This was probably a good time to fill in some of the gaps.

"We are not the first to do this," she said. "The year 1000 marked the first time God required the Seals to be ministered by seven righteous men."

"You mean here?" said Marion. "They came here?"

"Yes," said Etienne.

"Who were they?" said Lareggia, laboring from the effort of merely walking. Each word sounded like it might be his last.

"Arabs and Christians. One was, in fact, a Maltese Knight," she said. "You may know of the story of Rolandus, Brother Sforza."

Sforza grunted in the affirmative. "It is a fragmented legend," he said. "There are several versions that describe him facing down Lucifer on a giant sundial, and also at the entrance to the pit of Hell itself."

Etienne smiled. "Yes, and both are true, in the way that all legends are true. In the 800s, the great caliph of Baghdad, Harun al-Rashid, had a son, Abdullah al-Mamum, who became one of the most enlightened rulers of the age. He became a scholar, scientist, explorer, and philosopher. His expedition was the first fully and completely to explore and map out the interior of the Great Pyramid—although many say he did nothing but desecrate it. One of his descendants, Masudi al-Kaisi, returned to this site one thousand years ago to stand for what is good in us, along with Saint Rolandus and five others."

"Seven Keys to Seven Churches," said Marion.

"Yes," said Etienne. "There are always seven. For every season."

"Except for now," said Marion.

"What do you mean?" said Lareggia

"There is only one left."

"It will be sufficient," said Etienne. "Trust in our God."

"What is the name of this person," asked Sforza.

Etienne smiled as she thought of him. "He is a young man. His name is—"

HUANG XIAO

His route had been tortuous as he wound his way south from the high ceilings of the earth in Nepal. Travel by motorized vehicle was not the easiest thing to achieve in that part of Asia.

With each hour he endured, he became more aware of a great pressure building, and the weight of his journey grew more oppressive. Sleeping in sewers, packing crates, abandoned sheds, anywhere he wouldn't be seen. After two days of catching freight trains across northern India, counting the passing cities like beads on a string—Patna, Kanpur, Agra, Delhi—he ended up at an ASL (air/sea/land) container dock in Peshawar. Being very careful, he spent almost twenty-four hours deciphering and tracking endless containers until he had figured out the dock's basic layout and what containers were designated for what destination.

Time was his primary concern. He *must* arrive in Giza as soon as possible. Ideally, he'd wanted to find a container designated for Cairo, but the best he could do under the time constraints was Port Said.

The container was filled with construction supplies and equipment, and Xiao was able to open several cartons and make an acceptable bed out of excelsior and bubble wrap. The container was slipped into a cargo plane as he slept.

The flight to the Middle East required only four hours, and then the container was deplaned, loaded onto a flatbed truck carrier, and driven to a distribution center east of the Said docks. When Xiao heard the clanging of the huge latches of his container, he tried to remain unseen between packing crates—at least long enough to assess the number of people he would need to avoid.

From the quality of the light seeping into the opened container, he assumed he was indoors, most likely a warehouse. Footsteps echoed against the walls of the container punctuated by the harsh grunts and mono-syllables of the laborers, who had begun sliding ship-ping crates toward the open end of the container. Stealthily, Xiao kept something large between himself and the workers. As if playing a gigantic game of check-ers on an invisible board, he gradually worked his way forward, closer and closer to the opening.

Whatever awaited him out there, he would worry about it when he encountered it . . . or it encountered him.

He did not have to wait long.

As the last of the larger crates were unloaded, Xiao slid along the outer wall of the container and slipped around the corner. He heard no one shouting in his direction and assumed he was unseen, at least for the moment.

Quickly, he assessed the layout: a huge warehouse, swarming with laborers, an unloading dock where hun-dreds of boxes and crates were waiting for storage or further shipping by truck. He'd seen similar arrange-ments throughout his travel across Asia and knew he had to get clear of the area as soon as possible.

Xiao ran toward a series of aisles and warehouse shelving. As he did this, somebody finally saw him—unintelligible shouts followed him. Xiao continued to run as fast as his young, lean body would carry him.

He headed down a long aisle where several laborers

were stacking medium-sized boxes. They looked up at him but either did not care or simply chose not to try to stop him.

When he reached the end of the aisle, he chanced a left turn, which looked to end in a set of double doors. Racing toward them, Xiao glanced back, but the way was clear other than a few totally disinterested laborers who were probably thankful that he was the one in trouble instead of them.

Bursting through the double doors, he found himself in a narrow passage between buildings. One end was blocked by a parked truck; the other was open. As Xiao ran between the buildings, someone emerged from a side doorway, shouted and began running after him. Looking back, he saw a man dressed in some sort of uniform and brandishing a sidearm. Xiao sped up and dodged from side to side. He'd almost reached the open space when another uniformed man suddenly appeared, also holding a weapon and pointing it squarely at Xiao's face.

Xiao reacted on pure instinct, diving forward and tucking into a roll that launched him past the shooter. As he did this, the man fired his weapon several times, the reports resonating off the walls. Springing up, Xiao looked back to see his pursuer lying on his back, his chest stained with blood. The second security man had rushed to his comrade's side, and Xiao kept running, through a chain-link gate and past parking lots full of trucks.

He had no idea where he was. All he knew was that he had to get to Giza. And so, onward. . . .

PAOLO CARDINAL LAREGGIA

Why had he agreed to come along?
Because Peter would probably have had him killed

if he'd remained in the Vatican, came his response to his own question.

Paolo wheezed, laboring to keep up with the others. They seemed to have been walking for hours. The drudgery of the trek had been countered by Etienne's stories, but even so Paolo was exhausted. His heart jackhammered erratically in his chest. He was too old and unhealthy to keep up this pace.

But he knew that he no longer needed to survive the ordeal. After the flaming tree and the hosts of angels in the skies above Africa, he knew that God's hand stirred the mix. And that was enough of a sign to indicate that perhaps he might be forgiven for the prideful thing he'd set into motion, bringing Peter to life. He expected that he would soon die.

Oddly, the prospect no longer filled him with dread.

PETER CARENZA

The change in strategy had been a very good idea.

The helicopter hovered, waiting while the Egyptian Tourist Agency and Parks Police cleared a landing zone for them and sent troopers to secure the entrance to the Great Pyramid. Returnees to Giza were always shocked to see how egregiously commercial the area had become. Overrun by souvenir stands, eateries, hotels, mendicants, con men, and tourist guide operations, the place had achieved a level of ugliness that was almost profound. When the authorities swept through this backwash of mercantilism, more than a few people got upset. Peter watched the operation with a wry smile.

His pilot leaned on the stick. The helicopter touched down in a maelstrom of flying sand. Before the rotors had stopped spinning, Egyptian authorities rushed to the craft—two quasi-military-looking young men employed as security for the National Park Service.

"Your Holiness," said one soldier, snapping to attention, "I have been ordered by our President to welcome you and to report his surprise at your unannounced visit to our monuments."

"Thank you," said Peter. "I regret being unable to inform him in advance of my trip."

The young soldier nodded. "What can my government do for you to make your visit as comfortable as possible?"

Peter smiled, put his hand on the man's shoulder. "Do you really want to know?"

"Yes, Holy Father."

Peter continued smiling, but in a way that he could tell was making the young man feel uneasy. "I would be best served if you could leave me alone."

"What? I do not understa—"

"I have an appointment with my God—in your shrine. It is a private matter. I am afraid I cannot explain it in any other way."

"I see," said the soldier. "One moment, please." He stepped back and began an exchange through his two-way radio, which lasted several minutes.

Peter waited. Beyond the perimeter of the landing zone, a small crowd had gathered, but it did not appear that anyone recognized him. Peter felt so good at that moment, it was as if he were intoxicated. No, more. He'd never felt such an incredible combination of emotions and sensations, all suggesting that he was invincible and omniscient. Looking up into the bronzed sky, he regarded the sun as an old friend.

The soldier returned. "My government is happy to help you in any way," he said. "But I must act as your guide while you are in the pyramid, for safety reasons."

"Very well," said Peter. "I would like to enter right away. Can we get started now?"

The young man conferred with his partner, then said, "Let us go. Is there anything in particular you would like to see?"

Peter chuckled. "Yes, I would like to see my mother."

MARION WINDSOR

They were almost there.

The Queen's Chamber. Etienne told them it had been misnamed by the Arabs, who had pillaged this incredible structure, carting off the shining outer stones to build the mosque of Sultan Hasan. They didn't know that the ancient Egyptians didn't consider women, even a queen, worthy of such a tomb. Etienne told her listeners that in fact this was the focal point of the entire structure.

They had been walking in a straight line on a very slightly inclined plane, for a time Marion could not estimate. Etienne was leading them through the darkness, she thought, both literally and figuratively. Suddenly she stopped.

"What's the matter?" asked Marion, unable to see very far ahead of the nun.

"This is as far as the passage goes," Etienne said.

Marion followed the beam of Etienne's light to where it played on a blank wall of large limestone blocks.

"Now what?" she asked.

Etienne smiled a small, slightly impish smile and pointed her beam straight up, above their heads. "We go that way."

"That looks very tough," said Marion. Her own flashlight illuminated a perpendicular shaft with a beautifully detailed ladder inlaid into the wall of one side of the shaft.

"Etienne," said Francesco, "how do you *know* these things?"

She looked at him, still smiling. "How do you know God loves you?"

Francesco nodded and said nothing more.

"How far up do we go?" said Sforza, dropping down to one knee and opening his backpack. "We're going to need to set this up."

"A rope ladder," said Marion. "How?"

"You will stand on my shoulders, drive these pitons into the seams of the blocks anywhere near the first steps in the shaft. Can you do it?"

"I can do it," said Marion.

And she did. Within minutes, everyone was ready to ascend the ladder.

Everyone except the Cardinal. "I can't!" he said, almost crying. "I can barely walk on level ground. There is no way I can lift myself into the bowels of this place!"

"If you stay here, you may die," said Francesco, looking at his colleague with an expression of true concern. "Paolo, I mean it. Please, don't give up without trying."

"Thank you, 'Vanni. But I must stay right here."

Lareggia held the base of the rope ladder stable for everyone else, then watched sadly as they moved upward. Marion noted that the rungs and handgrips cut into the stone made the task of climbing as comfortable as possible, but the idea of doing it for hundreds of feet was daunting.

Soon, the small square that marked the entrance of the shaft below them had dwindled to a tiny spot of yellow light from Lareggia's torch.

As Marion climbed, trying not to think of what she was doing, she once again thought back over the past several years. Her entire life and, more important, her basic understanding of life, had been tremendously altered by events so strange that she could hardly believe they'd actually happened. And if she had such trouble imagining how it had all started, picturing how it might end was even harder.

It had something to do with the sun, that she knew, but no one had been very interested in talking about it. Even when she had the chance to read or view scientific discussions of the solar prominence activity, it was obvious that no one wanted to dwell on the worst implications of the volatility of the sun. Mainly because there was nothing, the scientists believed, that humans could do about it. . . .

But that's where they're wrong, thought Marion.

There is something to be done, and we're doing it.

"Almost there," said Etienne in a soft voice. He words were spoken without strain or sign of exhaustion. "I can see the opening!"

"Thank God," whispered Marion, suddenly realizing how true her automatic exclamation most certainly was.

"I am in the chamber!" said Etienne. Her voice resonated as though she stood in some vast, acoustically perfect place.

Marion's heart stepped up in rhythm as she pulled herself over the edge. Looking up she saw something that could not be possible. . . .

PAOLO CARDINAL LAREGGIA

He could hear the sounds of their voices cascading down the shaft like a delicate waterfall, but their words commingled during the descent, and he could comprehend nothing.

Paolo had passed the time by praying. And he was happy with the tenor of the words he composed for his Creator, because they were not the self-serving, groveling bequests of someone who is afraid for the fate of his soul. Paolo felt privileged to have been touched by and been witness to the manifestations of God. Very few mortals ever received such a gift, yet lately, it seemed he had begun to live every moment under the endless counsels of the Lord above.

Paolo found himself smiling as he looked once more up the shaft, where his brave and infinitely more fit companions had now vanished. He moved slowly to the wall, leaned against it, and sank to a sitting position. His great bulk settled so completely he wondered if he would ever have the strength to raise himself. He began to doze as the relentless exhaustion finally caught up with him—

He heard footsteps.

Instantly, he opened his eyes in immediate and tingling alertness. Adrenaline pulsed through him like electricity.

A rasping, pulsating sound echoed off the tight walls of the corridor, making the short hairs on his neck grow rigid until he suddenly realized he was listening to the bellows wheeze of his own breathing.

Feeling silly, he held his breath for several seconds, testing the atmosphere for silence.

Far, far away, it seemed, were the syncopations of footfalls, a cadence that grew louder with each repetition. Louder and closer. Paolo let out his breath in an abrupt release of air, but not tension. He was reminded of Shakespeare's classic line of impending dread: *Something wicked this way comes.*

The footsteps grew louder.

Paolo pointed his light toward the darkness, its beam reflecting off millions of dusty fragments of limestone dust, bouncing back to him like headlights in thick fog. He could see nothing beyond an embarrassingly short distance.

"Who is there?" he shouted.

The footsteps stopped, but for only an instant.

Paolo opened his mouth to speak again as he kept the beam pointed straight ahead, but no words would escape him. He sat splayed out against the far wall, with no place to go, no way to escape whatever was homing in on him like a hound from hell.

Then he saw movement in the muddy light, coming forward, resolving itself into a figure at first vaguely human, then more so. Another step, and he would know, he could see—

A young man, barely out of his teens perhaps. An Asian with a shock of dirty black hair, deep-set dark eyes made deeper by hideous purple circles under them. His cheekbones, though high, were sharply angled, giving him an oddly menacing, aspect. His sweater, trousers, and jacket were filthy, half in tatters, and he stank. Even from the distance of ten paces, Paolo could smell his pungent body odor. The boy paused to protect his eyes from the lance of the electric beam of light. He looked scary and fragile simultaneously.

But he possessed one other attribute that superseded all the others, and it made Paolo suddenly understand what the artists and illuminators of centuries long past had been attempting to show—this ragged young man walked toward him, his movements softly muted and traced by a pale, ghostly aura, and around his head what could only be described as a halo.

HUANG XIAO

He held up his hands, waiting until the man directed the flashlight someplace other than the center of his face. Xiao turned his head at an angle, trying to see who lay in wait along the corridor he'd been "directed to" as though in a kind of trance.

Ever since he jumped from the panel truck on the Alexandria Desert Highway, he'd felt as though he had been walking while half asleep. But now, as he studied the man who lay sprawled against the wall in front of him, he knew his journey must be close to over. And he felt suddenly very much awake.

The man was very large, obese like a sumo wrestler but without the underlying cords of sinew. He was of an advanced age, but Xiao was not sure due to his abundant flesh. At first Xiao had thought he was injured, but he did not appear to be hurt, and he looked quite benign.

So Xiao stood before him and bowed. His English was limited, but he tried, first touching the center of his own chest.

"I Huang Xiao. I . . . the Lady . . ."

The fat man smiled. "Etienne!" he said, and Xiao knew instinctively that this was the Dream Lady's name.

He nodded enthusiastically.

The fat man pointed to the rope ladder, jerked his thumb upward, and nodded.

Without hesitation, Xiao grabbed the ladder and began to hoist himself toward his destiny.

ETIENNE

She had no idea how it was happening, but she certainly knew why.

Despite being entombed in a chamber hundreds of feet beneath millions of tons of stone, they stood looking up at the endless vault of the sky beyond the milky blue atmosphere and off into the limitless wonder of the galaxy.

The thirty-ton blocks of stone had become *transparent*!

"Behold," Etienne said as she dropped to her knees, "the wonder of God's hand."

In silence, Francesco, Sforza, and Marion followed her example. The expressions on their faces ran the spectrum from awe to sheer terror. Even Etienne felt overwhelmed by the stunning majesty of this display. Transfixed by the darkly shimmering dome, Etienne felt the light of all the burning stars like tiny fingers of warmth all over her body.

They knelt for a time unmeasured, while the universe caught its breath and the jewels of creation sparkled down upon them.

It was Marion who finally broke the silence and anchored them once again to their task. "How is this happening? Etienne? What does this mean?"

Etienne looked at the three of them and felt the words flow effortlessly off her tongue. "This chamber represents the exact center of the pyramid. All lines meet here. Everything that emanates from the Churches of Earth travels the dragon paths to here. The Seals are nothing more than signposts along the endless road. Like the loop of the Möbius, the Seals, when opened, all lead to the same place . . .

" . . . *here*.

"This is the crucible where consciousness first was fired."

Etienne closed her eyes. She could feel the end of all this labor looming just beyond the veil of what they could now see. She knew now that the deaths of the righteous had been necessary—as death would always be—so there would be life, and the life of the just would always purchase more than that of the malign. Almost everything made sense to her now. She felt as though she'd been granted the briefest glimpse of a vastly complex mechanism.

Almost everything had fallen into place.

In that oddly prescient state of mind that touched her with unexpected frequency, Etienne knew that all would soon be unraveled.

The juggernaut that was the fate of the world clanked ever closer, and she believed they were prepared, despite her perception of a missing piece.

Marion, still looking up at the vault of endless space surround them, spoke as though in prayer. "It is so beautiful."

PETER CARENZA

He heard the words as he entered the Queen's Chamber with the Egyptian guard, and for an instant he was transported back, far, far back, to a night beneath an Indiana sky, when Marion had spoken similar words about their situation, their knowing of each other, and a certain innocence long lost.

"Yes, Marion, it is, isn't?" he said. His words had the effect of both mocking her and announcing his presence. The guard who had led him into the room stood in silent terror, looking at the yawning well of stars that threatened to suck him down forever. The man fell to his knees screaming and crying, then looked about him in search of an answer that would let him stop being so terrified.

"This is the place of the Creator," said a stocky man next to the gaunt Francesco. He stood to face Peter. "I am Brother Sforza of the Holy Order of the Knights of Malta. By the power of all I have sworn to protect, begone!"

"Very dramatic," said Peter, smiling. "Did you rehearse those lines for very long?"

Sforza reached for a weapon on his belt and Peter extended a single finger in the man's direction. There was a soft burst of light, like a cheap flashbulb going off. Sforza screamed and fell to his knees, twisting in pain. His right hand and wrist had been transformed into a smoldering stump of charcoaled meat. He waved it about in agony, then collapsed to the floor and passed out.

"You don't dare try to stop me," said Peter in the softest voice he could manage.

"He's in shock," cried Marion as she knelt beside Sforza. "Damn you!"

"Too late, I'm afraid, for that," said Francesco.

The Egyptian guard pulled himself to his knees and began to crawl clumsily toward the place where the entrance to the chamber would be were it not transparent. Peter looked down at the man and despised his cowering weakness. He kicked him in the stomach with incredible force, feeling the soft tissue rupture under the blow.

The guard's fear for his life must have superseded the debilitating pain, because he struggled to his feet, then launched himself down the access corridor, howling in fear and agony.

"Is that what you have in store for all of us?" said Francesco.

"Worse," said Peter. "And I won't have to even touch you."

Etienne smiled with sweet sadness as she regarded her son. "Do you see? He cannot even look me in the eye. His own mother. What is it, Peter? Shame? Or do you loathe me so much?"

Still not looking directly at her, Peter faked a smile and said, "That's it, you've got it, *Mother*." He spoke the last word with as much sarcasm as possible, trying his best to sound like a bored Valley girl.

"I am sorry, my son, but I do not believe you."

"In a few minutes, it won't matter *what* you believe." He smiled at them again, but it still didn't feel right.

"Peter," said Francesco, "does it have to be like this?"

"Yes, my dear foster father," he said to the Jesuit with a mock frown, "I am afraid it does."

Giovanni Francesco shook his head. "I used to be a young man, and I believed I was capable of anything," he said. "I no longer believe that—but I do believe you will fail."

Peter was getting a little pissed off that none of them had greeted him with any of the surprise or fear he would have liked to have seen. Something was wrong.

"Giovanni, do you also believe you will be the one to stop me?"

The old Jesuit shrugged. "No," he said. "I believe that, ultimately, you will stop yourself."

"Well spoken, Father," said Etienne.

His mother's gaze was locked onto him like a predator selecting its next meal. He glanced, but he could not dismiss the image of her eyes—cold and dark, hard and reptilian.

Something was *wrong*.

Why had he been told by . . . by the "seminarian" . . . to come here?

"Giza . . . get there," the seminarian had said. But

why? Because they were winning? Because they had to be stopped? None of that made much sense. Peter obviously had the advantage here. Only one of the Seven had slipped through his net. Ah, that was why he was here, wasn't it? To finish him off.

To finish the whole business.

That last thought weighed on his mind as though carved out of lead, then it began to sink, slowly, into the deepest part of him. There was a certain appeal to that idea, and he'd never stopped to wonder why. But Peter was beginning to understand . . . he was beginning to grow tired of the entire . . . game. And that's what it was, when you looked at it closely—just played out on a bigger board, a bigger field.

Several years ago (but it seemed like several *lifetimes*), when he'd been a parish priest in New York, he remembered hearing the elderly tell him they were tired, and ready to go. *Tired* was the word they'd used, and Peter realized he'd been listening, but had never really understood what the old people had meant when they used that word. They were weary and bored and uncomfortable and unable to enjoy the things in life they once had. Life had not become worth living. Sounded so simple, but it underscored an essential philosophical question: Was it *ever* worth it?

As if seeking an answer in those who faced him now, he could feel as well as see the conviction in their eyes, seething and boiling in the cauldrons of their souls. They believed in *something*, and that faith superseded any silly questions about existentialism.

Maybe they needed a demonstration to—

At that moment, he perceived an odd glow leaking into the chamber from the vertical shaft at its center. Everyone watched the square aperture with curious fascination. The sound of boots grinding on the stone rungs of the ladder began as a rhythmic whisper, then grew progressively louder.

This was it, thought Peter. The reason for his coming here.

The glow became alarmingly brighter. Suddenly, a young man appeared at the top of the shaft, and as he did so, the entire structure of the chamber, perhaps the Great Pyramid itself, seemed to swell and contract, all in an instant. The transparent vault of the galaxy hanging all around them shimmered and warped for a moment.

The young man looked around the chamber, his expression awe-filled but resolute. Standing, he stared at Etienne with a look of recognition. He was young, Asian, and looked close to exhaustion. His clothes were torn and ragged, and he smelled bad, but there was an aura surrounding him, a surreal and faintly visible glow that Peter knew would not be perceptible anywhere but in this place, this focal prism of primal forces.

"I am Huang Xiao, Dream Lady," he said to Etienne. "I have come to you as you asked."

He spoke in a dialect of the northern provinces of China, but Peter could understand the words, and he suspected that everyone else could too.

Etienne smiled. "The Seal is open."

"The Seal means nothing!" said Peter. "I know the Secret of the Seven. The world will never end as long as one of them lives. And this boy is the *last*."

Etienne looked at him with her raven's eyes, and he chose to look at Xiao. "The world is not so bankrupt that God cannot select seven more," she said.

Peter smiled. He'd learned his lessons well. "Only if there is no one to oppose Him. And this time, there *is*— thanks to the metaphysical meddlings of Father Giovanni Francesco and his friends."

"I renounce you," said Francesco.

"Oh," said Peter, "I am *so* scared."

Holding his hand in the direction of the Chinese boy, Peter opened his palm. Xiao cried out, arcing his back as he began to slowly levitate into the center of the chamber as though he had become a spatial body around which the galaxy rotated . . .

. . . and perhaps he was.

"It is time we ended this," said Peter.

And Xiao began to scream.

GAETANO

He pushed the humvee to its limits, banging and crashing its wide carriage and outrageous suspension over rock and sand with impunity. Clearly, this vehicle was built to be abused. Using its onboard GPS computer, he had homed in on the suburban Cairo district of Giza and figured he would be able to tell where the action was by looking for the right signs when he got there, which would be any minute now. He had glimpsed sapphire bends of the Nile as he headed southward, and the peaks of the pyramids, looking very much like the labels of the old Camel cigarette packages, were visible through the morning haze.

If anyone knew he had taken the vehicle from the Alexandria street corner, they had not seemed to care. Gaetano tried not to think of the immense machinery that clanked undergound throughout the world to allow men like himself to move with the ease and shadowlike presence the rest of the world never suspected. He had to laugh at all the people with their visas and passports and permits and the way they submitted so faithfully to all that supposed security.

They didn't realize that the ones who needed to be

screened and controlled by all that crap never submitted to it in the first place.

Gaetano shook his head, replaying the frenzied sequence of events getting him this far. D'Agostino had taken care of him. There had indeed been a shoemaker shop in Anzio, and the proprietor was a real cobbler—the kind you never saw anymore—and when Gaetano told him *sonny-boy is home,* everything was taken care of. Solotano was old, but he was prepared for the worst, and he had connections to all the right people. Within an hour, Gaetano had been riding a powerboat across the Mediterranean to an Egyptian fishing boat three miles off the coast of Alexandria. Three salty characters had taken him aboard, dressed him like themselves, and brought him ashore with nets full of silvery fish he did not recognize. From there, he was directed to the intersection of Tobruk and Malamein, where "formidable transportation" awaited him.

The humvee bristled with weaponry and other lethal accessories like concussion grenades, SAM missiles and personal launchers, flame throwers, and a variety of things with sharp points and edges. Gaetano had packed as much of the small, portable stuff into the safari vest he now wore and kept several sidearms on the passenger seat.

He hit the pyramid area at an oblique angle from the access roads and parking lots, coming in from the northwest to avoid an immense concentration of tourist facilities. As he drew closer to the largest of the huge pyramids, he saw the trucks and cars of Egyptian authorities were clustered around a sleek helicopter and a large area designed to be a controlled-entry area to the Great Pyramid itself.

Nothing like the direct route, he decided as he downshifted the humvee and punched the gas pedal. It responded by literally leaping over a sand dune. With great rooster tails of sand marking his path, Gaetano careened up a steep grade and slid to a stop only yards from the entrance. Feeling the focused attention of crowds of tourists and the Egyptian authories, he grabbed an Uzi and a Ruger .45-caliber semiautomatic assault rifle.

"Hey there!" yelled one of the guards, rushing up to the driver's side of the vehicle. Gaetano floored him with the open door as he vaulted from his seat. The guard's compatriots, five in all, hesitated, trying to decide whether to unsnap their little .32-caliber snout noses, or call in the big boys from the regular army.

Gaetano didn't really care what they did. He fired a few warning blasts into the air with the Ruger and disappeared into the passageway. When he'd gotten about thirty yards in, several of the guards made the mistake of not only following him but firing a few shots at him as well. Turning back for a moment, he sprayed the small corridor with slugs, rolled a concussion grenade toward the entrance, and ran.

Very fast, up a gradually ascending slope, wanting to get as much distance between himself and—

—the *blast!*

It recoiled and rolled up the passage and hit him like the wind of a passing freight train. The force of the explosively compacted air knocked him down and continued to funnel upward into the heart of the pyramid. Getting up, Gaetano raced after it—to get away from the fireball right behind it.

MARION WINDSOR

"Leave him alone!" she shouted as Xiao slowly turned in the air as if on a barbecue spit, his face a hideous mask of agony.

Peter looked away from his prey for a moment and tried to smile at her. But there was nothing left in him even to pretend such warmth, and all he managed was a grim parody of the out-of-control emotion she'd seen boil out of him the night he'd killed Daniel Ellington.

That had been the night she realized she'd crawled into bed with a monster.

Something rumbled up the corridor through which Peter had arrived. He stood in the entranceway as the shock wave of the explosion reached him. He stood firm and screamed triumphantly, as if the blast of superheated air had been a signal, cueing the end of all things. Marion watched, locked in some atavistic paralysis, as Peter held his hand over Xiao's head, closing his fist and dropping it as if throwing something to ground.

And Huang Xiao, who'd been twisting and screaming in Peter's demonic grip, was flung toward the floor. For an instant, as Marion watched the boy hurtle toward the transparent barrier of the chamber's bottom layer, she imagined that Xiao would spiral toward the distant stars.

But he did not.

And when she heard the bone-crunching impact of his body upon the invisible stone, she knew he had achieved the true status of saint . . . and martyr.

Something had gone terribly wrong. The Seven were no more.

"It's over!" cried Peter, whirling around and pointing into the starry night that surrounded them.

He'd gestured toward the sun, and Marion knew that Peter had done it; he'd triumphed over all they worked for and believed in. Tears of sheer panic burst from her as she watched a huge fiery arm suddenly extend from the coronosphere of the sun, whipping across the gulf of space like a cat-o'-nine-tails . . .

. . . but it did not reach for Earth . . .

Instead, twisting and curling in upon itself, the monstrous solar prominence touched something else, something on the farthest side from where the planet spun and hurtled along its well-worn track. And whatever the flare so touched flared briefly, like a piece of tinder that drifted through a flame, and then was dark again.

For an instant, they all stood silent and stunned.

"What—?" Peter shouted, wheeling about to glare at the little woman who was his mother.

"One more," she said in a very soft voice.

"What?" said Marion, barely able to hear what she was saying.

"One of the Seven you killed was not the one you truly sought," said Etienne.

Peter appeared confused. He looked at the well of space behind him, then at Etienne. "What are you saying, woman?"

Etienne took a step toward him, and he hesitated, stepped back.

"You *know*," she said. "You have always known."

"No!"

Etienne stepped closer to him, and Marion understood. She could feel her heart jumping. Everything pulsing, flowing. This was it, this was *really* it.

Armageddon, family style.

"Take me, Peter, and everything is *yours*," said Etienne.

PETER CARENZA

It was so *wrong!*

The thought twisted through his mind like a piece of barbed wire. And then everything felt like it was spinning—the chamber, the stars, his hold on reality. Peter fought to get control and make sense of what he must do next.

He must commit the ultimate sin.

God had not played fair because he didn't have to, and Peter could fully appreciate that, but he had not expected the wheel of destiny to turn so tightly upon him.

The ultimate sin.

Etienne stood within arm's reach. He wouldn't even need to touch her and she would die, and so would the world. He hesitated as his thoughts continued to boil through him. He felt skewered on the bitter irony of the moment—because he knew then he'd never been what any of them had expected, including himself. A curiosity, a weird metaphysical hybrid, a cosmic joke who had refused to look deeply enough into the dark pool of his soul to understand his true nature.

"You were born in deceit, Peter," said Etienne.

He looked at her and felt tears stinging his cheeks. "Do you know what Hitler said just before he killed himself?"

"No," said his mother.

"He said, *'I never asked to be born.'* "

Etienne looked at him with no emotion. Her calm seemed weird, because something was churning up his insides pretty thoroughly.

"Do you feel that way, too?" she asked.

"I think that maybe I always have . . . that maybe I always knew on some level . . ."

"Knew what?"

"That something was wrong," he said. "With *me.*"

"You are the Abomination," said Etienne. "You were not born out of love."

"So be it," he said, feeling sadness run through him like spilled acid.

"Choose, Peter," said Etienne. "I cannot stop you. I will not try."

"I choose—"

"No!" screamed Francesco.

Peter looked down at the skinny old priest with bony cheekbones and the gray buzz-cut. He was kneeling over the fetally positioned Sforza and had a small plastic or porcelain weapon held in both hands, pointed vaguely at Peter.

"Father, no!" cried Marion. "He'll kill you!"

"You are the beast," said Giovanni Francesco.

Peter grinned weakly. "Maybe."

"I gave you life," said the priest. "Now, death."

The distraction of Francesco was just what he needed, giving him the strength to break away from his mother's imprisoning gaze. He felt himself spinning away from her, a dark energy gathering once again in him. "Old man!" he said loudly. "You do me a favor!"

Peter's words were consumed by a series of explosions rumbling up the passageway behind him. His chest erupted in a spray of pink mist. Something red-hot slammed into his back, hurling him forward into Etienne's arms. Fiery pain flowed outward from his bowels like seething magma. He could feel his breath leaking away, but he lacked the power to call it back.

Someone was wailing, as if from a great distance. He was vaguely aware of someone holding him in her arms as he looked up into a thickening fog. There was a man standing over him, a man who looked oddly familiar. Peter had a brief flash of memory of another man, very similar to this one, pointing a gun at him, and then bursting into flame.

" 'Vengeance is mine, sayeth the Lord,'" the man said. "But it is also mine, you *bastard!*"

Peter looked at the person holding him—a woman

with short, dark hair and soft almond eyes, ageless and quietly beautiful, and full of a love he had never known.

"I only . . . need one . . . thing," he said, each word a serrated blade being drawn up his throat. Something wet and heavy was pooling in the center of his chest, making each movement a terrible labor.

"Tell me," said his mother.

Other figures wavered in the fog as they gathered around him, looking down as though from towering, impossible heights.

"For . . . giveness," he said, and closed his eyes.

MARION WINDSOR

She hadn't been prepared for any of this.

Her entire body was shaking from the preternatural coldness that had swept into the chamber. As she looked down at Etienne holding Peter, Marion felt brushed by the gauzy curtain of déjà vu, even though she'd never witnessed such a scene before.

But it had been eerily presaged by Michelangelo in his *Pietà*.

"I forgive you," said Etienne.

Francesco knelt and placed a hand on Peter's forehead. "*In nomine Patris . . .*" he began, quickly murmuring the ritual prayers of the sacrament of Extreme Unction, the Last Rites.

Peter's eyes remained closed as his final breaths bubbled out of him.

Then he abruptly opened them, startling Marion so much she gasped. For a moment, Peter appeared flushed with energy, and he looked from one to the other as he said, "Thank you." His gaze ended on Gaetano; "Especially *you.*"

When he closed his eyes, they would open no more.

All around them, Marion noticed, the stars seemed to grow brighter.

EPILOGUE

The New York Times (AP) In the months since the spectacular solar prominence that reached and partially burned the surface of the planet Mercury, the erratic activity in the coronosphere of our sun appears to have stabilized. This is the latest conclusion announced by scientists at the California Institute for Solar Research in Mojave Center. "All unusual and erratic patterns of solar flare activity have ceased," said Dr. Warren Kimball of CISR. "The signs of basic change we observed in our sun have ceased, and it appears to have returned to a more predictable pattern." Dr. Kimball was asked if he had any explanation for what had been happening on the surface of the sun, but he only smiled and held up his hands, saying, "You know, science does not always have all the answers."